Identicality

Hi Michael
— Thanks for reading
my book. Best to you —
and to your replicant.
Koppelman

Jay L. Koppelman

Identicality

Published by Wheatmark®
2030 East Speedway Boulevard, Suite 106
Tucson, Arizona 85719 USA
www.wheatmark.com

ISBN: 978-1-62787-973-6 (paperback)
ISBN: 978-1-62787-974-3 (ebook)
LCCN: 2022906894

Bulk ordering discounts are available through Wheatmark, Inc. For more information, email orders@wheatmark.com or call 1-888-934-0888.

For in much wisdom is much grief.
And he that increases knowledge increases sorrow.

—Ecclesiastes 1:18

Be yourself. Everyone else is already taken.

—Oscar Wilde

Acknowledgments

When I set out to write *Identicality*, I thought it would be easy. How's that for nuts? It turned out that there was so much I didn't know enough about. So I started by reaching out to people I know and then went on to others well beyond my sphere of acquaintance. I needed to know about the law and about lawyers, about the organization of businesses and about startups. Then there was aerodynamics, aviation, physics, biology, computer science, and medicine. How does medical research work and what goes on in hospital emergency rooms, police departments, and government agencies? As I sought answers to my endless questions, I found a bounty of enthusiasm from so many wonderful and generous people.

Here's a short list in alphabetical order that makes mention of a few people who were especially helpful in educating me about writing and about content, both technical and otherwise.

Jay Goldman is a physician working in emergency services for Kaiser Permanente who helped me understand medical research, hospital administration, and emergency medical care.

Lori Conser is my project manager at Wheatmark. She guided me through the publishing process, keeping me on track and constantly providing me with ideas, insights, and critiques.

Andrew Hoy, the founder of Affinity Aviation, is an extraordinary corporate jet pilot who made it possible for me to introduce some realism to the flight emergency.

Ann Jensen, a voracious reader and a retired librarian from UC Berkeley, provided the enthusiasm and encouragement that propelled my earliest efforts.

Dara Pincas is incredible. She's a vice president and head of Healthcare Law at Genentech who took time to provide me with essential insight that enabled me to capture the complicated relationship between Adam Braudy and Shari Williams.

Maxim Shusteff is a scientist's scientist. He's a group leader at Lawrence Livermore National Laboratory. Okay, so my grasp of science needed a little grounding. Maxim, please accept my apology if my fiction has gone and spun too far off into a black hole.

H. William Taeusch, since his retirement as professor of neonatology at the University of California in San Francisco, has gone on to become a very talented writer and is the author of *Baby Doe*. Check it out. It's a great read. He offered lots of encouragement, was a careful critic of my writing, and was a source of much-needed knowledge about writing, publishing, and medical practice.

Monica Wesolowska is a writer and an incredible editor. She tried her best to teach me how to write. I wish I had paid closer attention.

Hilary Zaid is an editor, and a writer too, who offered much needed assistance. I didn't implement all that she suggested. So honestly, any shortcomings are all my own.

In addition to these few, I want to extend my utmost gratitude to so many others too. You, my beta readers, were of enormous assistance. You were careful readers and were willing to be frank about changes, both additions and deletions, which have made *Identicality* better. You found all kinds of faults—some literary, some logical inconsistencies, and others as well. Thanks to all of you. This is not a work I could have done alone. I needed you all. I am forever in your debt. And please forgive me if in error I have lost sight of anyone not properly acknowledged:

Vicki Bagrowski, Sophia and Boris Burshteyn, Nancy Cahners, Patrick and Mila Feigelson, Fred Gans, Hank Hanig, David and Vera Hartford, Joanne Jagoda, Joe Jensen, Carrie Andrea Koppelman, Ed Kriete, Paul Panish, Jerry and Nancy Rauch, Ulli Rotzscher, Paul Schwartz, Sheldon Whitten-Vile, Fred and Christine Zhang.

But of all my supporters, one stands out like no other. My wife, Phyllis, offered her endless enthusiasm, relentless patience, and critical judgment, all of which were ingredients without which this book would not be possible. No, Phyllis. You can't have a byline.

Chapter 1

When the Angel of Death came to inquire into the life of Adam Braudy, it was not clear what testimony Charlie Wood would enter into evidence. Charlie, as a best friend, knew Adam well and had spent a lifetime admiring him, even revering him. A bond of love and loyalty joined them one to the other. But then there was resentment too. Adam's rocket didn't kill Charlie, but it left him blind in one eye and disfigured. And there was the expectation that Charlie, whenever called upon, would do Adam's bidding. But worst of all, Charlie, despite his own notable accomplishments and not insignificant wealth, was left to feel that he was just a bush-league player alongside Adam, who, having achieved the heights of wealth and industrial accomplishment, still had room to run.

As a kid, Charlie wanted to be just like Adam. He got into the habit of drumming his fingers on the table because that's what Adam did. He even adopted Adam's head twitch until his father shouted at him, "Knock it off, Charlie. I don't want to see you doing that anymore."

As eleven-year-olds, Charlie and his buddies looked up to Adam, and it wasn't just because he was the tallest. Besides being tall, he was as skinny as a fence post despite the fact that he was always devouring candy bars or munching on chips. Maybe that was because he only ran at one speed—and that was a constant go. As a sixth grader with a big mouth, he often spent more time in the principal's office than in the classroom. But after school during baseball season, he whacked more than his share of homers and pitched a sizzling fastball. When it came to basketball, he sank most of his layups, was famous for his free throws, and hit a fair number of three-pointers. His buddies didn't have to hold an election to know that Adam was their leader. They just knew who to follow.

One hot summer afternoon, while Adam's mom was gone for the day, she worried about all the mischief her wayward son had been instructed to avoid. Charlie reminded Adam of his mom's insistence, but that didn't stop him from enlisting Charlie and half a dozen buddies to join him crouched behind a rusted metal cabinet junked in Adam's backyard weed patch. Their hearts raced as Adam struck a match and lit a gasoline-soaked string. The air was thick with anticipation and the mix of pungent vapors from the gasoline and the burnt match. Charlie worried about the danger and warned Adam but to no avail. Then, despite his reluctance, Charlie nevertheless sought Adam's favor by poking his head up from behind the cabinet and timed a countdown to match the pace of the flame as it crept along the string heading for the kid-rigged rocket built just the way Adam had instructed. It was nothing more than a chunk of metal tube stuffed up tight with a full load of severed match heads.

Charlie finished the countdown. " . . . three, two, one, blastoff."

But it didn't blast off. It blew up. Everyone but Charlie was safe from the fiery spray of metal shards. The explosion pounded Charlie's ears and set them ringing. His gasp left him choking on the thick pall of sulfurous smoke. Charlie felt like he'd been battered by a blast of molten lead. One shard gouged a deep slash in his forehead, splattering a gush of blood. Another sliced into his right eye.

His buddies, all of them scared out of their minds, took off at the sound of Charlie's shriek—all, that is, but Adam. He bolted to Charlie's side and then stood frozen in stunned silence, his blank face blanched as if it were his own blood draining onto the ground. Emerging from a vacant trance, he pulled his shirt off and pressed it over Charlie's gaping wound, where it quickly became soaked with blood. That's when Adam ran off too.

Dazed and writhing in pain, Charlie cried out, "No, don't leave me."

Abandoned and left with the taste of blood in his mouth, he knew he'd surely die. But then Adam was back.

"Don't worry, Charlie. Everything'll be alright. Help is on the way."

Charlie heard a siren wailing and figured the police were coming and would throw him in a dungeon for juvenile delinquents. But it wasn't the police. It was an ambulance. That's all he remembered until he awoke from surgery. His mom and dad stayed by his side and comforted him throughout a day and a long night of delirium. He wasn't able to cry when they told him his mangled eye had to be removed. Instead, he sank into a dark pit of unresponsive silence, which only deepened at week's end when the bandages came off, and he and his parents saw his vacant eye socket and disfigured brow. He saw that his hideous deformity would doom him to the life of an outcast freak.

Through his window, Charlie saw Adam's hesitant approach. He saw him stop a couple of times to pick up and throw a few rocks before tripping on the stairs on the way to the front door. He pressed the doorbell while staring down at the welcome mat. Charlie's father yanked the door open.

Charlie heard his father shout, "Get out of here and don't come around again. We don't want you anywhere near Charlie—not now, not ever."

Charlie glimpsed Adam's rigid stance and saw him turn away when the door was slammed in his face. Charlie's father, his face red, stormed into his son's bedroom and with a failed attempt at calm said, "You are not to have any more to do with Adam—not at school or anywhere else. He's nothing but trouble."

His disfigured forehead and the loss of his eye were bad enough, but now the loss of his best friend left Charlie abandoned and shaking in uncontrollable sobs. But Adam wasn't deterred. Charlie heard him coming around once or twice each day, each time followed by the sound of his parents chasing him away. And day after day, Charlie sank ever deeper into depression. After a week, Charlie's mom told her son that they would allow Adam brief visits. Throughout the weeks that followed, Adam became Charlie's constant companion and a household fixture, often invited to dinner. Adam read to Charlie the science fiction works that lay at the center of his imagination and, at Charlie's urging, read *The Time Machine* twice. When Adam tired of reading, they watched *Star Trek* reruns, allowing Charlie to adjust to a world seen through a single eye.

The knowledge that Adam's rocket had caused Charlie such a grievous loss, together with that long week of caring for him, left Adam imprinted with an obligation that would last a lifetime.

Every day for forty years, whenever he looked in a mirror, Charlie heard his fateful countdown, felt the blast of fiery shards. But on the morning following his office party extravaganza, he was feeling something else as well. He was feeling large. When he looked in the mirror and ran his forefinger along his scarred brow, he saw that it lent character to an otherwise ordinary face. He saw that his glass eye contributed a curious expression of mystery that begged for explanation.

Later that morning, he peered out a window in his corner office, high up, in the heart of San Francisco's financial district. He saw himself not just as the City's preeminent lawyer but rather as a mighty warrior assessing the lands of his latest conquest. He was ensconced in one of those high-rent office buildings where the big dogs run off leash. He reached for the phone when he saw that it was Adam Braudy calling.

Adam's exploits had landed him near the top of the Forbes list of multibillionaires. A hotshot inventor-entrepreneur, he had started out small time and quickly went big. By this time, he was into heavy lift rockets, electronic gear for satellites, high-performance computers, and anything else that challenged his curiosity. That made him a titan of industry but also the guy who couldn't, wouldn't, or, in any event, didn't make it to Charlie's splashy party.

That party was a big deal, at least for Charlie—for Adam, apparently not so much. Charlie and his partners had celebrated the expansion of their law firm and the twentieth anniversary of Charlie's solo law practice that had given it birth. And they had a big win to celebrate. There had been a rash of news about a revolutionary household insulation material that besides saving energy also caused lung cancer, or so they said. Charlie's firm got a class-action lawsuit going and won it, getting a hundred-million-dollar award for the aggrieved parties and a healthy chunk of that for the firm. Now that was something to celebrate.

As Charlie picked up the phone, he pictured Adam, his graying hair askew, working away on a computer in his Austin office, dressed in tired jeans and a University of Texas sweatshirt. That would be the one he got, along with accolades aplenty, for endowing the university's Center for Nanotechnology.

"You missed one hell of a party last night," Charlie said.

"Sorry I missed it, especially since there's a story going around that your partners gave you some kind of an honorary award."

"You sound surprised. Some say you had something to do with it—that it was your bright idea."

"Not saying one way or the other. Call it strategic ambiguity. So let me hear all about it."

"You know Ivan Chau," Charlie said. "Old man Chau isn't satisfied just being mayor of San Francisco. It looks like he's gonna run for governor next time around. My partners invited him, his wife, and his entourage to attend our party. They enlisted the good mayor to present me with an award. It was a trophy bearing a statue of a hideous cyclops. It's one ugly sucker. The engraved message said, 'Awarded to the One-Eyed Monster at the Bar for Accomplishments Way Over and Far Above the Call of Duty.' Everyone got a good laugh at that—at my expense. Very funny, Adam. I hold you personally responsible."

This was one more reminder to Charlie that his deformity didn't diminish him and told him once again that Adam would never forget his responsibility.

"Okay, Charlie. I'll share the credit along with your loving partners."

"By the way, Adam, old friends of yours were hoping to see you. I had to wonder if they came to celebrate with me or were just hoping to rub shoulders with you."

"Get over it. Maybe they didn't come for you or me. Maybe they came to strut their stuff at the Fairmont while soaking up the free booze and gobbling the tasty chow. Anyway, how 'bout I figure out a way to make it up to you?"

"I'm sure there's a way. Give me a moment to make a list."

"No problem. We can talk face to face tomorrow morning in Austin. I've sent a plane to pick you up."

"Sorry, can't do it. How 'bout next week?"

"That won't work. This is not a pleasure trip. It's time-critical."

Screw you, Charlie said to himself. He didn't ever worry about their friendship. It would always endure. But he didn't want to endanger their business ties. Now and then, Adam would call on Charlie to help hire legal and technical consultants or to represent him or BrauCorp in meetings and negotiations. He made it clear to Charlie that he sometimes needed an outsider who wouldn't be chatting it up either around the watercooler or after hours at the bar. Charlie didn't need the hourly billings but would never want to give up the big payoffs. And there were plenty of opportunities for that.

Although Adam organized BrauCorp as a closely held corporation owned by just him and his wife, Shari, he created separate entities for his separate projects. When they demonstrated potential for success, he would take them public and organize each one with its own officers and board of directors. Adam was generous in granting lucrative stock positions in these entities to key employees and associates. As a contributor to the success of some of these fledgling startups, Charlie was rewarded with highly lucrative stakes.

As a result, he had already pocketed a bundle. One startup, a wisp in the wind, went bust in the first stern breeze. Two were rock solid and on track to go big time. And then there was the one that went mega. Oh, yeah, Charlie liked that—didn't mind banking those millions.

Though Charlie's twenty-million-dollar share was a bonanza, it rankled him that his take was mere chicken feed alongside Adam's billions. Even so, a call from Adam always left Charlie wondering about his participation in his friend's next big deal.

Charlie understood that Adam sincerely felt that his work was top quality, that he had a special talent. On more than one occasion, Adam had told him that he had a way of seeing things that others missed, that maybe he lost his eye in exchange for the power of insight. Still, Charlie couldn't escape the sense that his participation was more like a charity case than as a valued counselor. Adam understood Charlie's dilemma but grew tired of hearing about it.

"My calendar's crammed," Charlie said, "and tomorrow I'm scheduled to meet with Oskar Himmelmann. How is it that everything with you is right now, right away? I'm not going to cancel a meeting with a world-renowned composer. He's stashed away a handsome portfolio and has a ton of business dealings we can help him with. And his list of referrals is worth gold."

Charlie awaited Adam's response, but there was none. Adam didn't say a word. He didn't have to. Was Charlie just imagining that he heard Adam's fingers drumming on his desk? Charlie was pissed and wasn't about to blink first—until, once again, he buckled.

Charlie knew well Adam's compulsions. When there was something weighty on his mind, he worked all around the clock. He missed meals. He slept an hour at a time only to be interrupted by one scenario after another. His employees and associates were bombarded with tasks. Shari, his wife, became embittered. His kids felt ignored.

"Thanks, Charlie. I've got a project with huge issues—legal, technical, moral, and personal. It looks like I've got myself jammed into a nasty corner. Maybe you can help me out. It's highly confidential. I need the kind of judgment and discretion that only you can render."

Charlie accepted Adam's sincerity, recognizing that he rarely felt obliged to finish with smooth edges. But Charlie wanted to know more. What was so urgent and confidential?

Adam said, "This requires face time. Wrap up your day and fly here to Austin tonight. Don't press me with questions."

"Tonight? Come on. I hate red-eyes."

"I don't think you'll have any complaints once you see the new plane I've dispatched for you. Scott will be your captain. He told me he sometimes lets you play flyboy. Maybe he'll let you fly this time too. Wouldn't that be a kick? Megan's new. She's Scott's copilot. She flew fighters in the navy."

"Does that mean she can land your fancy new play toy on the deck of an aircraft carrier?"

"You can ask her yourself. Look, I gotta run. I'll be at the airport when you get in. See you then."

Though obstinacy festered, Charlie also felt flattered and intrigued; besides, the kid in him wanted to fly Adam's new plane.

Chapter 2

Charlie downed a cup of black coffee and shifted into hyperdrive. He overloaded his assistant and called in his partners together with their assistants to distribute his workload. They were pissed. None of them were slackers, but they all had their own full schedules.

"Charlie, we're all working hard here. We don't need to take on your load too. How is it in our interest to do your work while you go off and chase your fortune with Mr. Big?"

"Do I really have to spell it out for you? Try to remember that I invited each of you to participate with me in this partnership. Make no mistake: I do understand that you all work hard, but the business I bring to the firm is greater than that of the rest of you combined. The referrals that come from Mr. Big, as you call him, are a significant part of what we do here. Why don't you think of my brief sojourn with him as my effort to pull in more business for all of us?"

It was past eight when Charlie finished doing everything he couldn't leave for the others. By then, he didn't have to worry about rush-hour crowds, but even so, his eye twitched as he rushed home to see Laura.

Only half in jest, Laura quipped, "How is it that you always manage to be late on nights when you're supposed to fix dinner?" Charlie knew that as an environmental consultant, she was under a lot of pressure during this busy reporting season. But he was too. He had no time for either a bite of sarcasm or leftovers.

"Adam's leaning on me hard. He's got this new project he won't talk about on the phone. He said it's huge. He wants me in Austin overnight."

"I thought you were all excited about your meeting with Oscar Himmelmann. Did he cancel?"

"No, I had to ask George to step in."

"Just like that? Adam skips your party and then calls you to dance for him, and you just cancel your plans and say, 'Okay'?"

Charlie saw what was coming and knew it would go on way too long. His stomach churned, and it wasn't from hunger.

"Do we really have to do this?" Charlie asked. "How 'bout you think of Adam as an important client—actually my most important client? He says he's got a big problem. When he's got a big problem, that usually means there's a lot of money in play—and that means some of it is for you and me. Maybe a lot."

"Is that all you care about? We've already got plenty of money. Are you trying to compete with Adam? Oh, you'll make a lot of money alright. I guess our millions aren't enough for you. Is it the billions you're after? What more do you want? You're the big shot at San Francisco's biggest law firm. Maybe you want all of California too. You're the poster boy for the California Bar Association. You're on the mayor's—maybe the governor's—short list for consultants, confidants, and appointees. Money, clout, respect: haven't you figured out that however long you play second fiddle to Adam, you'll never catch up? I love you, Charlie. I'm proud when I see that so many people have such great respect for you, but it pains me to see that the only thing you're short on is self-respect. Do you really think you're going to find that by sucking up to Adam?"

Charlie's allegiance to Adam was indeed complicated. He knew that Laura was right, but she was wrong too. He did want the greater wealth that he knew would be his if he continued to participate with Adam, even as a junior partner. And he saw that when it comes to respect, even self-respect, is there ever enough? Even if he couldn't rise above second fiddle, working as a number two to someone at the pinnacle would put him in play in one of the world's greatest games.

Charlie looked at his watch, turned away in anger, and ran upstairs to pack a bag for a few days away. He took a deep breath to calm himself as he came back downstairs.

"Look, Laura, can we continue this when I get back. Adam's got a plane waiting for me at the airport. I have to get going."

"Oh, a plane all for Charlie. How quaint. Is this a plane with a well-stocked liquor cabinet, a fold-out bed, and a friendly stewardess?"

"Are you really gonna go paranoid on me? Come on . . . give me a break."

"With your history, I'm surprised you think you deserve a break."

"For crying out loud, Adam's planes are business tools. Guess what? We're doing business."

"Funny business, Charlie? Is that it?"

"Damn it, Laura. I'm not going to Austin to fuck some mile-high bimbo. I'm going to help a client with a business problem. I'm going to help a friend who reached out to me in need."

He cleared his throat, relaxed his shoulders, and measured out the cadence of his speech. "Okay, I've got a history, and it's not one I'm proud of. But that's what it is: history. I know I've hurt you, and I know it's a hurt you'll always live with. I'm sorry. But we've moved on. I can't keep begging for forgiveness."

He took a deep breath, paused, looked into Laura's tearing eyes, and said, "I love you very much, but I really do have to go. We can discuss this again when I get back in a couple of days."

―――――

At the executive lounge at Buchanan Field, Charlie found Scott looking out the window, his eyes fixed on Megan as she checked out the plane and double-checked the work of the ground crew. Charlie was fond of Scott, whom he had come to know over a period of years. He didn't look the part of a jet jockey. He was fiftysomething and stood about five foot six with a rounded belly that suggested an indifference to his middle-age appearance. He started working for Adam when Adam had bought his first jet. His qualifications were impeccable, and he'd lived up to them with every flight.

"Adam wants us back in Austin ASAP," Scott said. "He's got a big bug up his butt, and I think it's crawling."

Following a thumbs up from Megan, Scott said, "Looks like the plane's ready, and our flight plan's filed. Let's mount up and get out of here. With a quick clearance and decent weather, we should be in Austin by three a.m."

"Is that the new plane Adam told me about?"

"Yep, and she is a beaut. It's a Gulfstream G650."

"You're gonna let me have some stick time, right?"

"I don't know, Charlie. This one's got an awful lot of lights and buttons, not to mention the computer stuff. Besides, neither Megan or I have racked up a lot of time in it. The checklists are a bear. I'm glad Megan's got it down real good. I'm lucky to have her for my copilot. But, hey, maybe we can get her to take a break and give you a chance to play flyboy."

"Okay, but don't just give me straight and level stuff. The autopilot can do that better than I can."

"Hey, this plane's loaded with automation. It can do almost everything better than any of us. Except for a malfunction or an emergency, I don't think the damn thing needs us at all. Just last night, I was going over the plane's flight operations manual for the millionth time and found the section where it makes a recommendation for the ideal flight crew."

"Do we measure up?"

"Almost. It says the ideal crew consists of the aircraft's flight management system, a single pilot, and a dog."

"Come on, Scott."

"No, really. The flight management system flies the plane, and the pilot feeds the dog."

"Okay, Scott, I'll bite. Tell me. What does the dog do?"

"The dog's there to bite the pilot if he tries to take the controls away from the flight management system."

"Okay, very funny, but do I get stick time or not?"

"Yeah, we'll give you a shot at it, but if I were you, I'd keep a close eye on the dog."

Charlie smiled and followed Scott onto the tarmac, where the sweet, lingering kerosene smell of Jet-A1 fuel teased his craving for stick time. Scott introduced Charlie to Megan. She stood a statuesque five ten with an athletic build, all topped off with a shock of fiery red hair cropped short. Her steely demeanor didn't obscure the softness of her pretty face. Charlie wondered what it might take to make her smile.

"I understand you flew fighters in the navy."

"Yes, sir, I did."

"So can you land this plane on a carrier deck?"

With the smile that Charlie was looking for, she said, "Well, if I had to, I'd pray first and then give it a go. We might pull it off, but it'd probably mess up the plane a bit."

With a self-satisfied smile, Charlie shook her hand and turned to head up the stairs. At the cabin entrance, Scott introduced Charlie to Melissa, the flight attendant. She welcomed Charlie on board with a warm smile. He smiled in return, but behind his cheerful mask, a wave of melancholy swept over him. In her twenties, she was about the age his daughter would have been and seemed every bit as sweet.

"Hello, Mr. Wood. I hope you enjoy the flight. Please let me know if there's anything I can do to make your flight more comfortable."

"Thank you, Melissa. Please call me Charlie."

"Of course, Charlie. Can I get you a drink while we prepare for takeoff?"

"If you've got Laphroaig on board, I'll take it neat."

"I'll have it for you by the time your seatbelt's fastened. Then it'll be a short taxi before takeoff."

Twenty minutes later, Charlie was nursing his Laphroaig and enjoying its peaty smell as the G650 surged down the runway, quickly gaining speed and eager to leap into the air. And leap it did as its nose rotated well above the horizon and continued to accelerate into a gentle banking turn.

Once aloft, Melissa served Charlie the cheeseburger and garlic fries he chose from the flight menu. She set the tray down on the table in front of him and took a seat across from him following his invitation. They fell easily into conversation.

"This is a great job. I've met some really interesting people. I actually got to meet Senator Parton a few weeks ago. He was so nice. That was really cool. It's perfect for right now, but I'm not sure how long I'll stay on."

She spoke about her love for horses. She worked around them as a kid and later rode in competitions, which she frequently won. Veterinary school was next for her and then on to a career working with horses. Charlie was a good listener, but pounding waves of melancholy kept him from grasping the whole of what she said. He heard only bits and pieces: *hanging with family, dreams of marriage, raising kids.* Those were her dreams; so many of his were awash in sorrow.

In turn, Charlie told her that he and Adam had been friends since childhood and that they sometimes worked together. And he talked about Laura and their son, Joel. After a pause in their conversation, Melissa hesitated before saying, "I don't usually get to chat like this with our flight guests. I've enjoyed meeting you. Thank you, Charlie."

She got up from her seat and cleared the table. "Let me know if there's anything else I can get for you."

"Thanks but right now, I'm going to lay back and relax for a few minutes."

"Okay. If you doze off, I'll wake you on our approach into Austin."

By this time, Charlie felt exhausted and didn't care if he flew the plane. There would be another chance on the way home. He leaned his seat back and turned off the overhead lights. His body settled lazily, the muscles of his shoulders giving way to the gentle contours of the cushioned recliner. Half asleep, his thoughts turned to Adam and what he might have in store for him. Why the urgency? Why the mystery? These questions repeated themselves until they faded into nothing more than a white noise that finally delivered him, despite his angst, into a deep sleep.

In his slumber, Charlie found himself at the entrance to a cave, where he heard Adam calling from within. Peering in, he caught sight of a quivering light. Stooping low, he started into the bowels of the tunnel and, like a moth, headed straight toward the light. He reached out in front and to the side, where he felt a slimy wall. He was Jonah in the maw of the whale. The sodden air reeked with the stench of a muck he felt underfoot. All along the way, he heard echoes of Adam's repeated calls. The light drew him onward. He saw that it was cast by the flame of a single candle that flickered wanly far into the tunnel. He stumbled repeatedly on scattered rocks and debris. When he picked himself up after a trip and fall, his pants were ripped and soaked, his left kneecap skinned and bleeding.

Approaching the candle, he saw that Adam held it in his outstretched hand, his face blank, his cheeks marked by tracks of tears. Taking the candle from Adam, he continued past him into the darkness beyond. The light from that solitary flame was the only light to guide him along the path he felt compelled to follow. He waved his free arm to swipe aside a thick mesh of nearly obstructing spider webs. As the mesh collapsed in a heap, he heard a fearsome rumble and felt a violent quake. Underfoot, the floor of the tunnel started sliding and then fell straight away right out from under him. He was in a panicked freefall.

Awakened in terror, it took a long moment of confusion to realize that his nightmare had just begun. The plane had pitched over, trembling amid a brutal turbulence while plummeting straight down like a roller coaster falling off its track.

Chapter 3

Charlie's seatbelt bit deep into his lap and anchored him, keeping him from flying out of his seat. He felt his heart pound hard and fast against his ribs. He nearly puked while gasping to reclaim the breath that heaved from his chest.

The plane was sucked down into an abyss. In the darkness out the window, the moon was a blur that moved swiftly past the window time and again as the plane plunged in a steep spin.

Charlie looked around the cabin in search of a hopeful sign, but what he saw only added to the horror. Melissa, who had been moving about the cabin, had been thrown up against the ceiling. Her head hit hard. Her neck whipped back. Her limp body thumped back onto the floor.

The spinning slowed, but when it finally stopped, the plane was still pointing nearly straight down. Charlie wondered what he might have done to anger the gods, or was it Adam who had roused their fury? They poured forth a vicious blast of wind that battered the plane and threatened to rip away the wings. Charlie's stomach churned and left him sickened as his guts were shoved and squeezed by the acceleration forces that accompanied Scott's struggle to pull the plane from its dive.

At last, with the shuddering gone, the plane appeared to be in level flight. Charlie's attention turned to Melissa. When he tried to unbuckle his seatbelt, he couldn't make his shaking fingers work. He finally managed to release the buckle and made his way to Melissa's side, where he knelt down beside her to offer whatever assistance he could. He had been of no use to his daughter when she lay dying, but he prayed that there was something he could do for Melissa. Her eyes were opened wide, her pupils unresponsive to the shadow that passed before her as Charlie moved his hand back and forth between her upturned face and the light above. He swept aside a strand of her dark hair as he felt for a pulse in her oddly bent neck. He couldn't find one. Melissa, so young and full of life only moments before, was suddenly dead.

He hardly knew her, but within their shared hour of conversation, he had felt visited by a vision of his own lost daughter. Melissa's death brought Sandra to life and then back to death all over again. His throat ached. His eyes teared. Though it was Melissa who was dead, all he could see was a grownup version of Sandra. He lunged forward, arms outstretched, his forehead pressed onto the carpet. He hammered his fists against the floor and cried out in unrestrained grief, a grief that had been bottled up tight for a long, long time. Sandra was dead and now Melissa too. Yet Charlie lived as if for no reason other than to endure Sandra's loss all over again.

He wanted to cover Melissa but couldn't find anything that might offer even a measure of dignity to her sad repose. Desperate to know what had happened, he left Melissa and stumbled forward toward the cockpit. Was the plane okay? Would they make it to Austin? On the way forward, he passed the lavatory with its door ajar. Scott sat on the lid of the toilet seat and held his head in his hands, his shirt soaked with blood.

Scott's eyes rolled in their sockets as he babbled, "Check ground crew. Have to fill tanks. Gotta take off before flight plan canceled."

Charlie's legs started to wobble when he saw that Scott was dizzy and unable to stand, let alone walk to the cockpit and fly the plane. Charlie guided Scott to a seat and buckled him in. He applied moist towels to Scott's open wounds and was relieved when the bleeding stopped. He left Scott and continued on to the cockpit, where Megan was at the controls.

Megan had flown her F/A-18 for thirteen years. She knew it well. It had become more than a machine, more than an engineering marvel. The two of them shared a bond, an intimacy. It had become a part of her. As with an ardent lover, every flight delivered a rush. She delighted in its power and in her ability to extract the very limits of its capabilities. Every movement of the stick, every adjustment of the throttle, every button pushed and switch flicked was part of a spontaneous choreography—a study in synchrony. They were like skaters on ice teasing the boundaries that physics dared to enforce.

In time, she would know the G650 just as well, but now, despite a rigorous training routine including many hours of simulator time, it was still a new relationship not yet fully matured.

Entering the cockpit, Charlie cried out, "Melissa is dead."

"Shut up, damn it. We've got an emergency here."

That's when Charlie realized that Megan was on the radio with Houston Center. She was a quick study and had learned her lessons well, but the emergency checklist was not yet baked in. She acted with deliberation when reflex was called for.

"Gulfstream November Nine Victor Juliet, how do you read? Our radar indicates a rapid descent. Report your current status, please."

Megan's response was crisp. "Houston Center, this is Gulfstream Nine Victor Juliet. We encountered severe clear air turbulence at our cruise altitude—Flight Level 510. We experienced a significant loss of altitude as a result of a stall and spin accompanied by an engine flameout. We are currently in stable flight at ten thousand feet. Engine relit. I'm the copilot. Condition of the captain, a single passenger, and one additional crew member not yet known. Possible damage to the aircraft not yet known."

"Gulfstream Nine Victor Juliet, roger. We have you on radar. We show you two hundred miles short of your Austin destination at ten thousand feet. Report your condition when known."

"Houston Center, Gulfstream Nine Victor Juliet, wilco."

Not wanting to distract her from the emergency, Charlie told her as quickly as possible that Melissa was dead from a broken neck and that Scott was incoherent from a concussion or worse.

"Don't tell me Scott can't fly. We've got a big problem here. I was hoping to turn this mess over to him."

When Megan finally hauled the plane out of the stall and spin, they ended up in a steep dive. Outside of her F/A-18, she had never seen a speed so high. They had exceeded the plane's "never exceed" speed, a speed that invites structural failure. She recognized that the plane's sloppy roll response meant one or both ailerons were damaged. At best, routine maneuvering would not be possible, and at worst, they might end up spiraling into the ground. But in the back of her mind, what consumed her was something personal.

It was true that they had been walloped by unpredictable turbulence, but she and Scott had been probing the outer limits of their new plane's flight envelope. Like Icarus, they had flown too high and left themselves vulnerable. She feared that an inevitable investigation would reveal that their extreme altitude was too high given the heavy fuel load they had taken on board.

Her attention should have been fixed on flying, but in an unguarded moment, she let slip, "I'll be lucky if they don't pull my license. With Melissa dead, they'll hang me for murder or negligence or something. I'll be toast—maybe better off dead in a crash."

"Come on, Megan. Please, no more dead tonight. You can always kill yourself tomorrow."

After a sullen pause, she said, "Okay, but I'll need some help. You'll have to be my copilot."

With the sloppy ailerons, she couldn't get a proper control response. That meant there was no way the autopilot could fly the plane. She would have to handle the controls manually, which would be like steering a bicycle without hands. The challenge would be getting slowed down and maneuvered onto final approach. And then there was the weather. Conditions in Austin were not good. She would have to maintain a steady heading in instrument conditions and ease her damaged plane under a dangerously low three-hundred-foot ceiling. Even if she managed that, she would still have to execute a tricky crosswind landing with wind gusts of up to twenty-five knots and visibility of only one mile.

"Charlie, your job will be to read from the checklist."

"No problem."

"Okay, then. Hold on while I check in with Center."

She turned her attention. "Houston Center, Gulfstream Nine Victor Juliet. Level, stable, ten thousand feet."

"Houston Center, roger. Your altimeter: 29.55. Report your current condition."

"Houston Center, Gulfstream Nine Victor Juliet. We have a medical emergency. Our flight attendant is dead from a broken neck, and our pilot has sustained a severe head injury, a concussion at least. We're experiencing poor roll response. No visible damage, but we probably have some kind of aileron damage."

"Gulfstream Nine Victor Juliet, roger. Stand by."

One very long minute later, "Gulfstream Nine Victor Juliet, proceed direct to Austin. Contact Austin Approach on 127.22. We have advised them of your emergency. Good luck."

While Megan stayed busy coordinating with the various air traffic facilities, Charlie reviewed the approach and landing checklist that appeared onscreen.

With what seemed like a drunkard's stagger, Megan struggled onto final approach and listened for Austin Tower's landing clearance. "Gulfstream Nine Victor Juliet, good evening. Cleared to land runway one seven right. We are aware of your emergency and will have emergency medical services immediately available on landing."

With the landing only minutes away, Megan signaled Charlie to proceed with the checklist. He called out the next item: "Landing gear."

Megan checked the airspeed to make sure the plane was slow enough. Noting an appropriate airspeed, she responded, "Speed checks" and then threw the switch to extend the landing gear. The whirring of the electric motors was followed by two thumps accompanied by the illumination of two green lights on the instrument panel. When the whirring stopped, one yellow in-transit light remained illuminated instead of turning green. Megan's lament filled the cockpit. "Oh, fuck. Not now. Please, God, not now."

"What's going on?"

"Not entirely sure. It looks like something else got bent. There's a problem with the landing gear. If we can't get the gear down, we'll end the day shaving our abs on a belly landing. Not a great idea with all the fuel we still have on board. Right now, we have to abort our approach."

"What about Scott? We gotta get him to a hospital."

"Sorry. That poor bastard won't need a hospital if we crash and burn on landing."

Megan contacted the tower. "Austin Tower, Gulfstream Nine Victor Juliet. Missed approach. Got a landing gear problem. We're going around, standard missed."

Following instructions from approach control, she worked hard to coax her wounded bird over to the designated holding pattern. After running through the emergency checklist, triple-checking everything, there were still unanswered questions. Was the right landing gear down, and if so, was it locked in place?

Megan recalled that there was a camera on the plane's belly that might offer a view of the gear. Sure enough, she was able to see that the offending right gear looked extended, but was it locked in place? Would it hold the weight of their landing, or would it collapse on arrival? Megan cringed at the idea of a belly landing and declared her intention to attempt a gear-down landing.

Following vectors from approach control, she waddled back onto final approach. Once established on the glide path, Charlie read off the rest of the checklist while Megan struggled to maintain both their heading and airspeed. Worry stiffened their focus as they descended beneath the low ceiling and crossed the runway threshold. Megan was amazed she was anywhere near the runway centerline. But because of the crosswind, she still had to twist the nose to the right to align it straight down the runway while raising the right wing to keep weight off the right landing gear.

Megan was accustomed to touching down with just a kiss—but not this time. The plane was still askew to the left with the right wing elevated when it flopped down hard on the runway. The initial contact was absorbed by the left landing gear, but then they rolled right, slamming down hard on the cranky right landing gear. At first, they torqued and skidded but then careened down the runway with a destructive shaking. Fire trucks and two ambulances made up a caravan that followed along. Thankfully, much of their speed had dissipated when the right landing gear collapsed. The right side of the plane crashed to the ground, causing it to pinwheel around a fractured wing.

Megan feared sparks would ignite the fuel leaking from ruptured tanks or from ripped fuel lines. But even before the plane had whirled to a stop, firefighters were already spraying fire suppression foam. Getting off the plane was of paramount importance. Megan went through emergency shutdown procedures while Charlie stumbled through the cabin and opened the cabin door.

Because the plane was aslant, there was a delay getting the paramedics on board. Upon entry, one paramedic rushed to Melissa, still lying face up on the floor. Charlie watched and clung to a fantasy that he was mistaken and that she was still alive. That fantasy was crushed when the paramedic confirmed her death, lifted her body onto his shoulder, and headed to the exit. Charlie and Megan were urged off the plane, but both refused to go until they saw that the second paramedic had tended to Scott and helped him off.

Before Charlie could leave the airport, he had to endure a quiz by paramedics to ensure his health and by airport officials who were opening an investigation. He learned that Scott was in stable condition and had been rushed away to the hospital. Megan was still being debriefed. He worried about her, knowing that a guilty party had to be identified. Would she ever fly again?

When Charlie left the airport administrator's office, he found Adam's wife, Shari, waiting for him. Charlie was exhausted, completely disheveled, hair messed, shirt sweat-soaked. He felt drained, his knees wobbly. They sat down together in the office waiting area. He could hardly do more than sit still.

After a minute of silence, Charlie said, "Is Adam here?"

"No. He's at home. He needed a quiet place to call Melissa's parents and Laura too. I wouldn't want Adam's job, not today for sure. He said that he didn't know what he was going to tell her parents. He said that it was his job to reach them before some airport official or, God forbid, some reporter scrambling to make a deadline."

Charlie said, "Shari, before I say another word, I need to call Laura."

Chapter 4

Charlie was passing time on the Mediterranean island of Mallorca, where he and a friend had landed for a week after six months into a post-college interlude of pointless wandering. They made their way to the beach at Cala Agulla under a clear blue sky, marked with a few wispy clouds. A gentle breeze tamed the heat of the day. They found the beach packed with a bunch of hotties clad in skimpy bikinis. Charlie looked around and imagined which one of these beauties might be his treat for the evening. After tossing a Frisbee for a while with his friend, Charlie took careful aim and deftly flicked it to land close up alongside a sexy young woman in a yellow bikini.

"Sorry. I didn't mean to disturb you," he lied.

In American-accented English, she answered without turning, "No bother."

That was Laura. She and two friends were treating themselves to a European adventure after graduating from college. She had left behind a boyfriend she had broken up with and vowed she wouldn't get involved again any time soon.

Charlie pressed on. "You know, it's not always easy to get it to go where you want it to."

Laura laughed as she turned her head to match the playful voice with a face. Her coy smile marked by dimpled cheeks and sparkling brown eyes lasted but a moment. On eye contact, her smile went flat.

That was the usual reflex. Charlie long ago came to understand the unease that people felt on first sight of his glass eye and mangled brow.

For Laura, it was a forced act of compassion for her to shift back to a smile, guarded though it was. She picked up the Frisbee and passed it to Charlie, saying, "Oh, is that so? It looks like you're pretty good at it."

Charlie took that for an opening. "Hi, I'm Charlie."

"Nice to meet you, Charlie. I'm Laura."

She accepted his invitation to toss the Frisbee, which opened the door to a flirty banter. Charlie noticed she enjoyed the pleasure he took as he watched her run and stretch to reach the Frisbee tosses he floated just beyond her grasp. Charlie had reason to feel hopeful about the night ahead.

"Hey, Laura, what do you say we go for a walk, check out the town? I think our friends can do fine without us."

As the sun set, they found their way to a candlelit restaurant. Laura was getting to like Charlie, maybe a little too much. She reminded herself of her vow to avoid romantic entanglements at least for the duration of her travels. She had to do something to dampen the rising intensity of the evening.

Charlie found her to be much too earnest and felt disappointed when he realized there was no way he'd get this girl to bed. But as the conversation went on, as serious as she was, he felt drawn to her.

He wondered if she was trying to bore him to death when she spoke about her family life, or was she just responding to the sincerity of his interest? She spoke with a smile when telling him how her parents worked long hours to build a successful printing business and needed her to play "mommy." With pride rather than complaint, she described how she juggled her household duties and childcare responsibilities for two precocious younger brothers. She recounted the odd jobs she worked to make ends meet while attending college.

"I love dogs, so it was a pleasure and distraction to make a little money walking them. Then for a while, I clerked at a campus bookstore till I got fired when the manager overheard me making snide remarks about her. After that, I got a job as a bindery clerk in the campus library. That was a great job. I got to poke my nose into a lot of journals and magazines I'd never otherwise know anything about."

She was comfortable when she talked about her life and wasn't shy quizzing Charlie about his. He thought it bold of her when she asked, "So what's the story with that horrible scar? Did you get it vanquishing some dragon monster while saving a damsel in distress?"

They both laughed, and with lingering smiles, Charlie recounted his misadventure with Adam's rocket. "Adam's my best friend. He says that having lost an eye, I have the advantage of half an extra sense— that I can see things that others can't. Besides, now I've got one hell of a story, this glass eye, and a scar—sexy, don't you think?"

In the flickering candlelight, Charlie thought he saw tears well up in Laura's eyes. She hesitated for a moment but then extended her arm to reach out and run her finger across his scarred brow. Charlie wondered if this was an offer of comfort or an expression of desire. Whatever it was, she wasn't finished with her queries. "So what's next for you?" she asked.

"Well, I graduated college almost a year ago and always wanted to travel. It would take days to tell you about our adventures."

Charlie was taken aback when she asked, "So are you going to tell me what's next for you?"

That was a question that had lingered with Charlie for a long time. Indeed, what was next? What he knew instinctively was that he liked Laura a lot and grasped that she wouldn't be much interested in a wanderer. On the spot and without much thought, he was as surprised as anyone could be when he heard himself declare, "I'm planning to go to law school and practice law."

A year later, Charlie and Laura were married. He was in his first year of law school at Boalt Hall, and she had begun her career as an elementary school teacher. Charlie thrived in the law school environment and got excellent grades and recommendations. During his third year, he sought an interview for a position at a top-ranked San Francisco law firm. His grades and recommendations had gotten him the interview. To get this job would be incredible.

He wanted it, and he got it—but not without an edge. While Charlie had worked his way through college and then law school, Adam had spent those six years developing a range of lucrative products. Charlie wondered if he had gotten the job on his merit alone or because of an encouraging word from Adam Braudy, by then a boy wonder and the law firm's most promising client.

In drunken celebration, Adam had said, "Was I supposed to leave it to them to hire someone from a list of a half dozen highly qualified prospects, or was I supposed to suggest they hire the best? My answer was clear. What would your answer have been?"

In any event, it was a plum job, and Charlie had found himself excited and challenged—but what a slog. He worked long hours under a partner's wicked lash and too often came home late complaining to Laura. After five years, he had questioned his career choice. "I like the idea of practicing law but not like this. I thought I wanted to make partner, and with all the hours I'm billing and all the clients I'm bringing in, it looks like I'm on track, but the partners work their asses off. They work long hours and chase lifestyles they can't afford. Too many of them end up in divorce."

"So go out on your own. You're a great attorney. You'll do fine."

"Are you crazy? How do you think we'd manage with two kids on just your teacher's salary?"

Laura had a clear recollection of her parents' struggles with their family business and had no illusions about the risks and hard work required. With the boundless confidence that was her nature, she pronounced, "Don't worry. We've got some savings put aside, and it won't take you long to get up and running. At worst, I'll finally hear different complaints."

With Laura's encouragement, Charlie established his own practice and, over a period of several years, managed to build up a respectable client list. In the beginning, a handful of referral sources brought clients to his door, but none matched the bounty that came from Adam, who once again stepped in to make an assist. And, again, Charlie wondered if he could have succeeded without Adam's help.

Soon, Charlie's client list had gotten long enough that he could screen for new clients whose interests aligned with his own. He took satisfaction in helping them with their business issues, investments, and estate planning around their charitable giving.

Life seemed simple. Success followed success in Charlie's law career and family life. By then, he and Laura were parents of a couple of kids and happy in their marriage. Sandra, their firstborn, was beautiful and bright. With pride, Charlie imagined he would advise her on her education and career choices while shielding her from the many unworthy suitors who would inevitably compete for her attention. And at just two years of age, he dreamed that their son, Joel, had the skills that would propel him to a professional athletic career. Everything seemed right.

On a romantic anniversary, out to dinner at a favorite restaurant, Charlie handed Laura a gift box wrapped in glossy red paper. He raised his champagne flute while she unwrapped his offering. She gasped when she saw the dazzling diamond necklace.

"I love you, Laura. You are a dream come true. The reality of you far exceeds my fondest dream. Here's to us, to a long and happy life together."

Charlie took Laura in his arms and kissed her sweetly. They spent the night at the Fairmont Hotel and made love over and over again on silken sheets, waking in the morning to the first day of the rest of what they knew would be their happy life together.

But among Charlie's clients, he witnessed divorce, untimely death, ill health, and problems with kids. Even so, he supposed that an impenetrable bubble of immunity shielded him and his family. It was impossible for him to see how turbulence would buffet him. How his career might play out other than according to plan. How so many challenges, threats, and torments would bring pain and unhappiness into his life and to those he loved.

Chapter 5

Shari saw Charlie frisking his pockets, hunting for his phone without success. A call to Laura was clearly his first priority. "Here, Charlie, use mine."

At nearly two a.m., Charlie knew he'd wake Laura, unless she had already heard from Adam. Charlie was glad she hadn't, knowing that she'd be relieved to talk directly to him. The night's horror weighed on them, but sharing the burden made it more bearable. They discussed plans for her to join him, but did she really mean it? Details would have to wait until morning.

"Don't worry, Laura. I'll be fine. I'm just a little shook up. A good night's sleep is all I need. Let's talk in the morning."

After Charlie said goodbye to Laura, Shari whispered, "Let's get out of here."

They rushed past newspaper reporters, left the office building, and got into the backseat of Shari's chauffeured car. She said, "Michael, get us out of here. Don't stop for any reporters. We're not in the mood for Q and A."

"Not a problem, Mrs. B. I'll have you home straight away."

Michael was more than just a driver. His demeanor was calm and deliberate, which was unusual for a young man of only twenty-nine. He stood six feet two and weighed about 220. He would have looked more intimidating except for his clean-cut baby face and playful smile. An ex-Marine with combat experience, he was able to handle himself in any violent confrontation. Recurring training in high-performance driver courses enhanced his expertise, and constant practice honed his skills. And because he was also personable and charming, he was Shari's pick for a chauffeur.

Once clear of the airport grounds, Charlie asked, "So how's Adam handling all of this?"

He was unprepared for her response. "How's he handling this? I don't know anymore—not this and not much of anything else. The man is so focused, so driven. His focus even excludes me and the kids and almost everything else in his life too. And the worst part is I have no idea what the hell he's focused on."

Adam's intensity was no surprise to Charlie. It was a recurring theme in his own relationship with Adam. What surprised him was that Adam's focus even impacted his relationship with Shari, a relationship that Charlie had come to idealize.

"I'm sorry, Charlie. I shouldn't be bothering you at a time like this. Please forgive me. My emotions are all jumbled up. I'm a mess. I can hardly stand myself."

This wasn't the Shari he had come to know.

———

Adam and Shari had met and married young before Adam made his first serious money and before there was any reason to think about the enormous wealth they would ultimately command.

Shari was working as a development associate at a product development firm. Every day, her assistant would sift through dozens of proposals and forward the few that looked professional and well documented. Adam's proposal intrigued her. She was not disappointed when he called to follow up. He spoke with confidence and conviction. He sounded like someone who knew what he was talking about.

Over a period of weeks, their phone conversations, always professional, became ever more playful, even flirty. She played in his fantasies. Every phone conversation added an expressive stroke to a portrait he drew of a charming young woman with an alluring smile. Adam wanted to meet her.

In conversation with Charlie, Adam spoke of Shari. "I think I'm in love."

"Who with now, one of your rolling regulars?"

"No one I've talked about before. I haven't even met her yet—except by phone."

"Now there's the making for a love match. At least you got pictures, right?"

"No, not even that, but she sounds a lot like Melinda. You remember Melinda: medium height, short blond hair, hazel eyes, curvy figure, lilting voice, and great sense of humor. Shari reminds me of Melinda, but Melinda got away 'cause I was too slow. There's something about Shari that makes me want to move a little quicker. I've already booked my flight. She's kind of brainy. Hope she doesn't think I'm too light in that department."

Shari had protested, "New York's a long way for you. Don't bother just yet. I've still got research to do. But I can tell you that the way your project is shaping up so far, I expect it won't be too much longer before we're going to meet."

"Don't worry about me. I need to be in New York for some other business. I want to meet you while I'm in town. We can do some business first and then go out to dinner."

"If you're coming to New York anyway, I'd be happy to schedule an appointment with you but, sorry, can't make dinner. Conflict of interest, you know."

When Adam arrived for his appointment, he was greeted by a receptionist on the twenty-second floor of a prestigious Manhattan office building. The receptionist let Shari Williams know her visitor had arrived and then escorted him past a lavishly appointed conference room into Shari's spacious office. She explained that Ms. Williams would be joining him in a moment. Adam stood waiting for several minutes before taking a seat. When he heard footsteps approaching, he turned to see a tall black woman with maybe a dozen tightly woven braids draping her shoulders. She walked in carrying an armful of files, which she neatly deposited on Shari's desk.

"Will it be much longer till Ms. Williams steps in?" Adam asked.

"Your wait is over. I'm Shari Williams. Glad to meet you, Adam."

Instantly, he was on his feet. Even standing, Adam had to turn his eyes up to look into hers. He immediately judged her capable of some hefty powerlifting and recognized that this was a woman who would add a sizzle to any issue of *Sports Illustrated*.

Shari couldn't mistake the surprise in Adam's expression, a playful smile with a broad grin and a spirited laugh. "What's so funny?"

"You're not at all what I expected."

"I'm not what you expected? What did you expect?"

Adam's tongue was tied but only for a moment. "Do you ever wonder how we create images of people we talk to on the phone? I had an image of you as a beautiful woman, fair complexion, medium height, and slender. I never imagined I was talking to a tall, gorgeous black woman."

"Does that make a difference to you?"

"Are you asking if it makes a difference to me that you're tall and gorgeous or that you're black?" He didn't leave the question dangling long enough for her to respond with the answer he already knew. "I don't know if it makes a difference, but I'm sure we can figure it out. Let's talk business here and then go to dinner. If you'd like, we can even talk about race in America today. How's that for an offer you can't refuse?"

"Sorry, Adam, I have to refuse. I've got too much left to do. Let's go over your proposal here in my office. Maybe we can do dinner another time."

"No, no, no. The truth is I came all this way to meet you. I know you're not going to deny me the pleasure of your company."

"You can enjoy the pleasure of my company right here in my office."

They spent the afternoon digging into the details of Adam's proposal. It was nearly six when they finished, and Adam, undeterred, again suggested they go to dinner.

"Like I said, tonight won't work."

"I'll be here in town two more days. How 'bout tomorrow night?"

Shari, annoyed and feeling awkward, blurted, "No, Adam. Not tomorrow night either."

"Okay, I get it. You turn into a werewolf at night. So let's go to breakfast tomorrow morning."

"Don't you ever give up?"

"Nope. Sooner or later, you're gonna have to say yes."

Sorry, Adam. You seem nice enough, but I don't date clients."

"Okay, okay, I get that. Let's not go out on a date. But you do go to lunch with clients, don't you?"

"Yes, Adam. I do go to lunch with clients."

"Well, I'm your client, right? Let's go out for a six o'clock lunch."

"What's with you anyway? Do you think you have to impress me with your racial tolerance in order for us to buy into your project?"

"No, Shari. I guess I can accept that you might be suspicious, but frankly, on the receiving end of your suspicion, it feels like a slap in the face. You want to know what's with me? Here's what's with me. We've been on the phone for weeks now, and after every conversation I've embellished my image of you as a bright and captivating woman, one I wanted to meet. Okay, so I got the color of your skin wrong. So what? I don't believe you have other plans tonight. So what do you say? Let's get out of here and get some lunch."

———

Shari had grown up in a middle-class neighborhood in Queens, New York. Her father raised her alone after her mother died when she was two years old. He was the son of a sharecropper who had struggled to eke out a living for his wife and four kids on a depleted plot of parched earth. Her father was the first in his family to go to college.

After graduation, he went on to law school and then straight to work as an assistant district attorney in New York City. Determined that his daughter would not be denied a good education, he enrolled her in an academically rigorous private school. In high school, she was often point leader on the varsity basketball team and served as captain of the championship debate team. She would have claimed a 4.0 grade point average except for the blemish of a B+ in AP History because her teacher, an antiquated curmudgeon, couldn't see her way clear to accommodate Shari's athletic and debate team schedules. Nonetheless, Shari gained early admission to New York University, where she graduated magna cum laude. She had planned to work for a few years before going on to law school. She wanted to practice law like her father.

At "lunch," Adam was careful to confine his conversation to business matters but spiced it up here and there with small talk. A funny thing happened halfway through the bottle of wine that Adam ordered undaunted by Shari's unpersuasive protest. They drifted into stories drawn from their family histories and spoke about their hopes and dreams. In hindsight, he thought it odd that it didn't matter to him that she was black. Odd because, given his background, it would have mattered. Was it the quiet ambiance, the delectable food, or the wine, that aged vintage imbued with a hint of berries and oak? Whatever it was, her blackness faded from view. Her blackness—whatever that even meant—escaped his attention. At that time, in that place, he no longer saw it. He would have to weigh it soon enough, but for that moment, it had no weight. It did not compute. She wasn't black. She wasn't white. She was Shari.

All the things he had come to like about her he saw in her sparkling eyes, on her smiling lips. When she spoke of values and attitudes, he saw her as a person of strength, intelligence, and good humor. When she laughed, he laughed too, a reflection of her cheerful disposition. After dinner, they walked the neighborhood and stopped at a bar for drinks. The evening scurried along unnoticed and snuck up near to midnight. Shari welcomed Adam's suggestion that he walk her home. They hardly noticed the full moon shining down on them. At her door, he didn't expect her to invite him in, and she didn't, but Adam told her that he'd like to see her again and that just maybe then they could go out on a date.

Two years later, Adam and Shari were married in a private ceremony attended by Adam's mother and Shari's father. Charlie and Laura were also there along with one of Shari's closest friends. The two parents, wary of each other though they were, found they had something in common. They both questioned the wisdom of their children's interracial marriage. At the ceremony, they both appeared sober in expression rather than somber, and both managed to be cordial and keep their opinions to themselves.

As Adam and Shari began to accumulate wealth, Shari took the lead in directing their private investments and philanthropic interests. Though unpretentious in her daily routines, she always dressed with elegance on formal occasions and managed with grace the attention drawn to her, both fawning and sincere. Her sparkling eyes accompanied a dazzling smile—when it was offered. But she could also manage a piercing stare, which she wielded with fire or ice when ministering on behalf of the philanthropic boards on which she served. She had never been just a donor or a passive board member basking in the glow of virtue. No, where she had invested money, she had invested her vitality right along with it. Ever mindful of her father's emphasis on education, she founded and for a time chaired EIN, the Education Initiatives Network. In that capacity, she had been a vigorous fundraiser and largely responsible for EIN's success in funding innovative educational programs implemented nationwide. Adam supported her activities with enthusiasm and always expressed pride in her aggressive skills, except when he'd been the one on the receiving end.

Charlie couldn't conceive of Shari as jumbled up and a mess. "Shari, this doesn't sound like you. You don't have to apologize to me. Do you know that Adam called me and expected me to drop everything and fly out here overnight to meet with him about some new project? Is your complaint connected with that project?"

"I don't know. That's part of it. I know he's working on some big project he doesn't want to talk about. His focus, drive, determination—they're relentless. It drives me nuts and the kids too. The guy's got a lot going for him, but he's not perfect, you know. His major fault is the same as his major strength. He's a driven man: determined, relentless, insistent, unyielding. When he's on task, he doesn't sleep. His emails go out before dawn so their recipients have marching orders before they brush their teeth. I don't know how he manages to keep people working for him."

Shari complained about how Adam comes up with ideas and then pursues them with a determined single-mindedness. "In the past, there were breaks when our family life seemed almost normal. We made time for love and affection, for family and friends, for vacations and other interests too. But this time it's different. There are no breaks. There's only Adam's project. That's the beginning, and that's the end—day after day with no end in sight."

Charlie knew that Shari didn't tolerate her discontents for long. "Have you called him on this? Has he been at least a little responsive?"

"I can't get a conversation with more than a few grunts before his eyes wander. I can say something to him, something important, at least to me, and when I finish, it's like he wasn't even listening. For a while, I thought he needed his hearing checked, but that's not it. He can hear fine when he wants to. It's the listening that's a problem. You know I love Adam. We've had a long marriage—a successful one, I think. Or at least I thought so. We've had a lot of happiness and worked through whatever problems there were, but now this thing . . . it's different. I don't know what's going on. I've started to wonder if he's having an affair."

Charlie and Adam had graduated high school together and went on to the University of California Berkeley, where they were roommates. Adam was frustrated by the classes that didn't interest him, and the ones that did interest him always moved too slowly. He talked about dropping out. Charlie knew that was a bad idea and that if he did drop out, a decent job and successful career would forever elude him. Charlie had tried to talk to him about it, but there was no way to change his mind. Adam had had enough and dropped out before the end of that first semester.

Adam had gotten a job busing tables at a high-end restaurant. On a Saturday night a couple of months into the job, a waitress called in sick at the last minute. With a packed reservation list and unable to find a fill-in, Adam's boss, the restaurant owner, turned to Adam in desperation.

"There's a clean pair of pants and a nicely pressed shirt in the closet. It may not be a perfect fit, but it's close enough. Put it on. You're a server tonight."

Adam was surprised but figured he had nothing to lose. After getting dressed, his boss rolled his eyes as he inspected his new server's ill-fitting clothes. He briefed Adam on serving etiquette and on the evening's specials and then turned him loose, for better or worse.

Adam's charm made him an instant hit with the restaurant's affluent clientele, and his boss was impressed with his knack for upselling.

At night's end, Adam's boss said with a stern expression, "You're fired. I won't have you busing tables anymore. From now on, you're a server."

That was fine with Adam, who loved pocketing the generous tips he collected. The job was perfect. He worked evenings, which left his days free for his projects. His first invention was a kitchen gadget—a vacuum container for storing food. He had gotten his boss to put up a few thousand dollars. Once perfected, he sold it to a kitchen product marketing company. He split the modest profits with his boss and used his share to design a heavy-duty version for commercial and industrial use. He sold that design too, but this time negotiated a percentage of the profits. It was a big success. Adam was on his way.

Later, he cooked up a sensor and computer algorithm that cut fuel consumption in internal combustion engines and improved gas mileage by two to three miles per gallon. Automakers, under pressure to improve mileage, loved it and paid him handsomely for every car they produced. That was a lot of cars and a lot of money.

He subsequently figured out a way to purify wastewater to near perfect purity, and do it with half the energy consumption of alternative methods, and then adapted the same technology to desalinate seawater.

Water scarcity was on his mind when he developed a device to extract water from the air. How was that for a trick? Water vapor in the air is not insignificant. *Leave it to Adam to figure out a way to extract it even in dry desert regions,* Charlie thought.

Then there was the GPS algorithm that delivered better accuracy while requiring simpler hardware. That meant smaller-sized GPS gear that consumed less power. *Was he joking about putting it in a golf ball?* Charlie had wondered.

That was only a small part of Adam's story. How did he do it? He took his own ideas, and those of others, and elaborated them. Then he applied them to a wide variety of consumer products and industrial processes. The guy was also a natural promoter. At just thirty-five years of age, he had become fabulously wealthy, which enabled him to pursue his interests on an ever-widening scale.

Chapter 6

During the rest of the ride to the Braudy estate, Charlie and Shari continued their troubling conversation bracketed by long moments of uneasy silence. Charlie was dead tired, emotionally drained, and now burdened by the anticipation of seeing Adam in an unfamiliar light. He became wary about how their conversation might go as he and Shari passed through the guarded security entrance onto the estate grounds.

The Braudy estate consisted of forty acres of gently sloping land rising uphill from the entry gate to the home site, where their mansion commanded an elevated 270-degree view of a bucolic river run and thickly wooded hillsides. They drove slowly up a long, winding driveway and passed by manicured gardens, finally reaching the home at the top of the slope. Adam and Shari had worked with a renowned architect who was well regarded among old-veau and nouveau riche alike. From the architect's plans, the home Shari and Adam had built presented a traditional appearance from the front but gave way to a broad expanse of glass in the back overlooking the river valley below. The views were resplendent.

Adam was outside on the entry terrace when the car pulled up. He was clad in sweat pants and a limp T-shirt, which hung from his slumped shoulders. His recessed eyes were mere squints draped behind sagging lids. He accompanied Shari and Charlie inside and led them to the library. Adam's offer of whiskey was most welcome.

Adam began, "I woke them up—Melissa's parents. They were

probably deep asleep. Who knows? Maybe I woke them from sweet dreams to tell them their daughter was dead. At first, I don't think they knew who the hell I was. They must have wondered if my call was some kind of prank. At first, they were mute. I heard Melissa's father tell his wife what I said. That's when I heard a scream, a wailing sound. A sound like I've never heard before. A sound I pray I'll never hear again. It was the collective shriek from a thousand tortured sinners flayed skinless and burning in Dante's hell. Between wrenching sobs, Melissa's father struggled to make his questions known. But what for? There were no answers."

Adam drained his glass and poured more whiskey. He took a seat, and with his glass of whiskey in one hand, he ran his fingers through his disheveled hair with his other. His face was drained of color.

He spoke in a morose whisper. "I tried. I really tried. But there was no way I could comfort them. I kept saying how sorry I was and how we all came to appreciate what an extraordinary young woman she was. I offered that they should call me if there were anything I could do. But what could I do? Then we were both silent until he said . . . I can't believe what he said. He said, 'Thanks for calling.' And then he hung up. I've never felt so inadequate in all my life."

Adam turned his sullen gaze toward Charlie, cleared his throat, and said with uncharacteristic timidity, "As I spoke with Melissa's father, my perception of time and space skipped awry, fell backward. I couldn't help feeling like I was trying to comfort you. Melissa's death must remind you of your own loss."

Charlie said, "You know, under ordinary circumstances—as if you could call what happened tonight *ordinary*—to witness Melissa's death would be horrific, but in my case, it's—"

"I know," Adam interrupted.

Even after so many years, every reminder still caused Charlie heartache—and that was just a prelude to depression. The slightest hint conjured a palpable apparition of Sandra, Charlie's sweet firstborn child, who died from a freak bacterial infection when she was just five years old. Laura and Charlie had thought their bond was unbreakable. That bond was cruelly tested.

Why had he let Sandra play in the garden with his rusty tools? Why didn't Laura take her to the doctor sooner? Crippled by depression, convicted in courts of their own imaginings, they were sentenced to dangle from ropes made of the twisted strands of their confessed guilt and the unutterable accusations with which each charged the other. Without even the possibility of appeal or parole, their sentences inflicted a cruel penalty that by far exceeded their guilt. C h a r l i e could not dwell on their loss, could not talk about it. He pretended that he could move on, but any mention or recollection would disable him. Laura could not focus on anything else. She pretended that re-thinking every detail, recalling every misstep, was the only way to find some meaning in their loss and expiation for their sins. Between them there was no common ground. Their exuberant family life, once filled with hopes and dreams, became unsustainable.

Intimacy became impossible. Laura gave up her work as a teacher and spent hours each week in yoga and therapy. Endless conversations with friends over coffee and on phone calls early in the morning and late at night rounded out her daily routine. Charlie bought transient moments of release in anonymous sexual exploits. A woman he had worked with as co-counsel offered understanding and advice. Long evening hours spent together in case preparation soon became long hours spent in bed. But her assurances were hollow, and the sensual pleasure only reminded him of his failure as a husband. And yet, and yet, he longed for Laura, not the grief-stricken woman but the woman he could still recall: his bride, his helpmate, his nymph, and the mother of their son. Those recollections lingered even as the gulf between them widened.

Laura's discovery of Charlie's indiscretion proved both horrific and a blessing. It became a turning point. They had to decide which way to turn. In painful conversation, they recognized that each of them in their own way had abandoned the other. They realized that they could never go back to what they'd had. To go forward and rebuild, forgiveness was their only way.

—

Charlie wanted to move on, needed to, and said to Adam, "I understand that you called Laura too."

"Yes. She's anxious to see you. I sent a plane to pick her up. It'll be waiting for her at the airport. She can be here sometime tomorrow, whenever she wants."

Adam and Shari walked Charlie upstairs to a gracious guest suite. Alone at last, Charlie went to the bar cabinet and poured himself half a glass of whiskey. He drank a good part of it before setting the rest aside. Exhausted and tipsy, he pulled off his clothes, dropped them in a heap on the floor, and crawled into bed. He lay there, his head awhirl, worried that the constant spinning would keep him from sleep. But exhaustion won out. Though he fell into darkness, rest eluded him. He was haunted over and again by nightmares of Melissa crashing into the ceiling, the sound of her neck snapping.

Chapter 7

Charlie could not sleep and arose to find his memories were as bad as his nightmares. A hangover weighed him down, eyelids drooping low over his dry and itchy eyes, his face sagging. He wobbled to the bathroom and tried to refresh himself with a shower. Afterward, he searched and finally found his cell phone in the pocket of his coat, which lay in a heap on the floor like yesterday's refuse. He was anxious to talk to Laura.

She answered his call saying, "Are you okay?"

"I don't know. Didn't get much sleep. I feel lousy. How 'bout you?"

"The same. After your call last night, Adam called. He filled me in on more details. He said that he and Shari would take good care of you and told me he'd have a plane waiting for me at Buchanan Field. It's probably there already. I gotta get out of bed and tell Joel what's going on. You know how your son is. He's just like you. He'll want to hear all the details. Then I'll be on my way."

"So you're planning to come?"

"What do you mean? Of course I'm coming. What did you think?"

"I don't know. I wasn't sure. When I left for the airport, it seemed like things were horribly unsettled between us."

"Unsettled, yes, but, Charlie, I love you. I always will. I'm definitely coming."

"What about business? Are you going to be missing anything important?"

"Don't worry about that. I can do business with just my cell phone and a Wi-Fi connection."

After Sandra died, Laura had tried to go back into a classroom, thinking that it would be good for her. She loved the children but was overwhelmed by grief. Instead, she went back to school, got an MBA, and embarked on a new career as an environmental consultant.

Charlie and Laura continued their conversation, once again reliving the details of the dreadful night. Though it was left unsaid, they each recognized in the other that Melissa's death was one more reminder of Sandra.

Charlie looked in the mirror and ran a brush through his hair. He went downstairs and headed straight for the kitchen, where Adam and Shari were drinking coffee and catching up on the news.

Shari looked up. "Good morning, Charlie. I hope you were able to sleep."

"I slept like a rock and feel great."

Adam said, "That's funny. You look like crap."

"I think I'm alright. What do you see in the news—anything about last night?"

"Oh, yeah," Shari responded. "There's plenty. You know, Adam, it's a good thing you spoke with Melissa's parents. It would've been horrible if they heard about it on the news."

That stirred Charlie's memories yet again. He started to ramble. "You know, I thought about them, too, and about Melissa. Last night, I felt the immediacy of my own certain death, a panic I can't describe. But that wasn't the only thing. I saw Melissa thrown up against the ceiling. I saw it happen, and suddenly, just like that, she was dead. Now she's gone. She knows nothing. She feels no pain, no grief, no loss. While she was alive, her essence, her most private sense of self, was the center of her consciousness. She must have known happiness and felt pride in her strengths and accomplishments, and she must have known sadness, too, and felt melancholy about her flaws, shortcomings, and inadequacies. Now, though, suddenly there's nothing. Or is there something more?"

He couldn't stop himself from going on.

"For those who knew her, it's an entirely different story. They're the ones who suffer. They're the ones who know the pain, grief, and loss. They're the ones who are denied the unfulfilled potentialities of her life, now suddenly lost. It's as if her life wasn't her own. She may have been the bearer of it, of course, a most intimate custodian of it, but in a way, her life truly belonged and still belongs to everyone who ever invested themselves in it."

Adam was tempted to interrupt Charlie and save him from himself. This could only lead to more misery.

"When I first realized she was dead, I was confused. You know, I'm not so naive about death. I've seen it up close before. That lowland valley, for me, is not entirely unfamiliar terrain, but the immediate juxtaposition of Melissa's death with my survival evoked a senselessness that I can't dismiss. How could a sweet young woman, full of life one minute, suddenly be dead the very next? Melissa is dead, and I'm alive. Sandra is dead, and I'm still alive. What meaning can I find in their deaths? Hell, what meaning can I find in my life or any life, for that matter?"

Shari finally intruded. "Charlie, those are fair questions, but not every question has an answer."

Charlie paused and said, "Okay, so what's for breakfast around here?"

Adam left the room when his cell phone rang, leaving Shari and Charlie alone at the table. Charlie said, "Look, about last night, about you and Adam. I don't know how I'll handle it, but it's on my mind, and one way or another, I'll talk to Adam about it. I wish I could offer more comfort than that."

"Charlie, your presence last night was a comfort to me. Don't make this your responsibility. If there's a way, I know you'll find it, but you and Adam have your own relationship to manage."

"Shari, know this: I will find a way."

Two aspirins and two cups of coffee didn't touch his hangover or the headache. He was surprised that his bowl of granola stayed down.

When Adam came back to the kitchen, he appeared anxious to move on. Charlie understood that there was a reason Adam had called on him to fly out in a rush. What was it that Adam wanted of him?

"Okay, Charlie. If you're feeling up to it, let's get out of here and head on over to my new campus. After nearly five years, phase one construction is finished and partly occupied. I want you to see it up close and personal, and I want to tell you what's on my mind, what I've been thinking about for quite a while."

Adam turned to Shari. "Charlie and I are going to take the Porsche. Do me a favor and tell Michael I won't need him today."

Adam enjoyed his wealth, but along with it came some complications, personal security among them. Adam had many sleepless nights, many attributable to his busy mind grinding away, plotting and planning next steps. But, lately, more of those nights were spent half awake, wrestling with sheets and pillows in futile attempts to evade one monstrous threat after another. Was he an assassin's quarry? Were his wife and kids kidnap targets? Those fears dominated his nights, but by day he pretended indifference.

Shari had her own worries and was more realistic. They had invested a lot of resources in assembling a security team. Its task was much larger than just protection from physical assaults. They had to anticipate danger from any quarter and were prepared to deal harshly with even the most sophisticated threats.

Shari protested, "Adam, you can't just run around without protection. That's not smart. We've been over this before. We've got Michael for the extra security we both said we want. Do you really think you'll be safe driving around by yourself?"

"I know. We need security but not today. Today, I need to be in touch with the road and the world. Too much insulation is too much isolation. Some days I've got to have my life back."

"You should've thought about that before you made your first billion. You've got your life. It's just different than before. Get used to it."

"Thanks for the advice, honey. See you later."

They got into Adam's Porsche and waved to the guards at the guard post as they left the estate.

Chapter 8

Though Charlie had not yet seen the new BrauCorp campus, he had heard Adam's descriptions and frustrations throughout the five-year ordeal of design and construction. Along their way, Adam floored the accelerator. As they rushed headlong into the wind, every thought and emotion was cast aside. The sights and sounds of the road seized their attention. They felt more than heard the roar of the engine and its high-speed whine, the sound of the tires rasping over the pavement on straightaways and then skidding on winding curves.

After a time, Adam slowed down enough to invite a conversation. Charlie, mindful of Shari and her frustrations, took the initiative.

"So, Adam, you seem to be keeping uber-busy. How are Shari and the kids managing with all that?"

"They're fine. Shari's busy with her philanthropy projects and keeping tabs on the kids. We thought that things would get easier with Jessica off at college, but that's not quite the way it worked out. Jessica is nearing the end of her sophomore year at Brown. She's turned into a real case."

"What's the story with Jessica—boy trouble?"

Jessica, their firstborn child, took after her mother: tall and athletic with a powerful spirit. She excelled academically throughout high school and was ambitious enough to want an elite education. As a young woman of color, an appetite for human rights and racial equality was a part of her temper. She had decided that Brown would be just right for her. Adam was wary of her choice because Brown's political perspectives did not comport with his own. He argued with Shari over a period of a couple of weeks before reluctantly acceding to Shari's insistence.

"If she's got boy trouble, it's nothing we know anything about. I'm afraid the trouble is bigger than that. It's off to Brown she goes, and not even two years later she's figured out that her good old dad is a privileged white capitalist pig and a lousy one-percenter. Naturally, I had a few questions for her. I asked her which of my inventions would the world be better off without. How many people had jobs making the damn things I've developed? How much of our filthy lucre did she think we give to charity each year? How much won't she and her brother inherit because we give it away? She demurred on all counts. I told her she sounded a bit sophomoric. That's when the shit hit the fan. What I wanted to tell her was that she was being sopho-moronic. Glad I didn't. I think I dodged a bullet."

Their son, Steve, was a short kid who had trouble making friends, and both Shari and Adam were worried about the friends he did make. There were rumors that some of them were experimenting with alcohol and drugs. As a high school junior with a high IQ, he should have been focused on grades but wasn't. They had sent him off to a recommended boarding school, hoping the change in environment would make a difference. Then they worried when they found out he was spending a lot of time hanging out with a girl in one of his classes. But because she was a serious student, they decided that might be a good thing.

Adam was never uninterested in Charlie's life and asked, "How's Laura's work going?"

"She likes her work, but she's working too hard. Because of environmental regulations, her clients have stringent deadlines for reporting. And guess what? They all have the same deadlines. That means for part of the year she can coast, but then when reporting time comes around, she goes nuts. Right now she can coast."

"What about Joel?"

Joel had grown up in the shadow of his dead sister and felt that he was a disappointment to his parents. He spent much of his childhood alone, but by the time he had gotten to high school, he had become an accomplished athlete and a star on his school's soccer team. Because of his star power, he was widely respected by his classmates.

"Don't know what to say about Joel. Talk about coasting. He's not interested in school. His grades are lousy. He'll be going into his senior year without a clue about what follows. We're hoping to get him into a college somewhere, but we're not sure who'll have him."

"Charlie, don't forget my story. College wasn't my thing. Joel's smart—smarter than you give him credit for. He's got some of your brains and Laura's too. And I'm sure that on the soccer field, he's learned plenty about hard work, competition, and team play. If he doesn't want to go to college, have him call me. I'm sure we can find something for him to do."

They drove along a stretch of rugged flatlands. For a mile, on one side of the highway, there were dozens of wind-powered electrical generators. It looked like the Martians had landed and were preparing for their war of the worlds.

"Take a look at this, Charlie. We've probably got the biggest wind farm on the planet. It's one of our projects."

He explained that the wind farm generated modest amounts of electricity but a great deal of political capital. As a result, local, state, and national political figures had come to owe him. He expected to collect.

They turned off the highway and drove along a gravel road that bordered another edge of Adam's wind farm. They passed through a guarded security gate and then through a section of the wind farm before leaving the turbines behind in the dust.

Looking ahead, Charlie saw a monumental structure reaching over a hundred feet into the sky. It stood leaning with flowing feminine curves, its reflective black surface gleaming in the sun. "What the hell is that?"

"That's Black Beauty. She's magnificent, don't you think? I wanted to make a grand entry statement, but it's more than that. Inside that majestic beast is something I'm hiding in plain sight. I make big points when I tell Shari that she's the inspiration for Black Beauty. God knows she's got power inside her."

"It's beautiful, but what do you have to hide?"

Adam came to a stop alongside Black Beauty, got out of the car, and invited Charlie to walk with him.

"At this stage, we need to keep secret everything we're doing here. I've brought you here to let you in on the secret. We're developing some amazing technologies. They'll blow your mind."

The power requirements for Adam's projects were colossal. They couldn't be met by a wind farm or even by available commercial sources. He researched and then developed technologies to power his mystery project and, at the same time, deliver clean energy without practical limit.

"Adam, what are the technologies you have to keep secret?"

Adam had first thought he could meet his power needs with some kind of an electrical energy accumulator—an ultracapacitor, something like a battery. It would accumulate power from commercial sources over a period of time and then discharge it as needed in powerful bursts. Although the technology wasn't able to provide all the power Adam needed for his project, it worked great for other applications. Adam explained that wind and solar sources weren't reliable because they were intermittent, depending as they do on wind and sunshine. The ultracapacitors could make those intermittent sources more reliable.

Then Adam had applied the same technology on a smaller scale, allowing it to work in place of a battery. He saw that replacing bulky, limited-capacity batteries with ultracapacitors would solve the electric car problem. No more three-hundred-mile-range limits. An ultracapacitor sized for an automobile would cut size, weight, and cost and still allow for a range of over five hundred miles even uphill with the air conditioner running. After that, it could be recharged in five minutes. A colossal infrastructure program would be needed to serve the charging stations, but the economics allowed for that. Adam was already planning a business that would manufacture and install that recharging infrastructure.

"If the ultracapacitors didn't satisfy your power needs, where did you go from there?"

"We started thinking about making use of an experimental fusion reactor we've been working on. For years now, we've had some very bright people trying things that no one else thought possible."

Charlie knew that for sixty years, fusion research had been conducted in labs all over the world, and a workable reactor was always another twenty years away. What could Adam add to that?

Charlie said, "Yeah, that sounds great. Maybe you can just reverse engineer the one they got on Star Ship Enterprise."

"Laugh it off if you want, but we've already built one. What do you think is snugged away inside of Black Beauty? Inside her beautiful body is a fusion power plant."

"No, Adam, that's not possible."

"Yeah, it is."

Practical fusion power had proved elusive. Was it left to Adam to tame the hydrogen bomb and make its power available for peaceful purposes? Charlie understood that initiating a fusion reaction by slamming atoms together was as old as the hydrogen bomb. It was the containment of the raging fusion reaction that was the remaining challenge.

Charlie asked, "How is it even possible to confine a blazing sun or a hydrogen bomb explosion in a terrestrial box? You can't build a fire in a cardboard box."

"No problem. We don't have a fire. We only have sparks. Our approach works on a nanoscale. Here, take a look at this."

Adam reached into his pocket and pulled out a small raggedy rock furrowed with light and dark silvery streaks.

Charlie said, "So what's this—uranium or what?"

"No, uranium is old school. Uranium is for fission reactors. This is erbium. You can hold it. It won't fry you. When it's refined, it's a silvery white rare earth metal. It's used mostly in fiber-optic telecommunications. But we've been using it in our fusion research. We can purify the stuff in a special way and impregnate it with hydrogen atoms. Even impregnated within an erbium lattice, the density of hydrogen atoms is much greater than in any other state. When we focus an X-ray beam and zap a couple of these little hydrogen atoms, we're able to force a fusion reaction. Though the dimensions we're talking about are on the atomic scale, relatively speaking, a single fusion reaction produces a large amount of heat and pressure, enough so that it can initiate additional fusion reactions. Once begun, the reactions are self-sustaining, continuously producing billions of micro reactions. All we gotta do is aggregate the heat from those tiny reactions. We don't have a containment problem because we can regulate the aggregate temperature by modulating the density of the fuel molecules. We create a lot of sparks without starting a fire. That's the way we solved our energy problem, and along the way we've initiated an energy revolution."

But that was just the beginning. After establishing the practicality of his fusion power plant, Adam went to work miniaturizing it. If he could make it as small as a water heater, every home and building could have its own power source. That would put an end to the cumbersome and vulnerable electric grid and all the inefficiencies in the transmission lines, substations, and transformers. That would solve the infrastructure problem for the automobile charging stations as well. Make it still smaller, and electric automobiles and electrically powered vehicles of all types could be fitted with their own fusion power sources.

"With a miniaturized fusion power generator, all we'd have to do is replace a fuel lattice every once in a while, and a car would run for who knows how long. Now there's a problem. It would eliminate the need for our ultracapacitors and their supporting infrastructure right at the starting gate. How's that for creative destruction? Dead on arrival."

"So why aren't you electrifying the world with fusion power?"

"It's new. We're not ready, our government friends aren't ready, and, frankly, we're afraid of threats from hostile interests."

It didn't escape Charlie's attention that Adam had more than once tossed off hints about threats he didn't specify. Charlie was becoming unsettled.

"It won't be long till we're in the middle of an energy revolution. And what a revolution it'll be. If you own any oil wells, Charlie, or any oil company stock, this would be a good time to sell. But first we have some problems to solve."

Adam was frustrated by stumbling blocks. Safety was one. In the public mind, nuclear reactions meant violent explosions and radiation hazards. Those concerns had to be addressed, but Adam was confident they could be resolved. The real problem was in connection with economics. Yes, fusion power would be cheap, but its impact on the energy economy would be immense.

"It's the old buggy whip problem. You invent the car, and suddenly the buggy whip makers are shut down. Just imagine what gets shut down when fusion power comes along."

"Adam, energy cheap and clean sounds like a good thing. Obstructing that would be like putting a stop to the flush toilet."

"It may sound good to you but not to everyone."

Adam had a long list of opponents. It started with the oil companies and the businesses that serve them, but it was much more than that. There were unions representing oil field workers, natural gas drillers, coal miners, power plant workers. Then there were the oil transport companies—the ones shipping on rail, on the road, and on the seas. He even ticked off the pipeline managers and their workers. His list included the private and institutional investors who held substantial stakes in all aspects of the energy economy. They were all at risk. He cited statistics as he went along. Hundreds of thousands of jobs worldwide, maybe millions, would vanish. The impact on the American economy and on the economies of nations around the world would be huge. How many countries utterly dependent on oil production and export would be impacted? Many of them could collapse into a sink-hole and, while fighting for survival, could do unimaginable harm.

"Charlie, can you imagine all the pressure that our legislators and regulators are struggling with? They have special interests representing trillions of dollars pounding on their doors. And the state department has to be worried about global instabilities. Think about Russia, a nuclear power whose economy hangs on oil and gas exports. Are they just going to fade away? Yeah, maybe they will—but only after the fire and brimstone cools down."

"What about all the opportunities that will be created—the new jobs, new products, new capabilities?"

"Yes, of course, but government is an institution of the status quo. It weighs known and immediately foreseeable losses much differently than unknown and speculative possibilities. In the government mind, the palpable always wins out over the ephemeral. Revolutions are instigated by visionaries who, for better and sometimes for worse, dream of possibilities, some of which just might come to pass . . . or not. Bureaucracies and established interests resist revolutions."

"But, Adam, aren't we already in the middle of an energy revolution? The threat of climate change has instigated a huge movement toward clean, non-fossil fuel energy sources. Governments at all levels are all in on clean energy production. Of course, there are those who are resisting, but I'm not seeing the kind of opposition you're describing."

"You're right, Charlie, but for all the blather, current proposals for clean energy production don't amount to a large part of the world's total energy budget. Today's clean energy technologies may improve, but for now there's no way they can displace fossil fuels. Our fusion technology is a different story. It would immediately make fossil fuels obsolete. If you wanna see an oil derrick, you'll have to go to a museum."

Pushing for approval was a costly imposition. It was Adam's experience that it was cheap and easy to buy friends. But this time, nothing was easy. Every push got a pushback. That kept him from moving forward with his most important project, the mystery project that he wanted to discuss with Charlie.

"I don't know what it's going to take to get this to market. There are shadowy players in the mix, and they're pushing back with a lot of muscle and threats. Though they've kept us from commercial applications, they haven't kept us from employing it here for our own use."

There it was again—Adam's reference to a threat. Charlie dismissed it for the moment but took note and set it aside for further discussion later on.

"You've described your ultracapacitor and your fusion reactor. Did those discoveries solve your energy problem?"

"Not quite. We still had a problem. It was easy to couple our fusion reactor to an electrical generator and then feed the electrical power into our ultracapacitor. But then we recognized that because of the extreme power requirement, if we threw the big switch, we'd fry the power lines from the ultracapacitor to the application project site. We would have had quite a meltdown. We had to figure out a workaround. We settled on a superconducting medium to transport the electrical power. That meant researching and producing exotic superconducting materials and then optimizing cryogenic cooling processes that could cool the conductors down to a temperature just above absolute zero. That was a trick, but we did it. Now we have multiple cryogenically cooled, superconducting cables, each one about three feet in diameter and each one composed of dozens of separate conductors."

Charlie was in awe and asked, "How do you come up with all this stuff?"

Time and again, Adam developed things that had been nothing more than dream stuff. Little by little, Charlie had come to understand his friend's method. Adam didn't actually invent everything he worked on. The way he saw it, his job was to identify problems that called for solutions and pursue curiosities that cried out for answers. Sometimes a news announcement or a magazine article would excite his imagination. Once intrigued, he'd go to books, journals, and unpublished research articles. Because of his reputation, he had access to experts and geniuses in every field of human inquiry whom he might explore his ideas with. Most of the time, his ideas went nowhere. But that never slowed him down. He'd just put it aside and move on to explore another idea.

Whenever he would hit on something worthwhile, he would commit resources and funding to ramp up the research. If there was a business doing research that interested him, he'd recruit the researchers or even buy the company. When he bought a company, he'd keep the research and development department and then either operate the rest of the company as a sideline or sell it off. If the research was promising, he'd follow up with product development and turn it into a product.

Adam explained, "There's no way I could do any of this if it weren't for the experts I turn to. They're the geniuses. They're specialists in their fields—researchers, designers, and engineers."

"Oh, yeah, and you get the credit and make the big bucks."

"Charlie, you sound like a cynic. I think of it differently. I'd say that by their efforts, they become vested in the businesses that we jointly create to produce the products we develop together. Oh, yeah, when these products hit the market, they get lots of credit. They become highly regarded in their fields and enjoy much respect from their peers. In fact, a couple of these people are shortlisted for Nobel Prizes. How's that for credit? And then, because of their participation in the businesses we build together, they also reap the kind of credit they can take to the bank. I hold these men and women in high regard. And that respect is reciprocated. Later, when they come up with ideas of their own, it's not long before they come knocking on my door to see if we can do a redo. They know that my door is always open."

Adam wanted to move on and show Charlie the rest of the campus. They finished their walk around Black Beauty and, once back in the car, left her behind along with the fire and brimstone blazing inside. Some of the recent work Charlie had done for Adam was related to the construction and development of the campus, but all the energy technology was new to him. Charlie was overwhelmed. What else did he not know about? Seeing the campus was almost anticlimactic—almost but not quite.

Each of the twenty buildings articulated a distinct architectural style. Some recalled historical themes, others more modern. One expressively postmodern structure looked like a collection of boxes stacked in layers all askew. Had those boxes just tumbled into place, or were they about to topple to the ground? The landscape plan was a symphonic composition of grasses, bushes, and trees that meandered sinuously among the buildings, melding dissimilar architectural themes into a coherent whole.

A pair of buildings set apart from the others drew Charlie's attention. He learned that they were facilities devoted to medical research and that Adam's pet project depended on a team engaged in biological and medical research. This was a new direction for Adam—a move from the physical sciences to biology. Charlie could only guess at the direction of Adam's precocious intellect. *What might he be working on now—playing with life itself?*

Chapter 9

They drove through another guarded security entrance and into a subterranean driveway. Charlie didn't want to signal his worry, but the specter of one more guard post was one too many and spurred him to raise a question.

"Why all the security—your estate, your driver, your campus entry, and now your garage? Are these just the ordinary precautions of your everyday billionaire?"

"Yes and no. Obviously, wealth has its problems."

"Oh, yeah, Adam. I'm feeling your pain."

Even as he tossed off his smart remark, Charlie was thinking how he might feel if it were his family at risk. Wealth did have its problems. Besides, Adam's wealth was not the only lure. Some threats had nothing to do with his money. Modern-day Luddites were among those objecting. Not that their concerns were unjustified. Contemporary Luddites were well past worrying about the mechanization of textile industry jobs in nineteenth-century England. The modern variety feared being displaced by robots and artificial intelligence or, worse, being bound and enshrouded by the technological fabric of the times.

But Adam was not complacent about the economic and political actors positioned against him. As he explained to Charlie, they would feel the impact on their interests most directly and might do anything to impede or stop his energy revolution. And most worrisome of all was that they had the means at their disposal.

"Adam, is this paranoia talking, or are there specific threats?"

Adam had absolute confidence in Dean Fleck, BrauCorp's head of security. His appearance was quite ordinary: middle-aged, medium height and weight, modestly built, and slightly balding. Adam thought his beard looked attractive, but it bothered him that his "toothbrush" mustache looked like Hitler's. What was not ordinary about Dean was his intelligence and experience. Multiple times in the previous year, he came to Adam with warnings. On one occasion, a car had stopped on the street not far from the guarded entrance to the Braudy estate. A young couple had gotten out with their dog and walked toward the guard post. It was a sunny day, and they were laughing while throwing a ball for their dog to fetch. They took pictures to memorialize the occasion and even asked one of the guards to take their picture. They thanked him and playfully took pictures of him, some of which captured details of the guard post. Dean insisted this was surveillance.

On another occasion, a small plane had flown low over the Brau-Corp campus, making several slow passes and a few turns. Had the passengers been taking pictures? Then there was the janitor who, while cleaning, had been found in a research lab taking photos with his cell phone. Besides all of that, there were the relentless hacking attacks on BrauCorp's servers. Dean was charged with investigating all these suspected intrusions and heightening defenses against them.

"Yes, Charlie, we know of specific threats. We have quite a list. I'm not going to name names, at least not for now, but go ahead and make your own list of countries, especially the autocratic ones that are largely dependent on oil revenues. They have significant clandestine capabilities that we have to identify and protect against."

Adam drove along the underground driveway until they reached a basement parking area. They rode an elevator, only operable with a security key, up to the ground floor. The elevator door opened into a high-ceilinged warehouse space. Though it had just been recently occupied, it had already accumulated a surprising amount of clutter. There were multiple computer stations, racks of instruments with lights, dials, knobs, and screens. Hammers, screwdrivers, brushes, and pliers in assorted sizes were hanging on wall hooks. Others were scattered here and there along with drills, flashlights, and soldering irons. Vises, attached to edges of workbenches, clutched at gadgets on their way from what they were to what they might become. An office desk was in a corner. At one end of the work area was a roll-up door big enough to permit the passage of large pieces of equipment and bulk materials. The air was pregnant with a stew of industrial smells—a heady mix of alcohol, lubricants, ozone, formaldehyde, and animal odors, which combined to pronounce the imminent birth of discoveries about to be revealed.

"Adam, is this your play space? Is this where you do your magic?"

"This is the place. I love it. I love the smell of it—the machines, the chemicals. I love the sounds—the electrical hums and the whirring of my tools. Discovery is what I do here. It's a kind of magic, but it's for real, no illusions. See that device over there? That's a 3D printer. Do you know how a 3D printer works?"

"Sort of. It's like an inkjet printer, but instead of printing ink on paper, it prints plastic on top of plastic, one layer at a time, till an intended object is built up. Is that close?"

"Yeah, except that there's a lot of work being done developing printers that will build up objects like you described but using different kinds of materials besides plastic, like metal or even living cells. We're starting to see specialized metal parts printed and living tissues too."

Charlie figured that Adam must have been working on a fancy 3D printer, but knowing Adam, it would have to be more than fancy. It would have to be otherworldly. Adam pointed at two rectangular-shaped metal enclosures, each one about the length of a large van and tall enough to stand in. Windows made of thick glass or plastic were spaced evenly around each enclosure, and each was fed by wires and pipes. Charlie wondered what kind of magic Adam was about to reveal.

"One of those is a special kind of scanner and the other an extraordinary kind of printer. But before I show you how they work, I want to take you over to a med lab at the research center. There's someone there I want you to meet."

Chapter 10

Adam's lab had a door that opened directly to the outside, where they were greeted with a fresh breeze. They walked along a meandering concrete path in the direction of a multistory building about a hundred yards away. Ahead on the left was a putting green, and on the right a thicket of shrubs over six feet high was set back in the middle of an expansive lawn.

"Charlie, see those shrubs? They're laid out to form a maze. Every month or two, I have the landscape crew change them around. That way, even if someone has run the maze before, there's always another chance to get lost again. Wanna give it a try?"

"Do I look like a rat? Do I get a bite of cheese if I make my way through it?"

"Honestly, Charlie, you're so mercenary. Is it only the cheese you're thinking about? All you'll get is bragging rights. That seems to motivate more than a few people around here. By the way, you'll be pleased to know that everyone gets through it, some faster than others. In your case, I wouldn't recommend doing it alone near sunset. We haven't lost anyone yet, but you might be the first."

"I'll take that as a challenge. Let's have a go at it. What's your time? What do I have to beat?"

"Hey. No contest. There's no way you could beat me. I laid out the maze and supervised its installation."

Adam took out his watch and marked Charlie's start time. "I'll wait for you at the exit—however long that might take."

Charlie was determined to show Adam that he could find his way through the maze in record time. He hurried along but, time after time, had to retreat from dead ends. Without success, he tried peering between branches to see if he might cut his way through to a shorter route. In the end, it took eleven minutes. Charlie felt embarrassed that it had taken him so long, though Adam insisted that he was impressed.

"Not bad. The average time is a bit more than fifteen minutes, and only a handful has done eleven minutes or better."

They moved along toward the research center and entered an office on the fourth floor marked "Director of Research." The receptionist welcomed them and ushered them directly into the private office of Dr. Virginia Salter. It was a corner office furnished with impeccable taste. Set against one wall was a most unusual six-foot sculpture of Michelangelo's David. The left half was just as it is usually seen, but the right half was depicted with its internal organs on display.

Dr. Salter, a woman in her fifties with shoulder-length hair dyed brunette, was already in motion as they entered. She was quick to greet each of them with a warm smile and a firm handshake.

"Hello, Adam. Glad to see you. And, Charlie, please call me Gina. I'm pleased to finally meet you. Adam has told me much about you. I'm delighted that you'll be working on this project with us."

Working on what project? Charlie was surprised.

Adam said, "Gina, what do you say we take Charlie down to the lab and show him what we're doing with our rats?"

———

The lab bore the contending odors of disinfectants and those of the experimental rats whose purpose was to disclose the deepest secrets of human biology. Gina led the way to a maze.

"I want to show you how quickly a rat who has previously learned this maze can repeat its passage."

She picked up a rat from a cage bearing the letter A and explained that it took that rat about ten minutes to run the maze the first time. Then each day, for three days, the same rat ran the same maze several more times. On each subsequent occasion, it found its way in ever shorter periods. On this occasion, Charlie watched the rat race along a familiar route. When it reached the feeding station, Gina stopped her watch and reported the time.

"That was four minutes and twenty-three seconds. That's just about the same time as the last two times. I think that's the best we're going to see from this rat. We've performed the same protocol with the other nine rats in cage A, and with each one, we have obtained a similar result. Around four and a half minutes is typical."

She picked up the rat and placed it back in cage A. Then she took a rat from a cage marked with the letter B and ran it through the maze. She stopped her watch when the rat reached the feeding station.

"That was four minutes and thirty-five seconds. What do you think, Charlie?"

"What do you mean? I think you've got a well-trained rat."

"Now, Charlie, that's an entirely reasonable response—except for one minor detail, which I guess I forgot to share with you. This rat, the one you just watched run the maze in about four minutes and thirty-five seconds, has never run this maze before—never, not once. Four minutes and thirty-five seconds is an impressive time for a naïve rat, don't you think? How in the world does he do that? And if we run the other nine rats from cage B, you'd find that they, too, would run the maze in about four and a half minutes."

Charlie was confused. Were the rats from cage B a different, smarter breed? Had they infused the rats with some kind of brain juice? Was brain juice at the root of Adam's new project? Perhaps they actually trained the rat, only claiming that it was untrained. Or did they simplify the maze without Charlie's notice? Gina saw his puzzlement.

"Interesting, isn't it, Charlie? Now take whatever questions you might have and go along with Adam. I bet he has more to show and tell."

Gina extended her hand along with a playful grin and said goodbye. Charlie shook her hand and left the lab utterly bewildered, hoping that Adam could explain what he was missing.

Chapter 11

Adam saw that Charlie was baffled. "Cat got your tongue?"

"Well, yeah. So are you going to tell me how you got your lab rats to pull off the sleight of hand you seem so proud of?"

"All in good time, my friend. All in good time."

As they walked a little farther along, a playful smile widened Charlie's lips. "Adam, I know the scale is different, but that maze the rats ran in four minutes . . . is that the same maze I ran in eleven?"

Adam grinned. "No, Charlie, the rats' maze was much harder. Those rats are a hell of a lot smarter than you."

Their laughter wound down as they continued on their way back to the building that housed Adam's lab. They approached the main entry rather than the lab door and crossed the lobby to take an elevator to the sixth floor. The door opened directly into a reception area, where they were welcomed by Adam's executive assistant. They moved along to Adam's luxuriously appointed office.

Looking from floor to ceiling, Charlie said, "You sure got a lot of glass here. I guess you really like the view."

"I do. I like seeing all the buildings together and each one of them unique unto itself. Can you feel the dynamism? I love it. I can feel it in my bones."

"Why a solid wall here? Nothing to look at from this direction?"

"I had to put my big video screen somewhere. Besides, I need at least one wall for my Vermeer."

Adam directed Charlie to the adjoining dining room, where a table was set for two. Bill, Adam's personal chef, presented menus and described the offerings in detail. They indicated their selections, and Adam asked for the bottle of wine he had preselected for this occasion.

Bill returned with a bottle already uncorked and aerated. He poured a taste for Adam and one for Charlie as well. Adam swirled his glass and looked knowingly into it. He raised the glass to his nose and took several short sniffs, taking in the savory aroma. A small mouthful was all he needed.

"Ah, delicious. Charlie, do you agree?"

Before Charlie gave his approval, he asked to see the bottle and grinned when he saw the label: Château Lafite Rothschild 1996.

"Adam this is a memorable choice."

Smiling in response, Adam said, "On your account, my friend, a fine vintage. But don't think just because I can afford it, I ordinarily drink this well. I want you to know this selection is in your honor, to put a stamp on this consequential occasion."

Charlie heard the sound of a train coming into the station and felt the rumble of a big ask. Would he pay the price and step onboard?

"You know, Charlie, you surprised me this morning when you spoke with such emotion about Melissa's passing. Her death is a tragic loss. It can't be undone. But taken in hindsight, perhaps there's something for us to learn. There's a connection between my project and the circumstances of her death."

Charlie's head bobbed backward with his eyes widened in disbelief. After a pause, he managed to say, "Adam, what are you saying? Of course there must be something we can learn from her death. Any death presents an occasion to take stock, but her life and her death are not a message about your project. She doesn't have a part in your project. She's not part of a business plan."

"I'm sorry, Charlie. I know you had a rough time of it last night."

"A rough time of it? Are you kidding me? Now there's an understatement if I've ever heard one. I nearly died last night. I mean I went eyeball to eyeball with Dr. Death. And if that weren't enough, I had to witness the violent death of a sweet young woman. Sorry for what seems to you to be an excess of sentimentality."

"Charlie, I didn't mean to minimize what happened last night. I do understand it was a traumatic experience, but please listen for a minute."

"Oh, sure, Adam. Go right ahead."

"I can't bring Melissa back to life, but what if I told you that my new project is about restoring life?"

"Don't play with me, Adam. Give it up."

"I'm not playing. Like I said, I can't bring Melissa back to life. But what if I really could? Wouldn't that be worth your attention?"

"Sorry, Adam . . . or is it Dr. Frankenstein? This is bullshit. I'm not doing this."

Charlie got up from the table and walked away. He left the building and wandered back to the maze, hoping to lose himself among the shrubs.

Chapter 12

Charlie paced here and there, wanting only to be lost and in motion. After a time, he exited onto the surrounding grounds, where he took a seat on a bench with manicured shrubs and flowers nearby. He was thinking about Laura, hoping she'd arrive soon; thinking about Melissa and her parents; and wondering what Adam had on his mind.

Deep in thought, he was surprised when Adam sat down alongside him. He spoke in a gentle voice, one Charlie had never heard before.

"You know, I've never seen death before the way you did last night. When my mom lay dying from heart failure, I arrived in time to sit by her bedside, where I held her hand while the blessings of morphine comforted her as she slipped away into darkness. I've had friends and business acquaintances who have passed away, some suddenly and others with a warning, but I've never had to face the sudden violent death of anybody. There's no way for me to really know what that's like, what it must've been like for you."

A drape of sadness hung over Adam's face as he continued. "I've never felt death breathing down my neck. I haven't had to endure the almost certain expectation of death. It's not something I can even imagine."

"Adam, you're an amazing man, but you're a borderline lunatic. Actually, at times you're not borderline at all. I know your project is important. You couldn't have dragged me out here on such short notice if I hadn't grasped that much. At times, though, you're unbearable. Your relentless focus drives the people around you crazy. Your project is important. Okay, I get that. But for Christ's sake, your focus on your project to the exclusion of everything else—"

Adam interrupted. "What you mean is my focus to the exclusion of you and your sensitivities."

"Okay, yes. You're a smart guy. How come you couldn't figure out your timing might be off? From your remarks, it sounded like you anticipated my sensitivities, but then you went right along with your fucking agenda." He continued after a pause. "And it's not just me. Shari's having a hard time too. I've had to deal with your bullshit on the phone and now face to face, but Shari has to deal with this constantly. Okay, let's say your project is revolutionary or earth-shattering or whatever, but if you don't watch out, you're going to do irreparable damage. Maybe you don't appreciate how important Shari's love and loyalty are. Maybe you don't realize how badly everything in your life can go if you fuck this up. Is that really where you want to go?"

"Speak for yourself. Who the hell are you to be talking to me about my relationship with my wife? Who gave you permission to butt in?"

"Look, buddy, I've been your friend for a long time now, maybe too long. I claim whatever permission I need."

Adam responded with silence. His anger clearly registered despite a quiet patina that passed for calm. They settled into an uneasy silence, each weighing the import of this troubling exchange poised like an unbearable weight over the meaning of their friendship.

Adam got up from the bench and walked back and forth but never more than ten feet away. He sat down for a minute or two and then got back up again to resume his pacing. Charlie remained silent.

Adam finally said, "I can't talk about his now. Let's talk about this again after I've had a chance to cool off."

"Okay, asshole. You've got twenty-four hours."

They managed an uneasy laugh and settled back into silence, a pensive mood bearing hope and distress in equal measure. They spent five long minutes thinking their own thoughts before Adam said, "C'mon, Charlie. Tell me if it's too soon, but if you're willing, let's go back to my lab. I want to show you something that will blow your mind."

Chapter 13

"See this plastic box? Let's take it over to the scanner I showed you earlier."

Adam opened a door—a hatch, really—and entered the scanner room, where he set the plastic box down on a table. Machinery surrounded it on all sides, underneath, and overhead. They left the room, secured the hatch, and walked over to a computer console. Adam told Charlie to go over to the printer room, look through a window, and describe what he saw. Charlie said it looked like the scanner room except that there was nothing on the table. Satisfied with Charlie's description, Adam typed instructions on the computer keyboard. There was a loud whirring sound accompanied by a pervasive rumble, smooth and liquid in character. A greenish purple glow was visible through the scanner window along with intensely bright bursts of light. This sequence lasted over thirty seconds, after which a pale glow appeared through the window of the printer room. After another thirty seconds, the light in the printer room went out, and the whirring sounds and rumble went silent.

"C'mon, Charlie. Let's go see what's in the printer room."

They opened the hatch and walked in. Adam asked Charlie what he saw on the table.

"It looks like a plastic box, just like the one we put on the table in the scanner room. You look so proud of yourself, Adam, but isn't that just what a 3D printer does but without the twisted web of wires, pipes, and fancy gadgets?"

"You're right. That's what a 3D printer does, but look more closely at the box. See if it has a lid, one that you can open."

Sure enough, it had a hinged lid. Charlie lifted it, exposing the contents. He was surprised by what he saw. There were four articles inside: a gold necklace, a small bottle with a liquid in it that looked like dirty water, a piece of wood with writing etched into it, and a crumpled wad of paper.

"Adam, I thought that 3D printers printed with homogeneous materials, like just plastic or just something else. The items inside this box are made up of all kinds of materials."

"That's right, but before we move along, go back to the scanner room and bring me the plastic box you find there."

Charlie got the box and came back and opened it. As far as he could tell, the contents of both boxes were identical in every way. Charlie's curiosity drove him to unravel the wads of paper, one from each box. Both were one-dollar bills—both passable legal tender, both bearing the identical serial number.

Adam said, "Now take the bottle from the second box, the one we just printed. Open it and take a sniff."

"Geez. That stinks. It smells like shit. What cesspool did you get this from?"

"You have a keen sense of smell, my friend. Congratulations, you certainly know shit when you smell it. I got the water for the bottle you saw in the original box from our campus sewer line."

"You're not going to ask me to drink this, are you?"

"After all the shit you dumped on me, I guess I have justification. But no, we're going to take this water over to that lab bench across the room, the one with the microscope on it."

They walked over to the bench. Following Adam's direction, Charlie put a couple of drops of the water onto a slide, placed a coverslip over it, and positioned it under the microscope lens.

"Now take a look and tell me what you see."

"You know, I haven't done this since Zoology 1A."

Charlie peered into the microscope and immediately recognized the protozoans familiar to every student of biology.

"You've given me the wrong water sample. This must have come from the bottle in the original box that I retrieved from the scanner room."

"Why do you say that, Charlie?"

"Well, because there are bugs in it—little, creepy, living crawlers. I know you didn't print those little guys."

But even as he uttered those words, he looked around the lab and saw that, unless he missed a sleight-of-hand maneuver, the water sample did indeed come from the bottle in the copied plastic box. The implications of that simple observation began to sink in. The image of those little buggers swimming around in that drop of water was then and there forever burned into his brain. His field of vision narrowed and blurred into a white haze. The humming and rumbling of machinery may have been gone, but Charlie's whole world was shaking. He was stunned.

"Are you sure this is the water from the bottle in the box taken from the printer room? It's not the water from the scanner room?"

"We can redo the experiment as many times as you'd like. I've already repeated it dozens of times. In answer to your question, I'm sure that the water you're looking at came from the bottle in the box we took from the printer room."

"Adam, unless you're pulling a trick—"

"This is no trick. This device can replicate anything, inanimate or otherwise, living or dead."

Chapter 14

Charlie couldn't speak. His mind was racing. His thoughts were re-organizing themselves around a new, unbelievable reality. "The rats," he blurted. "The cage B rats, are they copies too?"

"Yes, there were ten rats in cage A. Each of them was trained on the maze. Once they were trained, we copied each one of them one at a time. Each of the ten rats in cage B is a copy of an individual rat in cage A. Each rat in cage B can run the maze in just about the same time that it takes its twin. Actually, that's not the word for it because they're more than twins. We use a different word for them. We call them 'replicants.' There's an original, and then there's a replicant. And we don't use the word 'copy' or 'print' to refer to the process. We use the word 'replicate.' As near as we can tell, our replicants are identical replicas, identical in every respect. At least that's the way they appear on close physical examination down to their genetic composition and even on to their memories too—at least their maze-running memory."

"But how can this be? I understand how one prints with ink, and I've come to understand how one might print with plastic, but what on earth are you printing with? I don't get it. How do you print a rat?"

"You've seen an inkjet printer, right?"

"Of course. We've got one at home and a bunch more at my office."

"Have you ever replaced an ink cartridge?"

"Well, yes, all too often."

"When you have a black-and-white printer, you only have to change out a black ink cartridge when it empties. With color printers, you have to change out multiple cartridges because printing in color requires combinations of primary colors. That means you have three or four cartridges, sometimes more. Sound familiar?"

"Yes, of course."

"Well, obviously we're not printing on paper. We're printing solid objects just like a 3D printer. But instead of using a homogenous substance like a plastic or a metal, we're printing with all the elements in the periodic table or at least a lot of them."

"There's a whole bunch of them, aren't there?"

"Yes, I think one hundred eighteen is the latest count."

"I get it. Instead of using colored ink cartridges, you're using one hundred eighteen cartridges, one cartridge for each element."

"You're getting close. We don't need to use them all. Some of the heavier elements are extremely unstable and decay rapidly. Besides, they have no place in any practical replication we have yet imagined. We only use the elements we expect we'll need for a particular replication. Mostly, it's a fairly narrow set. When we're replicating a living process, we're still using just a limited set of elements. For example, ninety-nine percent of a human body is made up of just six elements: oxygen, carbon, hydrogen, nitrogen, calcium, and phosphorus. Our scanner identifies the elements that are present in our subject. Some of what we find are just impurities or contaminants, and our replicant would be better off without them."

"So you can do without all the trace elements?"

"Maybe, maybe not. We don't really know all of the biology. When it comes to trace elements, we think we know most of what we need, but to some extent, we'd just be experimenting. We're not sure which elements we can eliminate. As a result, we actually do include some trace elements."

"No Frankenstein monsters yet?"

"Nope, not yet. Mostly, we think we can get by with a pretty manageable set of elements. We know we don't need any protactinium or mendelevium. We don't worry about them."

"The ones you need, how do you dispense them?"

"First we squirt them from their respective cartridges and ionize them. The resulting ions are dumped into a drum, kind of a cross between a mass spectrometer and a centrifuge. It's like a big tub of plasma in which electrical charges and magnetic fields get the ions spinning around in a vortex. Since we know the respective weights of the elements we want and we know the rate of rotation, we can figure out just about where within the vortex we can find the elements we want. Then we start scooping. We can't use a mechanical scooper. There's no way a mechanical device could carry the volume of material we need fast enough to do the job. That's why we devised an electromagnetic device that has the capability of virtually moving in and out of the vortex to scoop up just the ions we want when we want them. It's a kind of super-scooper. From the scooper, the ions are ported out of the tub to mix them up with other ported ions to form the molecules that we need to assemble our replicant material. It's more complicated than that, but those are the basics. Any questions?"

"Let's pretend that I really understood what you just said. It's actually a couple of off ramps past my exit, but let's move along. How does your replicator know which elements to pick off?"

"Now that's a question that will lead us to more of the magic. Remember the scanner room?"

"Yes."

"Think of the scanner as a kind of enhanced MRI imaging system combined with a CT scanner hyped with other exotic detectors. You can't believe the resolution. We can actually identify every atom in any sample we scan. And not just that. When we need to, we can also identify the quantum state of each and every atom and each atom's configuration space. We collect that data and store it in memory till needed."

"My understanding of physics is quite spare. How can you do all that detecting without destroying the object of your scan?"

"Charlie, am I ever impressed. That's a great question, one I can't answer because I can't get my arms around all the weirdness of quantum mechanics. The answer has something to do with entanglement, but I can't really explain it. If you want, I can refer you to our geniuses. Some of them have been working on this stuff for years. It's been a rocky road, and we didn't really know it would take us to where we've wanted to go. You can talk with any of them if you want, but I gotta warn you they only communicate in matrix math, statistics, number theory, and quantum-speak. Good luck."

"No, thanks. But, Adam, there must be billions upon billions of atoms in the objects you scan. I don't have any idea what you mean by quantum states and configuration space, but whatever . . . that's gotta be a whole lot of data. How much memory does it take to store all that?"

"It takes a whole hell of a lot. We found that conventional storage methods were inadequate. We had to create a new memory architecture that could handle this huge volume of data. We start with a lot of shortcuts. We can look at every atom, its quantum state and configuration space, but don't usually have to do that. If we're replicating a plastic box made up of a homogeneous plastic material, we're working with just a single molecule over and over again. We store the atomic details about the molecule just once. That way, we only have to store the description of each molecule's location. Or take that sample of sewage water. It's mostly water. We store details for a single water molecule, and then all we have to do is store the location of each water molecule we find. Or take the rats we ran through the maze. Most living things are mostly made up of water. That makes that part easy. And then let's look at the blood. A red blood cell is a red blood cell is a red blood cell. We describe a red blood cell once and then apply that description to every red blood cell that we map from the scanner. And it's not just blood cells. There are lots of tissues that are made up of cells that are virtually identical."

"But you're talking about the physical things. What about the more ephemeral stuff like your rats' memories?"

"Great question. You may think of memories as ephemeral, but fundamentally they're simply artifacts of physical processes. And that goes for behavioral traits too. In the case of our rats, we're most interested in their maze-running recollections. When it comes to memory, personality, and behavior patterns, we figured that we need to store much more detail about brain cells with all their axons and dendrites, not to mention their electrical processes and chemical products including neurotransmitters. That's where we need maximum resolution."

"You're making me dizzy, Adam."

"I can stop here if you want, but you're the one asking the questions. Shall I continue?"

"Why not? Even if I don't understand it."

"Here's something I'm especially proud of. We've devised a variety of computational algorithms that enable us to recognize fundamental numerical relationships among bits of data. That's what's known as principal component analysis, or PCA. We didn't invent PCA, but our researchers devised ways to use it to reduce the amount of data we need to store. It's like you're traveling along a straight path at a fixed speed. You don't need to record every location in time and space along the path. If you know the direction you're headed and you know how fast you're going, you can readily calculate every location just by reference to the passage of time. Similarly, when we recognize fundamental relationships among our data points, we computationally construct the data we need when we need it. And aren't we lucky? It just so happens that our scanned biological data is generally quite well structured. That means we can wrap PCA compression in along with the most efficient standard lossless compression algorithms that have been in use for decades."

"Oh, yeah, I can see that. That sounds easy—for you and for Einstein, maybe."

"Okay, maybe it's not easy, but we figured out a way to search for those relationships and apply them. We stick teams of supercomputers between the scanner and the memory. They search for patterns. When they find a useful pattern, the amount of data we need to store is substantially reduced. Oh, and those supercomputers, they're actually quantum computers. We were able to hire some world-class talent away from IBM. With them at the helm, we have exponentially expanded our computational capacity, and that makes it possible for us to run our algorithms on the fly."

"Adam, your shortcuts don't seem so short, especially the longer ones. Are we done now?"

"No, there's more. We've made impressive developments in our memory hardware. Instead of using transistors or whole areas of magnetic material, we found a way to store data on individual atoms. That saves us a lot of physical space. And then we leverage that methodology by using quantum mechanical methods. Each atom isn't limited to storing either a zero or a one because each one can be at any one of several or many different energy levels. We're still trying to figure out which atom to use in our memory. Right now, we're working with hydrogen, the smallest one. Hydrogen takes up the least amount of space, but then it only has five possible quantum levels. Larger atoms might work better because there are more quantum levels possible, but then we'd be dealing with larger atoms. We haven't optimized the trade-offs yet. For the time being, we're sticking with hydrogen. With five possible quantum levels, each hydrogen atom can represent a number between zero and four. That gives us a five-digit number system to work with instead of the two-digit binary system that is typical in contemporary computer memories. That multiplies the memory capacity of each storage element and, in turn, makes our memory capacity exponentially larger.

"The end result is that we use our quantum-leveraged, atomic-scale memory elements in conjunction with our various shortcuts. Given the enormous scale of our data requirements, we still need a large physical device to handle it. It won't fit on a data stick, but at least it can be contained in one large room. The value of this new memory architecture is enormous. Data needs in today's world are huge. This memory technology enables mind-boggling applications that can only work with access to vast amounts of memory. Whole new opportunities abound. Revenues from this development will be unbelievable. When I started this replication project, I thought of it as nothing more than an unrealistic curiosity. But the technologies that we've developed just to pursue this curiosity are of great consequence. And as you'll see, the replication project itself has incredible possibilities that go far beyond the satisfaction of curiosity."

"Okay, now that you've rattled my brain, let's see if I've got this right. First, you scan whatever you want to replicate, identifying each and every atom, its quantum state, and its configuration space. Then that gargantuan amount of data created from the scan is analyzed on the fly and stored in memory. From there, the data is fed to the printer to guide a spray of ions from your vortex tub in whatever combination you need to build the molecules that make up the objects that you're constructing, or, rather, reconstructing. Is that about right?"

"Yep, you've got it just about right. It's as simple as that."

Chapter 15

Until his phone rang, Charlie was unaware that the afternoon had crept into evening. "Laura, where are you? Are you here already?"

"Yes, we just landed. Shari met me at the airport. We're heading back to her place. Are you there?"

"No, I'm with Adam in his lab. We'll be heading home in just a few minutes. If you get there first, pour us a couple of drinks. Make mine a stiff one."

Charlie was anxious to get going, but Adam had one more piece of business. "There's something I must insist on. You can't discuss anything about this project with Laura."

"Okay, if that's what you're asking, but I don't understand why. Laura is certainly no more likely than I am to spill the beans to anyone."

"I know that, Charlie. But we're all vulnerable to slips, every one of us. The way I figure it, the fewer who know about this, the less likely there'll be slips. I haven't even told Shari."

"You've kept this from Shari too?"

"Yes, like I said, the fewer who know, the better. Tomorrow is another day. We can talk more about it then. Now let's get going. Shari and Laura will be waiting for us. We'll get together and enjoy a happy hour before sitting down for a late dinner together."

———

Adam and Charlie arrived back at the estate, but Shari and Laura weren't there waiting for them. They had said they were on their way. No matter, surely, they'd be along in moments. After another fifteen minutes, when they still hadn't appeared, Adam pulled out his phone and called Shari.

She answered breathlessly. "Adam, I'm scared out of my mind. We're on our way, but we're being chased. Michael saw someone suspicious tailing us. He got us off onto some lonesome country road. But they're still right behind us. I have no idea where we are."

"Don't worry, baby. Everything will be fine. I promise. Remember, our security guys know where you are. They're always tracking you. They'll get help to you right away. Just sit tight. Michael can handle this."

"We can't sit tight. Michael insisted we get down on the floor, so now we're being tossed around like a couple of rag dolls in a washing machine."

Adam ended his call with Shari and, within the same moment, was on the phone with security, who had just learned there was a problem. They had received an emergency call from Michael and had already jumped in response. Immersed in a flurry of activity, they dispatched a two-car security team to intercept the chase and a utility van to clean up. Their standard procedure included a directive to reinforce protective measures at the estate and to enhance protection for Adam and Shari's kids.

At the first hint of a threat, Michael placed his handgun within easy reach. His highly practiced driving skills were being tested as he accelerated rapidly when he could and turned sharply wherever an opportunity to evade presented. Too bad his extraordinary driving abilities were matched by the driver in pursuit. Under his breath, Michael lamented that he was tasked to chauffeur his client in a town car when what he would have preferred was something with a little more agility. Yet he appreciated that the town car was heavily armored.

Turning sharply at a bend in the road, Michael shoved the car into a controlled skid. He saw the dark-colored SUV attempt the same maneuver. It almost made it but skidded off the road and tumbled over and again down an embankment. Michael was satisfied that the SUV would no longer present a threat. He pressed a button on his GPS tracker to mark the location so his security team could locate the pursuers while he sped on his way.

His satisfaction was short-lived. Now there was a second dark-colored SUV in his rearview mirror. Michael resumed his darting maneuvers in this deadly game of keep away. He checked his mapper and saw that his security team was closing in and would be close to intercept within another couple of minutes. If only he could maintain his distance.

Then on a straightaway, Michael managed to gain a margin of distance. When the intercept team was within a hundred yards, Michael braked suddenly, throwing the town car into a sharp, skidding turnaround, forcing the pursuing SUV to brake to a stop. In an instant, Michael was out of the car and crouched behind the driver's opened armored door, his gun drawn and aimed. As three armed men emerged from the pursuing SUV, the intercept team pulled up with blinding strobes flashing and ear-splitting horns shrieking. The chaos was spiked by the explosion of several stun grenades that were fired at the armed men.

Members of the security team poured from the two cars. They moved like a torrent of flood waters, quickly engulfing and disarming the disoriented gunmen. Sam Galatine, the team leader, gave Michael a thumbs up, telling him that they were in control and that he could move with dispatch along his way.

———

Sam Galatine was one mean son of a bitch. At five feet five, he probably suffered from a Napoleon complex, but now at forty-one years of age, he hadn't yet met his Waterloo. Weighing in at 160 pounds, he had the hard-body musculature of an Olympic wrestler. His complexion looked like he must have used sandpaper and fingernails to treat a severe case of adolescent acne. His dark-brown hair with sprinkles of gray hung halfway down his back in a ponytail. His ears were cauliflowered, his nose askew from multiple fractures. He bore a scar over his left eye that extended from the midline of his forehead halfway to his ear. He moved about the scene with the dexterous agility of a ballet dancer. His raspy voice sounded like it was processed by a grinder. He snapped out one command after another, his teammates responding in quick time, suggesting a highly practiced routine and well-earned respect.

The security team was composed of Sam in one car with two other team members and three more team members in the second car. Sam couldn't do anything about the attacker's first SUV. Almost certainly the police would have arrived at the scene of that crash. That left Sam to devote his complete attention to this second SUV. Because Michael had led the chase onto a quiet country road, Sam figured his team would have enough time to be diligent. They photographed the vehicle inside and out. They took photos of the operatives and collected fingerprints, iris scans, and swab samples for DNA testing. They sought every bit of identifying information they could find, including clothing labels. They searched for the car's identifying information, even checking various locations for the correspondence of VIN numbers. They removed everything inside the SUV that wasn't tied down and some of the things that were. Cell phones, radio gear, and a laptop were collected along with sedating drugs, cuffs, ropes, tape, and an impressive arsenal of weapons. The would-be assailants were outfitted with automatic pistols, holstered handguns, and knives. In the SUV, they found additional ammunition for their various weapons and a box containing a dozen smoke grenades.

Although the team's training mostly prepared them for kidnap and assault scenarios, among them, Marty Sanders had been trained and tasked to search for bombs and detonation devices. In this case, they didn't want the SUV destroyed. They wanted evidence to help them understand the threat that was stalking their client. Marty reported to Sam that he had found a bomb and cell phone detonator.

Sam said, "Good going, Marty. That's the one they wanted us to find. Give me the cell phone and go back and find the other bomb. Look carefully but look fast, before their dispatcher figures out there's trouble here and decides it's time to blow this thing up and us with it."

By then, the utility van had arrived on the scene, and the gunmen, with their hands cuffed behind them and their mouths taped shut, were quickly herded into the back along with everything that had been removed from the attack SUV. Julio Sanchez was Sam's computer guy. It was his job to make sure that the laptop's data didn't get compromised. He quickly put it in the van in a compartment that isolated it from any network signals and went to work making sure that its memory didn't self-destruct following a programmed routine.

Once loaded, Sam directed that the van and the two SUVs be moved a safe distance from the attack vehicle while Marty continued his search for a second bomb. Having secured everything they could in the van, the team members fanned out to cleanse the site of any debris that may have been dropped or left lying around. They even swept up remnants and residue from the stun grenades and used a solvent and brushes to remove or at least age the appearance of the skid marks seared onto the pavement.

Sam's intuition was rewarded. The cell phone detonator received a call, which Sam presumed was intended to explode the discovered bomb. That meant he got his first clue and an opportunity to trace the call back to whomever might have been trying to set off the bomb. With everything on site cleaned up, Sam was anxious to leave the scene. He knew he had to move the attack vehicle but was reluctant to ask Marty or anyone else to drive it before being sure about an undiscovered second bomb. Sam was reassured, though, by Marty's thoroughness and by the fact that a detonation attempt had already been made. If there was a second bomb, it probably would have been blown too. With that in mind, Sam went to the van, retrieved a thickly padded fire-retardant suit, and tossed it to Marty.

"Here ya go, Marty. Let's be safe. Put this on. You'll look like an astronaut and feel like you're wearing a half-ton burka. Then get in the SUV and head for home but stay off heavily trafficked roads. I don't want any cops seeing you dressed for a space launch."

Chapter 16

Sam led his team to a work site set in a low-rent industrial park, sparsely populated by mostly spent businesses. Sam's vehicle went ahead while the others followed by alternate circuitous routes. Nearing the park, Sam watched for anyone who might have been following them and drove around the park's perimeter to check the neighborhood for anything out of the ordinary. Satisfied that all was clear, he entered and made his way to a large roll-up door marked with garish graffiti. While some of the nearby spaces had scruffy plantings barely clinging to life, this scrimpy plot was marked by weeds and a single dead bush. They had done their best to make their workplace appear unoccupied or at least poorly tended.

Julio was riding with Sam. He got out of the car and manually lifted the roll-up door, revealing what looked like an indoor wrecking yard complete with a junked car and an assortment of weathered auto repair equipment.

After Sam drove in, Julio lowered the door and then went to the opposite wall in front of Sam's SUV and slid it sideways. It looked like a filthy wall on which a variety of tools, advertising posters, and a five-year-old *Playboy* calendar were hung. With it opened, a more expansive interior was exposed to view. With Sam inside, Julio slid the wall panel back into its former position.

Over the next half hour, Sam coordinated the arrival of the other vehicles. One at a time, each followed his intricate routine. The hostiles were in the second vehicle admitted into the sanctum. They sat warily awaiting their uncertain fate.

When everyone had arrived, Sam issued his instructions. All the gear removed from the vehicles was placed for examination on workbenches. Julio took the laptop to his workspace, where he could more thoroughly examine the computer, its data, and its routines. The operatives, their mouths still taped and their hands cuffed, were hauled out of the van. They were stripped of their clothing. To avoid freeing their cuffed hands, their clothes were cut from their bodies with scissors. They were examined for additional weapons, drugs, or signaling devices.

Johnny called out, "Holy shit. Look what I just found on this hairy dude." He held up a little pill still stuck to a transparent Band-Aid.

Sam said, "Whoa there . . . it might be a spicy taste of cyanide. We need to know about that. Where'd you find it?"

"Sometimes I really hate this job. I found it taped to the underside of this guy's dick. How's that for a clever hiding place?"

"What about the other two? Did you find anything on them?"

"Nope, just this one guy."

Standing naked and cuffed, and with their mouths still taped, they were herded into a small room that was empty except for a couple of buckets to serve as toilets—no sink, no running water.

Sam spoke to them. "We're gonna do our best to make your lives miserable. There's nothing here for you to eat or drink. You may notice temperature extremes as we monkey with the thermostat. You'll be annoyed by loud sounds and flashing lights that will keep you from sleep. Tomorrow, we'll start the day asking questions—lots of questions. Cooperation might get you relief. Resistance will add to your miseries."

That was it. Sam uncuffed them, turned away, and left the room, securing the door behind him.

With his team assembled, Sam said, "Thanks for your hard work today. You've done a good job, but our work's not over yet. You'll have to pull one-hour shifts at the surveillance station. We're recording everything, but I still want you to log anything you notice. If they're scratching their balls or if they're farting, I want it logged. I want notes on any communicating gestures. Get some sleep if you can but plan on being out of your racks by six a.m. We're gonna have a heap of intel to review. That's it for now. G'night, gentlemen."

Four team members filed into a dorm room, where they settled into their racks. Johnny Falke had the first surveillance shift. The controls for the prisoners' thermostat and lights were programmed but had to be monitored. He sat down in front of the video monitors, put on his headset, and prepared for a dreary hour of tedious duty.

Sam went to his desk and picked up the phone to speak with his boss, Dean Fleck, the overall head of security operations.

"Hey, Dean, got anything for me yet?"

"Go to sleep, Sammy. It's time you were in your rack. I hope you'll sleep better knowing that we've already got hits on two of your bad boys. Nothing yet on the third. I'll send over details later tonight after we develop a more complete package but watch out. These two guys are real stinkers. They're responsible for some ugly hits and kidnappings. They don't appear to have any ideological commitments. They seem committed only to the highest bidder. That may make our work a little easier, provided they actually know something. That's about it for now. Get some shuteye. We'll have lots to talk about early tomorrow morning."

Sam judged that all was going well. He knew that the staff at headquarters and field operatives scattered around the world would be busy assembling information needed for the following day's interrogations.

Chapter 17

While Sam and his team had been cleaning up following the intercept and getting ready to head for the team's work site, Michael's job was to move his client to safety. While doing so, he was alert for other threats. Sensing none, he turned to reassure Shari and Laura that all was well. The two women, who were still crouched on the floor, were relieved yet still frightened. Back in their seats, Shari wrapped her arms around Laura's trembling shoulders. Michael's lighthearted nature was always reassuring, especially to Shari, who had a playful fondness for him.

"Well, ladies, are we having fun yet? If you're up for it, we can swing by some clubs on the way home."

Shari banished every hint of a quiver from her voice. "Thanks, Michael, but I think we'll go for a quiet evening at home."

"Well, okay, but don't say I didn't ask."

Shari had not previously experienced anything like this, but at least she and Adam had discussed security risks. For Laura, it was different. Not only had she never experienced any kind of physical threat, either to herself or any family member, but she had never conceived of herself as a target for anything of that sort. Shari had an intellectual context, a kind of preparedness. Laura did not.

Twenty minutes later, they pulled up to the entry gate at the Braudy estate. The guards had been alerted about the elevated risk level and were instructed to be suspicious of everyone who sought entry. The guards recognized Michael and Mrs. Braudy but not Laura and on that account awaited a veiled signal from Michael before opening the gate.

They pulled up the estate's colonnaded portico. Michael lowered his window when Adam approached him on the driver's side. "All's well, Mr. B. Sam did real good out there tonight. You might wanna tip him a couple of bucks for the special effort."

"A couple of bucks for sure and a pat on the back besides."

Adam opened the door for Shari, who stepped out with a bravado that belied the fear that still haunted her. Adam flung his arms around her and held her for a long time. Then he rubbed his nose against hers and kissed her.

Charlie opened the other door, reached in, and helped Laura to her feet. He held her in a tight embrace, sheltering her in his arms, her head at rest against his shoulder.

Inside, Adam poured double shots of whiskey. Shari and Laura related details of the assault while Adam and Charlie squirmed with rage. Adam knew the risk but was nevertheless shocked by the reality. For Charlie, like Laura, this was unfamiliar territory. He was confused and didn't know what to do with his anger.

Shari was obsessed with worry about their kids. Adam tried his best, without success, to reassure her that their security team was in full protection mode.

Charlie blurted out, "So where's the police? Why aren't they here already? What does it take to get them to do their job?"

Adam answered, "Charlie, we haven't been in touch with the police, and we won't be—not tonight, maybe never."

"What do you mean? What are you talking about? You want these guys to just get away with this? They tried to kidnap or kill Laura and Shari. No way can they get away with this. The cops have to track these guys down, drag 'em into court, put 'em in jail, and throw away the key. They've got to pay big time."

"There will be no police. We have a security apparatus that is world class. We have capabilities that go far beyond the police. We'll do this our way. We won't be bound by the legalities that constrain the police. Believe me, these people will pay dearly. And not just the monsters who were out on the road tonight, but their handlers, too, will feel our fury. I promise you. These despicable thugs, these moral degenerates, will pay."

Charlie was well acquainted with threats, but he dealt with them by brandishing demand letters, lawsuits, depositions, interrogatories, and courtroom oratory. He winced as he heard Adam's vituperations.

Chapter 18

When they finished their drinks and exhausted their capacity to vent, Helene, the Braudy's housekeeper and cook, served a light meal. They ate without appetite, chatting mostly about Shari and Adam's fears for their kids, whom they learned were well guarded and safe.

After dinner, Laura, Shari, and Charlie returned to the family room for another round of drinks in an attempt to further dull their anguish. Adam went off to call Dean Fleck at security headquarters. He returned and reported that the security apparatus was in full motion, that the assailants were successfully confined, and that there would be more information by morning.

Charlie rose from his chair. "Laura and I are exhausted. We need to get to bed. Your security team did a great job, but I'm pissed. I'm angry at our attackers, but I'm angry with you, too, for getting us into this mess."

Without expecting an answer, Laura and Charlie climbed the stairs to their guest suite, where they felt relieved to be alone behind closed doors.

They undressed and got into bed, hoping that sleep would envelop them. But it was not to be. They lay together, arms and legs entwined, exchanging intimate strokes and touches. Little by little, tension slipped aside, and sleep crept upon them.

Charlie was awakened from his restless sleep by Laura, whose sharp, anguished moans were muffled by her pillow and her slumber's thick cocoon. Charlie reached out to stroke her head, but the suddenness of his touch only added to her fright. She lurched up from her pillow with a shriek. At last recognizing that it was just a ghastly dream, she accepted the calming strokes of Charlie's fingers combing through her hair. He stroked to her eyelids and lips, where soft touches turned her frightened moans into cooing pleas for more. Their lovemaking extended into a long, passionate interlude that finally left them exhausted and short of breath. They laughed and fell into each other. At least for the moment, they felt cleansed by the torrent of sexual emotion that flushed aside the terrors that threatened to consume them. At last, they were left in a state of ease that welcomed a deep and restful sleep.

Chapter 19

They slept till after eight. Once awake, Laura wanted to make love again, but Charlie was anxious to find out what Adam had learned about the assault. Downstairs, they found that Helene had set out a breakfast buffet. They settled for their morning cups of coffee while waiting to see if Adam and Shari would join them. That's when they both heard Adam meeting with Dean Fleck in the adjacent room. They didn't want to violate his privacy, but curiosity won out, and they both ended up listening.

"Look, Dean, I'm not happy with the way this is going."

"I'm disappointed too. We did a thorough body search of these guys and turned up a cyanide tab on one of them. The other two were clean. But we screwed up and missed the second cyanide tablet. He managed to kill himself despite our scrutiny. It appears that he was the leader. He was the one who could have provided us with information. We haven't been able to ID him and probably never will."

Notwithstanding Adam's confidence in Dean, his piercing eyes expressed an anger and frustration that focused his query. "Tell me, Dean. Given all your scrutiny, how is that possible?"

"Well, the first tablet we found taped to the underside of the guy's dick. When we found the guy dead on the floor, we looked around and found a small capsule-like container not much bigger than a cyanide tablet. On examination, it appears that the container had been hidden in his rectum."

"So now we don't know who he is, and we can't question him. Now that's just great. How 'bout the other two?"

Dean was now playing defense. He spoke slowly, picking his thoughts and words with care. "The other two are plain vanilla—free-lancers, mercenaries for hire. They don't know anything of value."

With fingerprints, photos, and DNA samples that Dean's team had collected, they had been able to sketch out their identities. From questioning, it was discovered that they were recruited surreptitiously, picked up shortly before their mission, thoroughly briefed, and provided with everything they would need to get their job done. The entire operation was highly compartmentalized. It was a professionally engineered assault, but the engineer remained a puzzle.

Dean added, "We're still looking for clues from the cell phones, computer, SUV, and remnants from the bomb. Nothing yet, but we think we'll be able to turn up something. The SUV was really tricked out, not your ordinary vehicle—a lot of custom work with high-performance gear throughout and heavily armored too. There aren't a lot of shops where that kind of work can be performed. We're looking into that. The cell phones are no help. We might get something off the computer and maybe something from the bomb." Dean tried to sound casual in asking, "What do you want us to do with the two mercenaries?"

"Can you get any more information from them?"

"Doesn't look like it."

"Then wait a couple of days to see if there's a good reason to hold on to them. No torture unless there's information to be gained. After that, unless there's a compelling reason, I want them dead."

"Okay, Adam, we'll give it a few days. Let me know when you're ready."

As their conversation ended, Laura, sickly pale, got up with a start and retreated to their suite upstairs. When Dean left, Adam went into the dining room, where he was startled to see Charlie. Adam must have wondered, maybe worried, that Charlie had overheard his conversation. "So, Charlie, what do you think we should do about this?"

Charlie measured his response, knowing that Adam was too smart for him to pretend he didn't hear. "I'm out of my depth here, but you seem to be in your element. Hearing you command the execution of two men in premeditated cold blood was quite a shock. I've known you a long time. I thought I knew you but maybe not."

"It's a cheap shot for you to be cynically critical of me while you think it's okay to claim that you're out of your depth. That's rich. Remembering how angry you were last night and how badly you wanted the bad guys to pay, it seems odd now to hear you decline to offer a suggestion of your own. I ask again: what do you think we should do?"

"Why should I bother? You've already made up your mind."

"Tell you what. You heard me tell Dean to put them on hold for a few days. That means that nothing's going to happen to our bad boys until I give the say so. Let's make a deal. What do ya say? Even though it's me and my family whose lives are on the line, I'll put the decision into your hands. You want to be self-righteous? Go ahead. Tell me what you think we should do. I'll critique your plan, but I'll commit right here and now to go with your decision. You think you can handle that, Mr. Out-of-My-Depth?"

Charlie squirmed and said, "I remember a late night with a bottle of scotch when you claimed you were certain that capital punishment was wrong. So are you a hypocrite, or has time nurtured the cynic in you?"

"I've got an answer for you but not before I remind you that I challenged you with an honest choice about a fateful decision. In case you don't remember, I asked, 'What do you think we should do about this?' But now all you can do is parry my question into a discussion about capital punishment. Oh, how philosophical you are. Okay, I'll answer your question, but then I'll come back at you with my challenge. And think about this. In the absence of a decision from you to the contrary, those men will be put to death. That means that you can stop it from happening if you really want to, but if you don't, they will surely die. Their blood will be on your hands."

"Okay, I'll think of something, but go ahead and explain your hypocrisy. I gotta hear this one. You used to sound like such a humanitarian."

"I don't pretend to be a humanitarian. I live my life the way it makes sense to me. I have my own self-interests, and you well know that I pursue them with vigor and without apology. I don't think all life is precious. I don't think that the taking of life has to be left to God. Desperate circumstances call for desperate measures. As for capital punishment, I'm still opposed. It doesn't make me a hypocrite because I'm willing to kill this scum. Never before have I killed anyone or ordered a killing. I think of this as preemptive self-defense. If I'm threatened, do I have to wait for them to strike a blow? I'm prepared to kill these men and hate myself for it. I will feel guilt and seek some kind of redemption, but I won't stand by and let them kill me or my family."

"But we live in a nation of laws. We expect others to obey them, but how can we if we don't?"

"Laws are funny things. They're blunt instruments and crude. We need them, but sometimes they seize too much, sometimes too little. They're rarely sharp enough to get it just right. In the case of capital laws, that's not good enough.

"When it comes to capital punishment, I don't believe that the police are bad or that prosecutors are evil or that the courts are corrupt or that juries are incompetent. Oh, there's some of that to be sure, but I don't think that's generally true. That's not my issue. What is an issue for me is that these institutions are governed by human beings. Ah, the human element. These are people, no different than you and me. They wake up in the morning with hangovers. They're short on sleep after a night of arguing, or a night in the ER, or a night of bar hopping. They are distracted by illness or by personal financial issues or by problems with a spouse or with kids.

"Then they go to work. They're expected to succeed, to get results. The cop has to catch the crook. The prosecutor needs to win the case. The jury has to make a finding. The judge needs to impose a penalty.

Failure will impair a career, thwart an ambition. And overlying that are the political institutions and the politicians that have to answer to the passions of the public. Our institutions are susceptible to the shortcomings of the human condition. We need these institutions, but they're ultimately vulnerable to human weakness. To consign decisions of life and death to such vulnerable institutions and processes is, for me, a step too far."

"Hurrah for you. How eloquent, how elegant. But you, Adam, you're not susceptible to these shortcomings. You're above and beyond the burdens that afflict humanity. You can be the judge, jury, and executioner without fail because you are perfect."

"No, I'm not perfect, and yes, I am susceptible to human weakness. Shari is a constant reminder of that, and now I have you too. But I'm not acting as a third party. I don't have to worry about employer evaluations and career advancement. I have direct knowledge of these criminal acts. I am acting in self-defense both for myself and for my family and, frankly, for any who fall within my circle of proximity, which in this case, old buddy, includes you and Laura.

"Tell me, Charlie, do you have any question regarding the guilt of the scum we're arguing about? Do you want me to be more graphic about the personal history of the mercenary bastards we've confined? If you do, I can provide you with morgue photos of some of their victims. Do you think they were chasing Shari and Laura to deliver roses? Or do you think they might have been willing to torment your wife as a hostage and then take her life if so instructed? What do you think? How do you answer these questions? And finally, let's go back to my challenge, the one you've tried to dodge. What do you think we should do?"

Charlie tried to sound confident. "We should turn them over to the police."

"Okay, that's a thought. Let's work with that for a while and see if it truly makes sense. When we first learned that Shari's car was being pursued, are you thinking we should have called the police and left it to them? Were we wrong to send out our own security team to intercept them?"

"Well, yes and no. It's the job of the police to intercede in criminal matters, but your guys did one hell of a job."

"Well, thanks for the compliment, but we can't have it both ways now, can we? You said yes and no. Let's try to nail that down. You want to call that out as a yes or as a no?"

"Okay, you were right to send out your team, but you might have notified the police. Then they could have taken over upon arrival."

"Now, Charlie, when the police take over, they take over. That means they would have taken custody of the assailants and the evidence. Our friends would have clammed up till their sleazy lawyers sidled up alongside. That would have put an end to the questioning. I guess you can say that we didn't do much better with our *numero uno* now dead from cyanide poisoning, but that's looking back after the fact."

Adam continued. "Now let's talk about our illustrious police force. We know them. Our security team works closely with them. In fact, just between you and me, one of our associates is placed within the police department. We know a lot about what goes on inside. Do you remember there were actually two SUVs chasing Shari and Laura?"

"Yeah, Laura and Shari talked all about it repeatedly."

"And that means you remember what they said happened to the first one, the one that flipped and rolled."

"Yes, of course I remember. Laura and Shari said that your driver, Michael, reported the location to security so the police could be notified."

"Yes, that's exactly right. We went ahead and passed the information about the first SUV to the police. Isn't that what you suggest we should have done with the second?"

"Yes. I think that would have been best."

"Well, then you might want to know what happened to the first one. Let me tell you. This morning, oddly enough, the police department told us that they investigated our report and found nothing. Now I don't know about you, but I think that's a little suspicious, not to take anything away from our local police force. Unofficially, there's a little more to the story. You want to hear it?"

"Yes."

"Our inside associate tells us that shortly after our call, the chief received another call. We don't know yet who from, but the mystery caller asked for the chief's forbearance in their rush to the accident site. Now without speculating on the reason for the request, I find it most interesting that the police couldn't find their way to the site for over two hours. Now tell me, Charlie, your thoughts about our reliance on the police to fulfill our security needs."

Charlie was speechless and sat silent while a terrible anger welled up inside. He didn't know where or how to vent his rage. Was his fury with Adam, with the police, or with the scum? Or was he really enraged at finding himself defenseless and utterly dependent on others to act on his behalf, no longer knowing whom he could trust?

Adam saw that the thrust of his remarks had struck home. He wasn't gloating. There was no ironic grin. There was no expression of conquest. His face was drawn by a weight of melancholy that matched Charlie's own burden of despair, a despair born of Charlie's recognition of a personal inadequacy long denied.

Adam didn't ask again for Charlie's advice about the fate of the captives. He quietly watched as Charlie retreated to rejoin Laura upstairs.

Chapter 20

Laura was in tears and had just finished repacking the few things she had brought with her.

"Charlie, I gotta get out of here. I don't know where to go or what to do, but I can't stay here under Adam's roof, not for another minute. He's a monster. He wants to kill those men in cold blood. What kind of man is that? He's not a man, or if he is, he's a madman. We're not safe here. We gotta get away from here as fast as possible."

Charlie thought otherwise. Laura had witnessed the assault, and he had come to know all about it. Charlie felt that that made him and Laura vulnerable. He didn't feel confident leaving the safety of Adam's protection, and he couldn't let Laura go alone. Could he convince her to stay? She was in manic motion. Would he physically restrain her? He imagined that if he stood in front of her, he might be run over or swiped aside. He took the chance. He stood before her and embraced her. She didn't return the embrace but stood still, rigid and sobbing. He stroked her back and shoulders and then held her face in his hands and looked deep into her eyes. They stood that way for a while before he was able to seat her next to him on the edge of the bed.

"Come on, Charlie. We have to go."

"I understand. We're stuck. I don't know how to get us out of this, but let's talk about it before we do something we might regret."

"There's no way I'm going to regret getting out of here."

"Laura, we have our safety to be concerned about. Let's think about this before we put our lives at risk."

"What risk? Those monsters are confined unless Adam has already killed them."

"No, he hasn't already killed them, and it's true they won't harm us unless they're released. But the people who sent them are still a threat."

Laura leaned over and rested her head against Charlie's shoulder.

"Laura, I was as shocked as you were when we overheard Adam's conversation, but I spoke with him after you left. There's more to the story."

"What could he have possibly said?"

"The first thing I need to tell you before anything else is that Adam has left it entirely up to me to decide what to do with your assailants. It's up to me whether to kill them, let them go, or turn them over to the police."

Laura turned to Charlie with an expression of astonishment and relief. "So did you tell him to turn them over to the police?"

"It's not that simple. He shared some ugly realities with me. There's been no decision yet. There's no rush. We have time."

"This is dirty business, Charlie. I want no part of it. Just tell him to turn them over to the police."

"That's what I said—at first. But now I'm not so sure. You know how persuasive Adam can be. What he shared with me about the police left me feeling unsure of my judgment."

"Yeah, that's Adam for you. That's his great skill in life: seduction."

"You can say a lot of things about Adam, but to presume that his persuasiveness is merely seduction or subterfuge isn't fair and, more importantly, could lead us to a disaster of our own making."

"Maybe the master puppeteer has you dancing to his tune. Maybe you're just worried about your business investments with him."

"That's a cheap shot. Yes, Laura, my business interests are intertwined with Adam. That would be *our* business interests. But our business interests will always be secondary to our safety and personal well-being. Since you seem to have reservations about my judgment, instead of retreating up here and leaving it to me, why don't you go downstairs and have it out with Adam directly?"

Charlie wasn't surprised when Laura insisted she would do just that. She wiped away her tears and headed downstairs. Over an hour later, Laura swept back in on an angry wind.

"What's going on?" Charlie asked. "You look pissed. Did you come to blows with Adam?"

"Oh, I'm angry alright but not with Adam. At this point, I want to see those bastards dead. I'm now on the same page with Adam, except that he's not yet ready to hang the police chief by his scrawny little balls."

"Wow. That's a surprise. I thought you were pretty much locked in. What happened?"

"When I went downstairs, I was ready to call the police on my own. Then Adam told me more about what those vermin have been up to and what they've done. And he told me about the police chief's pathetic accommodation. While I was hearing him out, a call came in from Dean, his security guy. That's what put the final twist on my turnabout."

"What was that about?"

"You know that Adam and Shari sent Jess off to college at Brown. Did you know that she has her own security guard traipsing around with her on campus? She tries her best to give her guard the slip. She hates the idea that she has no privacy. And I don't blame her. Can you imagine a young woman off at college being followed around everywhere she goes by a babysitter? What kind of life is that? It turns out her guard noticed some suspicious characters tracking Jess. Jess thought she had given her guard the slip, and a potential kidnapper thought so too. When the kidnapper struck, the guard, a young woman, managed to jump into the middle of the mash-up, brought a knee hard up on the guy's balls, hammered his instep with her foot, probably breaking it, and then swept his legs out from under him. Damn those vile bastards. When I heard that Jess was a target too, something in me just snapped."

Laura was sobbing, gasping for breaths while trying to continue. "I had an image of our Sandra, all grown and off at college. I flipped out and went insane. What kind of monsters are these guys? Do I care what happens to them? You bet I do, and an easy death doesn't come close to what they deserve."

Laura was no longer crying. She was sitting in the stiffly erect posture of a tightly coiled spring, a taut expression of cold resolve etched onto her face. Charlie had seen that expression before but rarely. He knew that Laura was engaged. Nothing would change her mind.

Chapter 21

They took a few minutes to comfort one another before returning to the dining room to reconnect with Adam. They found him preoccupied with the multiple threats arrayed against him. For Adam, those threats were mere impediments to be parried. He issued instructions to Dean and then turned to Charlie and suggested that they return to his lab.

Charlie said, "I'm reluctant to leave Laura here by herself."

"Are you kidding me? She can handle herself just fine. She's tough as nails. She's got fire in her belly. She and Shari will be a comfort to each other. We may want to place guards on them to keep them from doing some damage. I wouldn't want anyone getting hurt, especially the police chief."

"Yeah, but what about us out there on the road? Will we be safe?"

"Safe? Sure we'll be safe. Michael will drive, and we'll have a security escort team along for additional safety. It'll work out fine—or then again, maybe it won't. What do ya say? Wanna come along and find out?"

Charlie wasn't persuaded by Adam's cavalier pretense. But could he, would he, decline Adam's invitation? On the one hand, he could stay at home safely guarded, or he could accept a risk of death in a fiery shootout with a bloodthirsty mob of mercenaries.

"Okay, but first give me a minute to put on my Kevlar vest, load my Glock, give Laura one last kiss goodbye, and remind her where she can find my will."

"Gotta love your drama. I'll have Michael pull the car around in front. Meet me there when you're Glocked and loaded."

———

With Michael at the wheel and a security team leading the way in a second car, they drove to Adam's campus. There, they met up with Gina Salter in the research center.

Gina said, "Hi, Charlie. Back already? I didn't expect to see you so soon."

"Curiosity's got the better of me. I came back hoping to see your rats do backflips."

"No backflips, at least for now. But if you liked the rat show and everything you saw before, you'll be amazed by what you'll see today."

When Adam left Charlie with Gina, she led him down a hallway to a dimly lit laboratory. There were instruments and computers set up around the lab and a surgical table in the middle. She put on an odd pair of gloves that covered her hands and arms up to her elbows.

"Charlie, here's a pair for you too. Go ahead and put them on but be careful. The material is delicate and has to be handled with care."

"What's it made out of? It looks like an odd mesh of something."

"There are several fine layers of material, each layer a matrix of conductive polymers. I won't bore you with details about their electromagnetic properties, but you'll see the effects momentarily. Watch this, Charlie."

Following the execution of a command on her computer, a hum filled the room, and an image began to form on the surgical table.

"That looks like the black box Adam showed me yesterday."

"Sort of. It's not the box or its copy. It's only an image of the box. It looks like the real article, but it's only a fine-resolution holographic image derived from the scan of the original box. Now watch this."

Gina reached out with her gloved hand and "grasped" the image. She moved her arm up and down, the image of the box moving with it. Then she rotated the box with a twist of her wrist. She noted Charlie's surprise and placed it back down on the table.

"Now, Charlie, you give it a try. Go ahead; pick up the box and move it about, but be careful not to move it beyond the lighted area. If you do, you'll crash this run. You won't do any harm, but we'll have to reinitialize."

Charlie reached out to grasp the image, but when he "touched" it, it wasn't a ghost. It was a solid object. When squeezed, it didn't give. Charlie brought his other hand into play, and upon redoubling the pressure, he sensed a slight give. When Charlie lifted the image and then released it, the image fell back onto the table, yielding the sound of its impact.

"Charlie, see if you can find the lid and open it."

Doing so, he lifted the lid to reveal the contents just as he had found them the day before.

"What do you think, Charlie?"

"What can I say? I think I must be visiting an imaginary world. Maybe it's another world or another universe, but it's no place I've ever been or could ever imagine. My God, Gina, where have you taken me, and can I ever go back?"

"Sorry, now that you've crossed this Rubicon, there's no way you're going back, not ever. But save some of your awe because we're not done yet. There's more—much more."

Gina retreated to her computer. The image of the black box decomposed, leaving nothing but a lingering memory. She executed another command, initiating the now-familiar hum. In a moment, an image of a rat formed.

"Go ahead, Charlie, pick it up."

It felt warm to the touch, soft and furry. Charlie petted it with his fingertip and could feel the softness of its belly and the hardness of its bony skull.

"Is it alive?"

"No, it's just an image, just like the box."

"You mean you can't make it sit up and nibble on cheese?"

"No, but how about an anatomy lesson?"

She grasped the scalpel, only an image really, and with a flick of her wrist made a lengthwise incision in the rat's abdomen, revealing its internal organs. She deftly removed its stomach, liver, kidneys and intestines, holding each of them up for her examination before laying them down on the table. Picking up a kidney in her gloved right hand, she spoke the command, "Zoom one." With that, the organ immediately increased in size. She repeated the command, and it increased in size yet again.

"At this scale, it's easy to work with even the smallest structures of the rat's kidney without being limited by my all-too-human dexterity. This zoom capability is one of my favorite tools. It's like working on pixels in Photoshop. And if you think this is crazy, wait till you see what's next."

At her command, the image of the dissected rat dissolved, and in its place the image of a naked man lying supine formed on the surgical table. He appeared to be a middle-aged man in good physical condition except for an amputated left leg. Using her mouse, Gina highlighted his whole right leg, executed a "copy" instruction, and followed that with a "mirror image" instruction. She picked up the image that she had just copied and flipped and placed it at the location of his missing left limb. She highlighted the location where she was about to attach the copied limb and spoke out her zoom command, but this time "zoom two." With the image enlarged once and then again, and with a full set of surgical tools available, Gina opened the stub and matched it with the image of the copied and flipped limb.

"I wanted to show you how we can attach all of the structures— the bones, blood vessels, ligaments, and nerves—but that would take too long. What you can see is that this type of surgery is possible."

"Well, I see the possibilities. It's an incredible revolution in surgical training."

"It's certainly that, but it's that and much more. Let's look at this stepwise. First, we scanned our subject, Mr. X. We projected the image of him. We then copied the image of his right leg and flipped it to make a mirror image. Presto, we had a left leg. In the protocol you just witnessed, we took the new imaged left leg and began attaching it to Mr. X's body image at the stub. But let's back up just a bit. What if instead of attaching the imaged leg to the imaged Mr. X, we printed—that is, replicated—the new left leg and then took it, in flesh and blood, mind you, and worked surgically to attach it to the real Mr. X? That's a tough surgery, making those many connections, but it can be done."

"No, Gina, that can't be. That's not really possible, is it?"

"Yes, it is. We've done it. Not on a human, at least not yet, but we've done it with pigs and sheep. The replicated limbs appear to be perfect, but the surgery is challenging. Sometimes the tendons don't heal well, and we've had trouble attaching nerves, but some of our animals have been restored to near normal function. It's taken a lot of talent working for a long time to get this far. We've overcome a lot of problems, and it's most encouraging to see our percentages getting better—way better.

"And we've done more than leg replacements. We've done other body part replacements too. When these techniques are perfected, we won't need dying organ donors anymore. In many cases, everyone can be their own donor. And that means because the replacement parts are from the recipient, we get perfect immunological compatibility—no more rejection."

"You mean you can replace a diseased heart, lung, or liver?"

"Well, we can replicate a diseased organ, but since it's not functioning, there's not much point in doing it unless we can repair it before transplantation. If a compromised organ can be fixed, then transplanting it would be a solution. Take, for example, a subject whose clogged arteries have caused a heart attack. If there were a scan taken before the heart attack, we could project the heart image, clear the image's arteries, and then print the repaired heart and transplant it. Problem solved, patient saved.

"Even if a diseased organ can't be repaired, we can almost always find a living subject with high compatibility and replicate that donor's organ, no dying necessary. There may be residual compatibility issues, but in most cases, we can deal with that."

"How about other kinds of diseases? Can you replicate organs riddled with cancer, repair them, and then transplant them?"

"Yes, we could, but cancer presents an entirely more complicated problem. We can work with a scan of the subject, including the cancerous organ. Then we can search for and find every cancer cell in the image. We can do a search and delete—no more cancer. Then we can take that clean organ and transplant it. But here's the problem: When an organ is riddled with cancer, chances are quite high that cancer cells have already metastasized throughout the body. That means that sooner or later, there will be metastatic cancers popping up elsewhere in the body."

"So you don't have a cure for cancer?"

"Not really. As I said, we can use our scanning technology to search out every cancer cell in the body. It helps to know exactly where the cancer cells are. We can eliminate every trace of cancer from the scan, but in the actual body, we're stuck with conventional therapies to eliminate cancer cells where we find them."

"If you've done a search and delete and you're left with a cancer-free scan, why not just replicate the whole subject?"

Gina's face suddenly changed. Eager, playful, even giddy in sharing her work with Charlie, she suddenly paused and turned her face away. When she turned back, the spirited smile that had animated her face was gone, replaced with an expression of caution and uncertainty. She was left speechless.

"You know, I just realized that I've been throwing a lot at you. Let's take a break and have Adam rejoin us. We can go back to my office, where the three of us can chat about what to show you next."

Chapter 22

On the way to Gina's office, neither she nor Charlie spoke. Charlie's mind overflowed with implications drawn from all he had witnessed. They moved past her receptionist and into her office, where she invited him to relax. Gina excused herself. She wanted a private conversation with Adam. Minutes later, she returned.

"We're in luck. Adam's been busy with security matters but will join us in just a minute."

It was clear to Charlie that Gina did not want to talk about her research. They were both relieved when Adam entered unannounced.

"Gina tells me that you've taken quite an interest in our work, but now is a good time to respond to questions you might have. In particular, Gina tells me that you stumbled on one of our greatest dilemmas, the dilemma that explains the urgency of your visit. We intended to demonstrate more about our project before discussing our dilemma, but now is as good a time as any. As I understand it, you wondered if we might cure a patient of cancer by ridding the whole body image of cancer cells and then replicating that whole image. Do I have that right?"

"Yes, that's the question I asked, but I asked it off the top of my head. In the several minutes since, I think I've figured it out."

"So tell us. What's our dilemma?"

"Well, it seems the replica, I guess you call it a replicant, is just that. It's not the actual subject; it's a replica, not the original."

"Yes, that's the start of it, but to fill that out a bit, let's look a little more carefully at our replicant. Remember that replicant is not just a copy. It's a perfect replica. It bears more than a likeness. It is more like an identity. For the moment, forget the cancer patient. Let's talk about a perfectly healthy subject whom we might replicate without any alteration. They are identical in every respect. Oh, maybe there's an atom or two that's misplaced here or there, but the difference is, as a practical matter, impossible to detect. Tell me, Charlie, who is real, and who is not?"

"The original is real. Isn't that obvious?"

"Of course the original is real. Yes, that is obvious, but the replicant is also real. It has all the physical attributes of the original subject, every freckle, scar, hair, and callus. And not just the physical features. Remember we've replicated all the nervous system pathways, every axon, dendrite, synapse, and neurotransmitter. That means the replicant has every memory and personality quirk as the original, the same temperament and proclivities. Side by side, you couldn't distinguish one from the other."

"What about the soul?"

"Show me the seat of the soul, and I'll show you how it's replicated too."

"That's creepy. You sound like you've already replicated a human subject. Is that true? Is that what you're telling me? What a thought that is! My mind is running from miracle to monstrosity."

"Rest easy. At least for now, we've not replicated a human subject. Everything I just described is gleaned from animal observations. We've gone up the evolutionary ladder and climbed up to mammals, though no primates yet."

"Why haven't you gone to primates, and why not humans?"

"We've avoided primates because we'd have to get regulatory approval. Without approval, we'd be in violation of the law. That would put our research facility and our researchers at risk of criminal prosecution. Can you imagine what damage a disgruntled employee could

do to us? For the time being, we can accomplish most of what we want with non-primate mammals."

"If you go to humans, how would you do that? Where would you go for that kind of regulatory approval?"

"There's no department for that one yet. To replicate a human, we'd have to go rogue. We'd have to accomplish a human replication with a bare staff, maybe just Gina and me—or maybe you, Charlie. We'd have to think hard about how to finesse the replication so it would not ever become known. That'd be a trick, but besides that, our technology isn't ready yet."

"You've successfully replicated a lot of mammals. It looks ready to me. If you can do it with them, why can't you replicate a human?"

"The higher up the evolutionary ladder we go, the more complex the organisms become. When we get to humans, we get a complexity we see nowhere else in the animal kingdom. We're not yet satisfied with the accuracy of the replication process. We've created a measure of replication accuracy. We call it *identicality*. Obviously, we're striving for an identical replica, but then there's the real world. We're laboring long hours to get our identicality score way down to near 1.0."

"What does that mean?"

"Identicality is a statistical expression we've cooked up; it's an expression of probability. It's a measure of the frequency of differences between successive scans of a subject or between the scan of an original and the scan of a resulting replicant. It's too complicated to describe, but for this conversation, we don't need to. If we can get to 1.0, that would mean we'd be almost certain that our replicant is the real deal. If we do two consecutive scans of the same subject, inevitably we're going to get two different outcomes. The scans can never be absolutely identical. That's a result of physiological functions going on in our subject. Because our subject is alive, it'll constantly have chemical and electrical processes going on. Any two scans separated by even a moment will yield different results. Our identicality score factors that in. It must alert us to replication errors while recognizing that some

differences are the result of normal physiological processes. When we do a scan, or rather a series of scans, we sedate our subjects to slow everything down and keep the time between scans to a minimum. Those steps improve the identicality score. If the score is larger than we expect, it might be because of a fart or burp or some other physiological event. Or it might be the result of an error in the process. We have to distinguish between errors and normal physiological events. At this point, we're seeing an unacceptable frequency of what we think must be errors."

"So what can you do about that?"

"Don't know. We're still learning. First, because the scan proceeds in a regular physical sequence, we can usually locate the spot where a difference appears. Then we look at the spot in both scans and try to identify what might be going on. Usually, upon investigation, it just turns out to be a routine physiological process. If that's the case, we disregard the difference. If we can't figure out what's causing the difference, we have to attribute it to an error. At this point, we are running multiple scans on sedated subjects and getting good agreement among the scans. Our most recent results are showing identicality scores of 1.4. We're making good progress but not good enough for a human replication. We want to see 1.0."

"So when you get 1.0, you'll replicate a human subject?"

"No, Charlie, not quite. We're constrained by more than the technology's shortcomings. We're also constrained by moral, ethical, and social issues. We need to think this through and decide if this is really something we want to turn loose in the world. We've already developed technologies and processes that are worth billions. Even if we shut down the replicator project, we have lots to show for our efforts. On the other hand, if we continue toward human replication, we need to understand the risks. That's why you're here."

"You don't really mean you need me in order to move on to human replication?"

"No, I need you to help *me* decide whether *I* want to move on to human replication. We used to drink wine, smoke weed, and talk about the big issues. It was easy then because there was nothing we could do about it. Now we're drinking scotch, and the talk's not as easy. Why? Because, regarding this issue, there's actually something we can do."

"Good God, Adam, why me? Why don't you just call in a priest or a rabbi or a philosopher?"

"Why call on a priest or rabbi when I have you? You're smart, you have good judgment, and you care about ethics. And don't forget, you're the cyclops, the guy with the extraordinary insight. Besides, I can always just say you're wrong and be on my way."

"You want me to drink scotch with you and moralize?"

"Hardly. There's more to it than that. I need you to immerse yourself in this technology and discuss it with others, even if only cryptically. I need a critic who is skeptical, someone who is wary of the implications. I need you to think about this deeply and share your thinking with me. I trust your insight more than you might imagine and certainly more than anyone else's I can think of. But I make no promises. You may come up with recommendations that I won't like. I might dismiss them out of hand. But if I do, it won't be without deep respect for you and high regard for your opinions. That much I can promise you."

"If you want someone who's skeptical and wary, you've got the right guy. Aren't you worried that I'll just derail your whole project?"

"Like I said, I'm not promising to accept your judgment as final. I know you're not a Luddite. I know that you don't reject modernity. Rather, you embrace it. I don't think in an earlier age, you would have rejected penicillin because it might have intruded on God's will in matters of life and death. I know you believe in God and that you believe that, for some ultimate purpose, God gave man free will. Frankly, I don't get it. It makes no sense to me. But your sensibilities, those that animate your belief, may enable me to gain a perspective that I might otherwise dismiss."

"Don't make me out to be religious. I'm hardly more than a hang-er-on at the edge of the cloth. You may think of me as a believer be-cause, at one time or another, I may have expressed a belief in God, but that's about it. No clergyman knows my name."

"I'm not interested in your religious credentials. I know you, Char-lie. I want you to do this for me, but first I want to show you one more demonstration. After that, you can give me your answer. You can take your time. I want you to be sure you want to do this."

"No, I'm already sure. I definitely do not want to do this. Look, I've got a very demanding practice. I can't just drop everything and run around chitchatting with people about something that looks a lot like science fiction. My partners would kill me. Besides, I've got political aspirations. You think I can put all that on the shelf and maybe come back to it later? No. I can't do that."

"I'm not yet ready for that answer. Let's go back to the lab for an-other demonstration. You'll find it difficult but illuminating."

Gina had been a silent observer of something that resembled a tennis match, all the while exhibiting an odd smile that suggested a foreknowledge of what would follow.

Back in the lab, Adam had a story to tell. "About two months ago, an employee came to me with a problem. Her father was seriously ill. He had suffered for many years with kidney disease and already had one of his kidneys removed. But now his remaining kidney was failing. He was on a list for a kidney transplant, but it was a long list. You might know that life on dialysis is difficult. Many patients prefer death. What with the chronic low blood pressure and recurring infections, it can be awful, not to mention the six hours, three times a week, spent in a dialysis lab. He was about to discontinue dialysis. He didn't want to live like that.

"Our employee was a good match immunologically. She wanted desperately to help her father and would have donated a kidney, but she only had one. As a child, she had been thrown from a horse. Her right kidney was ruptured and removed, leaving her with just her left kidney. She was devastated that she couldn't be her father's donor. She knew we were doing research related to transplants and had occasional contact with me. She asked me if I could help or at least offer some advice.

"I thought about it and brought it to Gina's attention. Gina has a lot of connections in transplant medicine. So, Gina, do you remember your response to my inquiry?"

"Yes, I do. I told you that the guy was toast. He was elderly, in poor health, and at the back of a long line of desperately hopeful patients. But then I said that in a couple of years, our replication procedure would solve this problem."

"Go ahead, Gina. Tell Charlie what you said next."

"I simply made an offhand remark that we could actually produce a kidney for him right now."

"Well, you know me. I said, 'So why not? Why not produce a kidney for her father?' That was obvious, but where, presumably, would this kidney come from? There has to be a documented trail. Fortunately, we operate a medical treatment facility within our organization. If our employee were to represent that she was donating a kidney, that source would not be questioned."

"Adam, don't tell me you replicated a kidney for transplant. This is all experimental. You've been dealing with rats."

"Remember the leg transplants on pigs? They were complicated surgeries because of the bones, tendons, and nerves. By contrast, kidneys are easy. So, yeah, we replicated a kidney. We made a complete scan of our employee, and from that scan we replicated her kidney. We studied it carefully in gross anatomy and in dissection and then histologically too. It was perfect. Of course, by the time we got done with the studies, the kidney was functionally disabled. So we replicated another one. We were in touch with the transplant surgeons who were caring for our employee's father and told them that the man's daughter had offered a kidney and it was ready for delivery. We packed it in ice and had it delivered to the hospital, where it was successfully transplanted. The man now has a fully functioning kidney and is living a normal life."

"This isn't legal, is it? Why would they accept a donated kidney from a research institute if you're not a medical facility that deals with patients? Can't you get into a lot of trouble?"

"First of all, we are an approved medical facility treating patients. We're not a general care hospital, but we've gained a well-regarded reputation in several specialties. We do transplant surgeries, and we deal with many orthopedic injuries. So if we offered a properly documented kidney, it would be accepted. But regarding your other question about trouble, yes, falsifying the source of the transplant kidney is certainly illegal. So, yes, I could get into a lot of trouble, but the man was going to die, and now he's alive. Without dialysis, he would have had only days to live. Legally, I guess there's a problem. Morally, I feel fine about what we did. What about you, Charlie? What would you have done?"

Adam paused to let his rhetorical question stir Charlie's conscience.

"Now, Charlie, if you're ready, we're going to produce an image from a scan and discuss its implications. I think you'll find it unsettling."

There was no difference from the previous sequence of events. The lights were dimmed. Gina went to her computer and moved her cursor down a list until she found what she was looking for. She double-clicked her mouse, and the familiar hum filled the room. Charlie's eyes were fixed where the previous images were formed, but this time there was no surgical table. As he watched, an image began to take shape, the barest outlines of a standing figure.

At first, he wasn't sure what or, rather, whom he was looking at, but by the time the image was fully formed, it was unmistakable. He froze in place. He was dizzy. Faintness left him wobbly. Was it really an image of Melissa?

"Adam, is this some kind of sick joke? What is this you're doing here? You know how Melissa's death has affected me. Her death and my barest escape are still fresh torments. We've moved forward only because I've managed to cloak my memories, but they're just barely out of sight behind the flimsiest of veils. And now you recall them in this most graphic way. Why on earth would you do that?"

"No, Charlie, this is not a joke. It's a part of what you will be dealing with as you work on this project with us. I don't want you working on machinery, stale philosophies, and hard data all disconnected from human experience. I need you to be personally vested in this deep down into your core. I need you to be working with blood, guts, and raw emotion. This is the reality of what we are doing. Just now, you're only looking at an image of Melissa, lifelike to be sure but just an image. This is just the start of what, no doubt, will be a troubling conversation."

"How is it that you have a scan of Melissa?"

"It was her father who needed the kidney transplant. She was the little girl who ruptured her kidney when she was thrown from her horse. She is the donor of the kidney that saved her father's life."

Tears welled up in Charlie's eyes. He said nothing while Adam continued in a tone and cadence that expressed great respect and admiration for Melissa.

"We were on a flight back to Austin. We had plenty of time to chat. She spoke about her father's condition. I decided to help her and her family. I didn't know how I could help until I had my conversation with Gina. That's when we had Melissa come into our lab for a complete scan. It was from that scan that we produced the kidney that saved her father's life. But here's the dilemma that you need to come to grips with. We have her scan. It's a complete scan. It captures every nuance of her being, both physical and psychological—and in your way of thinking, maybe even her soul. It's only theoretical now because the medical rescue team pronounced her dead at the scene, and a death certificate was issued. But what if we had taken her body and hid it away? What if we had taken the scan and created a replicant from it? Then Melissa, as far as anyone in the world would know except for us, would still be alive. She'd go to work, meet up with her friends, visit with her parents and brothers, and hopefully go on to live a full and happy life, one uninterrupted by an untimely death. And for all the people in her life, she'd still be alive. They'd know nothing about her broken neck. They'd be spared the grief of her loss, and hopefully they'd know her love and affection for the rest of their lives."

"But Melissa would be dead."

"Yes, she would. She'd be dead, but no one would know it."

"No, Adam, she'd be dead. She'd know it."

"No, how could she know it? She'd have all the knowledge and memories of Melissa. Well, almost all. She would lack memories of events that took place between the time of the scan and the moment of her replication. She'd have a memory gap, a sort of amnesia, but as far as she could tell, she'd be Melissa. She would be stupefied if someone tried to convince her otherwise. And to confirm her belief, everyone in her life would have no doubt whatsoever. They wouldn't know anything about her death, only that here she is and very much alive."

"You're talking about the replicant Melissa. I'm talking about the real Melissa."

"Charlie, I don't think you understand. What do you mean she'd be dead, and she'd know it? What's to know? The original Melissa would be dead. She wouldn't know anything. For God's sake, Charlie, she'd be dead. The replicant would become the real Melissa, as real as real can be."

"Adam, understand what I'm saying. I'm speaking metaphorically. She'd be dead, of course, but she'd have been deprived of her own death. I'm not sure how to put this in words, but she'd be deprived."

"I don't get it. What do you mean by 'she'd be deprived of her own death'?"

"Everyone in her life would go on living with a fraud, maybe not a conscious fraud, maybe a benign one, but a fraud nonetheless—someone who'd have taken over the real Melissa's life. For God's sake, it's like a body snatcher."

Charlie continued. "Melissa was alive; she lived a life, too short to be sure, but with a measure of fullness all its own, and then it's all over, done, ended, and there'd be no one to mourn. What am I saying? I don't even know. Just imagine Melissa's soul rising up to heaven, to be with God or to enter eternity, whatever any of that may mean, and as she rises, she stops for a moment and turns to take one last look at the life she lived, the life she's left behind. And imagine that what she sees is that no one even knows that she died. The two most significant events in anyone's life are birth and death. In her case, she would have died, but there'd be no one to even notice or to mourn her loss. How sad is that? The meaning of life is ultimately in how we live it, something only fully observable at its end. Honestly, why do we bother with funerals? Is it just to dispose of a rotting corpse? No, it's a time to take note of a life and its passage. There's something meaningful in that for all of us. It pays homage to the life that has passed, and it reminds us of the meaning of our own lives. Honestly, how would it feel to live your life and think that at its end no one even knew it was over? How lonely is that—how utterly empty and devoid of meaning?"

"Charlie, when you landed and I got medical confirmation of Melissa's death, I was on the phone calling her parents. It was the hardest phone call I ever had to make. They were utterly devastated. Their loss is beyond measure. I couldn't bear to think about my own children and how I'd feel if either of them died. In this case, Melissa's parents might have been spared that loss had a replicant been created. They would not have had to suffer that horrible loss, that parents' worst nightmare."

Charlie's response, without thinking, was shaped by the ever-present recollection of his own daughter's death, a sorrow that would forever dominate his anguished soul. That agony informed him that a replicant could never take her place in his heart but would for all his life be a reminder of his loss.

With his eyes watering and in an almost inaudible undertone, he said, "Her replicant would have been a fraud. Melissa died, and so did Sandra. No replicant could ever replace either of them."

"But, Charlie, you're talking like someone who knows there's been a replication. If Melissa went to the hospital and her parents were told that she had recovered, they would have no knowledge that their healthy daughter was actually a replicant. The same with Sandra. If her doctor told you that she had recovered, you wouldn't be in grief. You'd be relieved and give thanks for the miracle. You'd never know that she was a replicant."

"Of everyone I know, you, Adam, are the most direct, the ultimate realist. You're the one that's always saying, 'Get real.' You're the one that says, 'Get over it; move on. Quit burying your head in the sand.' Doesn't that sound familiar? That's the Adam I know. But in this case, you succumb to a sentimentality laced with saccharine."

"You're nuts, Charlie. I'm the one who had to make the phone call. How would you like to make a call like that?"

"I wouldn't. I don't know if I could have done it. I don't know how you managed to do it. That was the character thing to do. That's you, Adam. I'd like to think that if I had to make that call, I wouldn't deny death by substituting a fake likeness. We humans go to great lengths to deny reality, that thing that's ever with us. But reality doesn't go away just because we deny it."

Adam wondered if Charlie was talking about Melissa, or was it Sandra, when he said, "Death, and untimely death in particular, is a great tragedy that has always been a part of life. As painful as it is, our humanity has equipped us to deal with it. If we distort the meaning of death, we will, at the same time, warp the meaning of life. No, Adam, to deny death its due is to diminish life and deprive it of its meaning."

Adam fell silent for a long moment. "Now I'm more certain than ever. I want . . . no, I need you to take on this job."

While Charlie went off to weigh his options, Gina and Adam remained in the lab.

Adam said, "Do you think Charlie will be a help to us?"

"No, Adam. I think he's already made up his mind. He's going to come down against it. He may think he'll make a fair inquiry, but in the end, he'll turn thumbs down. I don't think that's what you want."

"Gina, I don't know yet what I want, and I don't need Charlie's approval. I don't want someone to support my judgment. I want someone to struggle with me and force me to think about things I don't want to think about and about things I might not think about on my own. I told Charlie, and I meant it. I can listen and learn from him and still reject his recommendation. It's not his decision; it's mine."

"He's biased. Do you want him swaying you from your independent judgment?"

"Of course he's biased. And you are too. He's a skeptic, and you're full on. On this question, I'd be a fool to rely entirely on my own independent judgment or yours. I want to be swayed forward and back. I'm not afraid of saying no to Charlie, and I'm not afraid of saying no to you."

"Adam, we've invested time, money, energy—lots of it. We've committed our full capacities to see this through. Do you really think that we might turn our backs on this at this stage, given what we've accomplished?"

"Like I said, it's my decision in the end, for better or worse."

"It sounds like you've already made up your mind about Charlie, and I don't like it one bit. I didn't come to work with you to see my very best efforts just shunted aside. You want to make this decision together with Charlie; it's yours to make, but don't expect me to sit around doing your bidding. You've got your options, and I've got mine."

"Gina, I know you've invested yourself in this project with a tremendous passion. I respect that, but before unleashing this technology on an unsuspecting world, I want to hear every contrary argument. I don't want to leave any stone unturned. Charlie will see to that."

Later that afternoon, Charlie went back to the lab expecting to meet with Adam and Gina. Adam said, "Gina got called away on another matter, so it's just you and me. Have you made a decision to join us?"

"I think that I'm just going to slow you down. You'll end up listening to Gina with one ear and to me with the other. Why invite that kind of contention? This could get really ugly."

"Damn it, I don't care about ugly. Don't you see? This is a contest that has to play out. If you say no to this responsibility, you'll leave a valuable perspective unrepresented. Is that really what you want?"

"Oh, when did it become my responsibility, one that I'd be shirking if I refuse to participate? Isn't that a little heavy?"

"Yes, it is. There's an important decision to be made, and you can play an important role in shaping it, or you can turn your back. What do you want to do?"

Charlie was quiet while he thought about the many times he felt persuaded—or had he been manipulated—by Adam. Was that, after all, Adam's great skill? He knew Charlie would be susceptible to feelings of responsibility, and he played that to the hilt. Charlie was responsive in that way, even as he felt humbled by a sense of misplaced confidence and flattery. But he was excited by, even craved, the prospect of participating in a historically consequential development. He felt charged with a sense of very great purpose. He sensed that this was something that was bigger than anything he had ever done before, maybe bigger than anything else he might do in his life. They were both quiet for an uncomfortable interlude until Charlie nodded his head, acknowledging consent. His fate was sealed.

Chapter 23

Home at last, Laura and Charlie tried to settle into a new routine. Charlie passed new client referrals on to his partners and engaged their assistance with existing clients. Laura's work suffered because of the emotional distractions that came along with their new lifestyle, which included the presence of a security routine established at Adam's insistence. Joel hated the security precautions that intruded on his friendships and his pool parties. All three of them wondered about the wisdom of Charlie's new position, a job with responsibilities that Laura never felt fully informed about. She understood that it was important to Charlie and reluctantly accepted his decision as her own.

They loved the home they had moved into when Joel was in kindergarten. It was spacious and bright and had a large, beautifully landscaped yard. It was a good fit for their casual lifestyle. They didn't want to move, but the security team insisted they were vulnerable because of proximity to neighbors and the lack of a secure perimeter. Charlie and Laura protested. Joel was furious. They gave in and made the move.

The new house was situated within the walled, fenced, and gated boundaries of a three-acre home site. The architecture was in good taste—but not their taste. It represented a level of luxury, opulence, and sophistication that they found hard to relate to, and the isolation seemed uninviting. Coming and going through a security gate was a constant reminder of the threat they had to live with. Nevertheless, it was a move for good reasons. They would adjust.

Throughout the summer, Charlie worked out an agenda with Adam. Despite a search, they uncovered no one working on replication. But they did find researchers working on technologies with broad societal impacts. Gene modification, in vitro fertilization, artificial intelligence, robotics, stem cells, brain function, and life extension were all classified as high-impact societal disruptors. Researchers working in these fields, along with philosophers, theorists, thinkers, and pundits, had things to say about these new-world technologies. Charlie's job was to identify the players, meet with them, learn about their work, and find out how they saw their work impacting modernity. What made them accessible was Adam's reputation. Some wanted to court his funding. Others wanted to rub shoulders in any way they could with Adam Braudy, the man and the myth. With just a mention of Adam's name, most doors would swing wide open.

In September, Charlie scheduled an early morning meeting at the Massachusetts Institute of Technology with a prominent researcher who was working on artificial intelligence. Charlie flew into Logan International Airport the night before, checked into the hotel, and took time to relax in the lounge. That's where he met Max.

"Hey, buddy, you new in town?" The slur of his tongue suggested a conversation Charlie wanted to avoid.

"Just got in. If you'll excuse me, my friend will be along in just a minute."

"If she's a real pretty friend, maybe she's got a friend for me too."

"Sorry, not that kind of friend. Would you mind giving me a little privacy here? I've only got a few minutes to do a little catch-up while I'm waiting."

The man moved on to the bar and ordered a drink. Twenty minutes later, he was back.

"Guess your friend's not comin'. By the way, my name's Max. Can I buy you a drink?"

Max was neatly dressed in a black pinstriped suit and an open-collared shirt. He seemed pleasant enough. Though tired, Charlie was bored.

"Okay, Max. My name is Charlie. Glad to meet you. If you're buying, I'm drinking scotch. Make it neat."

Max headed to the bar and returned with his glass refreshed and with a double shot of a tasty single-malt for Charlie.

"Thanks, Max. What brings you here?"

"I'm a sales rep for a plumbing fixture manufacturer. I'm here to visit several distributors in the Boston area. My boss is pushing me to get our sales numbers up. We need more business. If I can't push some product here in the next few days, we'll have to do some downsizing. We got a great crew doing real good work. I'd sure hate to see any of 'em let go. What about you, Charlie, you got any good news? What's your line of work? What brings you to Boston?"

"I'm an attorney. I help my clients with financial and estate planning and with their philanthropic interests. I'm here to meet with a client."

"So how's this economy affecting your clients?"

"Well, a lot of them went through a rough patch a while back when the economy got hammered, but they mostly got through it in good shape."

"Glad to hear there's some good stuff happening. Anyway, I see you've got your head buried in that iPad of yours. You must be reviewing stats for your client."

"No more stats for me tonight. I'm just relaxing around some light reading. I got a good sci-fi page-turner that no one's ever heard of."

"Oh, yeah? I used to read sci-fi when I was a kid. Haven't had much time lately. What's it about?"

"It's about a guy who's invented a replicator."

"What the hell is a replicator?"

"As the story tells it, it's a device that can replicate a human being together with all his mannerisms, memories, and behaviors."

"Oh, ya mean like cloning?"

"Not really. The author says that with cloning, you're just copying genes and growing a new organism from them. That way you end up with an embryo with the same genes as the donor. And then the embryo develops into a newborn, and the newborn eventually into an adult."

"So then you get an adult that's the same as the donor?"

"Kinda yes, kinda no. We're all a product of genes and environment. The cloned adult is always gonna be different from the donor. A lot different because it'll grow up influenced by an entirely different environment."

"You mean you can't just clone Einstein and get a redo?"

"You might end up with a brilliant guy, but maybe he bumps his head too many times as a kid. Or maybe he suffers an infection that fries his brain or at least diminishes it. Or maybe he gets pushed to be a genius and then suffers a burnout at an early age. Or maybe he's a certified genius but isn't interested in physics. Maybe this, maybe that. The possibilities are endless, but the one sure thing is that he's not going to grow up the way the original did. For sure, he's gonna be different."

"So how's the replicator different from cloning?"

"Well, in the story, the replicator doesn't just copy the genes. It copies the entire adult form, together with its memories and its learned habits and behaviors. It's different with a replicator. If you were replicated, the product would be someone identical to you, someone of your age and with every detail of your character, along with all your memories, insights, and experiences. And, I might add, the results of injuries both physical and psychological that you've sustained in life. For better and for worse, it would be indistinguishable from you."

"Whoa there, Charlie. Good thing this is just fiction. But hang on a minute."

Max rushed back to the bar to refresh their drinks. When he got back, it was clear that he'd been thinking about the replicator.

"Now you got me thinking. If my boss thought I was his best sales rep ever, he wouldn't have to troll for another hire. He could just replicate me. And, hey, if the Dodgers needed a pitcher, they could just replicate Sandy Koufax."

"The sales rep might work out, but another Sandy Koufax ain't gonna happen."

"Why not?"

"Sandy Koufax is an old-timer. His pitching days are over. You'd need to replicate him from a scan of him from back in the day."

"Oh, you mean like a recording or something?"

"Exactly. There would have to be a scan of Koufax from his prime. If there were such a scan, he could be replicated the way he was at the time of the scan."

"Oh, I get it. You wouldn't have to raise him from a baby. You wouldn't have an infant Koufax; you'd have an instant Koufax. Just put him on the mound and watch him throw strikes."

"Well, you'd probably wanna warm him up a bit in the bullpen."

"Hey, does that mean you can find the best and the brightest in everything and then just replicate them? If you need a doctor, just replicate the best one anywhere in the world, even replicate him as many times as you want?"

"That's what's in the book."

"Hey, raising kids is expensive and a whole lot of trouble, not to mention the worry and unreliable results. Why raise kids? The world wouldn't need 'em. You could just replicate what's needed. 'Hey, Joe, we need a half dozen sales reps over here. How soon can you deliver?' Or, 'Hey, Joe, we got a war goin' on. Can you fill an order for ten thousand Marines, the toughest ones you got?' Hell, you wouldn't even need to train 'em. They'd come pretrained. Oh, that's cool."

"Ya know, Max, you should have written the book. I hadn't really thought of all those angles, and I guess the author didn't either."

"Hey, look, I don't like to talk about it much, but my kids didn't turn out real good. They drove me and my wife nuts. We finally got a divorce. My son's doing dope, and my daughter, she's got tattoos and pierces everywhere on her body. Hell, she's probably got pierces where I got no business lookin'. And the creeps she hangs out with are scary. Maybe the world would be better off if we just replicated what we needed instead of playing kiddie roulette—trying to grow 'em up to be somebody you really want in the world but then ending up with crap."

"Max, you're painting an ugly picture. It never occurred to me that it might be used to populate the world."

"Well, what do you think, Charlie? Can you imagine big league baseball where every team's got a Sandy Koufax? Yikes."

Charlie washed down the last of his scotch and said goodnight. He left unsaid just how disturbed he was about the scenarios that Max offered. Back in his room, he lay in bed wrestling with his sheets for a long time before sleep finally interrupted his restless deliberations.

Chapter 24

On a Thursday afternoon in October, just a couple of weeks after a blistering Indian summer heatwave, an early cold front washed in from out of the west, bringing much-needed relief and over an inch of rain. Then it was over, and the skies cleared as if the clouds had been brushed aside by the fresh, blustery winds that followed right behind the front. The view from Charlie's office window was spectacular with a vibrant blue sky punctuated by bright, billowing cumulus clouds reaching high aloft. Charlie was drawn from the view by a phone call from Adam, who wanted an update and had good news to share.

Charlie said, "I've been doing a lot of meeting and gabbing. I've put the plane you provided me with to good use. I gotta tell you I started out skeptical, but the more I learn, the more I think the whole thing stinks. I don't like it. Last month I had a most amazing conversation with a guy who had way too much to drink. He scared the shit out of me. You're gonna hate me, Adam. I don't like this replication business. Not one bit."

"Save it, Charlie. Stick with it."

"I'll stick with it, but I'm not likely to change my mind."

"If that's the case, it'll be your job to change mine."

"You said you had some good news to share."

"Dean Fleck met with some guys who extended his senses into the darkest corners of the underworld. Despite the secrecy and compartmentalization that Laura and Shari's attackers used, Dean uncovered actionable information. Because of the unusual character and quality of the work done on the SUVs, he traced a path to a hack shop in Mexico City. They had turned an average soccer mom's family taxi into a high-performance attack machine. Dean applied enough pressure on the proprietors to get more leads, which he put together with information from decrypted files he found on the attack team's computer. He learned that the team was a product of the Secura Group, a private contractor based in Venezuela thought to be headed by a former CIA operative. Secura worked for wealthy individuals of a criminal bent, mob organizations, drug cartels, and governments who need to distance themselves from the mayhem they instigate. Dean was convinced that Secura could be neutralized, leaving the party or parties that hired them convinced that further assaults would lead to their discovery and to unwanted repercussions."

Adam added, "Dean has a plan. You may remember Sam Galatine; he's a key guy for us. He was the head of the security team that rescued Shari and Laura. Dean sent him down to Venezuela to scope out Secura's operation, identify their leadership, figure out who hired them, and discover their vulnerabilities. As soon as Sam reports back, I'll get back to you with more details."

Two weeks later, Adam sent an email saying he had just received a report that would be of interest and to expect a copy delivered by messenger. That afternoon, two men arrived at Charlie's office, identifying themselves as messengers carrying a package from Adam Braudy. Kay, the firm's receptionist, excused herself from the front desk and walked hurriedly to Charlie's office.

"Charlie, two big guys just walked into the office and want to see you. They look suspicious and said they have a package for you from Adam Braudy. Are you expecting this delivery? They said they have instructions to deliver it to you personally."

"Sorry, Kay. I forgot to tell you I was expecting a messenger delivery."

To be safe, Charlie didn't want to be left alone with them in his office and followed Kay back to the reception area, where he identified himself as Charles Wood.

"Mr. Adam Braudy has asked us to personally deliver this package to Mr. Charles Wood and to no one else. For purposes of identification, we've been instructed to obtain an iris scan. If that's agreeable, please simply stare at the target image appearing on the cell phone screen."

"Is this another one of Adam's inventions?"

"We don't know anything about that, Mr. Wood. We're only interested in securing your iris scan. Once we've done that, we can leave this package in your care."

Charlie gazed at the target on the cell phone screen. Within a moment, there was a beep, and a green graphic appeared.

"Thank you, Mr. Wood. Here's your package."

With that accomplished, the messengers turned and left while Charlie retreated to his office. He opened the package and found a handwritten note from Adam along with two bound documents.

Charlie, Here's a copy of Sam Galatine's report on his investigation into Secura and its head, Vincent Poole. You'll quickly see why I elected a secure delivery method rather than email. Please read it carefully, and let's plan on discussing further. I'll give you a call later this afternoon. I've also enclosed a copy of financial reports on one of our businesses along with some sensitive information regarding trade secrets. File that report in case we ever have to explain the nature of the delivery. After you've read the security report, destroy it along with this note. Adam

Sam Galatine's report was comprised of three parts. The first read like a business consultant's review and critique of the character and structure of a successful business organization. The second part read like a psychological profile of Vincent Poole. Lastly, the most disturbing part discussed the possible means to deal with Mr. Poole and Secura.

Though Charlie hadn't yet met Sam Galatine, he nevertheless felt forever indebted to him for aiding in Laura's rescue. His impression of him was of a trained killer, a shrewd man of violence, one with impressive leadership skills. More than that, though, the executive summary of the report revealed him to be a man of much intelligence and sophistication.

The Secura Group, a ten-year-old security firm, represents itself to be a leading provider of a variety of security services for both private businesses and government agencies. It maintains stylish offices in a prestigious high-rise building in Caracas, Venezuela. The firm was founded and is currently headed by Mr. Vincent Poole, an American citizen and former employee of the CIA who has been a resident of Caracas for over ten years. Many of the services Secura provides are typical of a private security agency, such as protecting key employees from violence and safeguarding critical operations from disruption. Formally, Secura maintains a staff of about fifty engaged in such defensive services.

Off the official roster, Secura maintains additional staff, perhaps numbering another fifty at any given time. They are deployed either locally or in various international locations around the world where they provide a variety of criminal activities for hire. These activities fall within several categories: (1) kidnappings, murders, and assassinations; (2) thefts and/or transport of documents, drugs, and arms; (3) intelligence gathering of commercial and government information; and (4) computer hacking for the surreptitious collection of digital information, the destruction of digital media, and/or the disruption of computer assets. They are considered highly effective in all these activities.

Mr. Vincent Poole, fifty-three years of age, was born and raised in Denver, Colorado. After high school, he went on to the University of Colorado, where he graduated at the top of his class. Upon graduation, he joined the CIA, where he was employed for fifteen years. He was considered a trophy hire, consistently exhibiting intelligence and initiative. He started as an analyst, in which capac-

ity he proved to be thorough and insightful. Eventually expressing an interest in clandestine activity, he was admitted to a training program where his analytic skills were matched with physical skills not previously recognized. Standing six feet tall and weighing a muscular one hundred eighty pounds, he became skillful in personal combat requiring stamina and excellent coordination. That proficiency, combined with intelligence and agility of mind, suggested a promising placement.

He was quite successful in his early assignments, repeatedly gathering important information under adverse circumstances while providing a human link to other undercover agents operating secretly in highly sensitive settings. Ultimately, it didn't work out. He came to exhibit a grandiose sense of himself, deserved to some extent but clearly to excess. Others were drawn to him because of his apparent prowess, conveyed too often by his own unsubstantiated claims of his exploits including accounts of promiscuous sexual conquests. He could be excessively competitive, bragging incessantly about his own feats, often accomplished while cheating, and all too often demeaning the efforts and accomplishments of others.

He thrived on risk-taking but frequently took unwarranted risks that might have jeopardized his missions, his life, and the lives of others. Beyond braggadocio, he was found to engage in lying, at which he was extraordinarily effective. During lie detector tests, he was able to pass the most sensitive scrutiny while relating information that was already known to be false. Finally, when confronted with one of his attempts at deception, he offered no apology or regret but instead became enraged and abusive, claiming that he was unfairly singled out as a target of unspecified revenge. He was recalled from field assignments but proved to be a disgruntled employee unable to engage constructively with coworkers. His employment was terminated.

At this point, his history was lost from view. There are rumors about his engagement with drug cartels and various foreign gov-

ernment agencies but nothing verifiable until ten years ago, when Mr. Poole reemerged as the founder of a small security firm in Caracas, eventually growing into Secura, an apparently successful organization in its current form.

Reportedly under the protection of the Venezuelan government, Mr. Poole and his organization appear to be immune from criminal prosecution and protected from violent assault. However, there are vulnerabilities. Although Secura is managed by a capable administrative staff operating in a formal organizational structure, because of Mr. Poole's paranoia, he has populated his organization with people who do his bidding but who do not have the skills and capabilities necessary to assume the leadership role in his absence.

This suggests that the removal of Mr. Poole is an obvious solution. There are several routes. The first is diplomatic. Secura is known to be heavily engaged in activities supporting drug smuggling into the United States. Thus, given our contacts in Congress, and especially within the State Department, at our urging, diplomatic pressure could be applied that might cause the Venezuelan government to initiate criminal action against Mr. Poole and Secura.

Secondly, the CIA has identified Secura and Mr. Poole to be engaged in clandestine activities, criminally targeting American companies and government institutions. In addition, Secura and Mr. Poole are suspects in deaths and disappearances of several US agents. It may be that the CIA, armed with more specific evidence delivered along with our encouragement, might take clandestine measures to terminate Mr. Poole.

Lastly, notwithstanding Mr. Poole's paranoia, given his appetite for risk-taking and his need for adulation and sexual conquest, he might be successfully targeted using our own resources.

Chapter 25

Charlie was trapped by circumstances beyond his control. There was no way to deny his complicity in the slaughter of the two hit men. He had dirtied his hands in slime. He felt responsible for putting his family at risk. He didn't know how to quit this horror. If they descended into the cesspool of Sam's third suggestion, to use Adam's resources to terminate Mr. Poole, Charlie would be immersed in utter filth. He was helpless and yearned for salvation.

By late afternoon, Charlie had read and reread the entire report several times. He recognized that Sam had access to people burrowed deep in the CIA who were willing and able to provide information on Vincent Poole. Charlie received Adam's call on line two, a facility used for encrypted communication.

Charlie said, "I was deep into your report within a minute of its delivery. I probably read it from front to back maybe three times. You really gotta stop and wonder what in the hell God had in mind when He created man. What a piece of work."

"I wonder about that every day, Charlie. But tell me, you got any questions for me?"

"You bet I do. Sam talks about contacts in the CIA, Congress, and the State Department. He made those connections sound quite intimate. What's that about?"

"I've mentioned before that we've made friends in the political community. Sam was simply referring to working those friendships as one possible approach."

"You said that you had close connections because of your development of the wind farm. Does that kind of friendship translate to political influence in Congress and the State Department?"

"The wind farm was just an example. An organization of our scale can't really function without constructive relations with governing authorities. Government is everywhere we are. It's gotten to be everywhere any of us is. There's no way to fight it. You gotta join it. I wish we were free to make our own decisions without interference, but that's not possible. Maybe it once was but not today. We maintain a substantial lobbying effort both internally and with the assistance of outside lobbyists. Those efforts keep us in sync with the government."

"Your lobbying is a way you plead your case?"

"That's the theory, and it would work out fine in the end if the regulators just did their job and made carefully thought-out decisions in pursuit of clearly defined objectives based on findings of thoroughly established facts. But that isn't the way it works. What usually happens is that there are competing political pressures forcing a decision one way or another. If we don't push our way, we lose out to someone else pushing another way."

"Are you talking about competitors?"

"Sometimes competitors but sometimes something else."

"Like what?"

"Like the head of a bureaucracy seeking more publicity, influence, and power, or a pol seeking votes, or a special interest pursuing an objective. For whatever reasons, a regulator or a politician might want to accommodate an interested party."

"So what can you do about that?"

"What do you mean? They lobby, and we lobby too. Regulators and pols may not respond to policy facts, but we have a way of being heard."

"With a bullhorn?"

"No bullhorns. You don't have to speak loudly when you say the things they want to hear. Let's use our fusion project as an example. We can't deliver votes because the millions upon millions of beneficiaries of fusion power are only prospective votes. We're not aligned with a currently identifiable voting bloc. But we can always find a way to be helpful. We can offer the means of getting votes. We give money. Or we give a wind farm if that's what they want. Or we give a manufacturing plant either here or there, as they might prefer. We have the means to be helpful, to be heard."

"That hardly sounds democratic."

"I'm not sure what *democratic* means anymore. We invest millions in pursuit of billions in potential revenues. If we just sit on our hands, the millions would be lost, and the billions would never accrue. In our case, those billions represent what would come from cheap clean energy and the new jobs and other benefits that come from that. We have the facts to be sure, but everyone's got their own facts. Like I said, facts aren't enough. More than just facts, we have friends. They help us because we help them. And considering how much we have at stake, we can make friends for small change, relatively speaking. It always surprises me how inexpensive it is to make friends. So that's what we do. We make friends."

"In the case with Mr. Poole, though, you're not asking for regulatory clearance for a power plant. You're asking for special treatment."

"Do you think it's wrong to ask your government for protection? Would you call the police if you feared an intruder? Look, we were personally attacked. Our lives were and are in danger. Aren't we permitted to ask for help?"

"Well, of course, but this is way out of the ordinary. Who can get this kind of special attention? You're buying special favors."

"Just because not everyone has immediate access to the police doesn't mean that someone who does have access shouldn't seek police assistance. We actually have a phone line that gives us access. I can wish that everyone could call their senator for the help they need. I know that's not going to happen, but I'm not going to let that sad reality prevent me from seeking help. If my contact can't or won't help, at least I've tried. And if my contact delivers, for whatever reason, then I will have gained my salvation. That leaves it up to the contact to figure out what's the right thing to do and then do it or not for whatever reason."

"I get it, Adam. Right now I'm just thankful I've got access through your good offices. And I guess what you just told me applies to both the State Department and CIA."

"Sort of. At the CIA, we don't go through outside political channels. We have friends and relationships and interdependencies directly within the CIA at multiple levels. There are individuals there who owe us big time. We work those relationships as needed."

"What do they owe you?"

"Some other time. For now, let's stick to particulars."

"Maybe I'm naïve, but isn't getting help from the State Department or CIA a long shot?"

"I don't want to prejudge it, but you're probably right."

"So if we can't get help, will we end up, in Sam's words, using our own resources?"

"Charlie, I know you don't like this. You may find it hard to believe, but I hate it as much as you do. But, unfortunately, this bullshit comes with the job. The answer to your question is if we can't get the State Department or CIA involved, we will solve this problem on our own. I will hate it, Charlie, but so help me God, I will do this if I have to. My life and the lives of people I love are at stake, and that includes you and your family."

Chapter 26

Adam said, "Charlie, I'd like you to reach out to one of our congressional allies."

"I don't know, Adam. I've done business with city council members and planning commissioners, but Congress is a different affair."

"Maybe some of the players are a bit more sophisticated, but this is not something that you can't handle. Harold Parton is the chairman of the Senate Foreign Relations Committee. We know him. He's a good friend. We've reciprocated with favors from time to time."

"Why put me in the middle when he's used to dealing with you?"

"Actually, he prefers not dealing with me, at least not directly. Except for demonstrably official meetings or social events, we almost always deal through an intermediary or even a chain of intermediaries. Go ahead and reach out to him. You'll find him readily accessible."

―――

"Hello, Mr. Rathman. My name is Charles Wood. I'm an associate of Mr. Adam Braudy. He asked me to reach out to Senator Parton."

"Yes, Mr. Wood. How can the senator be of assistance?"

"I need to meet with Senator Parton as soon as possible."

"Yes, of course. I'd be happy to make those arrangements. At the moment, Senator Parton is in the middle of a meeting, but I'll discuss your request with him as soon as he's finished. Perhaps you can tell me what you'd like to discuss with him and how urgent your matter is."

"We have some information regarding a person who may be of considerable interest to the State Department. We think that the State Department may want to initiate some action regarding this person. And, I might add, this person is of great importance to us. If a meeting could be arranged within the next week, it would serve all our interests."

"Well, let me assure you that Senator Parton always considers Mr. Braudy's voice an important one to be heard. I will bring this to the senator's attention right away and get back to you as soon as I can."

"Thank you, Mr. Rathman. We appreciate your help."

True to his word, Harvey Rathman, Charlie's new best friend, called right back and proposed a meeting with Senator Parton at nine a.m. on Monday morning. That gave Charlie a couple of workdays and the weekend to prepare and to get to DC.

Charlie called Adam on the encrypted line. He told him about the proposed meeting and asked Adam for a report that he could pass along to Senator Parton. "For the meeting, I'd like to have a report like the one you sent me that isn't so thoroughly footnoted. I don't want it to be clear that we have intimate contacts within the State Department and CIA. And I don't want to give him a report that discusses our third option indicating a willingness and capacity to take out Poole on our own."

"Good points, Charlie. I quite agree. See? You've just started with all this, and you already sound like a seasoned pro. I'll have the report that you already received edited as you suggest. I don't want to send it by email. I'll have it delivered to you by messenger at your hotel early Monday morning."

Charlie flew to DC late Sunday afternoon. He was awakened Monday morning by a call from the front desk announcing that a messenger was waiting in the lobby. Charlie quickly dressed and met the messenger, who confirmed Charlie's identity with an iris scan. He was a tall, beefy man who looked like his qualifications included an ability to deal with trouble. Charlie respected the man's muscle and asked for his company as far as the Senate office building. At the entry, the messenger handed Charlie the report and received an appreciative thank-you in return.

Once inside, Charlie wandered the hallways until he found Senator Parton's office suite. There, he met Harvey Rathman, who greeted him like an old friend. After providing Charlie with a cup of coffee, he ushered him in to see his boss, Senator Harold S. Parton, chairman of the Senate Foreign Relations Committee.

When Charlie crossed the room, Senator Parton arose from a large leather chair set high behind his expansive desk. He strode to meet Charlie halfway across the span of his spacious office. He was a tall, patrician character, dressed with crisp creases in a gray pinstriped suit. His thick dark-brown hair was dyed and coifed with every strand in its place. Charlie thought the senator's aftershave was a little too strong, but the musky scent emphasized a vigorous masculinity. He had expected a more officious interaction, but the senator extended himself with a warmth that testified to his friendship with Adam. Or was it his respect for how Adam might be helpful to him?

Charlie wanted to reciprocate the warmth but felt anxious. They sat in plush upholstered chairs facing one another across a small glass table bearing a vase with a fresh rose.

"So tell me . . . Charles, is it?"

"No, no, please call me Charlie. Otherwise, I won't know who you're talking to."

"Then Charlie it is. Tell me a little about your relationship with Adam. You know, he and I are close friends."

"Yes, he thinks highly of you and speaks of you with much respect, even affection, I might add. I've known Adam since we were kids. We grew up together and were roommates our first year in college. After that, we stayed in touch and over the years have done business together. On occasion, as in this case, he has asked me to get directly involved. That's it in a nutshell. Now tell me, how long have you known Adam?"

"Oh, it goes back about twenty years. It was shortly after I was first elected to the House of Representatives. I was as green a freshman as you could find. That's when we first met and found that we had a lot of similar views. He became one of my greatest fans and since then has been one of my strongest supporters. I really must say that my election to the Senate was due in part to his early support and not just his financial support. You probably know how well connected he is. His connections were significant in positioning me in the Senate race. And of course, his fundraising connections were of enormous help. Would I be sitting here today without him? I'd like to say yes, of course, but how would I know that? So that's my story. Now tell me what brings you here. How can I be of assistance to you and to my good friend?"

Charlie was touched by the senator's description of his relationship with Adam. It was more than just the words. The demeanor with which he spoke and his personal warmth and sincerity were convincing. But then Charlie wondered if that was just the essential skill of a successful politician.

Charlie told him about Vincent Poole and Secura and how they were engaged in a wide variety of nefarious activities, many impacting American interests. Charlie decided to tell him about the specific threat they represented to Adam and passed him the report with its included executive summary. He waited until the senator finished reading before he made his ask.

"So, Senator, American interests are at risk, and so are our lives. With the information in this report, which I'll leave with you this morning, we hope you will encourage the State Department to pressure the Venezuelan government to take action against Mr. Poole and Secura."

"Well, Charlie, I suppose you know that this is a difficult situation for the American government, for the State Department, and for me personally. Our relationship with the Venezuelan government is not good. I'm not sure what we can do."

"I know that. What I don't know is what pressure points exist that might be exploited. I understand that a constructive response from Venezuela would be the result of some quid pro quo."

"Charlie, I understand the importance of this matter. I get it. I want to be helpful. Unfortunately, I can't really offer you much hope, but here's what I will do. I'll be meeting with the Secretary of State later this week. I can at least promise you that this matter will be brought to her attention at that meeting. Beyond that, I can make no commitments. I'll let you know what transpires following that meeting."

"Thank you, Senator. We appreciate whatever you can do, but allow me to emphasize that Vincent Poole is a pernicious factor and a serious threat to American interests in general and a personal threat to our lives in particular. We must stop Vincent Poole. And we must identify whoever hired him in order to end the threat that they represent. There must be no misunderstanding here. This matter is of grave concern to Adam. He has every confidence in you and your ability to make things happen."

"Charlie, let me assure you I take your meaning. There is no misunderstanding. I'll do what I can and get back to you before the end of the week. That's my promise."

"One thing more," Charlie said. "I expect you'll find the report I've left with you . . . let's say *thought-provoking*. Please understand it's a sensitive document and should be taken as confidential, between us. Our concern is that from a careful reading, our sources might be deduced. That makes it important to exercise care in sharing the contents. We trust your judgment in how you use the report and the information it contains."

They rose from their chairs. The senator made no reference to Charlie's closing remark. "Give my best to Adam. Let him know that my wife, Charlotte, and I hope to get together with him and Shari sometime soon. And Charlie, perhaps you and your wife could join us too."

"I'd like that very much. I'll look forward to that happy occasion."

All the camaraderie and expressions of friendship seemed genuine, but Charlie felt like he had failed. It was a dead-end, an attempt worth the effort but one made in vain.

Chapter 27

On his flight back to the Bay Area, Charlie called to tell Adam about his meeting and that he feared his effort had been in vain.

"Don't be so harsh a judge. Hal is a good friend. The warmth you saw was not eyewash. His doubts probably reflect his unwillingness to make a promise he doesn't know if he can keep. From what you told me, I'm guessing he judges that this is going to be a hard sell. He's a savvy guy who knows how to press it, but he knows that even for him, it may be a step too far. It's too early to be pessimistic. Let's wait and see."

Throughout the week, Charlie expected the senator's call. As Friday afternoon dragged on, his patience wore thin. By four o'clock, he took note that it was way past quitting time in DC. But then the phone rang.

"Charlie, I promised you a call by this afternoon, and now, after an eventful week, here I am."

"Thank you, Senator. You're a man of your word. Do you have good news for me?"

"I do have news for you. And it's urgent that I get together with you and Adam to discuss this privately. I don't want to meet anywhere around here. I want to meet with the two of you in Austin."

What possible news couldn't the senator discuss on the phone? Charlie didn't ask. Without hesitation, without knowing Adam's sense of it or his availability, he immediately replied, "Yes, of course. When would you like to meet?"

"Right away. I'm available whenever you and Adam are."

"Pack your bags, Senator. I'll have our dispatch office let you know when our plane will be there to pick you up."

"Charlie, discretion is a priority. Keep this meeting and our travel plans quiet. The fewer who know about this, the better. Keep this away from your dispatch office. The pilot is going to have to know where he's going, but he doesn't need to know who his passenger is. Don't send a big plane into Reagan National. How about you send the fastest plane that can get in and out of Manassas Regional without having to take time to refuel. I want it to come in, pick me up, and get me out pronto. Get back to me with details."

Charlie was wondering what in the hell was going on but couldn't ask because the senator had hung up. Without a moment's delay, Charlie called Adam to let him know about the conversation. Adam was oddly quiet.

"Okay, Charlie, give me a few minutes to figure this out. I'm going to have to play dispatcher without our dispatcher. I'll get right back to you."

Adam called Scott, who was still off of flight status, waiting for a medical clearance following his concussion. Meanwhile, his skills were put to good use in the corporate dispatch office. But Adam didn't want this flight request to go through normal channels. He knew Scott could be trusted.

Adam said, "I need your help with an urgent situation. Discretion is of the utmost importance. I need a fast, low-profile flight into Manassas Regional to pick up a passenger and get him back here ASAP, without having to refuel at Manassas."

Scott was quiet long enough for Adam to wonder if he understood what he was being asked, but he finally responded.

"Okay. If you want to avoid the dispatch office, my suggestion is for me to check in with a buddy who runs a charter service in the DC area. If he's available, I can probably get him to fuel up at his base, scoot into Manassas for the pickup, and get your guy out here in a flash. That would be the quickest way to go if you don't mind a stranger in the mix."

"How well do you know this guy?"

"We go back a long way. We worked together for several years. He's a topnotch pilot, smart and professional, meticulous with his equipment, and from personal experience, I can tell you he knows how to keep his mouth shut. I don't think you can do better than that anywhere, except perhaps with me."

"Okay, I get it. You slipped that in nicely. We'll get you back on flight status as soon as you can convince our doc that you can hold on to your stick without shaking. Meanwhile, you know Charlie. He's the guy you nearly killed a while back. I'm gonna have him call you to get the details—that's if he's still willing to talk to you. Oh, and get a nice plane if you can, but fast is the most important."

Twenty minutes later, Charlie was on the phone with Scott. "Hey Scott, this is Charlie Wood."

"Hi, there, Charlie. You still talking to me?"

"Sure thing, Scott. After a couple of shots of whiskey, I was right back to my old self. How are you feeling?"

"I'm doin' fine, but I could be a whole lot better if I was back flying again. Put in a good word for me, will ya?"

"You bet, but let's do some business here. You got a flight for my guy lined up?"

"Yep, we're set. Just give me the go-ahead, and I'll have my old buddy Steve Balmer fly into Manassas to pick up your friend. He and his copilot have a sweet bird topped off and ready to fly. They'll hop over to Manassas from Reagan National in DC. It's a small jet but comfortable. It'll be about a three-hour flight."

Charlie asked, "Let's say your guy flies into Manassas and pulls up to the terminal at nine to board my guy. How will he recognize Balmer's plane?"

"That's easy. The plane's a Cessna Citation XLS and has a red and white striped tail. It's got a logo on it that reads 'ChartaJet.' What's your passenger's name? How will Steve know him?"

"Your guy probably won't recognize him, especially since he'll be traveling incognito. Let's have him identify himself as Mr. X."

"Charlie, you're creeping me out here. You gotta do better than that."

"How about 'Xavier.' Will that solve your problem?"

"Not really."

"That's the best for now. Anything else we need to do to contract this flight?"

"No, Steve knows we're good for it. He'll be at the Manassas terminal at nine sharp and be in Austin around midnight."

"Thanks, Scott. Oh, and by the way, whatever happened with that FAA investigation into our little mishap?"

"Well, the examiner grilled me real good. I thought for sure that my flying days were over, except maybe flying drones with the neighborhood kids. Then a couple of weeks later, I received formal notice that they were satisfied that we were unavoidably impacted by severe clear air turbulence and that the investigation was closed without any adverse consequences for either me or Megan. I could hardly believe it. These investigations usually drag on for months. Do you suppose Adam had something to do with it? I know he knows people in high places."

"I don't know about that, but it wouldn't surprise me. You'll never hear him claim credit for something like that. So I guess that means I'll be seeing you back in the cockpit soon. And when I do, don't forget you owe me stick time."

"I won't forget, Charlie. I owe you big time, stick time and a whole lot more."

With that settled, Charlie got right back on the phone and called Senator Parton. He seemed comfortable with the arrangements and agreed to meet Balmer's plane at nine. Charlie's flight would also be about three hours. They'd both be arriving in Austin at about the same time, just in time for a meeting in the bleary-eyed hours before sunrise.

But things went badly. En route, Charlie got an agitated call from Scott, a man of usually calm demeanor.

"Hey, Charlie, get a load of this. Some weird shit is going on here. What have you got me into? And what in the hell have I got Steve into?"

"What are you talking about?"

"Steve called me and said that when he went to check out his plane, an airport employee told him that the oxygen system mechanic who works on his plane had just left and told him that everything checked out okay."

"So what's the problem with that?"

"Well, here's the problem. It puzzled Steve because he hadn't called for any work to be done. His oxygen system had just been checked and filled earlier that day following a previous flight. Steve asked if he knew the guy. He said that he didn't, but the logo on the truck said 'OxAvia.' He even took a picture of it."

"Why would he do that?"

"He didn't want to forget the name of the outfit. He knows Steve is a sharp operator. He figured if anyone asked for a recommendation for an oxygen guy, he could tell 'em that Steve uses OxAvia."

"Do me a favor and send me a copy of that picture. What happened next?"

"Well, I told you that Steve's a smart guy. He figures that since everything is on the hush-hush, and we're sneaking in and out of Manassas on the QT, and our guy is only willing to identify himself by the name Xavier, he puts this together with an unknown mechanic fucking with his plane. That's when he decides that something funny is going on."

"So what'd he do?"

"Well, he sure as hell wasn't about to fly his Citation, not without it being thoroughly checked or, who knows, maybe even rebuilt."

"So how do we get Xavier to Austin?"

"Nothing to worry about. Steve takes another plane from his flight line. It's not as fast as the Citation—it's a King Air, a turbo prop—but it's already been fueled and ready to go. He figures he doesn't wanna stick around at Reagan, not even for another minute. So he lights his fires, winds up his turbines, and off he goes for Manassas. When he gets there, your Xavier guy recognizes the red and white striped tail feathers and the ChartaJet logo, but he's smart enough to know the difference between a jet and prop job. I guess your Xavier is accustomed to traveling in jets, and I'm guessing the big, sweet ones. He's getting suspicious and wondering if he's no longer important or if something funny is going on."

"This guy's an important friend. He and Adam are really tight. Could he really think we downgraded him?"

"I have no idea, but what I do know is that he almost didn't get on board. At that point, Steve decides he's gotta tell him the whole story. When your Xavier hears what's been going on, he decides it would be a good idea to get the hell outta Dodge. By then, a Piper Cub would have been good enough. So he hops on board with Steve, and it's up, up, and away they go, heading off for Austin. Bottom line, right now they're on their way. The King Air is a comfortable plane, but it's a lot slower than the Citation. They'll be along but a little late. Charlie, what in the hell is going on here? Is there something you wanna tell me?"

"No, sorry, I can't. What I can say is that you've done one hell of a job getting your buddy Steve on board with us. He's a good man. Adam will want to meet him. And he's going to rank you as some kind of hero. Hope you can live with that."

"I'll manage if I have to."

Charlie called Adam and got him up to date. Adam took most everything in stride, but this had him worried. They agreed that they would meet with Senator Parton upon his arrival and find out what was so important. The plan was to huddle with him and then go right into a second meeting with Sam Galatine and Dean Fleck. All this had profound security implications.

Senator Parton finally arrived at around one-thirty. Charlie had been at the airport since his earlier arrival and was waiting with Michael, Adam's driver, who was called on to drive the armored town car. When the senator got off the plane, Charlie didn't recognize him. He was dressed in jeans, a sports shirt, tennis shoes, and a baseball cap, clearly traveling incognito. Charlie welcomed him into the car and noticed the the senator lacked the exuberant self-confidence that had been so apparent at their Monday morning meeting.

Michael drove as fast as he could. They passed through Adam's security gate and drove up to the entry portico, where Adam met them. When they got out of the car, Adam extended a warm welcome to Hal and whisked him and Charlie inside and straight away into the library.

Adam poured ample measures of whiskey. Hal got right to it. "Tell me what in the hell is going on. My life was complicated before but manageable. Now things are spinning out of control."

"I understand exactly how you feel. I find myself in the same mess. I had no intention of compromising you in this way. This has taken me by surprise. Let's try to figure out what's happened. Talk to us about who you spoke to or met with after your meeting with Charlie."

"The first thing I did was read the report you gave me. At that point, I didn't talk to anyone about it. I reread it, reviewing several sections a few times. That's when I realized that either you were making speculative observations, or else you had some very, shall we say, unusual sources."

"Hal, the facts are the facts. They come from sources who we've found reliable in the past and who we have every reason to believe are still reliable. Please go on. Tell us who you spoke with."

"Well, as I promised, I met with Secretary of State Martha Saunders. At first, I didn't give her either the report or the executive summary since I thought it premature. I spoke in generalities. I described Vincent Poole and some of his activities as you described them. She seemed surprised and appeared interested in hearing more. She acknowledged that we do have objectives in our dealings with the Venezuelan government, and they, too, have objectives that we might accede to. The implication was that there was a possibility that some action regarding Mr. Poole might be taken."

Adam looked relieved. "Well, that's certainly good news."

"That's what I thought too. So partway through a productive conversation, Martha suggested bringing in the undersecretary for Latin American Affairs. That's George Carwell. I agreed, and the three of us continued our conversation, speculating on a possible plan—no promises, of course. By the end of our meeting, the way they were talking, I figured they were onboard with us. That's when I thought the particulars in your report would be helpful, maybe even essential. I handed over a copy and left it with them. Before departing, I told them that I needed to hear back from them by Friday. They said they'd certainly give me a progress report, but a definitive action plan would have to wait. That was it. I left."

Charlie asked, "Did you speak with anyone else about any of this?"

"Only my foreign affairs aide, Johnny Blackburn."

Charlie asked, "What did you tell him, and how long have you known him?"

"After my meeting at the State Department, I wanted to talk it over with someone I could trust. That's when I met with Johnny. He's a bright and reliable guy who's worked with me for over five years. I started our discussion with generalities, and then thinking that particulars were important, I gave him the report to read."

Charlie asked, "What's his background? Where did he work before coming to work for you?"

"He worked for a while in the State Department and before that at the CIA."

Adam jumped back in. "Okay, let's shift the conversation. You thought it was urgent to meet with us privately here in Austin, and you insisted on a rather unusual egress. What prompted that?"

"On Friday morning, I got a call from Martha Saunders. She was calling to give me the promised progress report. But her manner was different. She was blunt and insisted that after thinking about it further, she didn't see a way for the State Department to get further involved. I questioned her, trying to figure out why the change. She didn't say a lot, but from what she did say, I gathered she had reached out to the CIA to hear from them about what they already knew."

Adam said, "That's not really a surprise. We hoped for better, but that was always a likely response. Why not just report that to us by phone? What's the big deal?"

"You're right, no big deal. The big deal is next thing I know, I get a call from some high-level guy at the CIA who wanted an urgent meeting. He came right over and had a lot of questions. From the whole line of questioning and running comments, I had to wonder who you crossed swords with at the CIA."

"Well, let's be frank. We have useful contacts within the CIA who we rely on for our security needs. I guess you figured that out from our report. Since you passed it along to Saunders, she probably passed it along to the CIA. They probably came to the same conclusion. To my knowledge, those relationships were not previously known within the CIA."

"I gotta tell you, Adam, I guess they don't like that. I'd say that the CIA has you marked—for what end, I don't know. One thing I do know is they know my relationship with you, and in their book that makes me a suspicious character too. Anything else you can tell me about your relationship with the CIA?"

"Understandably, they'd be upset finding out that we have contacts inside feeding us intel, but there's another dimension too. We know that our fusion technology is an irritant to perceived American interests. The CIA could be working together with any number of foreign governments and industry insiders who don't want our fusion technology on the street. Up until now, we haven't been able to confirm CIA complicity in the threats arrayed against us, but maybe that, in fact, is the game. I would have thought we'd get at least a sense of that from our sources. I suppose that was a bad guess. The added element at this time is that because they now know that we've been able to identify Poole, they may be concerned that their role in this may be exposed. That has to be a big worry for them."

"Adam, you're a smart guy. Where do we go from here? What do we do about this mess? What do I do?"

"First, be suspicious of everyone on your staff and every mode of communication. Sweep your offices regularly for bugs. We'll check out your guy Johnny and try to figure out if his loyalties are with you or if instead they extend back to the CIA. In any event, paranoia is appropriate here. They, whoever they are, know about your visit here. Your friendship has always meant a lot, but going forward, I think you better close off your relationship with us, at least for now. Create some distance. We'll understand any public stance you decide you need to take. I don't want you further implicated in this. For our part, we'll be cautious in reaching out to you. We don't want to put your safety at risk. If you need help from us, make sure it's important and figure out a way to get to us without discovery. We'll figure out a way to respond."

Adam sighed before continuing. "I'm exhausted, and I know the two of you must be too. How 'bout we call it a day? Hal, I'll have Helene, our housekeeper, show you to your guest suite. We can continue our conversation tomorrow morning, and then we'll figure out how to get you back to DC."

Calling it a day was the plan for Hal, but Adam kept on moving. He brought Charlie along to yet another meeting, this one with Sam and Dean.

"Okay, guys. You were listening in. Let's figure this out. We gotta make a plan and execute."

Sam said, "We have several tasks as I see it. The first thing is that we already have a plan. We said that we would try the State Department and then the CIA. We did that. It doesn't look like we're gonna have any help from either. Unless something recommends otherwise, our plan calls for us to take action directly against Mr. Poole. We've got to get our hands on him and find out who's behind all of this. If we can't find out who the driver is, we're just gonna end up playing whack-a-mole."

"Okay, Sam, let's consider that, but you suggested several tasks. What else?"

"We've been receiving intel from several sources within the CIA. We have thought them reliable and comprehensive. We can no longer take that for granted. Either our assessments of them have been wrong, or something has changed. The CIA appears to be connected either directly or indirectly with Mr. Poole. We need to get a confirmation on that, and if there is a connection, we need to know if it's official or a rogue initiative. Either way, we need to know why our sources weren't able to give us a heads up. "

"Thank you, Sam. I concur. Dean, anything you want to add?"

Dean said, "I think Sam's nailed it. I'm for moving forward just as he suggests, but I'm concerned about Parton's foreign affairs aide. If our guys in the CIA aren't burned and are still able to help, we should get some intel from them on this Johnny Blackburn guy. If they can't help us, we'll need to figure out another way to find out where his loyalties lie."

"Good. Thanks for that, Dean. What else?"

"I also think we should double and then redouble our security measures around you. I don't necessarily mean in numbers of security personnel. I'm referring to intelligence activities, technology, and quick response plans for responding to incidents that may present."

"Excellent. I think we're in agreement. That means I can go to bed. But you, Dean, and you, Sam, still have some work to do. Sam, first thing, work up a plan to deal with Mr. Poole. We have to get our hands on him, find out who's directing him. And, Dean, for you, the first thing is to work up a plan for clarifying our relationships with our CIA sources, for figuring out the CIA's objectives and how to respond to them. We have to know if they have a role in Poole's efforts against us. Second, I want to know how we're going to check out Senator Parton's foreign affairs aide, Johnny Blackburn. Third, I want to see your plan for enhanced security. And then there's one more item we haven't discussed. The plane that Senator Parton was supposed to fly on was screwed with. The charter operator is having it carefully examined. I want you to coordinate with Scott to make sure that it's combed with extraordinary attention. I want to know if it was tampered with and, if it was, with what intention. I know detailed plans will take longer, but I want this sketched out immediately. I want to see early drafts of these plans in written reports by noon tomorrow."

After a pause, Adam continued. "And something else. I've put my life in your hands—and not just my life but the lives of my family and friends. I expect the best from you but haven't gotten it. We've been blindly relying on sources we only thought were reliable. That reliance has been horribly misplaced. There's no excuse. Your job is security. You've failed at that. I'll have better, or you'll be out of work. I want to see your plans. I want to be rid of this threat, whoever's behind it. If either of you can't cut it, tell me now. I want diligence, not dalliance. If you can't perform, I don't want you around here. Is that clear?"

Dean was visibly angry, "Look, Adam, we've done an incredible job. You don't know what we go through to protect you. We—"

Adam raised his right hand, palm forward, commanding an abrupt stop. "Dean, you can just bend over right now and kiss my ass. Yeah, you've done an incredible job, alright—incredible in the sense that I can't believe how incredibly vulnerable you've left me. You're right. I don't know what you do for me, but whatever it is, it's not enough. Your reliance on the perpetual allegiance of vital sources within the CIA is crazy. They have to be continuously monitored and tested. If there's a change, we have to know about it before it bites us in the ass. We . . . I can't be left to find out about this shit after the fact. After the fact, I'm dead. That's not good enough for me. It's up to you. Tell me now: are you up for this job, or are you out?"

Dean, still bristling but in painful recognition, said, "I'm in. You'll have my report by noon tomorrow."

Sam took it all in stride. "I'm in too. You'll have my report by noon."

Chapter 28

Several months had passed since Charlie had accused Adam of disregarding his relationship with Shari. On some level, Adam was aware of Shari's discontent, but he didn't fully recognize how heavily it clung as a weight on their marriage. With the heightened risk that bore down on him and his family, there came a shift in Adam's focus. He became fixed on securing the safety of his family. Going forward, the protection of his family would be first among his priorities.

Adam said, "Shari, I owe you something, a little surprise."

"Well, I've already got a surprise."

"What do you mean?"

"Just look at the clock. It's already seven, and you're still here in bed. Now that's a surprise."

"Funny girl."

"No, Adam, that's not funny."

"As you may recall, you went to bed alone last night. I was up late having a meeting on security matters."

"Yes, I remember going to bed alone—again. Did you think I wouldn't notice?"

"No, I didn't. I suspect that you've got a dirty little diary where you record those many occasions, probably a thick volume by now."

"As a matter of fact, there are several volumes. If there's going to be many more, I'll need a librarian to index them—or maybe an attorney."

"Well, I want to go on record. You're not going to need a librarian and certainly not an attorney. Things are going to be different. This past year, I've been consumed by worries about our safety. I don't know if you know just how worried I've been. I want you to know that we've made some decisions last night that ought to reduce our exposure. And I've made a decision to readjust my priorities. I'm not backing away from my business interests—far from it. But I realize that with my obsessive concern about security matters, I've let things get out of kilter."

"Wow, now that's what I'd call a surprise. How'd you ever figure that out?"

"I guess I've known it for quite a while, but I couldn't bring myself to do anything about it. Charlie said something to me on his trip here when he nearly got killed and you and Laura almost got kidnapped. He had the nerve to tell me I wasn't treating you right, and if it continued that way, I'd end up regretting it. I figured that if it was obvious to him, I'd better do something about it. I realized he was right. I love you, Shari. I love you very much. I don't want to lose you."

"I don't know what to say."

"You don't have to say anything."

"Yes, I think I do. You've made a generous admission, but it's only words so far, and it's been way too long in coming. Maybe it's my fault too for not getting on your case, but you need to know that I've felt dismissed. You can't imagine all the thoughts that have kept me up at night while you've been busy at your meetings or whatever else you do. I don't need to be at the center of your attention all the time, but did you really think I'd be content to continue things the way they've been going? Have you any idea how many times I've thought about getting the name of a good attorney from a friend? I never got that far because I couldn't imagine my life without you. But I didn't have to imagine. I've been having a life without you for some time. Now, just like that, you want to put it all behind. Well, how's that going to work? I sure don't know. What I do know is that you're driven by some unrelenting force. How are you going to free yourself from that?"

"You don't mean all that, Shari. I know you don't."

"Don't be so sure. You've opened a wound just now. I don't know how it's going to heal."

Adam had had to deal with Shari's anger and disappointment before, but this was different. He got up and said, "I'm not walking away from this conversation, but I need some space. I'm not going anywhere. I'll be back in a few minutes."

When Adam reappeared, he said, "I hate this. I'm trying to make things better, but it pisses me off that you can't accept that. Now it looks like I've only made things worse. Okay, I get it. You're angry too and skeptical about me changing. But you gotta give me a chance. You asked me how I would free myself from the 'unrelenting force' that you presume has been driving us apart. Well, think of it this way: it's that unrelenting force that will drive me to my goal of bringing us back together."

Shari didn't respond. She sat in stony silence.

———

At breakfast, they ate slowly, lingering over second cups of coffee. Adam took a chance lightly brushing her hand while describing their updated security situation and action plan.

"Adam, this sounds awfully scary to me. Somehow it seems worse thinking the CIA might be involved in this."

"I know, but the steps we're taking will make a difference. Eliminating Poole will put an end to the immediate threat. With that accomplished, the CIA is likely to feel vulnerable to discovery. Then with a little help from Hal Parton, we might be able to derail the CIA's appetite in pursuing us."

Chapter 29

Dean and Sam both had their draft reports delivered to Adam by noon. They were rough outlines but right on the mark. Within the week, both plans had been detailed with precision.

Dean had already determined that all but two of their inside contacts had been exposed and terminated from CIA employment. "Adam, I don't need to tell you that this represents a serious setback for us. We relied on those guys. We've still got two ranking guys in key posts, but we don't know yet if they're feeding us vital information we need or bullshit they've been told to feed us. We won't know for sure for a while longer yet. We're gonna have to tread carefully with whatever we get from them."

"Well, it's the kind of treading carefully we should have been doing right along."

"Adam, I got that, okay? Can we just move on?"

"Alright, let's move on. What else do you have for me?"

"The only good news is bad news. We've been able to determine that the CIA has indeed been involved in specifying Poole's mission, but they're not alone in this. There's a consortium of governments involved. It's an odd alliance composed of both friends and enemies working together under a common threat—the threat posed by your fusion reactor. That means that eliminating Poole might help, but that won't eliminate the threat from other sources."

Adam said, "I guess the prospect of abundant energy, both cheap and clean, is a threat they can't abide."

"That does appear to be the case. Looking at it from a different angle, we see the perfect example of friends and enemies coming together across vast political divides, working together to solve their problems cooperatively. You should be proud that you've been able to make that happen."

"I didn't know that political philosophy was one of your interests. Maybe this will qualify me for a Nobel Peace Prize. Getting back to the bad news, why is that good news?"

"It's rotten news, but the good news embedded there is that we were able to get this intel from one of our two remaining insiders at the CIA. I don't think she would have been instructed to pass this kind of intel on to us. Maybe she's still a reliable source. We'll keep a watch."

"What about Senator Parton's aide? Have we learned anything about him yet?"

"What we've learned, and this comes from sources outside of the CIA, is that he has maintained relationships with people at the CIA. What we don't know is whether he's providing them with inside information that your senator friend would prefer to keep under lock and key. Hope to get better info on that soon."

"Okay, Dean. Stay on it. It's urgent that I get actionable information to Senator Parton right away. I'd also like to tell him what we've learned about the tampering with his plane. Any information on that yet?"

Dean had overseen a thorough inspection of the plane, actually two of them. He insisted on double-checking everything. As a result, they turned up a device that would have registered a fire emergency in one of the engines. It would not have caused a fire or damaged the plane. It would have incorrectly alerted the pilot about a hazardous engine problem. The flight crew's immediate response would have been to shut down the affected engine and make an emergency landing. The fire emergency indication would have been triggered by a radio signal from some unknown source.

They also investigated the van with the OxAvia logo. The license plate from the photo was read, but it turned out to be a dummy plate. After further investigation, it became apparent that the van was connected to Secura. There was no way to know when the perpetrator might have triggered an emergency warning, but because of limited radio range and because they couldn't be sure of the planes routing, it was deemed likely that the false alarm would have been triggered on or shortly after takeoff.

Dean didn't think it was an assassination attempt. The report was clear that an experienced, well-trained flight crew would have been able to control the plane while shutting down the affected engine and then landing with just a single functioning engine. The report concluded that the objective was merely to rattle Senator Parton and disrupt his travel plans.

Adam was satisfied with Dean's progress but was anxious to know details about Sam's plan for dealing with Poole. Sam thoroughly briefed him.

"I'll fly down there with three of my teammates on a covert charter flight, not on one from the BrauCorp fleet. Before going, I'll arrange for the assistance from some local talent. We plan to get to Venezuela, do some training and team building with the local talent, and then lure Mr. Poole to a meeting where we can separate him from his confederates and then move him to a safe house for debriefing. We'll try extracting answers to a whole bunch of questions."

Adam asked, "What's your plan following the debriefing?"

"It depends. If we think he can be useful to us going forward, either cooperatively or otherwise, and if we have enough freedom of movement to get him home with us, we'll bring him back. Otherwise, we'll terminate him."

"How soon will you be ready to move on this?"

"I'm in the process of securing our Venezuelan affiliates. After that, all we'll need will be your approval."

"This is a good plan. I hoped that you could rise to the occasion, and it looks like you did. If you foresee a problem that requires a change of plans, check back with me. Otherwise, go ahead. You have my approval."

"Okay, we're on our way."

"We had a rough time last week, but I want you to know that I have every confidence in you. You've made your plan sound routine, but I know there's nothing routine about it. If anyone can pull it off, you can. If there's anything you need, just let me know. And let's not kid ourselves: The mission comes first, but your safety is important to me. Come back safe and in one piece."

"Thank you, Adam. I'll be back. Working for you is a privilege, one I wouldn't want to miss."

Chapter 30

Sam vetted some well-recommended affiliates. After exhaustive inquiries, he was satisfied that he had the best assistance he could hope for. A charter operator flew him into Caracas with three of his local team members. On arrival, he wasted no time connecting with his Caracas affiliates and acquiring vehicles, arms, and their necessary accouterments of battle. The combined team of ten trained together for an exhausting week built around strategies, practice routines, and team building. Through a vetted intermediary, Sam managed to arrange a meeting with Vincent Poole. He identified himself as a drug dealer willing to pay a substantial fee to Poole to eliminate a noxious competitor. The plan was for Poole to travel to a meeting spot about an hour by car outside of town, where they were to parlay.

Sam was satisfied with the local team. Juan was the first hire, and he recommended several men he had worked with on previous occasions.

Sam said, "Hey, Juan, here's what's happening. Poole will be traveling by caravan from Caracas to meet with us. I'm presuming he'll be suspicious and highly alert for trouble. Since our meeting spot is off the beaten track, if there's gonna be trouble, he'd most likely expect it at our meeting place. That's why I suggest we execute an ambush on the road along the way. Our IT guy will be watching for their departure from Caracas. He'll be able to give us a car and headcount and also place a GPS tag. That way, we can track their approach. You got any guess as to the likely makeup of their caravan?"

"I don't know what their routine is for something like this, but I'd guess there'd be at least three cars: Poole's car and one in front and another behind. How many more, I don't know. Let's guess four cars and four men per car. That means we're outnumbered from the start."

"Outnumbered, yes. There'll be just nine of us, but surprise will eliminate their advantage in numbers. We'll neutralize some of them at first contact. I'd rather take that chance than have to expand our team. I like our team the way it is. I went to a lot of trouble checking out you and your friends and then going through our training routine. Besides, the more guys involved, the more the risk of our surprise being detected."

Juan said, "I'll find a lonesome spot on the road, ideally a narrow valley where we can command some height on both sides."

"Good man. Let's get some kind of barricade we can cart around with us. As they approach, we can place it on the road. That will stop them at our ambush site. That barricade will also give our guys protected firing positions. From elevated positions on both sides of the road, we'll have our guys armed with RPGs. We'll use them to take out the front and rear vehicles at the outset. That'll even out the numbers nicely."

"Don't forget those cars are armored. I understand you've already had some experience with that."

"Yes, we have, but our RPGs will knock them out. Machine-gun fire will take care of any survivors who get out. At the same time, we'll be lighting off our flash-bang grenades and laying out our gas. That'll keep 'em rattled and hopefully incapacitated. At that point, we'll get up close and personal. That's when we'll ID Poole, bind him up, and swoop away with him."

"That's all fine if he survives the ambush."

"We want to take him alive. If he's dead, the most important part of our mission is a failure."

"What about survivors? What do you wanna do with them?"

"We're gonna have to clear the area pronto. If they're bleeding, let 'em bleed. We can't spend time with first aid. For the rest of 'em, I don't have the stomach for a mass execution. Just leave them bound up snug like and whack their knees real bad. That way they won't be fit for bothering us or anyone else anymore."

Chapter 31

The night of the showdown with Poole, Julio was waiting near the exit of the underground garage where Secura maintained its offices. About one hour before the scheduled meeting, four armored SUVs and a van like a Brinks armored truck left the garage together. Julio lifted what looked like a grenade launcher to his shoulder. It was, in fact, a grenade launcher but heavily modified with a custom silencer. It would quietly let loose a ball of putty-like material with a GPS tracker embedded. He took aim and fired and then watched the putty ball fly and impact the rearmost vehicle, where it stuck like glue. As the train of vehicles turned its first corner, Julio picked up his radio and informed Sam. Sam turned on his GPS tracking receiver and noted the target moving along one of several probable routes. Sam instructed Julio to take up his next position.

Sam directed his team members to take up their practiced firing positions and prepare their weapons with initial loads of ammunition and ensure that reloads were in easy reach. They were ready with their RPGs, grenades, tear gas canisters, and automatic weapons. An SUV with the barricade in tow was just out of sight behind a tree alongside the road. By this time, there was still another twenty minutes of excited agitation ahead of them.

Sam continued monitoring the caravan's progress as it snaked along, stopping here and there to disrupt the expected travel time. They were professionals exercising professional caution. Julio, also with a GPS receiver, watched and noted their cautious maneuvers while following carefully on his motorcycle a safe distance behind.

Noting that the caravan had come to a halt, Julio located a hill overlooking their position and saw that one of the four SUVs had separated from the others. When the remaining three SUVs and the van were back in motion, Julio updated Sam.

Sam was puzzled but noted that the caravan was generally moving along its way toward the meeting point. Perhaps the missing SUV was a scout vehicle taking up a leading point position. Sure enough, just about in time with the original routing plan, a dark SUV approached the ambush site. Sam's instruction was to let it pass unmolested, thinking it unlikely that Poole would be an occupant.

Julio reported to Sam that once again the caravan had come to a stop. This time they were unloading something from the van. Sam wanted to know, "Can you make out what it is?"

"Don't like the looks of this. Not sure. I think they're prepping a drone for launch."

Emotions ran high, and radio discipline lapsed.

Sam said, "A drone? What the fuck are they doing with a drone?"

"I don't know. Maybe they're gonna do some surveillance— lookin' maybe for some trouble, lookin' for someone like you. It's not big enough to carry anything they could shoot you with, but it's big enough to carry surveillance gear."

"Holy shit. I don't think we've got anything that'll take out a drone."

"Wouldn't do much good anyway. You knock out their drone, they'd know you're there."

"Keep your eye on 'em and keep me posted."

A few minutes later, Sam was looking for an update. "What's goin' on over there?" Sam's query went without a response. "Julio, do you hear me?"

Sam heard a *click-click* and some shuffling noises but nothing else. His attention was drawn away from the radio by a buzzing sound overhead. Looking up, he didn't see anything, but the sound came from something that seemed to pass along above the hillside, first on one side of the road and then back along the other. At one point, it seemed to come from a stationary position over the SUV parked with the barricade. Then it was in motion again, moving slowly back and forth along the hillsides, pausing here and there for closer looks. Suddenly it was gone, and the silence left a fearful chill.

"Hey, Juan, what do you make of that?"

"Señor Sam, I'm not worried about the buzzing of their drone. What I'm worried about is the thumping of their chopper. Poole's got a heavily armed chopper. If he turns it loose, we're gonna be sitting ducks."

"What the fuck? If you knew he had a chopper, why didn't you tell me? This is a hell of a time to find out."

"Sorry, señor. I didn't think of it. I didn't think he could use it for a nighttime operation. We better dig in deep if we want to see tomorrow."

Sam was not a guy to wait for things to happen. He didn't do defense. His default position was always offense. Waiting around for the chopper, hoping somehow to shoot it down, just wasn't his style. He quickly formulated a plan of attack.

"Okay, Juan, here's what we're gonna do in quick time. Get three of your guys into one of the SUVs. Move up the road *muy pronto*. Find that scout vehicle that passed through here and hammer it. Be careful. They're probably not far up the road. They're probably waiting and just itching to get back here to clean our clocks once the chopper whittles away at us."

"What about you, Señor Sam? You'll be a sitting duck waiting here."

"Don't worry about us, Juan. We'll mount the other two SUVs and head back to attack Poole's caravan. If both of us can surprise our targets, we'll have a chance of taking them out. Then with some luck, we can disperse before Poole's chopper arrives, but we gotta move fast."

Juan and his three compadres climbed into their SUV and accelerated up the road in search of Poole's scout SUV. They hadn't gone a minute up the road when they were greeted by an RPG round that impacted the ground immediately in front of them and brought them to a standstill. As a stationary target, the second round found its way and struck them on a side window. The blast disabled the occupants and left them mortally wounded. Poole's men confirmed their kill and then reassumed their positions to wait for any others who might follow.

Sam's GPS tracker indicated that he was approaching his target. He and his companion SUV slowed to a stop just around a bend in the road before reaching Poole's caravan. They threw themselves from their vehicles and scrambled with as much of their gear as they could carry. They immediately assumed lousy firing positions that had to be good enough. Two of Sam's men let loose with their RPGs, firing, reloading, and firing as fast as they could. At the same time, the rest of them added to the frenzied firefight with grenades and machine-gun fire. In short order, all was still. Every one of Poole's men was either dead or out of action. Poole was not among them. The survivors were quickly disarmed to eliminate any further fire while they awaited their deaths.

The thunder of a low-flying helicopter suddenly shook them from their elated sense of victory and filled them with dread. The chopper's machine guns began firing and raked over Sam and his men. They were cut to pieces, even as they attempted to return fire. Sam understood that he was bleeding out but lived long enough to feel the pain of defeat at the hands of Vincent Poole.

Julio, whose presence had been suspected, was able to retreat to a hiding place. From his position, he had been elated by Sam's initial success and then crushed by his grisly defeat. When the helicopter touched down, Julio watched two of its occupants swagger about and gloat over their handiwork. By then, Poole's scout SUV, with the only survivors of the encounter, pulled up to the scene. They quickly gathered as much material as they could in the hope they could identify Sam and his team.

On his return to Austin, Julio reported the details about the encounter to Adam. In his report, he praised Sam's courage and resourcefulness but didn't mention the high probability that Vincent Poole was never in the caravan—a terrible loss, all for nothing.

Chapter 32

In the course of his life, Adam knew many more defeats than success-es. He understood that defeat is the price you pay for the opportuni-ty to pursue success, but this was a defeat of an altogether different sort. Sam and his men had been a dedicated presence in Adam's life. They'd held his safety and the safety of his family in their hands. Sam was smart and able and principled. He had put his life on the line for Adam's sake. Adam was personally fond of Sam, and now he lay dead.

Then the headlines trumpeted more bad news: "Senator Parton Killed in Car Bombing." Dean, working with his contacts in the FBI, clearly understood from the methods and materials used that it was Vincent Poole's work. He made no effort to hide his tracks. He might as well have left his business card.

Adam yearned to be of comfort to Hal's widow. "Char, I just got the news. I want it to be all wrong. I can't imagine a world without Hal in it. I see his face right in front of me. I hear his voice. I feel his pres-ence. I'm haunted by the photos of his car all twisted and ablaze. I want to strangle whoever did this, whoever is responsible, and I will. I swear it. But first I want to be by your side, to be of comfort. Is there anything Shari and I can do for you?"

"Right now I don't know what we need. Hal's mom is here. We're doing the best we can. The kids are lost in grief. I don't know how to help them other than to just wrap my arms around them and hold them close. I know we'll get through this, but I just can't imagine how.

It seems unreal. I hear him walking around the house, opening and closing drawers. Ginger, our dog, ended up sleeping in bed with me. When I woke up in the middle of the night, I thought it was Hal. Can you imagine that?"

"First thing, Char, are you and the kids safe?"

"I don't know. How could I? We've been briefed by the FBI. They tell us that they're providing us with exceptional security protection. I don't know what that means. And they're helping out with the funeral plans too. Hal will be buried at Arlington the day after tomorrow. Good God, is that Friday already? It would mean a lot if you and Shari could be there."

"Of course we'll both be there. Shari will fly in first thing tomorrow. She'll give you a call later today. I'll fly in Friday morning. Please, Char, don't hesitate for a minute to let us know what we can do to help. It would be a comfort to us to be of comfort to you."

"Thank you, Adam. Your friendship has meant everything to both of us—and right now more than ever. Bye for now."

As Adam's losses compounded and depression sapped his strength, he turned to Charlie and was relieved he could reach him. "Charlie, you probably already heard that Hal's been killed. Dean is certain that Poole is behind it. I'm hobbled, first by Sam's loss and now this. I got Hal into this mess, and now he's dead because of me. I feel like shit."

"Don't be ridiculous, Adam. He's dead because Poole killed him. It's not your doing."

"Charlie, I got him into this mess by trying to use him to solve my problem. Now Poole has done this as retribution for my attack on him. He didn't need to kill Hal. He wants to kill me, but first he wants to torment me, show me how he can reach me and everyone I care about. No, Charlie, Hal's blood is on my hands. I can't escape that fact."

"Okay, Adam. If that's what you want to think, you're guilty as charged, but, for God's sake, before you hang yourself, at least do something useful. Go ahead; redeem yourself. Rectify your guilt."

"Oh, sure, Charlie. Easy for you to say. How do you figure I do that?"

"You started out to destroy Vincent Poole. You failed, Adam—you fucking failed. Now pick yourself up and finish the job. Failure is something you should be familiar with by now. Don't let it keep you from your success."

"Alright, Charlie, but first off, we need to get together face to face. Given the threats I'm living with, I've been doing a lot of thinking. There's a lot I need to talk with you about. I'm flying out to DC on Friday for Hal's funeral. I want you to meet me there. It'll give us a chance to talk."

"No problem. See you on Friday. Have someone call me with the funeral arrangements."

Chapter 33

Adam changed his plans and decided to fly out Thursday evening. He was reassured knowing that Dean's commitment to his security had become intense as never before. He saw that Dean had given extraordinary attention to his fleet of planes, especially the ones he would be traveling on. By Thursday evening, his plane had been checked, rechecked, and fueled for the flight to DC. He left the executive airport lounge and stepped into the near-freezing evening air, noting with pleasure the crystalline beauty of the vibrant, star-studded sky. As he neared the stairway to his plane's entrance, a gunshot rang out, and his now ever-present bodyguard suddenly threw him violently to the ground, turned around with his automatic pistol drawn, and contributed to a fusillade of gunfire directed at a window in a nearby building. Dozens of bullets peppered the side of the building. They shattered the window, but they couldn't stop a rocket launched from another window on the other end of the building. It shrieked low overhead.

Adam was barely conscious after hitting his head hard on the ground. And yet, through a veil, he sensed the proximity of death. In those last moments of life, he drifted above, looking down on his prostrate form lying facedown on the tarmac, rivulets of blood flowing from his head. The rocket's flight was only an instant, but that slender fabric of time, a sliver really, suddenly stretched into an infinity that folded around itself, embracing the past, present, and future within a locus of simultaneity. From that perspective, Adam saw the wholeness of his successes and failures, his joys and disappointments, his loves and losses, and he saw everything that came of them. He was ready for death.

Then the stretched fabric snapped back into the moment as the rocket impacted Adam's plane, rupturing a fuel tank and igniting its load of fuel. The blast shredded the plane into shards of shrapnel and produced a fireball that consumed everything within an angry radius of death.

Chapter 34

Once the fireball had receded and the smoke began to lift, the carnage could be seen all around. Charred and shredded bodies, severed limbs, and mangled debris lay everywhere. The inevitable sirens wailed while airport workers and bystanders assembled, warily questioning the safety of their presence in this grisly scene of devastation. The firefighters arrived first and lay down water and foam to put out smoldering hot spots and to suppress any possibility of further explosions. Only moments behind them came the emergency medical teams. They surveyed the scene of charred remains with dismay and concluded that their skills would not be needed. Their training pushed them from one corpse to another, forcing them to confront the grisly remains of what were once living, breathing human beings, now reduced to burned and contorted heaps of human flesh.

One of the EMTs came upon a large hump of remains and, on closer inspection, found that it was not one body but two, one stacked on top of another. Unbelievably, there appeared to be some movement underneath.

"Hey, Joe, get over here quick. We might have a breather here. Oh, Christ, what a mess. Give me a hand moving this top guy off of here."

They tried to move him by taking a grip of what must have been his shoulder, but it just pulled away in their hands, separating from the rest of the body like a drumstick pulled from a chicken in a pot of overboiled soup. They persisted and cleared the top body from the one underneath, who indeed was still alive. It appeared that one man had jumped to cover the other or fell atop him just before the fireball consumed all. As a result, the survivor was spared some of the ravages of the blast, but even if he did regain consciousness, he would surely know horrible suffering before joining his brothers in death.

They managed to get him onto a gurney and wheeled him over to the ambulance, where a paramedic went right to work. He got a couple of large-bore IVs plugged into his arm and started the saline running. Because he knew the victim's lungs and airway were fried, he repeatedly tried before finally managing to intubate him. He got an array of sensors connected up so vital signs could be transmitted to the hospital, where they could monitor the survivor's condition, render advice to the paramedic, and prepare to receive their patient. Knowing it was essential, the paramedic layered his patient with blankets. He initially feared for the pain he might be inflicting, but his patient knew nothing of pain. Given the extent of his burns and injuries, survival was inconceivable. The whole experience could be treated as a training exercise. Finally, the ambulance, with its lights flashing and siren blaring, rushed off to the emergency room.

The emergency room was prepared for an onslaught of injured patients, but there was just this one. The doctors and nurses pounced on their single charge. And here again was a training opportunity. They set out to exercise their best practices, challenged to see how long they might sustain life in this pitiful victim who was suffering from second- and third-degree burns over nearly his entire body. In addition, the patient was suffering from shock, smoke inhalation, and yet-to-be-discovered damage to his lungs and other organs. Their work was cut out for them.

The extent of his burns was incompatible with life. That was known from the start. They worked diligently to support his blood pressure with drugs and IV infusions. They managed to keep him well oxygenated despite burn damage to his lungs and trachea. A collapsed left lung resulting from a puncture required the immediate placement of a chest tube. Multiple vials of blood were drawn to run the diagnostic panels that would guide further treatment. X-rays were taken to identify broken bones and internal injuries.

Some of the diagnostic reports confirmed early diagnoses, while others revealed a variety of other life-threatening challenges. They found multiple rib fractures, which resulted in traumatic damage to their patient's lungs and liver. His liver was hemorrhaging, and his breathing was compromised by pulmonary contusions. Though he had sustained a head injury, they didn't see any intracranial hemorrhaging. That was the good news. The bad news was that he had multi-system organ failure as a result of shock, which at least for the moment could be treated, though precariously.

———

BrauCorp maintained its dispatch office and a security substation adjacent to the executive airport lounge. Among the witnesses were BrauCorp employees who knew Adam by sight. They were aghast to see their many friends and coworkers, including Adam, whom they regarded as an invincible leader, lying dead before their eyes.

Sally, one of the security office staff members, somehow managed to place a call to Dean. Crying nearly incoherently, she blurted, "Dean, it's awful . . . a disaster, an explosion. You gotta send help."

"Sally, slow down. Get a grip. What are you talking about?"

"An explosion, Dean. Mr. Braudy's plane got blown up in a giant fireball. Everyone's dead."

"Calm down, Sally, please. You're not dead. Tell me who's dead, how many?"

"The plane crew, the mechanics, the fuel guys, our security guys, and Mr. Braudy. Oh my God, Mr. Braudy . . . he's dead too. They're all dead."

"How many, Sally? How many are dead?"

"Oh, I don't know . . . maybe a dozen, maybe more."

"Sally, are you safe? And what about the rest of you in the office?"

"Yeah, it looks like the danger has passed. I think we're safe."

"How do you know Mr. Braudy is dead?"

"I saw him walking out to the plane just before it blew up."

"And there were no survivors?"

"There was one guy, looked like he was burned to a crisp. They took him away in an ambulance. The siren was blaring. I don't know. Whoever it is, who knows? Maybe he's still alive."

"Who was it, Sally?"

"I don't know. There's no way to tell. They took him away in the ambulance."

"Okay, sit tight. We'll get help out to you right away."

Dean directed a security squad to get over to the airport, telling them to call Sally for details. Then he called the hospital hoping to get an ID on the survivor. Was it one of his security team members? Could it be Adam?

No one knew the survivor's identity. With persistence, exasperation, cajoling, and threats, he finally got through to one of the nurses who had just come off shift after attending to the patient. Dean asked for a description.

"Are you kidding? You want a description? That's a trick. All I can tell you is that he's a male, probably around six feet in height. Don't know his weight, but I suppose he might be of average build. His hair is burned away, so I can't tell his hair color, but I can tell you that after we managed to get his burned eyelids opened, we found that he has hazel eyes."

"Thanks. Our Mr. Braudy is five ten with hazel eyes. I'll bring over medical info on him and on our security staff too. That might be helpful for identification."

Dean hung up the phone and placed a call to Shari, who was in DC visiting with Char. "Shari, this is Dean. Look, Shari, I don't know how to tell you this, but there's been a problem, and it doesn't look good."

"Dean, don't beat around the bush. What's going on?"

"Adam was getting ready to board his plane when a rocket blew it up, shredding it and killing a dozen or more people. We think Adam's dead."

"What do you mean you think? Why don't you know?"

"There was one survivor who's been burned beyond recognition. They don't know who he is. We're trying to get an ID on him. Whoever he is, he's in very critical condition and is not expected to live. We don't know much right now, but I wanted to let you know as soon as I could. We're trying our best to get an ID, but I don't know how long that might take. By the time we get one, he might already be dead."

Dean paused for a response, but there was only an eerie silence. Had the line gone dead? Dean raised his voice and said, "Shari, are you there? Can you hear me?"

He heard Shari's muffled shrieks as if from a distance. At last, someone said, "Who is this?"

"I'm Dean Fleck. I'm in charge of security for BrauCorp and the Braudy family. I need to speak with Shari. Please put her on the phone. This is urgent."

"She's half out of her mind. I'll try getting her on the phone."

A moment later, it was Shari's shaky voice babbling out questions, barely intelligible between gasps and sobs. "Gotta reach my kids. Are they in danger? You're supposed to protect us. How could you let this happen? Who's the survivor? Why don't you know? Gotta call Jess and Steve . . . get them home, Dean. And for God's sake, find out if Adam's alive."

Chapter 35

Dean immediately contacted Shari's pilot with instructions. He couldn't reach Jess or Steve but left messages presuming that they would already have heard from their mother about the explosion and explaining the arrangements he'd made for getting them home. Then he collected his staff's medical records and rushed to the hospital. On the way, he got Charlie on the secure line.

Charlie answered and said, "I'm gonna meet Adam in DC tomorrow for Hal's funeral. You gonna be there too?"

"Look, Charlie, the world just turned on its head. Adam's plane was blown up earlier this evening, and we think Adam's dead. He told me that in an emergency, I was to contact you for instructions."

"What? What are you saying?"

"Adam was boarding his plane when it was blown up. Everyone anywhere near the plane was killed in the blast—everyone, that is, except for one poor guy barely hanging on. We don't have an ID on him yet, but he's as good as dead anyway."

"No, Dean, that's not possible. It can't be."

"Yes, it can, Charlie. Not only can it be—it is."

"Fuck no. What do we do now?"

"According to Adam, it's up to you."

"You're telling me that Adam told you to take instructions from me? That's crazy. Is that what he's been thinking about and wanted to discuss?"

"Look, Charlie, I don't know anything about that. I just work here. I'm telling you what I've been told. I'll just do my job as usual. If I think I need to, I'll come ask you for instructions just like I'd come to Adam. If I don't like your instructions, I might bitch and moan just like I do with Adam, but Adam's my guy. Since he told me to come to you, that's what I'm doing. You got any instructions for me?"

"Give me a minute to process this, will ya?"

"Sorry, no time for that. My plate's overflowing. Give me a call whenever you need to. I've arranged for Shari's flight back tonight from DC, where she's been visiting Hal's wife. She should be back here in Austin in a few hours. I'm doing my best to get an ID on the survivor, though given his condition, it doesn't make much difference anyway. Meanwhile, I'm tightening up security measures for Shari and their kids. And we're snugging up security for you and your family too."

"Dean, they got Adam. Do you really think they're going to try for more?"

"I have no idea. I'm trying to find out. That's on my agenda. But for now, tell me . . . what's your plan?"

"I don't know. What in the hell is my plan? I have no idea. I'm going to hang up and go straight to the airport. I'll fly in to join you in Austin. I can't think beyond that right now. I've gotta get myself under control and get my thoughts together. I'll get back to you once I'm on the way."

En route to Austin and after a couple of stiff drinks, Charlie called Dean. "Any further news on our survivor? Do we know who he is?"

"We don't know who he is, and as far as his condition is concerned, all we know is that he's apparently still alive but barely."

"Do you know Gina Salter, Dr. Virginia Salter, the director of research at Adam's medical center?"

"I know who she is. I've met her, but I don't know her well."

"I'll call her right after we hang up and tell her to expect your call. When you talk to her, tell her what's going on. Make sure she knows there's a survivor. I know we don't know for sure, but until we find out, tell her you think it's Adam. She'll want to be in touch with the hospital to get the lowdown on their patient. If I know Gina, she'll want him transferred to her facility immediately. Listen carefully, Dean. Go through proper channels if you can, but do not, I say again, do not let yourself get bogged down in bureaucracy. Do anything you have to do to get Adam transferred. And I do mean anything. Speed is urgent. Is that clear?"

"All this effort for a dead man?"

"He ain't dead yet. I want him at her facility. I'm pretty sure Gina's going to want him there too. There's no way they can save him in the ER, but Gina can do magic if you're quick enough. It's your job to get him there without delay. That's my instruction."

"Okay, I get it. You got anything else for me?"

"Yes, this guy Poole has to be eliminated before he gets any more of us. I want a plan. I want Poole dead."

"We're working on it, Charlie."

"If you don't have a plan already, you're not working fast enough."

"Look, Charlie, nobody wants him dead more than me. He killed Sam, who was a good friend of mine. And he killed the three men Sam took with him to Venezuela. And then he killed my security guys out on the tarmac with Adam. These were good men. Some I've worked with for years. I'm not about to forget that. Believe me, I want him dead as badly as you do."

"Okay, Dean. Get me a rough plan in the next couple of days."

"Will do."

"And, Dean, Adam tells me that you can be a real pain in the ass, but he knows you've got his back. If Adam trusts you, and I know he does, then I trust you too. Keep me updated. I don't want to be out of the loop."

Chapter 36

"Hello, Dr. Salter? This is Dean Fleck calling. I'm Mr. Braudy's head of security."

"Yes, of course, Dean. I remember meeting you. I just got off the phone with Mr. Wood. He told me about the assassination attempt on Mr. Braudy and told me to expect your call."

"Charlie told me to get Adam over to your facility ASAP."

"I presume he told you the urgency."

"Yes, he did. I'm ready to move immediately."

"Good, but I have to warn you the hospital is not going to be inclined to release Adam, especially because of his extremely grave condition. That's because the transferring facility would be responsible for his death in transit. It would probably take Shari's permission or a court order. Since Shari's in flight, we can't wait for her arrival. I can contact our attorney to get the ball rolling, but I fear that ball will roll too slowly."

"Well, then, we'll just have to grease its path a bit. Do you know anyone in the hospital administration? And do you have a copy of a court order like the one we're gonna need?"

"Yes, I know Roger Walker, the hospital's chief administrator. I wouldn't say we're friends, but we're acquainted and on good terms."

"What about the court order?"

"I think I can find one. Why? What good would that do?"

"We can use it as a model to create a fake. With your help, and a lot of bluster, I'll give it a go, but only if you tell me that the urgency is genuine. Otherwise, I'm hanging my ass out there for nada."

"Let me put it to you this way. We're talking life and death here—Adam's life. Between Charlie's call and yours, I've already spoken with the hospital. From what they told me, if he stays there, he will die. That's not a guess. That's a certainty. If we can get him to our facility, there's a chance we might save him, but we have no time to waste. As to your question, the answer is yes. The urgency is genuine."

"That's what I needed to hear. Go ahead and scan the document and get it over to me right away. Then call me back so we can figure out how to deal with your administrator friend. Meanwhile, I'm gonna get an ambulance and an EMT crew for the transport."

"I'll search my computer for a representative document and send it over to you. Then I'll get over to our research center and get ready to receive Adam. We've got a lot of preparation to do. When you pick up Adam, be sure you get all of the diagnostic reports. They're required by law to provide them. I don't want to risk any slip-ups. You must ask for everything they've got, including notes taken during treatment."

Dean received a copy of a court order from Gina and immediately put one of his staff on the job of forging a lookalike. Meanwhile, Gina caught up with Roger Walker, who was still awake at home. Given his high profile, the chief administrator was glad to have someone else take responsibility for Adam's death. He just needed some cover. The court order would suffice, but they would have to have unequivocal evidence of Adam's identity.

Dean got an ambulance, a doctor, and two attendants from Gina's medical staff. He then called in a favor from the chief of police, who agreed that his officers would maintain a presence in two cars alongside the ambulance but would not otherwise interact with the hospital staff in any way. Dean figured that the mere presence of a couple of police cars with sirens and flashing lights would add official authenticity to the urgency of the court order and would lubricate the hospital's administrative processes.

When Dean arrived along with the ambulance and the police escort, Roger Walker was waiting. He seemed anxious but willing to help.

"Mr. Walker, I'm Dean Fleck. I'm here representing Mr. Braudy's interests. Here's a court order authorizing you to release Mr. Braudy to our care. As you can see in the document, we will be transferring him to BrauCorp's medical facility."

"Everything appears to be in proper order but there's just one problem. You are authorized to transport a Mr. Adam Braudy. Unfortunately, we don't know yet who our patient is."

"Let me help you here. You can see that like your patient, our Mr. Braudy, is five ten and has hazel eyes. Statistically speaking, that should be sufficient."

"That's what you might think, but try to understand that we're not permitted to transfer an unstable patient except in the most exceptional circumstances. This may be one of those circumstances. But that's a legal matter that requires our attorney's advice."

"Mr. Walker, earlier this evening, I brought over medical records that we have for Mr. Braudy and for the others who were present at the blast scene. Has your staff seen those records?"

"I don't know. I'm guessing their immediate concern is saving our patient's life."

"Of course, but I bet you got a thorough set of X-rays of your patient. Is that right?"

"Well, I'm not on the medical team, but that's probably what they did."

"Look here. Mr. Braudy had a left knee replacement, which can be seen in his medical records. I'll bet your patient also has a left knee replacement. Let's check his X-rays. That should serve as adequate confirmation."

"Interesting, but I have to check that out with our attorney."

"I understand, but if you don't want Mr. Braudy's death on your hands, you better stop screwing around and let me get him out of here."

"You know it's not that easy. If he dies in transit, which is highly

likely, the law makes that our responsibility. His dying here in our custody is one thing, but dying in transit pursuant to our release is another. Give me a minute. Our attorney is on call."

Walker returned, saying, "Our attorney says that your argument is
persuasive, but he needs a visual identification to confirm our patient's
identity. Are you acquainted with Mr. Braudy's appearance?"

"Yes, I work very closely with him."

"Then follow me. I'll take you to the trauma bay. I need to warn
you there's no way to prepare you for what you're about to see."

The two of them rushed down the corridor without further discussion, passed through a wide pair of swinging doors, and entered
the trauma bay. Walker halted and turned aside as Dean moved closer
to a table in the middle of the room. On it was a patient lying draped
beneath a blanket. A tangle of tubes and wires connected him to IV
dispensers, catheters, and electronic monitors of every conceivable
description. The attending nurse pulled back the drape and set loose a
putrid stench, the sickening vapor of burned flesh and opened wounds.
Could it possibly be Adam? Dean didn't really know who or even
what he was looking at. How could he? In places, the patient's skin
was entirely burned away, revealing bloody tissues usually hidden and
protected. What remained was charred in place. His skin, the shield
that protects a person's inner workings from an otherwise hostile environment, was mostly absent, leaving the man unprotected and ultimately vulnerable. What Dean saw left him feeling like he might vomit.
He managed to control himself but not for long. He turned away and
threw up on the floor. Still sickened, he retreated to rejoin Walker.

"Well, Mr. Fleck, can you identify our patient as your Mr. Braudy?"

Dean's mind reeled as he tried to focus on Walker's question.
Without his skin, there was no way he could discern Adam's likeness.
He was afraid to open his mouth to answer out of fear that he might
vomit again. He gulped down a dry swallow and blurted out with false
certainty, "Yes, that's him lying on your table. That's Adam Braudy."

Chapter 37

Walker called Dr. Raskin, the attending physician, to his side and directed him to prepare his patient for transfer.

Dr. Raskin said, "You gotta be kidding me. That's just nuts. This man is dying. Why in hell would we move him?" Then, rolling his eyes and with a shrug, he added, "Well, why not? I don't need another death certificate with my name on it. I've already got plenty of those."

He instructed his staff to join Dean's attendants in moving Adam, together with as much of the life-sustaining attachments as possible. Before leaving the hospital, Gina's staff physician spoke briefly with Dr. Raskin, asking for the full set of lab tests, X-rays, and reports.

"That's a lot to gather. It's going to take a few minutes."

Dean overheard that response and interjected, "We don't have a few minutes. We're getting out of here right now. It'll take us a minute or two to make our way down your hallway to our ambulance. If you can't get your shit together by then, we're gonna be out of here. In that case, you can hand it all to one of the cops outside, who'll stay behind to rush it over to us."

"Sorry, I can't release your Mr. Braudy without a personal handoff of those documents and disks."

"I'm sorry, too, Doc. If you can't get it together fast enough, we'll be out of here, and you'll be the one in violation. Let's not waste time beefing about it. Let's get busy."

Roger Walker nodded his consent. Dr. Raskin hurried off to gather the reports, which were produced barely in time to be handed off just as the ambulance was ready to pull away.

Gina's professional confidence turned to icy fear when she learned that Dean had succeeded in getting Adam transferred from the hospital. Now his survival would be entirely in her hands. The burden of that responsibility left her in a state of panic. She took a deep breath and let out a sigh that sounded more like a prayer. She managed to pull herself together and directed her staff to prepare for Adam's arrival. Within minutes of notification, they had surged into motion, assisted by their receipt of diagnostic information that had been transmitted by email. Upon evaluation, it was clear that Adam, despite his terminal condition, had received exceptional care from a competent staff operating in a well-equipped facility. Now it was up to Gina and her team.

Apart from the vigorous preparations taking place in her ER, Gina was anxious to prepare the replication printer for immediate use. It had been used many times in experimental routines, but except for the printing of a kidney for Melissa's father, this would be the only time living tissues would be replicated for human use. She sat down in front of her computer and quickly went through the list of scan files. She had several listed in a subdirectory titled "Adam." The earliest one was over a year old, but in the last several months, Adam had had a new scan taken every couple of weeks, the most recent just ten days earlier.

She double-clicked the file, and the imaging process began. Within a few moments, an image of Adam appeared, lying supine and naked before her. She looked at the body of a healthy man whom she knew would in no way resemble the burned and dying man she would be examining in just a few minutes. Her heart was pounding.

Dr. Paul Simmons was one of Gina's early hires. He had come to Gina's attention as a gifted surgeon and as a researcher at a prominent medical institute. His work was slow to take off at BrauCorp, but it was still early. He was excited by the idea of working with Gina on a project that held such enormous potential. Gina was relieved that she was able to reach Dr. Simmons, who was at home, deep in sleep. Following their conversation, he quickly headed to the research center, arriving in just twenty minutes.

"Paul, here's a recently scanned image of our subject. He's sustained extensive injuries that will require the replication of body parts—not sure which ones yet. He'll be arriving in the ER in moments."

"Gina, I've only been working on animal subjects. Are you sure you want to do a human subject?"

"Just between you and me, which means keep this to yourself, we've already done a human kidney replication and transplant. It worked out just fine. In this case, our subject is near death. No conventional care will save his life. If we don't work our magic, he'll be dead. We've got nothing to lose. Here's your first bite at the apple."

"I'm not sure that's the best metaphor. You sure you want to go with that one?"

"I'm sure. This sure as hell isn't Eden, and I'm not really worried about going to hell. I've already seen the diagnostics—not pretty. Here's what you're going to do. While I go down to the ER to examine our subject upon arrival, get on the computer and look over the diagnostics under the subject's name: Braudy."

"Braudy? Not *the* Braudy."

"It's a long story, Paul, but, yes, it is *the* Adam Braudy. Is that a problem for you?"

"Well, I'd be lying if I didn't say it makes me more than a little nervous."

"Nervous is okay, but can you do it?"

After a thoughtful pause, he spoke with a shaky voice. "Yes, of course."

"Good. I'm hoping that we'll be able to keep him stabilized for a little bit longer, long enough for you to get the replicator ready. I'll check out our patient and let you know which organs we'll need and in what order. Meanwhile, I'll work with our team to start cleaning his charred wounds. Following that, we'll use that new electrospinner to spray a protective mesh of nanofibers over his exposed surfaces. I hope it works as well as they said it would. If it does, it'll give him an artificial skin to help support his body temperature and give him a topical dose of antibiotics too. Now get to work and let me get to mine."

In the ER, Gina was shocked. Although she had seen the diagnostic reports along with attached photos, she was not prepared for what she saw before her. She was sickened by the sight of Adam burned beyond recognition, and she was humbled to think that his life lay in her hands.

She wasted no time and had Adam moved to the OR, where she applied the nanofabric and helped prepare him for surgery. By this time, Adam's kidneys were failing, and she saw that his ruptured liver was in need of replacement. Because his trachea and lungs were irreparably damaged, it was becoming increasingly difficult to keep him oxygenated.

Dr. Simmons had a long night ahead of him. First, he replicated and transplanted one kidney. The second one could wait. Then he replicated and transplanted the liver, followed by the lungs and trachea. The kidney transplant was easy, and the liver transplant went well, but the lungs and trachea proved to be difficult. Midway through the following morning, with the first round of surgeries completed, Dr. Simmons, near collapse, was amazed that Adam was still alive. He was moved in desperately critical condition to the ICU, where he was expected to die.

Chapter 38

When Charlie first heard Dean's report on the attack, he felt overwhelmed with emotion. Fear was dominant, first for Adam and Shari but also for himself and his family. Gina's report that Adam was still alive following the surgeries gave Charlie hope but not much. Immediately following his first conversation with Gina, he called Laura and shared with her the details he was aware of.

"Laura, I gotta get to Austin right away. I want you to come with me. Shari's really hurting right now. I think she could use our help."

"Of course I'll go with you, but I don't want to leave Joel behind alone. There's no way I can do that. Will we be safe traveling together?"

Charlie answered, "I honestly don't know. I think we'll be okay, but I can't be sure—not of anything anymore."

"Should we take separate flights?"

"I could arrange that if you want."

"What do you want?" Laura asked.

"I want us to be together, whatever may come."

Charlie reached his pilot and told him about the attack and to be particularly vigilant for anything that didn't seem routine. Two hours later, Laura, Joel, and Charlie, nerves on edge, were safe, at least for the moment, and heading for Austin with an expected arrival time of around three a.m.

En route, Charlie called Shari, who had already arrived safely at home. "Hello, Charlie. What a relief knowing you'll be here soon.

Please stay here with me and the kids. I need your support. It'll be better for all of us."

"You sure we won't be a burden? Laura, Joel, and I may be more than you want to deal with."

"You can't be a burden. You'll be a comfort. And I know Jess and Steve will both be glad to have Joel here too. I think you know Helene, our housekeeper. Please call her to make arrangements. I'll let her know you'll be calling."

Charlie asked, "What's going on with Adam?"

"They did a lot of surgery. Gina says he's doing better but is still critical. He's not conscious yet but may be soon. You can check in with Gina. She'll give you the details."

Charlie called Dean. "We'll be arriving around three your time. Have a car there to get us over to Adam's. We'll be staying there with Shari. Any more information for me?"

"You may want to know that following the attack, we were able to get our hands on two members of the assault team. We think there were just the two of them except for maybe a getaway driver. We're looking at video coverage to see if we can find their vehicle. One of the guys was probably a diversion. He fired at Adam and missed and then got showered with our return fire. He's really messed up. We don't think he'll live long enough for us to get much more information from him. But the guy who fired the RPG is alive. He's only suffering from bruises, contusions, and pain resulting from a nasty blow to his crotch. Probably won't be fathering any children."

"Do we know who sent them?"

"It's complicated because they're working through intermediaries, but it looks like the plot goes right back to our old friend Vincent Poole. By the way, we've reviewed the video from the scene. You might be interested in that."

"What's interesting?"

"Well, it was a chilly night. Adam's bodyguards, the four on the tarmac, were dressed for cold weather. Sean was a new hire. He signed on with us about two months ago—came with good recommenda-tions, a big guy, heavy, very rugged, lots of muscle. We put him through our training rigmarole, and we buddied him up with one of our regu-lars. He was wearing a heavy overcoat. When the shooting broke out, before returning fire from the attacker, he instinctively threw Adam down onto the tarmac. That's probably what caused Adam's concus-sion. Then when the rocket launched, he turned to find Adam, spread out his coat, and fell down on top of him. That's probably what bust-ed Adam's ribs. Sean's the guy responsible for Adam's concussion and broken ribs and for protecting him from the worst of the blast. He's a hero. The guy did it right."

"Does he have any family we can talk to?"

"Nope. He's a loner. He broke up with a short-term girlfriend in New York just before joining up with us. No former marriages, no kids. We know nothing about parents or sibs or anyone else who might want to know what he's done. We'd like to find a way to honor him."

"We will, Dean. We'll get together with your staff to let them know about this guy's courage and sacrifice. We owe it to him and to all your people. How many of our people were killed?"

"There were four bodyguards. Two of them were within the blast radius. They were fried. A third bodyguard died when a chunk of the engine smashed into him, nearly took his head off. Then on board the plane, there was the flight crew: a pilot, copilot, flight attendant, and the fourth bodyguard. Then there was a guy from the dispatch office who was keeping an eye on the fueling and on the maintenance peo-ple who were coming and going. At the time of the blast, two guys were fueling the airplane, and one guy, an aircraft mechanic, was dou-ble-checking the pilot's aircraft inspection. That's eleven dead. Let's hope Adam doesn't make it an even dozen."

Dean told Charlie he'd have a car waiting for him that would be accompanied, front and back, by escort vehicles carrying well-armed men.

Charlie called Gina. "I understand you were able to get Adam over to your facility. Tell me what's going on."

"First thing, you owe Dean Fleck a gold medal. I'd sure like to know what he eats for breakfast. He showed a lot of initiative and ingenuity. I'm not sure what you told him, but he went out and got Adam transferred. I didn't think he'd be able to do it, at least not in time, but he did. Then when I took a look at the medical reports coming in, I hesitated. I didn't want to take on that kind of responsibility. I almost wished Dean didn't get him transferred."

"What were the reports telling you?"

"The photos were gruesome. We medical folks see a lot of nasty stuff, but this was the worst I'd ever seen. And the diagnostics and write-ups were clearly describing a dead man with a heartbeat. The only chance we had was to fire up the printer and start replicating. Because Adam's been paranoid lately, not without cause, he'd been coming in every ten days to get scanned. So we had a current scan that allowed us to print the immune-compatible organs we needed. So far, everything seems to be working. Not sure how long that'll last."

"What about his concussion?"

"Don't know yet. Scans look okay. If he lives, we think the chance of recovery from the concussion is good. We put him through an MRI, which showed things as mostly normal, though we did see some minor swelling. We might have missed microscopic bleeds that could cause impairment, but there's not much more we can do for that other than what we're already doing. We'll run another MRI in a few days to note any changes."

"So how did the replication business go? Any problems there?"

"Not really. We had a lot of confidence in the kidney replication and transplant because of our prior experience. The liver transplant went without any problems, but the lungs were tricky. We had difficulties in surgery with both lungs and the trachea, but in the end, it worked out. Now the real test is in the patient's response."

For months, Charlie had wanted to find something good to say about Adam's replicator but was dissuaded by ethical considerations. But after hearing what Gina had to say, he wondered if, after all, there was an appropriate role for replication technology. Its capacity to save lives put the question of ethics into an entirely different perspective.

Charlie, Laura, and Joel arrived at the Braudy estate. They found Shari strong and remarkably able. She served as a pillar of strength for Jess and Steve. They all took turns going back and forth to the hospital to see a man barely clinging to life. On the third day, Gina took everyone aside and told them Adam's numbers were getting better and that he might become responsive before long.

Shari came for visits and sat for long hours in dark despair. Nearly Adam's entire body, including his head and face, were covered by the nanofiber mesh. That obscured the horrific sight of his damaged underlying tissues and left him with the appearance of a disfigured man, lying comatose and unrecognizable. She longed to see a sign of improvement or hear an encouraging word, but neither was in the offing. Though Shari was a woman of incredible strength, the weight of exhaustion and the gloom of depression left her nearly immobilized. She sat harboring her worries and fears while watching the IV bag deliver hope one drop at a time and the heart monitor confirm life, one beat after another.

A nurse was continuously in attendance or just a step out of sight. Gina checked on Adam every half hour and tried to be of comfort. She touched Shari's shoulder gently, not knowing what else to say or do, hoping her presence was more help than intrusion.

The next day, Adam's condition was not good. He was experiencing low blood pressure and had several episodes of ventricular fibrillation, which required the use of a defibrillator to shock his heart back into normal rhythm.

The day following, Shari was home with her kids when Gina called. As she reached for her phone, she felt her throat constrict, her heart skipping beats.

"Shari, it's me, Gina. There's been a change—for the better."

"Oh my God. Is he awake? Can he talk?"

"No, nothing like that, not yet anyway. His systems are showing progress. Heart rate is regular, beat is strong, blood pressure is stable, respiration is steady, and oxygen saturation is okay. He's still intubated, but we've been able to back off a little on the oxygen. His other numbers are seeing improvement too. I wouldn't say he's conscious, but he is responding to stimuli. His eyes are open, but that doesn't mean he sees anything. Maybe tomorrow we can run a PET scan to image his brain's metabolic activity. God only knows what he's cooking up inside that thick skull of his."

"Oh, Gina, I can't believe it. Can I come by to see him?"

"Of course you can—anytime. But don't expect to talk to him or even get a glimmer of recognition. That's still a ways off, no way to know if or when. He's still a man in critical condition, but he's making progress. We're starting to get hopeful."

"Thanks, Gina. I'll be over in just a bit. The kids are here with me. They'll be over the moon to hear this news."

"Don't let them get too excited. Things are still touch and go. Be sure to prepare them for what they're going to see. Take whatever time you need. We'll take care of everything over here. Give me a call when you're on your way over. I'd like to be there with you when you come in."

Chapter 39

Charlie needed distractions. He called his law partners for updates but ended up annoying them. Dean Fleck was also annoyed by calls from Charlie several times a day, anxious to hear when and how Vincent Poole would be eliminated. Dean was blunt and told him to stop annoying him, but then, not long after, he came to meet Charlie in Adam's library.

Dean walked in with an air of confidence. "How's Adam doing? Making progress?"

"About an hour ago, Gina called to tell us he's doing better, and to say she gives you high marks for getting him over to her in time. She's really impressed."

"Well, I just did my job. That's why I get paid the big bucks. What's amazing is that Adam's still alive. I actually saw him at the hospital. I heard what their medical staff had to stay. It seems impossible to me that he's alive, let alone responsive."

"Don't get too confident. He's not out of the woods yet. He's not even conscious. The only reason for hope is that he survived the surgeries, and his diagnostics are starting to improve."

"Let me know when he's conscious. I wanna be the one to tell him what I'm about to tell you."

"You sound awfully cocky. I'm guessing you have one hell of a plan to deal with Poole."

"Past tense. We had one hell of a plan. We executed our plan, and now I'm proud to say Vincent Poole is dead. Think Adam might wanna hear about that?"

"What? He's dead? You executed a plan without telling me? We wanted him alive. We wanted to find out who hired him."

"We wanted to take him alive, but things didn't work out. Things had a way of moving too quickly. In connection with Sam's trip to Caracas, we set up a surveillance operation focused on Poole. When Sam's attempt on Poole failed, we didn't terminate the surveillance. Even then, we figured we'd have to move on him again and again until we were successful. In the course of our surveillance, one thing led to another, and an opportunity presented itself. A door opened, and we went right in. We got him. Given the priority of eliminating Poole, and given the brevity of the opportunity, I assumed responsibility for the decision, presuming it would meet with your approval."

"Dean, you have a reputation for acting on your own. That's fine when you're successful. But at the same time, since Adam's made me a responsible party, your independence makes me nervous."

"Charlie, you're the boss. Adam has always allowed me to operate with a certain amount of latitude. If you don't tell me otherwise, I'm always gonna act on my own. If it looks like a tough decision and there's time to track you down and flesh it out, I don't need to assume that kind of responsibility. I'll come to you for direction, but too often, things happen too fast for us to sit around. I understand your concern, but in this case, I have no regrets and no apology."

"Okay, Dean. Fill me in on the details."

"There are no secrets we're keeping from you. Glad to give you as much detail as you want. Just be sure you really want to know."

Charlie's curiosity won out. "Gimme the scoop. I want to know if this is going to come back and bite us."

"That's not going to be a problem, at least not a bigger problem than any other way we might have dealt with Poole. I think there's a good chance that we'll never even be connected with his death. We'll have to decide whether that's really what we want."

"Okay, tell me."

"I think you know from Sam's report that Poole has or, rather, had a significant sexual appetite, one that he exploited to excess. He did like to get it on. We observed that he had become rather infatuated with a knockout beauty who also exhibited a significant sexual appetite. She introduced him to a club where he could indulge in a variety of sexual expressions along with a taste of various chemical elixirs."

"Come on, Dean, did you set this whole thing up? Is this your doing?"

"Like I said, an opportunity presented itself. It might be fair to say we might have helped it along just a bit. While Poole was engaged in a variety of activities, we were able to enhance his chemical experience. The poor guy succumbed from an overdose. Looks like he died doing what he loved most. What a way to go."

"So you're telling me he's dead. That's confirmed?"

"Yes, the police were called along with an ambulance. They were in no rush to haul the body away while they conducted an hours-long investigation. The women were known regulars in the trade. They were operating at a known establishment, a high-end club. The assortment of drugs that Poole ingested was the usual mix, just a variety of commonly used, readily available recreational drugs, though one of them might have been from a bad batch. Can't imagine how that could've happened. Other than that, there was nothing that would suggest anything especially deadly or out of place, just the usual drugs used to excess."

"Did you have to give him an overdose? If you hadn't, he might still be alive and talking to us."

"We got the drugs to him, but he elected the dose. By that time, we were out of the loop."

"So how is Secura handling this? Are they able to function in Poole's absence?"

"Can't tell yet. We're monitoring the situation closely. They probably will be able to maintain their legal operations but may have difficulty sustaining the illegal ones. That requires the leadership of a real badass. Poole was their guy. Not sure they've got anyone else to step up to that rank. They'll make every effort to maintain, but we expect that there'll be a rapid erosion in their capabilities. We'll test them on that and do what we can to help along their decline."

"Okay, Dean. It's a good news/bad news story. We wanted the intelligence, but at least we got the vengeance. I'll get you in to see Adam as soon as he's able to handle the good news. Meanwhile, stay on top of Secura and the other agencies. We need to anticipate their next steps."

Chapter 40

When Charlie next saw Shari, she spoke about the long hours she had spent at Adam's bedside. She described the spaghetti of tubes and wires that was still needed to tether him to life. Everything seemed unchanged from her previous visit. Gina, along with Dr. Simmons and a couple of nurses, had greeted her with smiles. They were pleased with Adam's progress: pinpricks had elicited muscle responses, and he opened his eyes briefly in response to loud commands. They spoke about removing the endotracheal tube, but that would be the following day at the earliest. Shari was clearly energized by the hope that Adam might be on his way to recovery.

The following days showed more progress. With the endotracheal tube removed, but with oxygen supplied through a nasal cannula, Adam's breathing was regular, his oxygen saturation good enough. His eyes were open for long periods, and he was observed tracking movement in the room. There were rasping noises from him as he tried clearing his throat, but still there was no conversation.

Another day later, Adam was able to recognize both Shari and Charlie as they came and went. He responded to Shari with a kind of facial movement that could only have been a smile, which left her in tears. He turned up his right thumb in a buoyant expression when Gina came in. When Charlie approached his bedside, Adam reached out a dressed hand that could not yet be touched. It was an extraordinary gesture of hope and confidence. All who saw him were affected by a sense of wonderment, a sense that they had witnessed a miracle. Was this just one more step in a long history of human accomplishment, or was it the work of God?

Following a week of continuing improvement, Adam was able to speak in three- and four-word sentences.

Charlie asked, "Gina, is he strong enough for conversation?"

"He's still extremely weak. Though he is speaking, conversation is another question. You have to understand that he's been very sick and has suffered a brain concussion, maybe some brain damage too. Don't forget he suffered a nasty hit to his head. It takes time to get over the effects of a severe concussion. Give him time. I think you'll see a lot of improvement."

"How long could it take?"

"It could take months, even more than a year, to see a complete recovery—that's if there's no permanent damage. And we might see different aspects of brain function respond differently. Some capacities may seem normal or appear to be recovering, while others may lag or maybe never fully recover. We just have to be to be patient. He's alive. That's more than we ever expected. The most important thing to keep in mind is that he's got a powerful will and lots of support. That will drive his recovery more than anything else we can do for him."

When Charlie entered Adam's room on his next visit, he was surprised to see a meeting breaking up. Janet Ralston, BrauCorp's CEO, and Gary Smathers, BrauCorp's general counsel, were just leaving. Charlie knew them but not well. He was acquainted with them because of his consulting work for Adam and his interests in a handful of Adam's ventures.

Charlie said, "Hey, Janet, Gary, what brings you two down here? Checking up on the big guy?"

Janet grinned. "Nope, wouldn't have bothered just on that account. Gary and I came down here because Adam called for us. Can you believe that? He's got business on his mind. Here he lies with all these good-looking nurses around him, and what he wants to do is talk business. And it's business that involves you in a major way. But I'm going to let Adam tell you, if he's still able."

"What do you mean if he's still able?"

"Well, his condition is fragile, but his mind is limber. He may have exhausted himself, but see for yourself. Afterward, come by my office for a chat. You're in for a big surprise."

Charlie found that Adam had drifted off to sleep. So he left the room and the building and meandered aimlessly around the campus grounds. The sky was a vibrant blue, and a fresh breeze carried a light floral scent. The grass underfoot was lush and moist. Charlie sat down on a nearby bench, took off his shoes and socks, and reveled at the sensation of walking barefoot through the grass.

Later, when he got back to the room, Adam was awake and appeared to be staring off into space. Charlie drew closer. Adam's vacant stare shifted to an expression of recognition. He turned his face toward Charlie but with weakness.

"Adam, I'm glad you're awake. I thought I'd never get the chance to speak with you again. But now you're back. Do you feel like talking?"

"Don't know."

"First, tell me how you feel."

"Like shit. Spoke with Janet and Gary."

"I did too. Janet told me to speak with you about a big plan you have that involves me. And then she said I should come by her office afterward. You got something to tell me?"

"Able . . . barely. You take over BrauCorp. You chair board. You direct, keep or change. But only if I die or when I say."

"If you die? Haven't you spoken with Gina? Didn't you get the memo? She says you're doing fine. Planning for your demise appears to be premature."

"Just spin. Don't believe. Must make plans. Go see Janet. Talk with Shari too."

"Damn you, Adam. Your realism is going to kill you. Didn't anyone ever tell you that there's a time and place for hope and prayer? Just this once, can't you have at least a little faith in your own survival?"

Adam replied, "Got faith. Realism too."

"Alright, Adam, but don't mind me if I plan on your complete recovery."

Adam's eyes wandered out of contact; his eyelids drooped. Exhausted, he drifted back to sleep.

Charlie went to meet with Janet. "Okay, Janet, I spoke with Adam. He says that in the event of his death, he wants me to take over BrauCorp. Is he nuts? Am I competent to take over? Is he competent to make that kind of a decision? Would that stand up in court?"

"Those are interesting questions that we could speculate on for hours, but the answer to your last question makes everything simple. Adam and Shari are the sole owners of BrauCorp. The rest of us, you included, hold interests in the operating spinoffs. If Shari were to dispute the decision, there might be an argument, but with her consent, there would be no problem. Gary and I are working up a mechanism to effect the change that Adam says he wants. Once we've worked up the details, we can get together again for a thorough discussion. If it sounds right to you and if it's okay with Adam, then you can explain it to Shari for her consideration. If it's okay with her, that'll make it a done deal."

"From a legal standpoint, it sounds fine, but me running BrauCorp? I don't get that."

"No insult intended, Charlie, but I don't get it either. The only thing I can say is that over the years, I've seen Adam make a lot of decisions. Some didn't make sense to me, but he's the conductor, and the train usually ends up running where he intends it to go."

"Well, yeah, but Adam isn't doing so hot right now. In his condition, is he really capable of good judgment?"

"It's anyone's guess, but think of it this way: We wore him out in our meeting. For most of it, although his eyes were rolling around a bit and his speech was sluggish, his thinking was nimble. Even now I wouldn't want to bet against him. Only time will tell. The other way to think about this is that he might fully recover, and then none of this will be a worry. That'd be the best solution."

"Yep, let's pray for that."

Just a day later, Charlie found Adam well rested. Though his speech was still sluggish, he seemed more alert. "You spoke with Janet?"

"I did speak with Janet. I told her I had reservations about your sanity, but she assured me you knew what you were doing. She told me that Gary was working first priority on getting paperwork together for us to review."

"What about Shari?"

"I did speak with Shari, but we only chatted about your condition. Adam, you should be proud of her. She's been solid through all of this."

"I know. What about changes?"

"I didn't speak with her about that. I figure I'd rather see the documents Gary is preparing. Then I'll have a better understanding of the arrangements and be able to discuss them more intelligently with her."

The next day, Charlie met with Janet and Gary. He was surprised that Gary had worked so quickly. Gary attributed the quick turnaround to the simplicity of the task and was astounded that Adam, though he had suffered a concussion and maybe worse, was still able to devise a plan and communicate it without difficulty. All that was left for Gary was to prepare a written outline and specify the documents needed to formalize it. The final documentation would be drawn only after both Adam and Shari agreed.

The plan called for converting the existing BrauCorp shares, all of which were held by Adam and Shari, to non-voting shares. At the same time, the couple would be issued additional voting shares amounting to 5 percent of BrauCorp stock, leaving them with complete control of the company. In the event of Adam's death or upon his direction, those voting shares would be transferred to Charlie, allowing him to assume unfettered control of BrauCorp and make him the owner of about 5 percent of the stock. That would leave the remaining 95 percent of non-voting stock in the hands of Adam and Shari. However, if those voting shares were transferred to Charlie at Adam's direction rather than on his death, Adam or Shari could reclaim the stock at a later date for value. They would have to purchase the shares, leaving Charlie without an interest in BrauCorp but with one to several billion dollars in hand. Gary went on indicating the various documents that would have to be drawn or modified.

Charlie was disoriented thinking about the enormous responsibility that might befall him and awed by the potential wealth that might be his. Amid a swirl of befuddlement, he indicated his approval. Next, Charlie and Gary met with Adam, who also approved the specifics of the plan. The last step was for Charlie to seek Shari's approval.

"Shari, I know this has been a grim time for you. I can't tell you how much your composure has strengthened me. I saw Adam earlier today. He seems to be recovering nicely. Of course, there are still risks, but he's amazing. He can do it."

"Charlie, you're making me nervous. Is there something I don't know? I feel like you're about to drop a bomb."

"No bombs. I'm just an instrument of your loving husband's obsessive compulsion to control. Whether he's living or dying, it all comes down to his control. Where did you find this guy anyway?"

She smiled. "You're not telling me anything I don't already know. Controlling a controller has been a real trick. Fortunately, I have my ways."

"I bet you do. Are you aware that Adam is hatching a plan for me to control BrauCorp in the event of his death?"

"He talked about a plan that would have to meet with my approval. Is that what you want to discuss with me?"

Charlie told Shari how he, Adam, Janet, and Gary had worked together to create a plan according to Adam's wishes, and her consent was the next step. "Whatever you say today is for today only. It's only the finished and signed documents that will make everything final. Till then, you can think about it; discuss it with Adam and with anyone else you want. You can say yes today and then change your mind tomorrow. With your approval, this plan will set up the mechanics for the creation of voting stock, which you and Adam will hold exclusively. Any subsequent transfer of the voting shares will only occur if Adam directs the transfer or in the event of his death."

"You said that you went back to Adam with the details, and he's in agreement? You think he actually understands everything?"

"Ya know, Shari, he actually dictated the plan to Janet and Gary. Gary spent the last several days fleshing out the details. When we got together with Adam this morning, he pissed and moaned about technical details and grammatical errors. His concussion might have caused some damage, but we couldn't tell. He's an impressive guy. What can I say?"

Charlie went through the outline in detail and answered the many questions that Shari asked. "It looks okay. If that's what Adam wants, I'm willing to sign on, but give me a day or two to think about it. Is there any rush?"

"Adam's making good progress. As long as that's the case, a couple of days is no big deal. It would only be a problem if Adam were to suffer a relapse or worse."

"Thanks, Charlie. You just spiked my heart rate again."

"Sorry, Shari. It looks like I've been hanging around Adam too long. He's now got me thinking in realist mode. Not sure I like it like that."

"I certainly understand that, Charlie."

Charlie felt uncomfortable hurrying her because he was a substantial beneficiary. But after a week, Janet was getting anxious and Adam too. If he took a turn for the worse, there would be a problem. Adam wanted it wrapped up.

Adam said, "Shari, why slow? I want it done."

"You think I don't know that? But it's too painful. To think about this means I have to accept the possibility of you dying. That makes it nearly impossible for me."

"Get over it. Want to rest. Can't like this. Why delay? Worried about Charlie?"

"That occurred to me, but no. I trust Charlie. He and Laura have always been such close and sincere friends."

"You want to chair? I can agree. Just want settled. Need to rest."

"I've thought about that too, but I don't want to take that on. I'd rather leave it to Charlie."

"Give Gary okay. He'll draw docs. You can change your mind till signed."

That afternoon, Shari called Charlie to give the go-ahead. He said, "I know it's been a difficult decision. Frankly, I don't know if it's the right way to go, but Adam is convinced, and that's good enough for me. I'll tell Gary to produce the final documents. Figure on a week to get them in order. Then we can put this behind us."

During that week, Adam continued to gain strength, making good progress. Day by day, one by one, the tubes and wires were disconnected. The nasal cannula was gone. Adam was breathing entirely on his own. Everything was on track for a successful recovery until Adam registered an elevated temperature. A drip line that had been feeding a steady stream of antibiotics to ward off infections was reinserted. The medical staff was in a flurry with blood draws for culturing. They were determined to identify the infectious agent and cleanse it from his system.

Several of Adam's surgical sites became swollen with blue-green pus and had to be drained. He was not a whiner, but he complained that his sleep was interrupted by aching joints. Even with the antibiotic drip back in place, the infection dragged on. His hundred-degree fever was not itself a problem, but it warned of a threat. Different antibiotics in a variety of combinations were tried but to no avail. The fever persisted. The infectious agent was found to be an antibiotic-resistant

Pseudomonas aeruginosa, the scourge of burn victims and a frightening challenge to Adam's recovery.

Though the infection began to weigh on Adam's stamina, he was still alert enough and determined to see the documents that Gary produced. He studied them with remarkable acuity and insight and insisted on changes he declared in brief utterances. With the changes made, the final copies were printed and ready for signing. Shari was expected at any minute.

Shari and Charlie both signed the various documents. Adam scrawled an unrecognizable signature that would only be held valid with the signatures of two nurses acting as witnesses. Afterward, Shari asked everyone to leave. Adam was finally at ease while Shari gently patted the top of his head. She leaned over and kissed him gently as he drifted off to sleep.

Chapter 41

The next day, Adam's condition worsened. His fever was over 102. The infection was resistant to every antibiotic they tried. With each attempt, there was an encouraging response that dissipated in a fog of hopelessness. Gina and her team were running out of ideas, grasping at straws. Charlie went to visit Adam and found him lying amid a fresh tangle of tubes and wires. He was weak and spoke only with difficulty.

"Glad you're here. Want to talk."

"Glad to see you too," Charlie said.

"Shari signed. Good job. Was hard on her?"

"No, she's smart and resilient. She made sure she understood what she was doing. She was right to take her time."

"About my bug. Gina said it could kill. If worse, you must help."

"Adam, this is not going to kill you. Gina will figure this out, and I know you know that too."

"No denial. You sound stupid. This bug can kill. My plan. You part of it."

"I thought we had a plan. Didn't we sign your documents? Isn't that your plan?"

"More. Discussed with Gina. You work with her. Must replicate me. Promise. Do this before I die. Want to see."

"Adam, you know how I feel about your replicator. I don't like it. What are you trying to accomplish? You think that you'll live on, that you'll cheat death. We've talked about this before. You'll be dead as a doornail, only thing is that not everyone will know it."

"You right. Can't cheat death. I know. Not what I want."

"Well, what the hell do you want? I've been trying to figure that out for a long time. Is it perpetual wealth if not perpetual life?"

"No. My life has purpose. I made a difference. Things left undone. Need replicant to finish. Must know will be finished."

"You think that only your replicant can possibly carry on? Are you so vain to think that even with your notes and records, there's not someone born of a woman who can pick up where you leave off?"

"You know who can?"

"Not off hand, but maybe you're afraid I can find someone better. You want to give me time to work on that? I'd rather spend my time doing that than creating an Adamstein monstrosity."

"Adamstein . . . that's funny."

"Don't just laugh it off. You haven't even achieved your identical- ity 1.0 criteria yet. You're stalled at 1.4. There could be a lot of horror in the difference between 1.4 and 1.0. Do you really want some fake lookalike running around with your name and identity? What if your replicant isn't quite up to snuff? Can't you see that it might be flawed and acting in your name? Now there's a legacy I wouldn't want to have. Is that really what you want? Is that the kind of accomplishment you want connected to your name? I don't like it, not at all. I need a break. While I'm gone, think about what I've said. We can talk further when I get back."

When Charlie got back an hour later, Adam was awake. He spoke a few words at a time, spaced by long pauses. "You hate this . . . always did. I have reservations too. You persuasive . . . that's why wanted you. Knew you'd fight me, make me stretch. I stretched but haven't changed. Will get Gina to do herself . . . no need for you. Only need you if prob- lems. Need you to counter Gina . . . to pull plug."

"That's crazy. I want to pull the plug right now."

"Gina will go without you. Work with her. You'll see problems . . . quicker to stop. Be opposition. Dearest friend, with last breaths . . . must count on you."

Charlie cried. He sat alongside Adam in silence with tears running down his cheeks, his lifelong friend dying at his side. Should he say yes and one last time defer to Adam's bidding? Or say yes but then not do it? Or should he allow Adam to die with his refusal foreclosing his friend's last dream?

"Adam, I don't have it in me to tell you no. I don't have anything more in me to fight you with. Once again, you get your way. I will honor your request, but do me a favor. Don't die."

Chapter 42

The infection ran unabated. Adam suffered chills while his fever spiked to 106 before coming back down to 104. Despite his rapid breathing, his oxygen saturation declined. As a result, the nasal cannula was put back in place. His heart rate sped up, while his blood pressure went down. He tried eating but couldn't keep anything down. That called for placing a feeding tube. During the night, he was restless. During the day, there were periods of wakefulness but mostly on the edge of delirium. His urinary catheter was reinserted, but there wasn't much urine production to drain. There was bleeding around his green and swollen surgical sites. Repeated lab results showed a rising white blood cell count and an advancing prevalence of Pseudomonas. A chest X-ray revealed pneumonia. Adam was in grave trouble.

"Gina, what's going on? Why can't you do something?"

"Charlie, I hope you understand we're not sitting around here doing nothing. We're doing everything imaginable. Adam is critical. He's suffering from a horrible infection. It hasn't responded to our most aggressive antibiotic treatments. He's falling into septic shock. We're not sure what to try next. We just have to keep doing what we're doing."

"Can I see him? Is he conscious?"

"Of course you can see him. Is he conscious? That depends on what you call *conscious*. He goes through periods of delirium and confusion but then emerges into something like consciousness. I'd say his consciousness is episodic. If you want to talk to him, you gotta catch him when you can. Keep in mind he's critically ill. We've held off on the morphine drip at his insistence, but without it, he's suffering anxiety from breathlessness."

With Gina alongside him, Charlie stepped in to see Adam in the ICU. He was awake, with Shari in tears by his side.

Charlie said, "I'm sorry, Shari. We didn't mean to intrude."

"Don't be sorry, Charlie. Adam and I have just had some sweet time together—in fact, a lifetime of sweet time. Now he's made it quite clear that he wants time with the two of you. He's all yours. And as for you, Mr. Braudy, play nice with your friends. I'll be checking up on you."

She stood up, carrying a heavy weight of sorrow, and leaned over to kiss Adam on his forehead. Then she turned toward the door and walked out without looking back.

Charlie's throat was choked with emotion, and he could hardly speak. He looked at Gina and saw her eyes glistening with tears. Adam struggled to speak between labored breaths. "Any hope for me?"

"There's always hope, Adam, but your numbers are not looking good. They're getting worse," Gina replied.

"Can I beat this?"

"If I look at you clinically, you're as good as dead, but I've seen this before. The human organism is a miracle, and I've got to tell you, miracles happen. I've seen it time and again, infrequently enough to call it a miracle but often enough so that it's not a complete surprise."

"Percentage, please."

"I can give you a percentage, but the range of uncertainty exceeds the percentage. That means anything I tell you is meaningless."

"Just give it to me."

"Okay, Adam, let's say it's 2.5 percent, plus or minus twenty percent. Does that help you in any way?"

Adam was silent while he struggled with his breathing.

Gina said, "You made me promise not to ask again about the morphine. But I have to remind you that it will ease the breathlessness that's causing your distress."

"One-way street. Must talk first."

Gina said, "What is it, Adam? What do you want to talk about?"

"Need paper to transfer to Charlie. Need witnesses. You must replicate me. Gina, you want to. Charlie, you hate. But I want. You must. Wake me when done. I must see for myself. Promise me. Tell me yes."

Gina nodded, and with an unmistakable expression of sorrow, Charlie did too.

Chapter 43

Gina sought two staff members to witness Adam's signature on the directive that would transfer BrauCorp's voting stock to Charlie. One was the supervising nurse then on duty. The other was Paul Simmons, Gina's close associate. With those signatures, Charlie became the unquestioned head of Adam's business empire and, as the holder of five percent of BrauCorp stock, a man of substantial wealth. He was at once in awe of this newly bestowed status and submerged in a black bog of angst and regret. Afterward, Gina called in a nurse and instructed her on the introduction of the morphine drip. Charlie and Gina walked to her office, where they could discuss the next steps.

"Gina, let's talk about the process, but first I want to tell you about my last conversation with Adam. He told me that if his condition worsened and death appeared near at hand, he wanted his scan printed. He already knew, but I told him again, that I thought the whole enterprise was morally and ethically wrong. I told him that I didn't want to be a part of it, but that didn't stop Adam. He pulled out the stops and insisted that I work with you to create his replicant. I fought with him but ultimately agreed. I promised him that I would work cooperatively with you to see the replication through. It's only fair that you know that."

"Charlie, I appreciate your candor, but that's no surprise. You've made your distaste known from the start. I hear your words. I don't know how much I can count on you, but since you're telling me that you're willing to go forward with Adam's last request, I'll take your word for it. Let's start talking process."

Gina exhaled and continued. "When we leave here, we'll go to the lab where you've been on several occasions. We'll call up Adam's most recent scan, scrutinize it, and run several routines to ensure that the scan projection is as accurate as possible. Then we'll cut and paste."

"Cut and paste? What do you mean?"

"Well, you've seen Adam. He's not looking real pretty. His skin is not yet healed. He looks hideously disfigured. He's got surgical scars that make him look like he's been run through a meat grinder. His body took quite a beating in the original explosion and then, too, with the surgical procedures that followed. It's true there are always miracles, but if we suddenly replace a dying man suffering from devastating burns with a perfectly healthy replacement, it'll raise questions that are impossible to answer. We have to take the scan image and alter it. That way, when we print the replicant, it will look like Adam as he is now down in the ICU or as he might reasonably look following a miraculous recovery. Only then can we do a print run."

"Gina, that's ghoulish. When I talked to Adam about his replicant, I told him he was going to end up with an Adamstein monstrosity. And now you're making that come true."

"It's not as bad as it sounds. Of course, there will have to be alterations to his most evident injuries, but those alterations we make will heal rather quickly. As far as the symptoms of his concussion are concerned, we can manage those with drugs, which we can withdraw over a period of time."

They walked down the hallway to an unfamiliar lab, where they met two of Gina's most highly trained and trusted associates. Inside the lab, the equipment was ready to go, but Gina's first order of business was to introduce her associates to Charlie. The three of them had been working together for several years before moving to BrauCorp. Her associates were talented postdoctoral researchers. Because a lot of their work had involved contact with patients, Gina needed them to have clinical training. Medical school would be too long a slog and would interrupt their work. Instead, they both went through a nursing program. When Gina had signed on with Adam, she insisted on having her two associates come with her. Adam agreed without hesitation. Gina had absolute confidence in their technical competence. Their loyalty was beyond question. When Adam had met with them, they were excited to be part of the team and pledged themselves to the advancement of the replicator project.

Charlie guessed they were both in their midthirties. Alan Samuels was tall and gaunt. His head was a fuzz ball that looked like he had neglected to keep his bald head shaved. He had stooped shoulders, probably from spending too much time hanging over a computer keyboard. He had an engaging smile with unblinking eyes as he shook Charlie's hand with a firm grip.

Debbie Grant was of medium height. She wore fitted jeans and a T-shirt that was snug enough to complement her slender figure. Her dark hair was cut short and crisp, accenting her obvious vitality. She extended her hand with confidence along with a polite smile.

After exchanging pleasantries, Gina, along with Alan and Debbie, went through the lab routines that Charlie had previously witnessed. This time, the image that appeared was Adam Braudy's, lying naked and supine. Gina, working with Alan, ran several diagnostic routines over and again to ensure that the scan data transferred to the image processor was perfect. Then, working from photographs of Adam taken in the ICU, Gina and Debbie did their best to approximate Adam's current appearance. It wasn't perfect, but it didn't have to be.

"Charlie, we've done it. The image is as good as we can make it. We're ready to print."

"Just like that? 'We're ready to print.' For God's sake, Gina, we're making history here. Doesn't this occasion warrant a little drama? You know, like 'one small step for man, blah, blah, blah.'"

"Charlie, I know you're struggling to make the best of your promise to Adam, but your reluctance and cynicism are showing."

"You're right, but at this moment, at this precipice in history, can you please take a moment to reflect on what we are about to do here? I don't know why, but I think the occasion warrants it. History will appreciate it. I will appreciate it."

"Okay, Charlie, see how you like this: we take this leap today into the unknown, a leap that once again demonstrates the human capacity to change the world around us, hopefully a leap into a better world."

"That's good, Gina. There's pride in accomplishment there and humility too. It's memorable. I like it. I hope we can keep this in mind as we move forward."

"Charlie, now it's your turn. I await your command to initiate the print run."

Charlie wanted to shout out, loud enough for all eternity to hear, "No way. I will not do this." But his promise bound him, as he and Adam both knew it would. After a pause that must have left Gina wondering, he said, "Initiate the print run."

Chapter 44

Gina pressed a button, and the print run was underway. The printer was like the one that Adam had demonstrated months before when he first introduced Charlie to his project. Then it was a plastic box. Now it would be Adam Braudy. Just as before, the loud, all-pervasive rumbling hum of the apparatus filled the room with an astonishing sense of power. It felt like the currents that ran the universe were flowing underfoot. At the same time, pulses of light could be seen flashing brightly behind the printer's windows. This went on far longer than Charlie recalled from the earlier run in Adam's lab, but it finally slowed down and then ended, leaving just a colorful glow before going dark.

The printer was located on one side of a room large enough to accommodate it within an elaborate, state-of-the-art medical suite. The suite was filled with the medical tools and devices that would be found in an ICU. It was in every way prepared to receive its first human patient.

With the print run complete, and the lingering afterglow faded from view, Alan and Debbie rushed to the printer, opened the hatch, and went inside. Within moments, their patient, lying on a gurney, was wheeled out of the printer. As the man's body was lifted onto the hospital bed, diagnostic and support paraphernalia were rapidly attached. When Gina had replicated her rats, pigs, and sheep, the experimental subjects were almost immediately conscious, with normal bodily functions intact. Though the new Adam appeared dazed, he was awake and aware. Gina quickly injected her new patient with a sedative that rendered him unconscious. She wanted time to check his bodily functions and figure out the next steps. A plan to introduce this new Adam into the hospital ICU and then into his new life would require thoughtful planning.

———

Gina insisted that, except for Alan, Debbie, and Paul Simmons, no one working a full shift in the ICU would work there again for at least ten days. That way, no one—not a doctor, a nurse, an administrator, or a custodian—would witness Adam's treatment on consecutive days or his inexplicable gains from day to day.

"Okay, Charlie, here's the plan. When everything looks ready to go, we'll assign Alan and Debbie, along with Paul, to staff the ICU. The quietest part of the daily schedule is the early shift around three or four in the morning. That's when we'll move Adam upstairs for 'special procedures.' If we can rouse him, we'll inform him of our success. Then we'll move our new Adam to the downstairs ICU for his continuing care. Alan, Debbie, and I will attend to him there. Upstairs, we'll care for Adam as best we can."

"'As best we can'? What the hell does that mean anyway? We'll have two Adams, and upstairs we're going treat Adam 'as best we can'?"

"Charlie, I understand this is a highly charged loss for you, but you really must understand that Adam is as good as dead. His sepsis is re-lentless. Nothing we've tried has helped. We're out of ideas. He's close to circulatory collapse and total organ failure. The end is in sight. I'm not sure we can even rouse him to consciousness to tell him about the successful replication. Maybe it'd be a waste to even try."

"No, Gina, we will honor our promise to Adam. We created his replicant, and we will do everything we can to let him know."

"Okay, Charlie, that was our promise, so that's what we'll attempt to do."

All that day and into the night, Gina, Alan, Debbie, and Paul worked to examine the new Adam in every dimension, doing everything conceivable to determine the authenticity of his replication. They ran dozens of diagnostics: blood tests, X-rays, CT scans, MRIs, PET scans. Everything was perfect. The only thing that remained was an examination of his cognitive function, but that would have to await his "recovery" in the ICU.

At last, they acknowledged to themselves that they had done everything practicable to demonstrate a precise replication. They meticulously prepared the upstairs lab to receive Adam. What was designed as a high-tech state-of-the-art medical facility was then readied to provide hospice care for their dying patient. Downstairs in the ICU, everyone was scheduled to go off shift at midnight. That's when Adam would be prepared for his move upstairs. And at three a.m. sharp, that's what they did. Once in the lab, they worked quickly and diligently to restore the machinery of care.

"Okay, Charlie, here we are. To honor our promise to Adam, we'll need to discontinue his morphine drip. If he regains consciousness, and that's a big if at this point, he'll be quite anxious because he'll be suffering from respiratory distress. It's how you'd feel if you had a plastic bag over your head or if you were waterboarded—not pleasant. If he becomes conscious and cognitively aware, we can give him the news about his replication, but then within moments, our humanity will demand that we reestablish the drip. I'm telling you this because I want you to be sure that you actually want us to wake him from his peaceful decline."

"Gina, we've been over this before. I trust that you mean well, but my promise, which I didn't give lightly, demands that we follow through. You're making this hard for me. Leave it alone. Just do it."

Gina reached for a particular IV line and shut the valve, stopping the morphine drip. Minutes went by as Adam became restless and then breathless, but still he remained unconscious. Hoping to rouse him, Gina administered a small dose of naloxone, an opium antagonist. Gina and Charlie stood by his side, where Adam could see them.

Charlie said, "Adam, can you hear me?"

He couldn't speak between gasps of breath, but his eyes indicated recognition.

"We've done it. Do you understand? We've done it."

He nodded again.

"We've put him through all kinds of diagnostics. He's perfect, Adam. He's you. If you can turn your head, you can see him just there across the room."

Charlie stepped forward and helped Adam turn his head to the side so he could cast his glance. There, the body of a man lay covered under a sheet except for his head, which, even in profile, yielded an appearance of Adam. Adam turned his head back and mumbled between breaths.

Charlie wondered if he said, "Thanks, you've been a loyal friend."

Charlie managed a tearful grin and said, "You've been a pain in the ass, Adam, but I love you. You'll always be with me."

He grinned back as Charlie nodded to Gina, who opened the valve, allowing the morphine to flow, easing Adam back into the quiet darkness of a very long night.

With that done, Debbie and Charlie remained with Adam while the rest of the team accompanied the new Adam back downstairs to the ICU, where they reconnected the tubes and wires that provided the accoutrements of sustenance to an almost perfectly healthy Adam Braudy. During their shift, they made entries to the record of diagnostic results to indicate a slightly improving medical condition. Exhausted and exhilarated, they stood by and took additional shifts until they were relieved the following midnight.

Charlie couldn't leave Adam's side, dying though he was. He spent time thinking about the many years of their friendship and also how he might manage the governance of BrauCorp. At the same time, Debbie maintained a routine of monitoring the continuous readouts indicating Adam's condition, checking the flows of life-sustaining elixirs, and, in between, checking her email or clicking from link to link on the internet.

"What are you looking for, Debbie? Looks like you're addicted to the internet: Facebook, recipes, shoes, or what?"

"No, I'm still hoping to find another way to overcome Adam's infection. That Pseudomonas is mean shit. For years, the threat of antibiotic-resistant bacteria has been growing, but Pseudomonas is the worst of the worst. It has mechanisms that make it naturally resistant to antibiotics, but it's also able to mutate and then propagate new strains that are resistant to new antibiotic treatments. It's a real killer. Once it puts the grab on you, it just won't let go. Look at Adam. We've tried every conceivable antibiotic and even combinations. Nothing works for long. We just tried the latest and greatest on him, but it's just like the others. It starts to work, but then the infection just comes roaring back."

"So you're just hopping around the internet, hoping to find some cure?"

"Hey, it can't hurt to look. This past week, I've felt like a kid on monkey bars. I've been handed off from one researcher to another, trying to find something new to try. On one hand-off, I got passed along to some guy in France doing pharmaceutical research. Get this. He scooped up a bunch of crap out of the sewer and found viruses there that kill bacteria without killing the people infected. Does that sound like a scam or what?"

"Sounds stinky."

"Well, yeah, but don't laugh it off. It turns out this guy's a real player, Dr. Jean Foliere. It's starting to sound legit. After a phone conversation, he emailed a peer-reviewed paper he's written. It sounded interesting. I started to think that I might have stumbled on to something important."

In a follow-up conversation, Dr. Foliere referred Debbie to a researcher at Emory University in Atlanta who had successfully replicated his work and isolated a batch of viral phages that proved effective against Pseudomonas.

Debbie said, "I guess the sewage in Atlanta isn't much different from French sewage. Shit is shit."

She followed the trail and spoke with Dr. Abigail St. John, who encouraged Debbie and agreed to provide her with a batch of phages. Debbie told Gina, who, after speaking with Dr. St. John, reported to Debbie that she made arrangements to have the batch picked up.

Debbie said, "I don't get what's going on. I just got this email from Dr. St. John, who says the batch has been ready, but no one picked it up."

Charlie asked, "Why not? What happened?"

"I have no idea. You'll have to ask Gina that one."

"Debbie, I'm going down to the ICU to check in with Gina. Call me if there's any change in Adam's condition."

Charlie expected to find Gina exhausted, but she was euphoric. She looked like a kid at Disneyland. "Gina, I was talking to Debbie. She told me about a viral treatment for Adam's infection. She said you made arrangements to pick up a batch of something from a researcher at Emory University. Now she tells me she got an email saying the batch is still waiting for pickup. What's up with that?"

"Did she tell you that the pharmaceutical company is pushing the hell out of this thing, trying to turn shit into greenbacks? There's a lot of junk research out there. We really don't have time to screw around with it."

"She must have told you that there's a peer-reviewed article out on this particular shit. You told me we tried everything. You told me we would try anything."

"Yeah, anything with promise. I'm not trying organic poppyseed extract activated with refined earthworm castings. I've exhausted myself trying things. I'm worn out."

"Gina, I don't get it. I saw you upstairs in the lab moving around with a spritely gait and now, after a sleepless night, you're dancing around down here like a school girl. It's hard for me to tell just how worn out you are. I don't know; I'm not seeing exhaustion."

"I've told you, Charlie, Adam is as good as dead. We did everything we could, and now he's dying. There's nothing more we can do."

"No, Gina, you're wrong. I'm no medicine man, but from what I learned from Debbie, I don't think there's nothing more we can do. I want to see this phage tried out. It looks like you never made an effort. I'm gonna get it here, and when it arrives, I expect you and your staff to put out maximum effort to treat Adam with it. That would be the upstairs Adam, not your preferred Adam down here. If you've got a problem with that, you can let me know right now."

"Okay, Charlie, okay. You're the boss. If that's the way you want to play it, get your magic potion here, and I'll treat our patient with it. Just keep in mind that you're playing for miracles here."

"That's alright. I'll take a miracle wherever, however I can find one."

It was hard for Charlie to imagine that Gina no longer cared about Adam. He figured that for her, the opportunity to do a human replication was such an accomplishment that she didn't want a distraction getting in the way. For her, a man at death's door was only a distraction. What was the difference between one Adam and the other? They were identical, weren't they? One was the same as the other, except that one was damaged goods and dying, while the other was the picture of health.

Charlie grabbed his phone, called Dean Fleck, and explained that Adam was in desperate need of medication. He gave Dean contact information for Dr. St. John and told him to coordinate with her and contact the flight dispatch office to scramble a plane for an emergency run. Charlie knew that Dean would do his utmost, but he worried about Gina. Would she provide the level of care that Adam's precarious condition required?

Dean did his magic and had the batch of phage back before the end of the day. Charlie was there with Gina when Dean delivered the material personally. Gina seemed engaged as she briskly gave directions to her staff. The previously placed artificial skin appeared impregnated by underlying necrotic tissues and had to be removed. Then the underlying tissues had to be cleaned to remove the greenish-tinged bacterial-infused products of the Pseudomonas infection. Once again, the artificial skin had to be sprayed on, but first the phage treatment had to be applied. Gina used half of the phage material to create a solution that could be applied topically with a spray applicator. Afterward, the nanofabric was overlaid. The remaining phage material was used to create a solution that could be administered intravenously.

"What do you think, Gina? Is this gonna work?"

"Charlie, try to remember this wasn't my idea. No, I don't think it'll work. Give me a break. You think you're going to cure Adam with sewage? You wanted to try it. Okay, we've tried it. If this doesn't work, maybe you can come up with another batch of slop."

"Okay, Gina, I get it. You don't like it, but I'm counting on your professionalism to see to it that Adam is cared for with perfect attention."

Chapter 45

The next day, nothing much had changed, but at least Adam wasn't worse. The second day, he seemed to be doing a bit better. By the third day, even Gina acknowledged improvement. Was the phage treatment really working, or was he improving because the infected skin had been removed and the underlying tissues cleaned?

"Gina, I'm gonna call Shari and give her the good news."

"Hold on a minute, Charlie."

"I know, I know, you wanna wait and see if his recovery is real."

"That's not what I was going to say. What I was going to say is that Shari already knows Adam's recovering. I told her a couple of days ago."

"But we're just now starting to see improvement. What would you have told her a couple of days ago?"

"I told her he was finally making progress. In fact, she's already visited with him downstairs in the ICU. Just between us, let's call him Adam B."

"What are you saying? That's not Adam."

"Everyone else thinks so. You're the only one who doesn't. Look, we've been over this before. In every imaginable way, that is Adam downstairs. Go see for yourself. What you see up here in this lab is a sick man, critically ill. Despite the improvement you think you see, he's still going to die. I know you're having a hard time coming to terms with this, but even if he did miraculously survive, he'd suffer serious, probably incapacitating, handicaps. Which Adam do you want for a friend? Which Adam does Shari want to live her life with? Who would you pick to run BrauCorp?"

"That guy downstairs, your Adam B, is a fake, a fraud. I can't call him Adam. Maybe he doesn't suffer handicaps, but that's not Adam. This man here is Adam."

"I think you need to think this through. Why don't you go downstairs and see for yourself? Go talk with Shari. She's wildly excited now that she's seen Adam B recovering. Whatever you tell her, for God's sake, don't tell her about our lab experiments. That's gotta wait."

"You expect me to play along with your fraud?"

"Fraud? Don't make me into a criminal. Do you really want to throw Shari into a hellish turmoil? At this point, she's finally feeling hope that her husband might actually survive, and now you want to come along and crush that hope? Do you really want to tell her that the man she thinks is her husband is not really her husband? Do you want to tell her that her real husband is the terminally ill invalid hideously sequestered away in our lab? You're nuts. You can't do that."

"What am I supposed to do—lie to her?"

"This is what you do. You go down there. See for yourself. Meet Adam B, the new Adam. Talk with Shari. Then ask yourself which Adam she should choose to make her life with."

"You've put me in a box. Adam was still alive when you invited her to visit the fake Adam B. Why would you do that? We were still trying to keep Adam alive."

"Because there was no hope. Adam is terminal now. He was even worse then. There was no hope."

"No, you denied the hope. You're utterly infatuated with your experiments. You couldn't see that there was still hope. Now you've created something . . . I don't know what you've created."

"You're way off base. That something isn't something I created. As I recall, it's something we created. Get it? We did it together. And we did it following Adam's instruction. Like I said, go downstairs and see for yourself, but don't tell Shari. We'll worry about that later, if we have to."

"Okay, I won't tell her for now. I can't, but you better watch over Adam up here with the best possible care. I promise you, if he dies, there's going to be an investigation. I'll see to that. I don't think you want that to happen."

"You got that right, Charlie. I don't want that to happen."

Chapter 46

Charlie went downstairs and was relieved that Shari wasn't there. He knew he couldn't look her in the eye. Adam B was alone, attended to only by medical staff. He was resting quietly. The artificial skin that was protecting Adam upstairs was gone. This Adam had been made to look like his own new skin was growing in. The tangle of spaghetti that was sustaining Adam's life upstairs was no longer necessary downstairs. There still were IV lines and sensor wires but not nearly as many. He was not intubated as Adam was upstairs, and neither did he need an oxygen cannula. It was amazing. He had the appearance of a victim of violent trauma but looked more like a patient at rest than a comatose man lying near death. And despite the induced disfigurement, he was immediately recognizable as Adam. Charlie wanted to reach out, touch him, rouse him. He would tell him how relieved he was that he was recovering. But then he remembered this was not Adam—or was it?

Just then, Shari walked in. "Charlie, where have you been? You've been staying at my house, but I haven't seen much of you. And now that Adam's finally making progress, you're nowhere to be seen."

"I'm sorry. I've been sleeping here at the hospital, keeping a watchful eye on Adam. I wanted to get back to you at home, but I couldn't leave. Too much going on."

"You've been here with Adam? Why haven't I seen you? Where have you been?"

"There's been too much going on: reviewing medical protocols with Gina and handling business matters with Janet and Gary."

"Oh, Charlie, it's a miracle. I thought I said my last goodbye, but now Adam's survival is looking possible. Gina says they expect to see signs of consciousness within the next few days."

"Well, I'm sure she knows what she's talking about."

"What's wrong, Charlie? You don't seem happy or hopeful. Is there something you haven't told me?"

"No, I'm just exhausted. Adam's survival is a miracle. Gina's a miracle worker. I can't wait to talk to Adam. I hope to be here when he regains consciousness. That'll be cause for celebration."

Charlie couldn't tolerate being under Shari's watchful eye. He stepped out into the hallway pretending to answer a phone call. A few minutes later, back in the ICU, he told Shari he had to go upstairs to speak with Gina. As she turned toward him, he reached out beyond his guilt, took her in his arms, and enveloped her in a protective hug.

Clutching for his response, she started sobbing. "Tell me everything will work out. I have to hear you say it."

"Shari, everything's going to work out fine. And whatever happens, Laura and I will always be close by your side."

Charlie left Shari alone with whoever it was still lying unconscious in the ICU.

Chapter 47

For two weeks, Charlie was a haunted man. He sought relief but couldn't find it. The good news was that Adam, the real Adam, was definitely recovering. The viral phage treatment was working. The infection was stopped. The overcoat of artificial skin would soon be removed to expose his own newly regrowing skin. The bad news was that Adam, conscious and alert, appeared to be suffering from previously undetected brain damage. His speech was intelligible, but however complex his thinking might be, he could utter only short, choppy sentences. He had the strength to stand but couldn't coordinate his muscles or maintain his balance. Walking was nearly impossible. His gaze was more like a stare, and his responses were delivered in slow motion.

Gina's reaction was complicated. She had successfully treated and brought back to life a patient lying irretrievably doomed to death. This was a historical event. She could take credit for it, but she was conflicted by the fact that she had opposed the lifesaving therapy that made the recovery possible. Beyond that was the ultimate dilemma: how to adjudicate the conflicting claims to the identity of Adam Braudy. Downstairs there lay a conscious and recovering Adam Braudy, soon to be discharged, while upstairs was a brain-damaged Adam Braudy still suffering from disfiguring wounds and other profound impairments. The scars and injuries might be remedied with multiple surgeries involving replicated body parts. And with time, the miracle of brain plasticity might mitigate Adam's brain damage, but all that lay ahead.

Shari was visiting Adam B downstairs for long hours every day, relieved that her husband had been restored whole to life, even if he did suffer a curious amnesia. That amnesia saved him from the horrors of his nearly fatal encounter but also left him unaware of the events of the preceding week. Though Gina knew better, she and other consulting specialists expressed confidence that even those lost memories might eventually be regained. Regardless, Adam had his life back. He and Shari spent their time together declaring their love for one another and looking forward to his move home.

Charlie spent a lot of time tending to BrauCorp's business affairs and visiting Adam upstairs. One evening, Laura and Charlie were talking at home with Shari.

"Charlie, why haven't you been in to see Adam? He's been asking for you. He wants to see you."

"I've been in to see him," Charlie lied. "Unfortunately, he's been asleep so much of the time."

"He hasn't been sleeping that much, unless you're going in to see him in the middle of the night."

"Well, actually, my days have been a blur. It's a madhouse tending to everything that goes on at BrauCorp. I never imagined what Adam's days were like. He's been a very busy guy. Now it's up to me. I guess my visits were too late."

"In that case, why don't we go in to see him together? Do we really need to make a formal appointment?" she asked. "I know he'd like that. What do you say?"

"Sure, Shari. Let's do it tomorrow afternoon, say three o'clock."

Charlie didn't know what else to say. He had a visceral dislike for Adam B. His loyalty was bound up with the genuine Adam. He called Gina, told her about his planned visit, and instructed her to arrange for

Adam B to be taken out for any kind of diagnostic procedure at three o'clock. That would at least buy some time.

Charlie met Shari in the lobby and walked a long corridor with her to Adam's room. He was shocked to see him still there and tried his best to conceal his anger. Was it Gina's plan to force this meeting?

Adam B greeted Charlie with enthusiastic affection. "Where have you been, Charlie? I imagined you'd be the first person I'd see when I came back to life. Instead, it was some nurse. At least she was good-looking."

"You're looking great. You gave us quite a scare. We thought we said our last goodbyes. I guess you can't keep a good man down. Here you are, back to your old tricks. Good to see you."

"Shari tells me you've been incredible through all this, but what's kept you away?"

"I've been pressed into serving your business interests. What a lot of work. I don't know how you do it."

"Well, I'll be getting back to it soon enough. That ought to allow you to get back to your own life."

"My life will never be the same again."

"What do you mean?"

"Have you spoken with Janet or Gary yet?"

"Yeah. When I didn't see you, I put in a call to Janet. I wanted to get an update. I feel like the world has moved on without me. I need to get back up to speed."

"What did she tell you?"

"I'm not even sure what she said, but she thought it would be a good idea for me to check in with you."

"Well, the first thing to say is that you've got a case of amnesia. Not sure how current your recollections are, but we need to figure that out. But before we do that, I have to get to a meeting with Janet. Anything you want me to tell her?"

"Hey, what's going on? I talk with Janet, and she tells me to talk to you. You don't come in to see me, and now that you're here, you give me five minutes of your oh-so-valuable time, and then you want to turn around and bug out. Besides amnesia, am I nuts or something? Shari told me you've been out of touch with her too."

"Did she tell you I've been going nuts trying to manage BrauCorp in your absence?"

"She told me something like that, but she only mentioned it briefly in passing. Why do you ask? What's with all the questions?"

"Let's discuss it tomorrow. Right now I really need to move along."

"Fuck you, Charlie. I may still be in recovery, but I can figure out that you're not acting like a friend, at least not the friend you used to be."

"Look, Adam, you've been through a lot, but the rest of us have too. Let's talk more about this when I see you tomorrow. Right now I have to go."

Charlie felt like he was talking to a fraud. Adam didn't look like a robot, but wasn't that what he was? Just a fancy robot. But no one could tell, not even the robot. That was what made it so hard. The robot actually thought he was Adam. Charlie wanted to laugh out loud, but all he could do was smile and try to be nice. He never imagined he'd have to be nice to a robot. He could hardly stand being in the same room with him or it while the real Adam was upstairs, struggling to reclaim his life.

Charlie left the ICU and called Gina. When he told her he'd be coming over to her office, she said they should meet upstairs. When Charlie got there, he found her in conversation with an ever-more responsive Adam Braudy. Charlie was relieved that perhaps there was no brain damage after all. When Adam saw Charlie, he turned from his conversation with Gina and called out to him.

"Hi, Charlie. Glad to see you. Feel like shit but alive. Gina says I'll recover."

"Yes, you will. What a relief, though it will take time. That means you're gonna be one big pain in the ass until you're well enough to be left on your own. Damn, you look great. I can't tell you how relieved I am to see you."

"You'll give back BrauCorp? Thought wouldn't give up."

"Are you kidding? I think that for the past few weeks, I've done an acceptable job, but it's not for me. Glad to give it back whenever you're ready."

"Still feel lousy. Rely on you a while. Hope pay is good. All going well?"

Charlie lied. "Don't worry. Everything's going fine."

"Get Shari here. Anxious to see her. Tell her I miss her. Want her kisses."

Gina, who had been watching closely, coughed and turned away. Charlie stammered but finally managed to say, "Adam, we've got a little problem to discuss with you."

"Too many problems. Not now. Get Shari. That's first."

"That's not going to be easy, Adam."

"What? Shari's okay? More assassins? What's going on?"

"Adam, do you remember that last conversation we had before your lights went out? What do you remember?"

"All thought I was dying. Moved BrauCorp to you. Told you to make replicant. You did it, right?"

"That's right, Adam. We did it. We passed the voting shares of Brau-Corp to me, and we created your replicant. It was quite a success. You should be proud of your technology. It worked just like you planned. At least the replication went like you planned."

"There's a *but*?"

"Yes, Adam, there's a but—a very big but. You were going downhill fast. There was no way to save you. You were in shock, being consumed by a terrible infection. You were surviving on a mere trickle of blood flow from an unproductive heartbeat. There was no hope. Your organs were shutting down. But for a fading ember, you were already dead.

"But your replicant was alive. Shari came in to see you, but it was your replicant that she saw, an essentially healthy Adam Braudy. Her hopelessness, her devastating loss, was suddenly replaced by the reality of your survival. Or at least that's what she thought. When the sedation wore off, he became conscious. As far as Shari could tell, you survived, but in reality, it wasn't you; it was your replicant. She's been by his side ever since. He's conscious; he's whole; he's bright, conversant, and funny. He's you, Adam, in almost every way—except that he's not you."

Adam fell silent. His eyes had been locked on Charlie's but then closed as he turned his head away. Was he in denial, hopeless despair, or determined thought?

Gina knew Charlie needed a break and Adam needed to rest. She reached over and opened an IV valve that sedated Adam, allowing him a temporary reprieve from this new and perhaps most crushing ordeal.

Chapter 48

Charlie had to interact constructively with Adam B, but how? He summoned his courage and went back downstairs.

"Hi, Adam. Sorry I had to leave you so quickly before. I didn't want to end the day that way. Now that I'm here, let's chat a while."

"Charlie, I was awfully short with you before. I wasn't sure you were going to be back. This recovery thing has me a little jumbled and short-tempered. You know how I get when I'm not in control. And am I ever not in control. Truly, Charlie, I do have an idea of what you've been through, and I appreciate it. I know it hasn't been easy."

This was Adam's charm offensive in action. At least on this dimension, the replication of Adam was true to form.

"I need to get back into action. I need for you to catch me up from where I left off. This amnesia thing is weird. I can understand how it would affect my memory of the attempt on my life, the explosion, and the hospital stay, but I don't understand the lapse of the previous weeks. I need you to fill me in."

Charlie lied and told Adam B, "Gina told me that you'll probably recover those memories, though she couldn't say how long it might take. But never mind. I can fill in the blanks for you. Let's try to figure out what you remember. Do you remember the trouble we had trying to get Hal Parton's secretive midnight flight to Austin off the ground?"

"Yes, and when he finally got to us, scared half out of his mind, I remember him telling us about the State Department's unwillingness to help us."

"Do you remember Sam going off to Venezuela on his mission to deal with Vincent Poole?"

"Yes, I remember that, but I don't know how it worked out. If I know Sam, he got that bastard. Am I right, or am I right?"

"Adam, this is going to be hard. The mission was well planned to the last detail and then executed to near perfection. You wouldn't expect anything less from Sam, but there were things he couldn't possibly have anticipated. The mission failed, and the entire team, except for one of our men, was wiped out. Sam is dead."

A pall of sorrow spread over Adam B's face as he weighed this loss. Charlie watched him struggle with his emotions and forgot that he was talking to Adam B—the robot, the fraud, the usurper. Whatever or whoever he was, there was no mistaking the genuine anger and grief he felt over this loss. He was in pain, and the pain brought him to fury.

"Are you telling me that Poole is still alive? That son of a bitch is still walking this earth? I want him dead."

"Adam, he is dead. Even with Sam's loss, Dean immediately swung right back into action. I can tell you more details, but Vincent Poole is dead. There may yet be a continuing threat, but it won't be from him."

Adam had heard enough for the day. There was no way for Charlie to talk with him right then about Hal Parton's assassination.

Charlie said, "It's getting late. That's enough for today. I'll come in again tomorrow, and we'll catch you up the rest of the way."

Charlie got no pushback, which was not like Adam. Instead, Adam looked at him with sadness and nodded. Charlie touched Adam B on his shoulder. Adam B reached up to grasp Charlie's hand and held it firmly in his. It was warm to the touch. He was flesh and blood.

Charlie left flustered and pushed himself to go back upstairs to see Adam. When he came into the room, his friend was awake and staring out the window at a gloomy overcast sky. He turned his head slowly, cast a vacant gaze in Charlie's direction, and said, "Morning already?"

Maybe he was half sedated, or was he still enveloped in a fog of recovery? Was it depression, or was it something more long-term or permanent? Charlie told him he wanted to check in one more time before leaving for the day. Adam responded to Charlie's "goodnight" with a slow nod of his head.

That night, Charlie spoke with Gina. "I'm worried about Adam. He's not himself."

"Of course he's not, after what he's been through. Keep in mind that he's by no means recovered from his ordeal. There's going to be a lot more progress. But this afternoon, we performed a functional MRI study and found several loci of functional impairment."

Charlie knew an MRI was a high-tech gadget that had given him claustrophobia when he had to lie motionless in a terror tunnel while listening to hammers pounding his brain. But he had no idea what Gina meant by a functional MRI.

Gina kept it simple. She told him it's different from an X-ray or CT scan, both of which create images based on the fact that bone and other dense tissues are opaque or partially opaque to X-rays. She explained that in an MRI, a powerful magnetic field energizes individual atoms in the tissues being studied. When the magnetic field is relaxed, those atoms radiate energy. The energy measured is different for different kinds of atoms. Since different types of tissues are made up of different kinds of atoms, it's possible to distinguish among them. And because brain activity affects the atomic makeup of brain tissue, it's possible to map the location of brain activity.

But the simplest thing Gina could say was that in Adam's case, parts of his brain weren't functioning the way they ought to. What Charlie wanted to know was different.

"Is it permanent?"

"He suffered a major impact to his head when he was thrown onto the tarmac. Besides that, he was in shock, both at the time of the explosion and then again when he lay dying from the infection. On both occasions, his blood flow was so low that parts of his brain may have suffered from oxygen deprivation. That could have caused the brain damage we are seeing."

"So is your answer that the damage is permanent?"

"Yes and no. It's like with stroke victims. When there's damage to parts of the brain, there is some plasticity. That means that other parts of the brain, healthy parts, can take over for the damaged parts. It can take training and time, but there can be a recovery of lost functions. We're not necessarily going to see it in the short run. It can take months or even several years. Even then, there would likely still be a remaining deficit."

"Can't we just replicate brain tissue and replace the damaged parts?"

"That's an idea we've given a lot of thought to, but at this point, it's just experimental."

"So when Shari comes up here to see Adam, she's going to see a man compromised by the violence done to him."

"Well, only if she comes up here."

"Why wouldn't she come up here?"

"Because her husband is downstairs. We've been over this. Do we really need to go over this again?"

"Well, I suppose you could slip Adam B past her as the genuine article if Adam were dead. Even then I'm not sure that would be the right thing to do. But he's not dead. He's very much alive, and he's going to recover. What do you intend to do about that?"

"I don't know, Charlie. But I can tell you this: if you didn't go off half-cocked and get that sewage sludge therapy, we wouldn't be worrying about this now, would we?"

"Gina, you've been spending way too much time in your lab with rats. You really need to get out more often. There are human qualities that you seem to be missing. I guess it's true. You really were content to let him die. And now I suppose you want to cloister him away up here and maintain him as an experimental subject."

"Charlie, I understand your concern. Give me some time to think about our options. We can talk more about this later."

Chapter 49

The next morning, Charlie went back in to see Adam B to tell him about Hal Parton. Adam B recognized Charlie's reluctance, which put Charlie on edge.

"Adam, yesterday I had to tell you that Sam was killed. Today I have to tell you that Hal Parton was killed too. It was Vincent Poole's doing, but under whose orders we don't know. He was getting into his car. A planted bomb was triggered when Hal started his engine. It killed him instantly. He never knew what hit him."

Adam B turned his head away for a moment. When he turned his face back toward Charlie, his gaze was piercing, his complexion pale. "Leave me alone for a while. I'd like to be left alone."

"I understand. I'll check back with you later today. There's more we need to talk about."

Charlie's visits with Adam upstairs had left him resentful and angry with Adam B. But when he spoke with Adam B about Sam's death and then Hal's, he saw in him the heartfelt emotion of a troubled soul. Adam B was feeling the pain of personal loss. His grief and sense of loss were genuine. He was hurting.

Like a yoyo, Charlie went back upstairs to visit with Adam. The attending nurse was checking the readings on the various instruments monitoring his condition and ensuring that the IVs were feeding properly. When she was done, she stepped out of the room and left Charlie and Adam alone.

Adam turned his head to see for himself that the nurse was gone. He said, "Get me out of here."

"What? You're in no condition to be moved. There's no place to move you to."

"If not, I'm dead."

"What are you talking about?"

"Gina's strange. Used to be close. Always worked together. Fed each other hopes, dreams. Doesn't talk to me now. Only at me. Cold. I'm only a patient. Adam B taking my place . . . with Shari and now Gina too. I'm in her way. She must get rid of me. Get me out of here."

He sounded paranoid, but Charlie didn't think his worry was unfounded. He didn't know what Gina had in mind. They hadn't yet had their conversation about how to proceed. Despite his brain damage, Adam sensed something that Charlie was slow to accept, something he couldn't face. He wanted to tell Adam to wait and see, but Adam's instincts were almost always right. Charlie couldn't dismiss his concern, especially given his own conversations with Gina.

Adam was relieved when Charlie told him he would do it, but he didn't know how to make the move. Gina was the one person Charlie would have gone to for help, but who could he turn to now? Adam said, "Do quickly. No time."

Charlie decided he would turn to Dean Fleck. After all, he'd gotten Adam released from the hospital. In addition to Dean, medical expertise would be needed from someone who knew Adam's situation. It was risky, but he approached Debbie Grant, who had worked so hard to save Adam's life by tracking down the viral phage treatment.

"Debbie, I don't think I properly thanked you for all your help. Your initiative in tracking down the phage treatment was impressive. Gina got top billing, but you deserve a lot of the credit. Believe me, your achievements won't go unnoticed around here."

"Thanks, Charlie, that's a nice gesture, but I don't think I'll be around here much longer."

"Are you being recruited away? That would be a huge loss for us."

"No, that's not it at all. I've been content to work alongside Gina. She's amazing and has always moved Alan and me up the ladder right by her side, at least until now."

"What's happened?"

"She's been unhappy with me, angry in fact. I'm not sure why. Maybe she's embarrassed that she hadn't done her part to follow up with the pickup of the phage from Dr. St. John. Ever since then, almost every interaction with her has come with criticism—in my view, unwarranted. I don't think I have a future with her. I've invested plenty of time and energy with her, only to be discarded—a *persona non grata*. I haven't started looking for a job yet, but I probably should. I'm wondering what kind of recommendation I might expect from her. I don't think I'll get much of a job if she blackballs me."

"Don't worry about Gina's recommendation. I'll talk to her, and, regardless, you'll always get my recommendation. If that's not enough, we have lots of ways to get you a plum position. I'll see to that."

Charlie couldn't believe his good luck. The door had opened wide. He felt confident he could get Debbie to help move Adam and manage his care. "In fact, Debbie, I have a job for you right now. This is hush-hush. Not a word to anybody. I need you to keep everything I'm telling you to yourself. Adam and I, not Adam B, are convinced that Gina sees him as a problem, a threat to everything she's accomplished with replication technology, a threat to her personally and professionally. We fear that Adam's life may be in danger. We need to move him. You would work with our security people to move him to a safe place where we can properly care for him. You'll be happy with the pay, and professional opportunities will be abundant. I need you to work with us on this."

"Charlie, I can't believe that Gina would allow any harm to come to Adam."

"You're probably right, but remember her dereliction already almost killed him. In any event, we're not going to wait to find out. We have to move him now. I need your help."

Debbie was silent for a long pause while she chewed on her lower lip. Because Charlie needed her, he was anxious to offer more encouragement. But he knew that he should just keep his mouth shut, wait for her response, and be prepared to answer any objections she might raise. Charlie was relieved when she offered none.

With an expression tinged with uncertainty, she said, "Okay. I'll do it, Charlie, but it sounds creepy. If this creeps me out, I promise you I'll disappear."

"You don't have to worry. Your role in this is straightforward. It's not going to creep you out. If anything or anyone bothers you over this, let me know. I'll protect you."

Chapter 50

Debbie didn't say a word to anyone—not to Gina, Dr. Simmons, Alan Samuels, or even Adam. She consulted closely with Dean to help arrange for an ambulance with the equipment needed to ensure Adam's safety. With Debbie's help, Dean was able to find a ranch property for rent located not too far from a major hospital near San Antonio. The relative isolation of the ranch made it suitable for harboring a fugitive. The house was quickly outfitted with communications gear and medical equipment. Even though Adam was stable and recovering, and would be attended by Debbie, she and Charlie both thought that the presence of a skilled physician was advisable. Finding a suitable physician was a tall order. How many qualified physicians could there be who would be available on short notice to tend to a single mystery patient at a remote location?

Dean provided Debbie with the names of nineteen physicians along with their CVs. She had no idea how he'd come up with his list, but she quickly eliminated twelve of them and expressed serious reservations about the remaining seven. She asked Dean for more names. Within hours, he provided her with five more. She then dismissed the entire first list and was relieved to find two candidates on the new list who looked promising. For each, she placed follow-up telephone calls to references, former employers, and associates. She had video interviews with both candidates and was satisfied to settle on Dr. Warren

Paulson. He had experience as an ICU doc who was under a cloud of controversy because of accusations that he was screwing his nurses, which, of course, he denied. He was anxious to work and was immediately available.

Debbie and Dean decided the early morning would be the best time to make their move. Debbie got herself on the staff rotation for that shift. She also managed to get Pauline Mathews, a coworker Debbie was friendly with, assigned as the second nurse on duty. When Debbie and Pauline began their shift and when the two nurses on the preceding shift left after finishing their paperwork, Dean appeared in Adam's room. Debbie, who was Pauline's senior, explained the details of the transfer protocol as it was clearly outlined in the official hospital documentation. Pauline was a little taken aback but had no basis to question the transfer. Debbie enlisted her help in disconnecting the tubes and wires that wouldn't be needed until they could be reconnected in the ambulance. That would be a twenty-minute undertaking. With Adam secured to the gurney, they started wheeling toward the door.

That's when things went badly. Gina was a workaholic who put in too many long hours late into the night. That night, tired and bleary-eyed, she looked up from the clutter of papers that littered her desk and scanned the video screen she had set up to monitor Adam's room. What she saw triggered an outburst. "What in the hell is going on? What's Dean doing there?"

She bolted from behind her desk and dashed to check out whatever mischief was going on. Just before Debbie and Dean could make their getaway, Gina, in a mad scramble, nearly collided with the gurney with Adam secured on board.

She cried out, "What's going on here? Where are you taking him? Why wasn't I notified?"

Dean said, "We have instructions from Charlie. He's authorized this move. That's enough for me."

"Sorry, Dean. That's not enough for me. Unless there's some kind of emergency, nobody moves my patient without authorization from me or Dr. Simmons. Charlie's got no authority in this matter."

He pressed the gurney against Gina until she was forced aside. "We beg to differ."

"You can't get away with this. I'm calling security. They'll put a stop to this."

"Good luck with that. Those guys work for me. I'm kinda thinking that they're gonna be taking instructions from me."

Gina was furious and made good on her threat. Two guards came rushing to the ICU. Partway down a long hallway, they ran headlong into Debbie, Dean, and Adam.

One of the guards said, "We just got an emergency call from the ICU. You know anything about what's going on?"

Dean said, "Yeah, I know all about it. You don't need to worry. Everything's under control. You might as well get back to your security post, but be ready for a heap of questions and paperwork."

Dean and Debbie continued down the empty hallway to the waiting ambulance, where the crew helped load the gurney on board. Dean and Debbie clambered on right behind.

With necessary drip lines and wiring properly connected and everything secured, Dean said, "Come on, guys. Let's move out quick time. And stay off of highways and busy streets if you can. I don't really want to have to explain anything to the cops."

With lights flashing and the siren wailing, the ambulance lurched forward along its way. Two and a half hours later, they arrived at the ranch house that would be Adam's new home.

Chapter 51

Several days later, Charlie flew to see Adam at the ranch. Travel time by car would have been burdensome, but with a BrauCorp helicopter, it was less than forty-five minutes each way. Charlie boarded the chopper and took off from the BrauCorp campus, where he had established his office.

Upon arrival, Charlie found Adam sitting up and alert with only a couple of tubes and wires tethering him to machines. He saw that Adam's artificial skin had been removed, and his own skin was growing back. Though his appearance was hideous, there was hope that subsequent surgeries and skin grafts would restore a more normal look. A broad grin stretched across Adam's face. Charlie wondered if any of the IV infusions that Gina had ordered had contributed to his previous malaise.

Adam called out, "Hey, Charlie, glad to see you. Didn't think you'd be able to find your way to my little hideaway."

Charlie couldn't believe he was speaking in whole sentences. "I couldn't, but your pilot knew the way. You look great. How 'bout you introduce me to your two friends?"

"You already know Debbie. She's been a lifesaver—literally." As he spoke, he turned his head in her direction with a broad smile. She responded in kind.

"And this is Dr. Warren Paulson, my staff physician. He manages this extraordinary staff that's charged with keeping me alive."

Dr. Paulson, a tall, fiftyish man with graying hair, stepped forward and shook Charlie's hand with a hand that had never been acquainted with a blister or callous. "It's a pleasure to meet you." Charlie couldn't help but wonder about the truth surrounding the sexual harassment charges that upset his career.

Adam's speech displayed much of its former cadence and nuance. His vocabulary seemed expressive, and he projected his voice with ease. After a bit of chatter, he asked Debbie and Dr. Paulson to excuse themselves.

"Charlie, getting me away from Gina saved my life. I'm convinced of that. Within days of my escape, I started feeling remarkably better."

"Maybe you were already getting better. Regardless, you look good, and you sound good too. Maybe now that you can talk like a regular person, we can figure out a plan."

"I've been thinking a lot and have a plan in mind. I presume that no one knows about me and my replication yet, even Shari?"

"Yes, that's right. Shari doesn't know. Only you, me, Debbie, Gina, Alan, and Paul Simmons know. Oh, and Dean too. There was no way I could engineer your escape without that full disclosure."

"Does Adam B know? Does he know he's a replicant?"

"Not as far as I know."

"Does he know yet about the transfer of BrauCorp to you?"

"I don't know. Probably."

"Why probably?"

"Because he would have found out from Janet, who he would have consulted with right away. And he would know from Shari, who probably discussed it with him."

"Okay, then let's go with those assumptions until we find out otherwise. Keep alert and let me know if they prove wrong."

"Since we're talking about Shari, when would you like me to bring her out here to get reacquainted with her husband? As it stands now, she thinks Adam B is you. This is going to take some careful preparation. When she finds out that Adam B is your replicant, she's likely to suffer some kind of horrible shock. It'll be a nightmare. I'm not sure how we're going to pull this off."

"I can't worry about that now."

"What do you mean? You have to. She's your wife. She's making a life with Adam B. You can't just leave her like that."

"I have to, Charlie. There's no choice. I'd risk the disclosure of the replication project. There's too much at stake. I can't allow that to happen. Besides, if she saw me now, she'd prefer Adam B for sure. He's intact. I'm not exactly at my best."

"What are you talking about? You're not giving her credit. I think you owe it to her to confront her with this face to face. If you don't, you'll only be sorry later—very sorry."

"Charlie, I've thought this through. I've made my decision."

"It's a bad decision, Adam. You sound like an iceberg. Shari's your wife. You've got to find a way to bring her back into your life. And you've got to do it now before it's too late."

"Get off my back. I told you I made my decision. I don't need more of your advice on this. I'll get back together with Shari in my own way, on my own timetable."

Was Adam suffering from brain damage? His judgment about how to deal with Shari seemed crazy but otherwise, he seemed competent to resume command of his identity and his empire.

"Okay, Adam, let's hear your brilliant plan."

"The first thing I expect is that when Adam B finds out he gave you operating control of BrauCorp, he's gonna want it back. You will resist that."

"But the agreement says he can take it back. If he thinks he's Adam Braudy, how do we resist that?"

"He can't just take it back. He's gotta buy it back from you for value, right?"

"That's right. He just shoves a bunch of money at me, and he gets it back."

"No, Charlie, if he doesn't pay you enough, you won't sell it back to him. The agreement says he's gotta pay you for value. You got any idea what the value of BrauCorp is? I bet you don't, and neither do I. If we don't know, that means he doesn't know."

"But it can be determined."

"Yes, it can. If it came down to a dispute, there would be a legal action and an appraisal to make a determination of value. Do you have any idea how long that would take? Absent any mutuality, and with legal finagling, it could take years before he could regain control."

"That would only delay things. We'd just be buying time."

"That's all we need to do. We'll buy time while we work the rest of our plan. In time, he'll come to learn that he's not Adam Braudy after all. That will end his claim for good."

"Why not tell him now that he's not the real deal? That way, you can take back control and get on with your life."

"I can't do that. If I did, knowledge of the replicator would become public. I can't allow that, at least not now. I hate to say it, but you were right from the start. This technology is wrong. It's wrong for me, and it's wrong for humanity. We have to undo it without it becoming known."

"Adam, you can't undo it. The few people who know about it are already a few too many."

"We'll figure out a way to deal with that. The first step is to shut down the machinery before anyone gets wise to what we're up to."

"How do we do that?"

"That's where you come in. To start with, you're gonna block and deflect Adam B's attempt to take back control. To launch that effort, you'll fire Adam B. Get him off the campus and out of your hair. Make him unwelcome anywhere in or around BrauCorp. Get a restraining order. You're gonna cut off payments to him of every kind including the distribution of dividend payments on the ninety-five percent of BrauCorp stock that he and Shari still own. And cut off his computer access too. At the same time, you'll have to fire Gina and chase her off campus. Have her ushered out without access to her lab and files. Work with our computer techies to make sure she can't access or get away with any documents or data she presently has access to. She's probably feeling safe right now because she has an ally in Adam B. She's in for a big surprise. Can you do this, Charlie? It's gotta happen fast."

"I don't know. Your plan seems plausible. I gotta think it through. I like the direction. Can I get back to you on it?"

"Of course, take your time. Start your thinking and get back to me. You have five minutes."

"Seriously, how soon do you need to know?

"I'm not joking. You have five minutes. Don't let me down."

Chapter 52

During those first few days following Adam's escape to the ranch, Adam B was discharged from the hospital. At the estate, Shari and a nurse were at his call. On Charlie's first trip back from the ranch, he got a text from Adam B asking for a meeting as soon as possible. Charlie didn't respond. He had plenty to talk to Adam B about, but that had to wait. Charlie first had to have a conversation with Dean to ensure that a muscular security plan was in place to facilitate the terminations. Once back at the campus, Charlie called an urgent meeting with Janet and Gary.

"Thanks for making yourselves available on short notice. We've got lots to discuss."

Janet said, "I hope this won't take too long. There's a lot going on right now."

"Our meeting probably won't take more than an hour, but the follow-up will turn your schedules upside down. We have to plan for the terminations of two high-level employees."

They were perplexed. Janet was, after all, the CEO. Charlie and Adam before him were chairmen of the board. Her job was to run the day-to-day business of BrauCorp subject to the general directions of the board of directors. In the case of BrauCorp, even though the chairman functioned as the board of directors, terminations were "for cause" as determined by management, meaning by Janet or her underlings. Charlie's involvement would be an unconventional intrusion and clearly a departure from procedures established during her tenure as CEO. Charlie was about to let loose a tidal wave that would upset the established norm of behavior between CEO and board chair.

"Janet, this will come as a surprise, but it is my instruction that we must immediately terminate the employment of Dr. Virginia Salter and Mr. Adam Braudy. If located on a BrauCorp facility, they are to be removed under strictest supervision and are to be prevented from any access to any physical or intellectual property whether equipment—including computers—or files, either in hard copy or digital form. Further, we must ensure that they have absolutely no access to BrauCorp's computer networks. I want restraining orders secured. They need to know that we are determined to deny them any access whatsoever."

They were stunned and silent. From their expressions, Charlie could see that they were sure he had lost his mind. After a long pause, Janet said, as though she were trying to calm a lunatic wielding a gun, "Certainly, you have the authority to take these actions, but can we talk about this first?"

"We don't have time for that. This needs to happen immediately."

Charlie's urgency redoubled their judgment of his insanity.

"Would it be too much for us to ask why you want to do this?"

"I wish I could tell you, but I can't. I can assure you, though, that I'm not taking these steps lightly. These terminations are key to the survival of BrauCorp as a responsible corporate citizen."

"Look, Charlie, Gary and I have worked closely with Adam these past ten years. We've developed a collegial, professional relationship that has developed into a bond of respect, admiration, and even friendship. I don't know what to say about Gina, but regarding Adam, I can't see throwing him under the bus."

"There is much I want to tell you but can't. What I can tell you, though, is that this is ultimately in Adam's best interest."

"That's a good line. Why don't we ask him if it's in his best interest?"

"First, we don't have time. Second, he's not currently in a position to fully understand the direction we're taking."

"Let's see here: I've worked intimately with Adam for ten years;

I've had multiple visits with him this past week as he's prepared himself to take back control of BrauCorp; and he exhibits the physical, emotional, and intellectual capacities of the Adam I have always known. On the other hand, I hardly know you at all, though I remember you quite clearly questioning whether Adam was nuts to turn the chairmanship over to you. I'm beginning to think that's the case."

"And I remember you saying that Adam knows what he's doing and that you wouldn't want to bet against him. Maybe you remember that too." Charlie couldn't get their agreement. "Janet and you too, Gary, have my decision. I want these terminations to take place immediately. I understand and appreciate your personal loyalty to Adam, but if you can't act on my decision without hesitation, then I'm prepared to replace either or both of you. And if you refuse to perform in accordance with my directions, and if information pertaining to these dismissals reaches Adam or Gina, you will be held responsible for damages. Those damages will be extraordinary, and you'll be tormented for years by legal action I'm prepared to take. Why don't the two of you talk this over? I'll leave you alone for a few minutes. When I get back, I expect your answer."

When Charlie got back, Janet said with resolve, "Gary and I quit. We won't be a party to this. We're out of here today. When Adam takes back control, I'm certain we'll be back too."

"You better be prepared to find interim employment. It'll be quite a while till Adam and I work out a buyback."

"You know, Charlie, you're a poser pretending to be Adam's true and loyal friend. What a load of shit. You're the lowest scum. You're just another opportunist, a Judas, a schemer of the worst sort. You can rot in hell, where I hope you'll stew in the slime of your betrayal."

Charlie felt a thump in his chest. His stomach cramped. He did his best to hide his hurt. Janet's remark cut deep. Despite what he knew to be true, he felt the guilt of her accusation, though it was not really his to bear. Here he was, acting on Adam's instructions, working as best he could to restore him to the life from which he'd been swept away. Had

Janet known what he knew, she'd think him a hero. Instead, she saw him working his own interests, undercutting Adam when he was most vulnerable. He tried to take comfort knowing that she would eventually recognize how wrong she was. Until then, to her and to Gary, too, he was just slime, and with their slanders, he'd be seen that way in ever-widening circles.

So that made two more high-level terminations to manage. They would be tricky. Charlie spoke with Dean to let him know what was going on and then with Bob Winston, BrauCorp's CFO. Adam had told Charlie about him and said he might be able to step into Janet's role someday. Charlie thought it odd that Bob didn't seem concerned about the terminations. He worried that he might be morally indifferent, not a trait he wanted in a new CEO. Perhaps Bob recognized that there might be factors lying outside his purview. In any event, Charlie coordinated with Dean and took care of Janet and Gary, seeing to it that they were relieved of all their duties, cut off from any corporate access, and ushered off campus. He had the legal department begin preparing restraining orders for Janet, Gary, Gina, and Adam.

Then Charlie called and reached Gina in her office and explained that he was coming over for an urgent meeting. Dean and two of his security agents went with him. The two agents waited in the hallway while Charlie and Dean walked in. Gina's assistant showed them in to see her without delay.

"Glad to see you, Charlie, but I don't want to discuss anything with Dean here. He and I have had a difficult time recently, and because of that and other reasons, I think our conversation should be kept just between the two of us."

"It really doesn't matter. On my way over here, I've been trying to figure out the best way to tell you this, but I guess I should just come clean and tell you that you're fired. Dean is here along with two of his security agents, who are outside in the hallway. They will supervise your immediate departure."

Gina's face blanched white. She stood frozen, still as a statue. She and Charlie faced one another in awkward silence. She might well have tipped over and fallen to the floor, cracking into pieces. Finally, though her ashen pallor held fast, her eyes began to dart. Then her facial features stirred, and her shoulders stiffened.

She stammered, "You can't do this, Charlie. Adam's my boss, not you. Adam can fire me. You can go to hell."

"No, Gina, I can fire you, and I've done just that. Adam is no longer your boss. I am. And I can assure you I am not going to hell, though it wouldn't surprise me if that's where you end up. You have one hour to gather your personal property. You may not take with you any Brau-Corp property or work products. That means keep your hands off telephones, computers, and files. Dean, please call in your security agents. Oh, and Gina, it would be unwise of you to speak with Adam B. He doesn't know that he is a replicant. We will be taking steps to mitigate the problems arising from his replication. You will probably find it in your interest to cooperate with us in these efforts. If you discuss Adam B's replication with him or anyone else, you're going to end up in a professional ethics nightmare that could put an end to your medical career, not to mention the possibility of civil suits and criminal prosecutions."

Her demeanor pretended at calm as she spoke in a quiet voice. "You know I have an employment contract."

"Of course you do. Did you think we might have forgotten? No, Gina, you don't have to worry about that. We're more than happy to buy out your contract on very generous terms. You won't even have to hire a lawyer. We can discuss those financial matters soon, presuming, that is, you act responsibly."

With everything appearing to be under control, Charlie and Dean left Gina with her two chaperones while they headed off to the helicopter pad, where the chopper was waiting to take them to a meeting with Adam B at the Braudy estate.

The Braudy's neighbors didn't like noisy intrusions when helicopters landed at the estate, but because of the urgency, Charlie couldn't be concerned. Adam B was in shorts and a T-shirt, happy to enjoy the warm sunny morning while waiting at the landing pad. Upon arrival, Charlie and Dean stepped onto the pad as the whine of the chopper's turbines wound down.

As they approached, Adam B seemed surprised to see Dean stepping off along with Charlie, but it didn't keep him from displaying a broad smile with arms outstretched, ready to hug.

"Charlie, I'm glad to see you and especially to welcome you here at home rather than in the hospital. I can't believe I've got my life back. I know it's in no small part because of you. Thank you for all you've done, not just for me but for Shari too. You and Laura have been wonderful. We can never thank you enough. We are forever in your debt. And, Dean, that goes for you too. We're indebted to you. Your efforts have sheltered us from disaster. Your work has been superb. Thank you."

Charlie and Adam made small talk as they walked to the patio. Shari and Laura came out to join them. Helene had prepared coffee and pastries. It was one celebratory reverie among old friends with Dean standing in as a spectator. They enjoyed the coffee and pastries while taking turns recalling the threats and fears that had impacted them. It seemed like a long time before Adam B moved the conversation to plans going forward. "I'm glad you're here. We've got lots to talk about."

As if on cue, Shari said, "Laura, why don't you and I take off and leave these guys to their scheming? We've heard their stories. I don't think we need to hang around any longer."

After Shari and Laura left, Adam B said, "Several days ago, Janet briefed me on the agreements we executed creating voting shares of stock in BrauCorp, transferring them to you and then installing you as chairman. I've been told by everyone that you've done a superb job. And just between us, I understand there were some sticky issues that you handled quite skillfully. Thank you, Charlie, not just for your friendship but for all you did while I was out of action. Anyway, you can see that I'm the picture of health, healthy of mind and body. I'm ready to resume management of BrauCorp. I want to unwind those agreements. When everyone figured I was a goner, I can see how it might've seemed like a good idea but not now, looking back in retrospect. Let's unwind the deal and pay you handsomely for your extraordinary contribution."

Charlie had prepared for this moment and had rehearsed his lines out loud in front of a mirror. He was also buoyed by the successful experience he had when he fired Gina. But this was different, and Adam B noticed Charlie's delayed response.

"What do you say, Charlie? Cat got your tongue?"

"No, Adam. As much as I've prepared for this moment, there is no easy way for me to tell you that I must insist on standing with the agreement as it is written."

"What?" he blurted. "What's this about—money, power? You got used to moving in big circles? You like smart people coming to you with big ideas? You like the idea of being worth a few billion dollars?"

"Adam, there's no way I can explain this to you. I've got my reasons, and it's got nothing to do with wealth or power."

"Look, Charlie, we can find a role for you in BrauCorp that will make you a vital participant, a major player, not just in that company but in the highest ranks of the industrial world. We haven't even put a number on a settlement price. I'm prepared to negotiate with you around a substantial sum."

"Sorry, Adam. Like I said, it's got nothing to do with wealth or power. Let's move along. You asked me here, but I have urgent reasons of my own. I have to ask for your separation from BrauCorp in every capacity. I don't have to ask you to resign from the position of chairman since that's already done, but I do need to terminate your every connection with BrauCorp except as a passive holder of stock. That means severing your access to labs, offices, equipment, material, and files. Your computer access has already been suspended. A restraining order is being prepared to prohibit you from access to the campus and to prevent you from being in contact with any employee or contractor of BrauCorp. You have computer gear here at your home. I ask that you surrender it forthwith."

"Wow, Charlie, am I impressed. You were my buddy, a junior partner, my valued helpmate. Who knew that you had the balls to pull off this kind of shit? You are a piece of work. Gotta tell you I am impressed."

"Sorry it has to be like this. I couldn't figure out any other way. A signed handwritten note attesting to your resignation will suffice. Let's do it now."

"No, fuck you. I won't do it. You want to fire me? Go ahead. I'm not going to cooperate with you in any way. If you want my computer gear, you better get a court order and have your *polizei* come collect it. I'm not turning anything over to you."

Charlie reached into his breast pocket and retrieved a folded piece of paper, which he passed to Adam B. Adam B unfolded it and saw that it was a formal notice of the separation he had described.

"Ya know, Charlie, we've been friends since we were kids. You've been my closest personal friend. I've always relied on you. And I've been very generous with you too, always making room for you in my businesses. Where's the respect I'm due? Doesn't our friendship mean anything to you? What is it, Charlie? Have you been feeling diminished as a mere recipient of my charity? Where has my friend gone?"

Charlie recalled the many times that Adam was there for him. He was there when Charlie was courting Laura. He was at their wedding, the best man. When Sandra died, he and Shari dropped everything to be with Charlie and Laura, to support them through that horror. These and other occasions came to mind without him having to say a word. While Charlie felt those hammer blows inflicted in rapid-fire succession, he forgot that he was speaking with Adam's replicant and not with Adam. As was the case with Janet and Gina, he felt Adam B's accusations hit him where it hurt most. Indeed, what kind of friend was he, after all?

"Adam, I'm mindful of your many acts of friendship. They are not unappreciated. If you knew what I'm dealing with, you'd make the same decisions."

"What bullshit. I'd never treat you like you're treating me. I believe we're done here. Get your ass out of here. You and Laura have been our house guests. Get Laura and get your shit out of my house. You are not welcome here—not now, not ever. And, by the way, you can expect to be spending a lot of time tied up hand and foot with legal proceedings. I'm gonna sue your ass off. You may want to find an apartment near the courthouse 'cause that's where you're gonna be spending a lot of time. Just to let you know."

"I'm not surprised. We'll see how that's gonna work for you. I don't think you're gonna be happy with the results. Only time will tell. See you in court."

Charlie went into the house to find Laura. She was laughing and drinking coffee with Shari. Laura looked up and said, "Have you boys finished playing? Are you ready to move on to other things?"

"Laura, we've gotta get out of here. We've been told to pack up our belongings and get out. Dean's at the chopper, getting ready for departure. We need to cram and scram. I'll explain later."

She looked at Charlie in disbelief and then turned to Shari, who, like her, was left without words. Charlie grabbed her hand. She was startled into silence as he tugged her to her feet and towed her up the stairs to the suite. When the door was slammed closed, Laura started shouting.

"What on earth is going on? You can't just pop in and drag me around like you just did. I'm not a little girl or a rag doll. Who do you think I am? Hell, who do you think you are? You can't do that."

"I'm sorry, Laura. I truly am. You deserve better. I've just gone through a day filled with one nightmare after another. This one is the worst. I've come to sorrowful blows with Adam. I fear it's beyond repair. We have no choice but to leave right now without further discussion."

"Without further discussion? Are you crazy? You can't do something like this and tell me 'without further discussion.'"

"There will be lots for us to discuss, I promise, but it must wait till we're out of here. Please, Laura, trust me; help me. I need your help on this. Please don't fight me. Not now."

Charlie turned away and started stuffing their belongings into their suitcases. Laura reluctantly followed suit. Finished, Laura, still bewildered, followed Charlie back downstairs. As they passed Adam B and Shari on their way out the door, Charlie evaded eye contact with both of them. Laura and Shari exchanged expressions of puzzled confusion and sorrowful doubt.

Adam B called out, "Good riddance, you miserable son of a bitch."

Charlie said nothing but urged Laura on. As they approached the helicopter, its turbines were whining and its rotor turning. With their seat belts buckled, the pilot took note and lifted off for the trip back to BrauCorp.

Chapter 53

In the cabin, the pounding thump of the rotors was overwhelming. Laura's ears felt battered, but more distressing was her dismay at being ripped away from Shari without explanation.

"Charlie, what on earth is going on?"

"Adam is furious because I refused to transfer back to him the shares that he transferred to me and because I terminated his every connection to BrauCorp."

"You did what? I don't understand. Why wouldn't you give back the shares? Why would you terminate him? I don't get it. What's going on?"

Charlie knew what he had told her sounded absurd. He was confused and didn't know what to say. He felt bound by his pledge of secrecy, but with that secret kept, what could he possibly tell Laura that would make any sense at all?

Finally, he blurted, "I have my reasons. You have to trust me on this."

"Of course I trust you, but what reasons could you possibly have? Why won't you tell me?"

His mind tumbled as he struggled to think of an answer that might be convincing. "You know there are threats on Adam's life and on Shari's too. I have to keep what I know secret to protect them and to protect us from those same threats. If you were to know what I know,

I'm afraid that the safety of all of us would be at risk. Mine is already at risk."

Laura was quiet as she gazed out the window, looking down on the landscape below. From two thousand feet, who knew what love or turmoil might be found within the walls of the homes passing silently beneath them? And along that dirt road branching from the highway and winding its way through the hills, what peace or woe might be found around the bend at its unseen end? Tears welled up in her eyes and then trickled down her cheeks. Hurt and confused, she didn't know what to think. She brushed aside the arm Charlie extended to comfort her. She was in pain. Charlie felt abandoned. They were both trapped in a prison of promises and lies.

When they landed at BrauCorp, with a wall of silence between them, they went straightaway to a spacious penthouse guest suite set atop the tallest building on the campus. That would be their home until they could figure out a better plan. Charlie wanted to talk with Laura, but she repeatedly rebuffed him. He knew her silence was only temporary. Soon enough, she would have plenty to say.

Charlie needed to see Bob Winston, the new CEO, and was relieved to leave Laura and the pounding silence.

"Bob, are you seeing any problems with our terminated employees? How are the restraining orders coming?"

"We got Janet and Gary out without a lot of trouble. We did have a little argument over a laptop computer. That was resolved by letting Gary take it, but only after first removing the hard drive and wiping the computer clean. We were careful to remove everything. If he wants to use that computer, he'll have to reinstall a hard drive and an operating system."

"What about Gina? How did that go?"

"Not good. She's got one hell of a temper. The security agents got into it pretty good with her. There was a lot she wanted to take with her. She told us she'd sue us to get everything she claimed belonged to her. The agents took an inventory and pictures of everything she was claiming. Then they asked her to sign the inventory. She didn't want to do it. She finally did when they threatened to destroy the inventory list. Like Gary, she also wanted to take her laptop. When they told her she couldn't, things got a little physical. She was pissed and threw the damn thing at one of our agents. He dodged it, and it ended up on the floor busted in pieces. Don't think it's gonna help anyone now. She finally left with our escorting agents, leaving the busted pieces on the floor."

"How about the restraining orders?"

"They're ready to go. We'll get 'em over to the county courthouse tomorrow. We ought to be able to get a judge to sign off on them by the end of the day. How did it go for you with Mr. Braudy?"

"Badly. Whatever property Mr. Braudy holds is still in his possession. I'd guess he doesn't have too much on his computer. I think most everything he saves to memory goes straight onto the corporate cloud server. I hope he doesn't have a local backup facility."

"Well, we can file for a subpoena to seek access to any computer or corporate property he may have. If we can get a hold of his computer gear, we can find out about any backup facilities he's using."

"A waste of time. He can figure out a workaround. I just hope he's not holding on to important data or info."

Chapter 54

Adam insisted that he and Charlie should avoid the use of electronic communications. He was paranoid that his existence could be discovered, that his replication technology might be revealed. He insisted that frequent meetings would enable them to minimize vulnerable communications. That meant frequent flights. The question then became how to conceal Adam's identity from Tom Melano, the helicopter pilot, and from Dr. Paulson.

Tom Melano was a recent hire who was unacquainted with Adam. He was retired Army—short, grizzly, mean-looking, with never much to say. He carried himself like he might have when he was young, when he was muscle and bone. He was still muscle and bone, but now he carried a little extra baggage around his beefy midsection. After flying several thousand hours in military choppers, his Army career crashed with a smack-up in a poorly maintained Apache that left him with a nasty-looking scar and a military disability. His scrape might have scrambled the brains of a lesser man but not so in Tom's case. He got his job with BrauCorp by demonstrating remarkable flying skills and an uncanny calm under pressure.

Hiding Adam from Tom proved easy. But how to explain Debbie? Around the ranch in warm weather, Debbie often dressed in short shorts and tight-fitting tees. She looked hot. It was easy for Charlie to leave Tom with the impression that he was having an affair with her, and, in truth, he wished he were. Though shyly reluctant at first, she finally agreed to encourage that impression by greeting Charlie's arrivals with enthusiastic hugs. Because Tom also had to be kept away from the house, he was made to wait in the helicopter, the ranch guest house where Dr. Paulson was living, or around the grounds, never in the ranch house.

It was trickier with Dr. Paulson. He had a legitimate need to see Adam's medical records, but they decided not to disclose his identity. If there were a slip-up, there would be one more person who would come to know about the replication. Because they couldn't allow that, they redacted every reference to Adam's name in the records provided. Although that aroused Dr. Paulson's suspicions, it was unavoidable. In any event, that level of secrecy was part of the job description.

Because there was so much going on, Charlie flew to see Adam almost every day. He also spent a lot of time working with Bob Winston. But Charlie's work was, for the most part, as a stand-in for Adam, whose need to control was extreme. Adam would brief Charlie on what to say and to whom. Then, later, he'd debrief Charlie on all his interactions to mine the smallest nuggets of detail. Adam insisted that nothing was too inconsequential to be ignored. Charlie witnessed the relentless drive and focus necessary for Adam to accomplish all he had achieved.

Adam's recovery was now moving quickly. At last, he was free of his tubes and wires, but his body and especially his face were horribly disfigured. Debbie, who knew the capabilities of the replicator, assured Adam that after further healing, plastic surgeries using tissues they could produce would transform his appearance.

Dr. Paulson became restless and wanted to move on. He suggested that Debbie stay and supervise Adam's continuing progress. He offered to remain available for consultations, for periodic checkups, and for emergency visits should the unlikely need arise. With Debbie's concurrence, Adam reluctantly agreed but only on the condition that Dr. Paulson would stay on Adam's payroll and remain on call in the San Antonio area.

Charlie had thought that Debbie would be the first one to get cabin fever and want to move on, but that was not the case. He became aware of a warm and playful interaction between her and Adam. She appeared quite content to remain. Charlie and Debbie maintained the affectionate arrival act they had adopted to keep Tom suspicious of his "affair," but as time went by, she seemed less comfortable with the fiction and more comfortable with Adam.

On one visit, shortly before Dr. Paulson's departure, Charlie arrived and found Dr. Paulson alone in the house. Adam and Debbie, he said, were out for a walk. Charlie was anxious to intercept them. He feared that Tom's impression of Charlie's relationship with Debbie might be compromised if he were to see Debbie return to the house in the company of an unfamiliar man. The ranch property was expansive. It had broad flatlands and meadows, bare knolls, wooded glens, and swampy lowlands. Charlie headed out on a trail suggested by Dr. Paulson.

He'd been walking for about fifteen minutes when he saw Adam and Debbie partially hidden from view in the shade of several trees. They were naked, their clothes tossed aimlessly here and there. He couldn't keep himself from watching. Adam was lying on his back with a prominent erection while Debbie was straddling him and getting ready to mount. Charlie's eyes were fixed on Debbie's alluring body as she managed penetration and began gliding rhythmically up and down. Engaged as they were in their growing frenzy, Charlie didn't have to worry about them noticing him. Debbie started slowly and gradually built up to a quicker pace. Finally feeling embarrassed by his intrusion, Charlie had to haul himself away.

From a distance, he called out Adam's name. He wanted it to appear that he wondered where they might be. On hearing Charlie's call, Debbie quickened the pace that brought them both to a rollicking climax accompanied by a mix of moans and giggles. What followed was a flurry of activity as they quickly dressed and headed back in the direction of the ranch house.

When they caught up with Charlie, they agreed that he would go ahead and let them know when they could move quickly, unnoticed, into the house. Once inside, Adam asked Debbie to excuse herself while he and Charlie settled into a conversation. Adam was anxious to hear details about recent meetings and suggested solutions to current challenges. Then he moved to a different path. "I've been giving a lot of thought to our problem with Adam B. I've had a terrible time figuring out how to proceed. At this point, as hard as I've tried, I've only been able to come up with one solution."

"I've been thinking, too, but came up empty. What occurred to me was to give him a bundle of cash and have him go off and retire on a Caribbean island. Then I realized that would never work. He's just like you. Retirement just wouldn't suit him," Charlie concluded.

"You're right about that. The only thing that will work is to terminate him."

Charlie's expression was one of bewilderment. He remained silent while he struggled to understand Adam's use of the word *terminate*. After all, Charlie had already terminated Adam B's every association with BrauCorp. What was left? Sensing Charlie's confusion, Adam repeated his proposed solution.

"Here's the deal. Adam B has taken over my life. He's living in my house. He's fucking my wife. He's aiming to get BrauCorp back, and unless his fake identity is uncovered, he eventually will prevail. In that case, the replication technology will be exposed. I can't allow any of that to happen. He must be terminated."

Charlie got his meaning more clearly than he wanted to. "You know, Adam, I was beginning to think that you came through this assassination attempt in good shape, but now I think that you've got some wires crossed. Adam B's living in your house and fucking your wife because you gave him the keys. What in the hell did you think would happen? You could have included Shari. She's your wife—a loyal, loving wife, incredibly so. She's a strong woman and plenty smart too. She knows her way around. She could have been your partner. You abandoned her to Adam B. That was your doing, and now you want to complain that he's fucking her? That's rich, and all the while you're out in the pasture fucking Debbie. Now that really shows a lot of class."

"I've got my reasons."

"Yeah, I bet you do."

"Fuck you, Charlie. Debbie sees my disfigurement and looks right through it."

"Sorry, that doesn't wash. What makes you think Shari wouldn't see through your disfigurement? Face it: you screwed up real bad. How the hell are you gonna fix that now?"

"Like I said, there's only one solution. Adam B has to be terminated. By that I mean he must be stopped, put to an end."

"You mean you want to kill him?"

"No, not kill him. Maybe *terminate* is the wrong word. That word has too much baggage. The right term is that I want to turn him off. And for that, I'll need your help."

"I won't do it. I won't kill for you. That's murder."

"No, it's not murder. He's only a replicant, a robot. He's borne of a machine. Hell, he is a machine."

"I'm not gonna debate you. As far as I'm concerned, he has every attribute of human life. He's as alive as you and I. As far as I'm concerned, what you call *terminating*, or whatever word you want to use, I call *murder*."

"Charlie, he doesn't have a birth certificate. He has no independent identity, no family, no personal history. Hell, he doesn't even have a Social Security number. How's that for lack of identity."

"Very funny, but I'm not laughing."

"Look, he's nothing more than a fancy robot. Every robot has an on-off switch. Adam B has one too. All we have to do is turn him off."

"What do you mean?"

"Do you remember when you were concerned about creating a replicant, how wrong you thought it was? I was impressed with your judgment but felt I wanted to give it a go anyway. And do you remember when I was lying near death, pleading with you to be involved in my replication, and I wanted you to be a check on Gina?"

"What's that got to do with an on-off switch?"

"Even before you expressed your concerns, those concerns were already on my mind. That's why I programmed into the replication process an on-off switch. A replicant needs such a switch. It only needs to be activated. That's not murder. We'd just be turning him off, turning off a machine. He's a machine. That's all he really is. That was one of the roles I foresaw when I urged you to be a check on Gina."

"Adam, one of my biggest fears about creating a replicant was that it would harbor some dark flaw and turn out to be a monster. I was wrong; that's not what's happened. You created a replicant who, as far as I can tell, is a perfectly decent human being. Did you hear me? A human being. That's to your credit. He's no monster. The supreme irony here is that you created your replicant, and now it's you who have become the monster."

"Nice one. You want to make me the monster, but what are you? Have you forgotten that it wasn't me who created the replicant? It was you and Gina who threw the switch. I wasn't even there."

"What a load of shit; it was your invention, it was your decision, it was your pleading that insisted on the replication."

"Oh, poor, pure Charlie. You're the one who had all the ethical and moral reluctances. Where were you and your principles when push came to shove? You're all heart and soul now, but where were you when you violated your oh-so-deeply held principles? What other calumnies might you perpetrate if only I pleaded with you? Get off your high horse, and let's get down to the business at hand. You threw the switch to turn him on. Now you can throw the switch to turn him off."

"No," Charlie shouted. "I won't do it. Whatever harm I've caused is bad enough. I won't compound it. I'm done with this."

He turned away from Adam and stormed past a bewildered Debbie in the adjoining room. He shoved the front door open and fled the house as if it were on fire. Then he caught sight of Tom, who was waiting in the helicopter. Walking toward him, Charlie held up his right arm overhead and swung it in wide circles, signaling he wanted a quick departure. By the time he was seated, the turbines were already whining. Liftoff wasn't fast enough.

Charlie knew what he had to do. Without his assistance, there was no telling how or when Adam would make his next move. He couldn't take any chances. He had to get to Adam B and Shari to warn them of the threat.

Chapter 55

Charlie wanted to talk with Shari alone first but couldn't imagine how to do that without including Adam B. On the way back to Austin, he called Adam B, but the phone just rang. There was no answer. Was he refusing Charlie's call? He left no message but texted, "Life death. Must c u and shari. Arriving by chopper in 20."

Adam B was pissed but met Charlie at the landing pad. "What do you want? We have nothing to talk about."

"There are things you need to know. You and Shari are in grave danger. I need to talk to both of you."

"Dean's my security guy. Why am I hearing this from you?"

"First of all, Dean works for BrauCorp. He doesn't work for you anymore. Second and more important is that he doesn't know yet what I need to talk to you about."

"This better be good. Then I'll decide whether to include Shari."

"No, it's both of you or nothing. Let me remind you we're talking life and death, yours and Shari's."

After a searching pause, Adam said, "Okay, we'll do it your way. Wait on the terrace while I go find her."

Charlie walked to the terrace and took a seat. He had no idea how to talk with them about any of this. Shari didn't know the first thing about the replicator, and Adam B had no clue he was a replicant.

It was a restless five minutes before Adam B returned with Shari.

They took seats across from Charlie at their table. "Okay, Charlie, here we are. Let's get this over with."

"Remember when I was here last, I told you that if you knew what I was dealing with, you'd make the same decisions I made?"

"Nice cover. What a load of bullshit."

"No, not really. Now you're gonna hear what it is that I'm dealing with and what the two of you will need to deal with too."

"Enough drama. Just lay it on the table."

"Adam, you're not really Adam. You're a replicant of Adam Braudy. We know you as Adam B."

"Whoa there, asshole. That's a hoot. Is that the best you can do? If that's what you came here to tell me, you can get back on your chopper and get your ass out of here."

Shari, mystified, turned to Adam B. "What's he talking about? What's a replicant? Who's Adam B?"

Adam B grumbled to Shari, "Charlie and I are done here. Go inside. I'll fill you in on the details after I get rid of him."

Charlie cut in. "No, we're not done. Not by a long shot. You both need to hear this. Your life is at risk, and, Shari, your life is about to be turned inside out. Let's put this on the table, shall we, Mr. Adam B?"

Shari's plea was desperate. "Adam, please tell me what he's talking about. Do I have to hear it from Charlie, or are you going to tell me?"

"Look, it's just a project I've been working on."

"What kind of project would lead to this kind of trouble? Am I missing something? Have we talked about this?"

"No. I've been working on this for a while now." After a pause barely long enough to charge his courage, he added, "It's on the edge of fantasy. That's why I've had to keep it secret."

Hurt and dismay flushed over Shari's face. "You had to keep it secret from me? What kind of secret would you have to keep from me?"

"When I tell you, you'll understand. I've been developing a replicator."

"Oh, that explains everything. Now I get it. It's a replicator. That's why you had to keep it a secret. No, Adam, I actually don't get it. Don't you think this might be a good time to tell me about it?"

"I didn't mean to keep you out. I just lost perspective. It's complicated."

"Don't give me this complicated crap. Just tell me. Stop beating around the bush. What's a replicator?"

"It's a device that can copy anything, living or dead. It can copy a living animal, even a human being, together with its memories and behavioral traits. In the case of an animal, we refer to the replicated form as a replicant."

"You never thought to share this with me?"

"Let's talk about it later in private, okay?"

Charlie interjected. "No, we're not putting this off. We've got to deal with this right now."

"Adam, what does Charlie mean when he says that you're a replicant of Adam Braudy . . . when he calls you Adam B?"

"He's full of shit. He's playing some kind of angle here, and he thinks he can dismiss me—us—by claiming I'm not really Adam Braudy. You be the judge. Look at me. Look me in the eye and tell me who you think I am."

"I think you're my husband, Adam Braudy."

"Well, I'm glad you got that right."

"No, that's not right," Charlie said. "You are not Adam Braudy, not in the literal sense. You were created by a replicator, by a machine. I was there. I'm a witness. Adam Braudy was dying from his injuries and wanted to see himself replicated. Much to my regret, we fulfilled his dying wish and created you."

In utter disbelief, Shari turned to Adam. "Is this even possible?"

"I promise you I know nothing about this. I mean, of course I know about the replicator. It's my invention. Yes, it's possible to replicate a human, at least in theory. We haven't actually done it yet. Hell, we've replicated a lot of rats, that's for damn sure. I promise you I know nothing about me being a replicant."

"I'm dumbfounded," Shari said. "How is it you never told me any of this? How can I believe you about anything? What else are you hiding from me? Tell me, do you have a lover too?"

"No, it's nothing like that. I never imagined that it could come to this. And I'm telling you, Shari, I still don't believe it. Am I supposed to believe it just because this asshole makes this crazy claim? I don't think so."

A heavy silence descended. It was finally breached when Adam B, shifting to take the initiative, launched a challenge. "What's your angle on this? Are you presuming you can keep me from taking back Brau-Corp because I'm not really Adam Braudy? Is that it?"

"No, that's not it. I'm trying to protect you."

"You're trying to protect me? That's a laugh. Is this how you go about protecting me? Even if what you say is true, how do you imagine that it's protecting Shari and me to start stirring this up? Why wouldn't you just keep your mouth shut? Isn't that what your dying Adam Braudy would have wanted?"

There was no way for Charlie to soften the blow. If there was, it was beyond his grasp. "I told you that as he lay dying, Adam pleaded with me to create his replicant. And I've told you that I fulfilled his request and that you're the result. What has brought me here to tell you is that Adam Braudy, beyond anyone's imaginings, survived and is recovering. He literally came back from the dead and now wants his life back, the one you've taken from him."

"Oh, tell me another. Who writes your material?"

Shari bolted from her chair, saying, "I can't listen to this anymore."

Adam B, with a sudden thrust of his hand, desperately reached out to grasp hers before it might be lost to him forever. He managed to catch it, but she reflexively yanked it away. "Leave me alone. Who are you anyway? You might be Adam Braudy, but does it even matter? I don't know you. You cut me out of your life. You're not the Adam Brady I thought I was married to."

Shari turned and walked away. Adam B ran after her and spoke to her, hoping that Charlie couldn't hear. "Don't leave, not now. You can leave later if you have to. I know listening to this bullshit is hard, and I know you're angry and don't trust me, but we have to hear him out. Then we can judge it. I don't want this to break us apart. We're stronger than that. But if nothing else, let's at least hear what Charlie has to say. Then we can move forward one way or another, separately or together."

She looked into Adam B's eyes hoping to burrow into the place where truth resides. She was moved by what seemed like candor even while she remained guarded by her doubts. "I'm scared and don't know that I can trust you. I don't know what to think. I don't know what to do."

"I don't either. I want to kick Charlie in the ass and get him out of here. I don't trust him after what we've been through. But then I think we owe it to ourselves to at least hear him out. I need you to hear this too."

Adam B guided Shari back to the table with a gentle touch on her back. He said to Charlie, "Why should we believe anything you tell us?"

Charlie's throat seized up, threatening to choke off what he had to say. "There are a few people who are aware of your replication. If you could trust any one of them, maybe that would persuade you. Or you tell me. You know the replication process. There must be a way to tell a replicant from an original."

Adam B's face went blank and cold, color draining away.

"What's the matter?" Charlie asked. "What are you thinking?"

Adam B remained silent as Shari watched his stoic expression. She said, "You know something, don't you? What is it?"

He sat dismally silent and brooding. "I'm suddenly more frightened than I've ever been in my life—that's if I've ever even had one. God help me. I don't want to know."

Shari said, "You don't want to know what?"

"I'm suddenly afraid to find out whether I'm Adam or Adam B."

"I understand," Charlie said. "But you have to know. Things can't go on like this. Tell me now: is there a way to determine who's who?"

Adam B explained, "When we designed the replication process, we knew we had to be able to distinguish between an original and a replicant. We figured out a way to place markers in the unused sections of DNA, the sections that don't code for anything. Except for occasional errors in cell division, every cell in the body has the same DNA. Those are the genes that determine every aspect of each of us and make us, genetically, who we are. They're identical throughout the body. That means all we need is a DNA sample from any cell. We can grab a little DNA from a single hair. Then just examine it to see if it bears the marker. If there's no marker, we're looking at the original. If there is a marker, we're looking at a replicant."

Chapter 56

"I'm going to give Gina a call," Adam B said. "I bet she can clue me in on what's going on."

More than anyone else, he knew she would be able to testify to his true identity. But it wasn't just her testimony he sought. He wanted evidence. He wanted proof. She could analyze a specimen of his DNA.

"No way," Charlie exclaimed. "I fired her. She's a killer. She tried to kill Adam. You can't trust her. Stay away from her. There are other ways to examine your DNA."

"No, Charlie. You don't trust her, but I do. I have no idea why she'd want to kill Adam, but she handled me like I was her baby. Besides, do you really want an unknown lab looking at my DNA? If I'm a replicant like you say I am, they're gonna see my markers and wonder what planet I came from. I don't think you want that any more than I do."

"But I fired her. She no longer has access to our lab. How can she test your DNA without a lab?"

"That's no problem, Charlie. You'll give her access to your lab."

Like Adam, Adam B was ultimately persuasive. But how to reach out to Gina? Given the nasty confrontation, Charlie could only guess how badly their next conversation might go. It didn't surprise him when Gina didn't answer his call, but a day later, she responded to his voicemail with a call that was thick with caustic animosity.

"Well, Charlie, it's nice hearing from you after all this time. I hope BrauCorp is tanking under your pathetic leadership. Tell me, what's the occasion for your call? What is it you want from me that I won't do for you?"

"Come on, Gina, don't be bitter. Can we cut the crap here? You must know I wouldn't call if it wasn't important."

"Important for who—you or me?"

"For all of us. It's urgent. You have to speak with Adam B and let him know who he is, how he came to be replicated. I told him, but he doesn't believe me. He wants you to test his DNA, to report on the presence or absence of the replication markers. He trusts you. There's no one else."

"I can't do that. He knows that I won't. Many months ago, in thinking about replicating a human, it was clear to both of us that we'd never divulge that kind of information to a replicant. In the event of a human replication, that would have become an ironclad protocol."

"No Gina. You created your protocol in an entirely different situation. That was then. This is now. Everything's changed. The protocol you discussed didn't presume a living original. In this case, Adam is still alive, and he wants his life back. I don't know what he's going to do next. He wanted me to terminate Adam B, meaning kill him. Right now I'm trying to protect him. I've warned him, but he doubts my intentions. If you don't help, Adam B will write off my warning as a conniving plan to steal his identity. I need your help."

"I can't believe this. This is your doing. If you had just let Adam pass on, we wouldn't be in this mess."

"I don't want to reopen a debate with you. What's done is done. Let's move on. Can I count on you?"

Charlie desperately wanted her help but wondered why she might agree. Would it be out of sympathy for Adam B, the product of her relentless effort to perfect the replication technology?

Adam B was relieved when Charlie told him that Gina would help and would welcome his call. He spoke with her, saying, "That snake Charlie claims I'm a replicant and Adam, the original, wants me out of the way. He calls me Adam B. How's that for a laugh?"

Gina grasped that Adam B wouldn't accept any assertion she might make without evidence. "Adam, why are you calling me?"

"Charlie claims you were involved in my supposed replication."

"If I told you that you're Adam Braudy or if I told you that you're Adam B, would you believe me?"

"Look, at this point I don't know who I can believe about anything. I know who I am. I am Adam Braudy. I'm not a replicant. I want you to test my DNA. To make sure the results aren't faked, I want to work side by side with you. I want to eliminate any uncertainty. As it stands now, Shari doesn't know what to believe. I want to dismiss this sick joke and get on with my life."

"I guess you know that Charlie fired me. I don't have a lab."

"Not a problem. Charlie agreed to let us use the BrauCorp lab for this single occasion."

"Do you want me to tell you right now if you're the real Adam Braudy?"

"No, that won't do. All I really care about are the lab results. How's nine tomorrow morning?"

———

The next morning at the lab, they sat down over a cup of coffee and brushed up on lab procedures. Adam B was already familiar with them but appreciated the review. Afterward, they started by taking three samples: a strand of hair, a bit of saliva, and a superficial scraping of skin from Adam B's forearm. They would test all three to check for consistency.

After a long morning, they sat together going over the test results. They saw that Adam B's DNA carried the replication markers. There was no outrage, no fury, but color drained from Adam B's face, and his expression went blank. He sat still like a dead man propped up. Fearing a violent explosion, Gina kept her distance. After several endless minutes, he emerged from his stupor. He was devastated but surprisingly unsurprised. A morose Adam B spoke frankly to Gina with an air of resignation and despair.

"I did recognize the possibility. When Charlie first made his claim, I was terrified, but it kind of made sense. I had a hard time imagining how I managed to survive intact from such a devastating explosion. And then that odd amnesia bothered me too. It didn't escape me that my missing memory went back to my last scan. I didn't want to believe it and hoped that our work here this morning would be a relief from a nightmare. I guess life doesn't always offer relief."

With a sympathetic tone that seemed strange coming from her, Gina asked, "What will you do now?"

"I don't know. I guess the first thing is to talk with Shari. I have no idea how to tell her or how she might respond. Since my return home from the hospital, we've enjoyed a sweet time, thankful for our life to-gether, maybe closer than we'd ever been. We had a homecoming and a coming together that flushed away a lot of the tension that we'd been living with for a long time. We felt cleansed. Then along comes Char-lie, who turned our lives into agony. Now I have to tell her I'm not her husband, that she's been sleeping with a stranger."

"No, not exactly. You're no stranger. Remember that you are a pre-cise replication of her husband. But there is a significant difference that you can't ignore. The original Adam has to live with his brush with death. That has left him with injuries both physical and emotional, in-juries that you don't bear."

"What do you mean?"

"He's got to be suffering from post-traumatic stress. I don't know how severe, but I bet he's not sleeping much at night. Although a lot of his injuries were fixed with several surgeries and organ replacements, his body can't have fully overcome the physical shock and distress he sustained. For another thing, he's suffered a severe concussion. We al-ways suspected brain damage. And he's horribly disfigured too. Maybe a good plastic surgeon can help, but these things together impact him and his relationship with himself and with the rest of the world. No, Mr. Adam B, the two of you may be the same in many ways, but make no mistake: you have become two very different people."

"Gina, we're like identical twins. We're fundamentally the same."

"Yes, that's exactly right, but identical twins aren't really identical. They share the exact same genes, and they certainly look alike, but from the moment the first division separates them into two separate embryos, they experience life differently. Maybe one has a better blood supply. Maybe one gets squished too much in the womb. Maybe one gets a headache from being the first to squeeze through the birth canal or gets yanked by forceps. Maybe a hundred maybes. And that's just at birth. Moving on through life, think of accidents and illnesses. People who know identical twins can nearly always tell them apart, even just listening to them speak. Like I said, you and Adam are two different people. Everything we do or don't do changes us in one way or another. Living life changes us for better and for worse. I don't think Adam Braudy has been changed for the better."

"That's all just a lot of theory. I have to deal with reality. I don't know how I'm going to do it, but I'm going to fight like hell to make my life whole. It's my life. There's no way I'm going to give it up."

Following his meeting with Gina, Adam B called Shari. "We have test results. I'll be home within the hour. We have lots to talk about."

"Tell me. What are the results? You're my Adam, right?"

Without hesitation, he said with a tenderness she had rarely heard from him, "Dear Shari, I can't answer that question. What I can tell you is that Charlie was telling the truth. I am a replicant. Whether I'm your Adam is another question, one that only you can answer. Let's talk when I get home. That is, if it's still mine to come home to."

Next, he called Charlie. "Well, you miserable son of a bitch, it looks like you were telling the truth after all."

"Of course I was. You may be a replicant, but you still know me.

How could you think I'd abuse you the way you feared? Look, there's no way I can know what you're going through. Your experience is unique in human history. But I'm Charlie Wood. Remember me?"

"Yeah, Charlie Wood. I do remember you. And I remember you saying that if I were in your shoes, I'd make the same lousy decisions that you've made. Maybe that's true, but there's something you said a couple of days ago that stuck with me. I'm still trying to wrap my head around it. You said something about replicating me and regretting it. Is that right?"

"Yes, there are moral and ethical dilemmas. Just look at the mess we now find ourselves in. For me, the whole idea of replicating humans is repugnant. Actually, I find it inhuman."

"Well, try this on for size. When Shari was pregnant with Jess, we were filled with hope and joy. Wanting to be good parents, we thought it would be a good idea to get together with friends who were in similar circumstances: new parents, pregnant couples like us, or couples hoping to get pregnant. We invited experts to come speak with us. We had a pediatrician at one meeting, a noted child psychiatrist at another. We had a midwife nurse come talk to us about birthing, and on another occasion, we hosted a rabbi."

"What? You, the ultimate skeptic, turning to religion?"

"No, not me. It wasn't my idea. This rabbi comes in dressed all in black. It's a hot day, but he comes in wearing black pants, a long black coat, and a tall, wide-brimmed black hat. His long beard is streaked with lots of gray, and he's got long curls of hair, also graying, hanging down in front of his ears. He walks around the room with a gentle smile, introducing himself as Rabbi Goldshteyn, and shakes hands with the men and nods politely to the women. Anyway, early in the discussion, he asks us to think about the greatest gift we ever received. I was hoping he wouldn't ask me directly because the first thing that came to my mind was the red Ferrari that Shari bought me when we first started making serious money. I was relieved that he didn't ask me, but he did ask Shari. What do you think she said?"

"I have no idea."

"She said that I was the best gift she ever received. Boy, did I blush over that one and felt really silly for thinking about the Ferrari. A friend, a new dad, said their newborn baby girl was the best gift ever."

"How did the rabbi respond?"

"He applauded the suggestions but said we were missing something fundamentally important."

"What was that?"

"He said that each of us had received the gift of life. He said that was the most precious gift of all. And he added that it was to our credit that we were now, in turn, giving that most precious gift to children of our own. In that capacity, he said we were serving as instruments of God. In that way, we were approaching the divine."

"Why are you telling me this now?"

"Because, you jerk, you gave me life. You brought me in from out of the void. Do you truly regret that?"

"You don't understand. This has been a never-ending nightmare."

"For you maybe, but however troublesome it may seem to you, for me it's life. I don't know where or how we go on from here or how much pain we'll have to endure, but I'm alive, Charlie. I'm alive. I don't regret that, not for one minute. And I'm not too proud to say to you *thank you*. I'm not so sure about you being an instrument of God, but there's no doubt in my mind that I'm indebted to you for my life."

"I hadn't really thought of it that way. I gave you life. I did that." A proud smile took form on Charlie's face. "And I didn't even have to change your stinky diapers."

"That's right, but we still have a cleanup job to do. For the first time in my life, I have no idea how to move on."

"Let me have a shot at it. Let me go back to Adam and let him know about your discovery and your recognition of how complicated this is. Maybe that's a way for the two of you to come together."

Chapter 57

That afternoon, Charlie flew out to see Adam. As the chopper touched down, the blast of air thrust down from the rotor kicked up a thick curtain of grit and dust. Waiting for it to settle gave him a moment or two to collect his thoughts before facing Adam.

Once in the ranch house, Charlie found Debbie looking tantalizing. She was wearing her white shorts and a peach tank top stretched thin. It was practically transparent. It was hard to imagine that Adam, though sitting at his computer, had been hard at work.

Adam didn't greet him. Instead, he said as though he were tossing crumbs over his shoulder, "When you left here last time, you were plenty pissed. I didn't expect to see you again or at least not this soon. Did you forget something, or is there something you want to tell me?"

"I didn't forget anything. I remember it all too clearly. I came back because there are developments you need to know about. I remember, a while back, struggling to find my way out of your maze. I did it then, though with difficulty. Now we've got a mess of a maze. Maybe we can put our heads together and find a way out."

"Oh? Now, it's 'we've got a mess.' Well, that's progress. Have you decided to pull the plug on that nasty little irritant?"

"No, I haven't. I'm not gonna kill for you, and I'm not gonna change my mind. What I came to tell you is that I spoke with both Adam B and Shari. I told them that he's a replicant and that you're still alive and want your life back."

Adam was quiet except for the drumbeat of his fingertips beating on the tabletop as he considered a response. For several long moments, he struggled to contain his anger. "I thought we agreed that we wouldn't tell him about this."

"A lot has changed since then. I have a plan I want you to consider. If you don't buy into it, this whole debacle will spin out of your control. You may not like my plan, but it will allow you more control over the consequences than any other option you have."

"I can't wait. Let's hear it."

"I want you to meet with me, Adam B, and Shari. It will be the first of several meetings during which we'll figure out how to divide up your respective interests."

"You're nuts. How would we divide up our interests in BrauCorp and its intellectual property? How would we divide up my wife and family?"

"I don't know, but unless you start talking, you'll end up with nothing or worse. How do married couples settle their differences in a divorce? And how do disgruntled business partners split up their interests? I'll tell you how. There's an impossible negotiation followed by an unsatisfactory settlement. But keep in mind that a settlement means an exit from purgatory. I know you're enjoying Debbie's company, but do you really call what you have here a life, sequestered here in the outback? This would be a chance to work out this problem and move on to a new life. There's no other way."

"Nice try, but my solution's better. Just turn him off."

"Sorry, there's no way your solution's gonna happen. Adam B has protection from threats of every kind, including you. I've seen to that. If something happens to him, you'll be a primary suspect. You may think his death at your hand wouldn't be considered murder, but I will find a way to see you prosecuted. Make no mistake about that."

"Since you don't sound much like a friend, you can get your ass out of here. Consider both you and your proposal dismissed."

Charlie didn't argue. He felt that Adam needed some time to

think. He left hoping for a response, and sure enough, the next day, Adam texted, "Idea has merit. Let's explore."

Charlie called Adam B and told him about Adam's willingness to meet. At first, Adam B sounded optimistic, but that was followed by a tone of wariness. For a man dismissed as a mere replicant, a pretender, he suddenly found himself established as an odd kind of peer. He understood something that Charlie missed. It wasn't possible for Adam to have moved that far that fast.

The next day, Charlie flew to pick up Adam B and Shari at their estate. As they got on board, there was no conversation between them. All the way to Adam's ranch house, their silence hung heavy between them. Was it the strain of their unsettled relationship, or was it worry about their encounter with Adam?

As the chopper settled for a landing, a gust of wind shoved the craft down hard. Wrenched and rattled, they fled the cabin without speaking a word. Charlie felt a knot in his stomach. Shari's eye twitched. Adam B wore a stoic mask that concealed his worst fear. Charlie was the first in the door and was relieved to find Debbie nowhere in sight.

Adam said, "Well, Charlie, welcome back to my humble home. I see you've brought some friends along. Won't you please introduce us?"

Shari, next in the door, was greeted by Adam saying, "Hello, Shari. I'm glad you're here. I've missed you."

Shari was frozen in place. She dismissed Adam's words, which were expressed without feeling. She was immobilized, tears welling up in her eyes. She gagged on a breath of air and began to cry, whimpering at first and then falling into sobs. Disfigured though he was, he was without a doubt Adam Braudy. She understood that Adam B was a replicant, but this meeting was the concrete evidence that made the replication real and undeniable.

Standing tall at her full height, Shari was nevertheless left trembling and in need of comfort. Adam didn't know what to do. Charlie knew it wasn't his role to intercede. It was Adam B who, after what seemed like an eternity, finally approached her and wrapped his arms around her. He combed his fingers through her hair and placed kisses on her cheek.

He had no idea what he meant when he whispered in her ear, "It'll be okay. We'll find a way out of this mess."

Seeing Shari comforted by Adam B's embrace, Adam recognized his failure. He bit his lip and cried out, "I can't do this. This meeting is over. Get out of here, all of you."

"No," Charlie exclaimed, "it's not over. There's too much at stake. This is probably the hardest part. We have to stick with it."

Adam picked up a large glass vase from the table and threw it, shattering it against the far wall. He stormed out and into an adjoining room, where objects were being thrown and were heard crashing on walls and floor. The sounds of heaving grunts were heard, a measure of Adam's fury.

Then there was a panicked woman's voice crying out, "Oh my God, Adam. What's going on? What are you doing?"

Debbie, who had been banished to a bedroom down the hall, was not about to be ignored any longer. She helped calm Adam and then went with him back to the meeting. Attired as she was, she made a most alluring entrance. Adam was rattled; Adam B was dumbstruck. Shari said, "Adam, what do we have here? Or, rather, who do we have here?"

"Shari, this is Debbie. She's a nurse and research assistant. She's been here monitoring my recovery."

"Well, Debbie, glad to see that he's in such good hands. What do you think? How's Adam's recovery going?"

With a sidelong glance in Adam's direction and the barest hint of a smile, Debbie said, "He's doing fine. I'd say he's mostly recovered, just a few issues left that require continuing attention."

"I'd say you appear well equipped to ensure that all his bodily functions are performing well."

This was going badly and could have gotten a lot worse. Charlie interjected, "Please, Shari, let's not lose this opportunity. Don't forget what we came for."

What did they come for? Charlie, Shari, and Debbie witnessed Adam and Adam B costar in the world's strangest performance. Adam walked up to Adam B—who was then standing—reached out his hand, and stroked his face. Gently pinching his skin, he was amazed to see that it was indeed really human. Emboldened by what she had just witnessed, Shari walked up to Adam and ran her fingers along the crusted fissures that scarred his face. Walking behind him, she saw that the scarring was also etched into his neck and the back of his head. She tried to hold back her emotions but then began to cry. She reached out and hugged Adam as if to recapture the love of their entire lifetime together.

Charlie was relieved, actually surprised, to find Adam and Adam B seemingly good-tempered, even revealing a kind of intimacy. They were partners lost together in some unknown dimension.

Feeling hopeful, Charlie interrupted. "I encouraged this meeting because I truly believe that you, Adam, and you, Adam B, can work out a settlement. I think this is a good start. Now that you've had a chance to get acquainted, let's schedule a meeting for next week to hammer out a plan."

Adam said, "I'm truly amazed. I knew human replication would work, and now I can see for myself that it does. But that doesn't mean I need a plan. There's really nothing we need to settle."

"Much too early for that," Charlie said. "I believe we've established a point of connection. That's already an accomplishment. Let's not prejudge anything else right now. Let's get together next week and see where it goes. For that meeting, I'd like each of you to sketch out a plan you think might work."

Charlie stood up to leave. Shari's eyes looked vacant, her expression flat. Neither Adam nor Adam B pressed any expectations on her affection. The three of them glanced in turn at Adam, communicating something more than goodbye, and then left the house.

The trip back to the Braudy estate was once again weighted down with silence. On arrival, Shari and Adam B departed the helicopter without a word. Shari walked quickly ahead of him by several paces. Charlie wondered how they would spend their time until their next meeting.

During the following days, Charlie spoke with both Adams, asking about their progress in outlining a settlement.

Adam said, "He gets nothing from me."

"You're gonna have to stretch here," Charlie said. "Remember, he can expose your technology. You don't want that, do you?"

"No, but I can't stand the idea of giving him something he doesn't deserve."

"I'm not going to argue with you about what he may or may not deserve. That's a fool's errand. There may be another way to think about this."

Adam barked sharply, "You're getting a little too smart."

"No, not smart enough. Believe me, I wish I were smarter. Wanna hear what I have to say?"

"You want permission? You got it."

"Let's say a rich, married dude is getting it on with his sweet honey and gets her pregnant. And let's say that Honey Suckle, for whatever reason, doesn't want an abortion. Do you think she 'deserves' a settlement? What the hell does *deserve* have to do with it? Nothing. Does our friend settle up? Yes, big time, and not because Honey Suckle deserves it but because he fucked up. That's the way I see your situation. You fucked up, and now it's time to settle. Maybe Adam B doesn't deserve squat. I don't know about that, but I do know that there's still a price to be paid. You're gonna have to pay up."

Adam closed off the conversation abruptly. "Thanks for nothing. I don't need or want your advice."

Later, in a conversation with Adam B, Charlie asked, "What are your thoughts about the settlement?"

"I don't know. Like Adam . . . geez, I hate using my name when I speak of him. Like Adam, I don't feel much like settling. I like it the way it is. I just want him to go away."

"It's not going to work like that. He's not gonna go away. You're smart enough to know that. And you're smart enough to know that you have a lever. So use it."

Adam B was quiet, lowering his voice. "If we're talking money, that's one thing. If we're talking about BrauCorp or the estate, that's another. But what I can't begin to imagine is how to divvy up Shari and the kids. Adam and even you are thinking that he's the Adam who married Shari, lived a life with her, and raised children together. But think about it: I have the exact same memories and feelings about Shari and the kids. These memories and feelings are real. They're etched into the deepest parts of me. They may be Adam's too, but by God, they are also mine. There's no way you can convince me otherwise. We are talking about my family."

"You're right. Part of me sees you as a recent arrival, but don't think that I don't understand your claim. I don't know how to work this out. It's out of my hands, but divorces happen. Not to you maybe, but these kinds of torments are all too common and then, after brutal struggles, get settled. And you know what? The parties move on. They make the best of a rotten situation."

"That's different."

"Different how?"

"Each party in every divorce has a contributory role in the break-up. I don't. I'm an innocent. Adam did this. I had no role. I'm the victim here."

"You're gonna play victim? Oh, that's interesting. I've known you since we were kids. I've never, ever known or imagined you to play the victim card. That is way out of character. When I told you that I regretted replicating you, you confronted me and thanked me for giving you the greatest gift, the gift of life. Well, welcome to life. Life does its thing, and we struggle with it as best we can. You're neither an innocent nor a victim. What you are is just one more player in the game of life. It's up to you to get on with it."

———

On the day of their next meeting, Charlie, Shari, and Adam B flew back to the ranch. They walked into the house and saw that Debbie had joined in, this time wearing a loose-fitting pair of black crepe slacks and a modest white linen blouse. Without much more than a polite greeting, Adam took charge by turning to Adam B, saying, "I have my own proposal, but if you don't mind, I'd like to hear yours first."

Adam B spoke in a firm, clear voice. "Okay, I'm willing to start. I propose that we split BrauCorp fifty-fifty. I'm willing to relinquish corporate governance to you. Outside of the corporation, I'm willing to split personally owned assets fifty-fifty. The exception is the estate, which I'll forgo entirely. For me, the most important thing is my claim to family. Shari and the kids are my family and my life. That I cannot, will not, concede."

Shari looked directly at Adam B with a startled expression. Adam burst out with an ironic laugh that built to a raging blast. "Fuck you, you lousy little piece of shit. How in the hell do you have the nerve to sit there and pull this kind of crap? Who do you think you are?"

With a proud smile, Adam B asserted, "I am Adam Braudy, husband to Shari and father of Jess and Steve. I'm president of BrauCorp. If you can't understand that, there's really nothing much we can talk about."

Taking the cue from Adam B, and with a determined calm, Adam replied, "There's no way you will take my place with my family. Don't even think about it. Just because you slipped into bed with my wife, that doesn't give you any kind of claim. We're talking about my family, not yours. Never yours."

Charlie and Shari turned their attention to Debbie, wondering what she was thinking about Adam's pledge of unwavering attachment to Shari and his kids. They took note of Adam's fleeting glances in Debbie's direction. Watching the two men fighting over her and her children filled Shari with righteous anger that made her bigger and stronger than she had ever been in her life. Her face was armored with a determined scowl, while her throat prepared itself to cast her fury.

She stood up and with a bitter, scornful blast said to both of them, "Who the hell do you think you are? Am I just a slave or a piece of meat and my children mere chattel? You two are nothing more than jackals fighting over scraps. Who knows? Maybe you think we can settle this with a *ménage a trois* or, with Debbie thrown in, maybe a *ménage a quatre*? No. As far as I'm concerned, I want no part of either of you. I'm ready to file for divorce. Debbie, you can have this dog. Adam, you've run from me and hidden yourself away, not caring a whit about the kids or me or even who I share my bed with. And all the while you're carrying on with Debbie. What kind of man does that? And now you want it all back again just like it never happened? And you, Adam B, or whatever your name is, I don't know you. You've been kind to me, and I understand that you thought you were Adam, but you're not Adam. I don't know you, not really. I don't care what your memories are. I have my own memories. Don't ever pretend to lay claim to me. Charlie, get me out of here."

Charlie tried to calm things down but without success. Shari was storming, unstoppable, as she headed out of the house toward the helicopter. Adam and Adam B stood for a time in silent confrontation until Adam B decided to follow Shari out the door.

Adam said to Charlie, "Aren't you going too? You'll miss your flight."

"The helicopter isn't going anywhere without me. You sure made a mess of things. Anything you want to say before I'm out of here too?"

Adam looked upset, maybe by the anger or maybe because of the lost opportunity. "You don't have to say anything. I admit it. Maybe I was too hasty. I got a little too emotional and lost control."

"Well, that's an understatement. What are we going to do now?"

"I don't know, but I don't really want to end our negotiations. Maybe we can restart."

"Am I really supposed to go out there and tell them to come back in?"

Charlie could see that Adam had something in mind and that he didn't want to give up. "Yeah, tell them I want to give it another try. Tell them I regret my behavior and that you think I'll be a little less emotional. Tell them anything you want, but you have to get them back in here."

Charlie was startled. He thought for sure that the day or even the entire negotiation was shot. But maybe there was still a chance to make some progress. With a buoyancy borne of pride in his success as an intermediary, he stepped outside and spoke with Shari and Adam B.

"Let's go back inside. Adam wants to give it another try."

Adam B said, "What's there to talk about? I thought he made things perfectly clear."

Charlie said, "He knows the deal breakers, and he still wants to talk. That has to be a good sign. We've got nothing to lose."

Shari said, "I'm not going back in. These two assholes are gonna start all over again fighting over the kids and me. You can go in there if you want. You don't need me. I'm not going."

Charlie pressed on. He knew the meeting wouldn't work without her. "Shari, there's nothing more to lose. You said your piece. Your position has registered. And if you're really serious about divorce, you don't want to be left out of this discussion. Let's give it a go."

In the end, they both reluctantly agreed and headed back into the house, where Adam oddly welcomed them on the porch as if nothing had happened. Was this the same Adam? Once inside, he turned and closed the door behind him. They all took seats opposite Adam, who was seated on the couch with a briefcase at his side. His demeanor was calm, his voice smooth as he said, "I've been doing a little planning for this meeting and want to show you something I've prepared."

He opened the briefcase. No one could clearly see what was inside, but it resembled something like a small oxygen tank. Maybe it was one that had sustained his life during his recovery. He reached over and twisted the handle. The sound of escaping gas filled the room.

"What's this?" Charlie asked. "Is this some kind of demonstration of what you had to live with as you struggled to survive?"

"Yeah, this is a kind of demonstration alright, but it's not oxygen. This stuff is argon gas. I told you, Charlie, that our replicant has an on-off switch. For real humans, this gas is harmless except at very high concentrations. But it's not harmless for a replicant whose DNA has been coded to induce a devastating immune response." He turned to face Adam B. "Well, Mr. Adam B, I'm turning you off."

All eyes focused on Adam B, who jerked to his feet in a panic and raced for the door. When he got there, he found it locked with a keyed deadbolt. It looked like he might attack Adam out of anger or in an attempt to get the key, but instead he tried picking up a chair to crash it through a window. By then, his eyes appeared glazed as he started to wobble. In confusion, he turned aimlessly in no particular direction. His cheeks flushed, and his face began to swell into grotesque proportions. His eyes squeezed shut, and his lips ballooned. Gagging and wheezing, he struggled in desperation for air. Debbie ran to him as he fell, hoping to start resuscitation.

That's when Charlie turned his attention to Adam and saw that he, too, was swelling up while gagging and choking. And to his utter astonishment, so was Shari. Charlie was unaffected by the gas but was staggered by the shock of seeing the hideous death struggles of people he dearly loved.

Chapter 58

Although she tried heroically, there was nothing Debbie could do. So rapid and desperate were their final moments that Charlie and Debbie, the incredulous survivors, couldn't even offer comfort. All three of them died right before the survivors' disbelieving eyes. Charlie was slow to grasp the implications. From what Adam had said about the on-off switch, he understood what happened to Adam B, but he couldn't imagine why Adam and Shari were victims, while he and Debbie were left unaffected. As he regained his senses, he realized that Adam and Shari, like Adam B, were replicants too.

Charlie didn't know what to do. He couldn't just abandon the scene, and he couldn't call the police either. Debbie got bed sheets from a linen closet and draped the bodies. Then the two of them sat down to think things through. It was Debbie who suggested they call Dean Fleck or Gina.

"Yes, Gina might know something about this and what to do. Dean could help with the coverup."

Charlie took out his phone. "Gina, this is Charlie calling. Get back to me immediately. We have an emergency. No games. Just call me ASAP."

Because Charlie worried that Gina would nevertheless play games, he had Debbie call her too. When she answered Debbie's call, Charlie took her phone. "Gina, don't hang up. We have a disaster here. Adam released a load of argon gas to switch off Adam B. Now not only is

Adam B dead, but Adam and Shari are too. What's going on? What do we do now?"

"Oh, shit. I knew something awful might come of this. Don't you see? That's why I wanted to see Adam pass on when we printed Adam B. How many Adams do you think we could juggle at the same time?"

"You mean you knew that Adam was a replicant? You didn't think to tell me?"

"Yes, I knew. And Adam, the real Adam, told me not to divulge this to anyone, not even you. Adam and Shari were exhausted from their worry about the threats of assassination. As inconspicuously as possible, Adam called me into his lab and told me about his plan to replicate himself and Shari. They wanted to escape into a self-made witness protection plan. I told him I couldn't do it. By that time, like you, I had my own doubts about the ethics, especially since we hadn't yet achieved our identicality criteria. I told him it was a bad idea."

"Then what happened?"

"He leaned on me hard. You know how he is. I finally conceded. It was just the two of us. We worked together, no one else involved. That was tricky. We replicated him first. We were encouraged by the result, so we went ahead and replicated Shari. We tried to be careful. I think we did a good job."

"You mean to tell me that Adam and Shari are still alive?"

"Yes, that's right. I don't know where they are, but I do know that they have an anonymous, encoded method of accessing the BrauCorp network. That way, Adam can keep an eye on what's going on, and I can get messages to him."

It had been easy for Charlie to think of Gina as a mad scientist, but it turned out to be more complicated than that. He'd had good reasons for the way he treated her, but he had regrets too, especially now that he needed to work closely with her to clean up all the raggedy ends.

The first thing for Charlie was to bring Dean up to speed, who immediately took charge of the cleanup. Debbie was having a hard time. Witnessing three deaths was bad enough, but Adam had been a sincere love interest. She suffered his loss badly. Her expectations may have been unrealistic, but her heart had been committed. Charlie pleaded with her to keep what she knew in confidence and offered to assist her in any way he could. Though in a state of loss and confusion, she agreed.

———

Two days later, Charlie met with Gina at her urging. When they met up, she was more than collegial; she was genuinely compassionate and acknowledged how this lengthy interlude had affected her and how she imagined it must have impacted him. After further discussion, she handed Charlie a letter from Adam.

Dear Charlie,

There's no way I can adequately apologize to you for what you've suffered on my account. Shari and I were frightened for ourselves and for Jess and Steve. We had to make a change. I have many regrets about the replicator project, of course, but regrets about the fusion project too. About the latter, in my enthusiasm for the idea of unlimited and inexpensive electrical power, I just couldn't imagine the magnitude of the threat it represented to so many powerful interests. Experience had always taught me that my perseverance would ultimately be rewarded. It was hard for me to see that I had met up with such formidable adversaries. As for the replication technology, I came to share your concerns. You were persuasive. I was on the cusp of shutting it down when I thought that replication was the only way Shari and I could free ourselves from the threats that haunted us. So I replicated both of us and pulled the kids out of school. I never imagined what would flow from that fateful decision. Believe me, I didn't intend to trap you in such a dreadful dilemma.

For now, I must remain hidden from the world, officially dead. I must ask that you continue operating BrauCorp in my place. My

Adam replicant, let's call him Adam A, did a good job placing you in command. Let's leave that standing. Going forward, I leave all decision-making in your capable hands except for two decisions that must be for me to make and for you to implement.

First, put a stop to all work on the fusion project. Yes, it's virtually complete, but you must withdraw the licensing applications and halt, at least for now, any further development that might appear to advance it to commercial implementation. That means no research and no engineering. It's to be frozen in place. Someday it will be thawed out and become a highly valued human resource. But for now, freeze it.

Second, utterly destroy everything connected with the replication project. That means all the hardware, lab notes, and files, both paper and electronic—anything that might testify to its existence. The technical knowledge we developed must be eliminated. It must not befoul our hands hereafter, and it must never fall into the hands of anyone else. I have discussed this with Gina, and she is agreeable. Have frank conversations with anyone else who has any knowledge, however peripheral. Be as generous as you need to be to ensure that they are loyal to this principle. If you suspect anyone who you think might want to trade on any part of this knowledge, I must be informed immediately so that necessary action can be taken.

Your insights, your principled behavior throughout this ordeal, and your loyalty to me are well noted. You have been a true friend even as I have proven myself undeserving. I wish you well and will always be close at hand.

Adam

Charlie was relieved to have evidence that Adam and Shari were indeed alive and well, but he didn't understand why Adam had printed Adam A without sharing that information. He could only wonder if Adam genuinely valued his friendship. True enough, Adam couldn't have foreseen the particular consequences, but it couldn't have escaped him that much chaos would ensue.

Charlie went ahead with his management responsibilities, which included the suspension of work on the fusion project. He was relieved, thinking that the announcement of Adam's death, the public funerals, and the withdrawal of the application for licensing would end the assassination attempts. Perhaps that was only wishful thinking. Regardless, Charlie ensured that their guard remained on high alert.

He offered to rehire Gina and was delighted that she agreed. Together, they set about eliminating anything that might disclose the existence of the replication project. They even euthanized and destroyed the replicated rats to ensure that a careful examination wouldn't reveal DNA matches between originals and replicants. Every piece of specialized equipment was dismantled and thoroughly torn down to such an extent that even upon close inspection, no one could surmise their intended functions. Gina, with Dean's assistance, had every conceivable network facility searched to locate every email, scan file, and any other file, technical or otherwise, that might have dealt with replication. Backup systems and cloud storage resources were combed. Nothing was to escape their attention. Every file they came upon was deleted from its discovered location and moved onto a single computer unattached to any network. From that computer, those many files were scrutinized and their contents used to create search terms to help widen their search. When at last they were satisfied that every hint of replication had been removed from every conceivable source, the two of them got together to complete their task by obliterating the consolidated memory media.

But then they hesitated for a moment of reflection.

Gina said, "I think we're ready. Let's get on with it."

"I don't know, Gina. Are you sure that Adam wrote that letter?"

"What do you mean? You saw it. Who else would have enough information to write that letter? It would have to be Adam who wrote it."

"I know we have lots of security, but could it be possible for someone to have gained enough access to write that letter?"

"No, I don't think so. It's too specific. Besides, it sounds like Adam."

"What about another replicant? Could it have been written by another Adam replicant?"

Gina didn't answer, but her eyes widened. She was left speechless but her expression said, *Oh no, could that really be? I just don't know.*

"Since Adam and I were kids, I have always looked up to him. He's an amazing guy. He's been like a big brother. He's been there for me as a friend, and I've always deferred to him. As far as Adam's replication technology is concerned, I never liked it. You know that. But I was repeatedly persuaded to assist him in getting us into this mess. Now, after all we've been through, I realize that I don't really know if that letter was written by Adam or by a replicant or some other interloper. My judgment says that we should preserve what we have here and revisit our decision at some later date when we may come to a better-informed perspective. That's my decision. We will preserve these files."

So they shut down the computer and built around it an unbreachable vault, where it would reside in the meantime.